THE BLOODSTONE

Also by the author

Adventures in Godhood

Imaginary Friends

Weekends Can Be Murder

The End (forthcoming)

The Nash'terel books

The Earthborn

The Bloodstone

SIC TRANSIT TERRA
(Edge Science Fiction and Fantasy Publishing)

Book 1: *The Genius Asylum*

Book 2: *The Otherness Factor*

Book 3: *The Relativity Bomb*

Book 4: *The Genome Rally*

Book 5: *The Cockroach Crusade*

Book 6: *The Identity Shift*

The Stragori Deception (forthcoming from Brain Lag)

THE BLOODSTONE

A novel of the Nash'terel

ARLENE F. MARKS

Milton, Ontario

Brain Lag
Milton, Ontario
http://www.brain-lag.com/

Library and Archives Canada Cataloguing in Publication

Title: The bloodstone : a novel of the Nash'terel / Arlene F. Marks.
Names: Marks, Arlene F., 1947- author.
Identifiers: Canadiana (print) 20230586651 | Canadiana (ebook) 2023058666X | ISBN 9781998795093
  (softcover) | ISBN 9781998795109 (EPUB)
Subjects: LCGFT: Paranormal fiction.
Classification: LCC PS8561.R2868 B56 2024 | DDC C813/.54—dc23

Content warnings: Child death, death, gore

There is a legend on Rin Yeng, the fifth planet of the Gorna system. It concerns a mineral with mysterious properties, and a lost people called the Nash'terel, which in the Yeng tongue means "secluded ones".

The story goes this way: one day a curious young Nash'terel was exploring a cave deep in the mountains around the isolated valley where his people lived. He came across a strange and beautiful rock deposit in the cave wall. In his haste to break off a piece of it to study, he cut his hand.

He watched in fascination as the chunk he was holding absorbed the blood from his wound. Then the mineral changed colour, the milky white blossoming into an entire palette of vibrant hues. He named this mineral "dashkra", which in Yeng means "bloodstone".

When he shared his discovery with the other Nash'terel, they were struck by its ornamental beauty and began mining it. Nash'terel artisans ground and polished the stone and made it into jewellery that became incorporated into rituals and ceremonies. Meanwhile, the fine dust they created as they worked with the dashkra was spreading throughout the valley. The dust became incorporated into the bodies of the Nash'terel and gradually transformed them into a new race... of shape-shifting vampires.

When the truth about "the secluded ones" finally came out, the Yeng were enraged and horrified. The emperor ordered his generals to assemble an army. However, when the soldiers stormed into the valley, their quarry had vanished, along with all the dashkra. The Nash'terel had apparently carved every last bit of the mineral from the mountain caves and taken it with them. Only the dust was left behind.

In some versions of the story, the dashkra dust settled on the boots and uniforms of the soldiers and was thus carried out of the valley to infect other Yeng, over time turning them into vampires as well. In others, the Nash'terel escaped by killing the soldiers and assuming their shapes, hiding in plain sight among the Yeng and spreading the "blood sickness" themselves each time they fed.

So the legend goes. The truth is probably something much more mundane.

Part One

2008

Three Months
Before the Purge...

Chapter One

━━━━◆━━━━

Gershred would have preferred to fly to Vancouver, but Maldemaur had remained adamant—the Trans-Canada train made more stops, giving them opportunities to escape if a Yeng assassin chanced to come aboard.

Maury's paranoia peaked every hundred years or so. That was how often the rift opened, linking Earth and their home world, RinYeng. Shred knew from long experience that there was no reasoning with his partner at such times. The only thing to do was go along with him. So, they shapeshifted their faces whenever the train pulled into a station. They shuttled back and forth between the passenger car and the one with the sightseeing bubble on top. They could have afforded better class tickets. However, all an upgrade would really have given them was privacy, and privacy would have handed the advantage to an assassin, if there happened to be one in the vicinity.

All of that aside, Shred would have found the journey quite enjoyable if only Maury had been in a more conversational mood.

For the past several hours, he hadn't spoken a word. He was

currently wearing his "do not disturb" expression, the one that looked like Chazz Palminteri with heartburn, and Shred could swear that at least three other passengers had made a point of walking past them to see whether either of them was wearing handcuffs. In truth, he was becoming concerned.

"Talk to me, Maury," he begged. "We know Bilyash and Angie are safe, so something else must be bothering you. You're not having second thoughts about making this trip, are you?"

Maldemaur exhaled audibly, as though Shred's voice had flipped an on/off switch. "What do I say to her? What *can* I say, when just the thought of being in the same room with that duplicitous bitch Vincaspera makes my fangs itch?"

"You say whatever it takes to close the deal and get us Middlevale at a fair price," Shred told him. "Once that's done, I'll stay out west and set up the training camp, and you can go back to Ontario and put her firmly behind you again. Are you certain the address you found online for that human cult she's running is correct?"

"Yes, and I'm betting it's bait in a trap, along with her current female shape. She's been calling herself Victoria Spears for quite a while, apparently. Not that it makes one iota of difference. To me, she'll always be the miserable cheat who got me expelled from the Science Guild on RinYeng all those centuries ago out of spite, because I spurned her advances."

"She was a pressure adept, as I recall, most likely an elemental master by now."

"So, she can use her mind to push things around," Maury huffed. "And you're a heat lord and I'm a light lord. What's your point?"

"That we're equals, with different talents but the same degree of power. That means we ought to be able to sit down and negotiate, like civilized beings. But if you simply barge in and confront her about the past—" He paused for a beat. "Nothing will be served by putting her on the defensive before you've even presented your offer to purchase the town."

Maury drew a deep breath before blurting out, "What are we doing here, Gershred? Not just on the train, but in general. We're Nash'terel. We're the secluded ones, and what we're about to do... Is this really who we are now?"

So he *was* having second thoughts.

Unsurprised, Shred turned his head and gazed out the window. They were following the course of an impossibly blue river, speeding along a broad ledge that had apparently been carved into the side of a hill. As far forward and backward as he could see, a carpet of evergreen treetops ran from the train track down to the water. On the opposite bank, the carpet continued, rolling away to meet a crenellated wall of purple-crowned hills. The sky overhead was cloudless and intensely bright. If all he and Maury did now was get off at the next station and return to Toronto, Shred reflected, the rugged beauty of that landscape alone would have made the trip worthwhile.

But of course, they couldn't. They'd begun a vital mission on behalf of their entire race and had to see it through.

Maury's "do not disturb" face had discouraged anyone from sitting down nearby. Now he and Shred were alone at one end of the passenger car, able to converse quietly with no fear of being overheard. Maury glanced around cautiously before continuing in a voice that was almost a whisper, "We have been living quietly on this world for a thousand and a half years, staying safe by being invisible. We've hidden out by spreading out and concealing our alien abilities from the human population, and for the most part the strategy has worked. But these new developments—the purification campaign by the Yeng emperor, the threat of assassins from both sides of the rift, their specific targeting for death of our Earthborn offspring—it's changing us, on a fundamental level. We're actually making plans to form and train an *army*. When have the Nash'terel ever gone that far?"

"Whenever we've needed to do it," Shred replied evenly. "Not all of us are cut out to be scientists and philosophers, you know. Some of us enjoy the discipline of martial arts and the adrenalin rush of combat."

"As individuals, yes. As a race, however, the Nash'terel have always been peaceful. Making war is not our way."

"It's not?" Shred had to work to contain his impatience. "You have a short memory. Before the Nash'terel drank life essence, we drank the blood of our prey. That was what made this planet perfect for us when we first arrived. The humans were constantly warring among themselves. We joined their armed forces so that we could quench our thirst on their battlefields. It's still there, Maldemaur—the thirst. It's why we eat our meat raw. So don't tell me that spilling blood goes against our Nash'terel nature.

"In any case, our conflict with the Yeng is not about land or possessions. It's about our continuing existence. Every Nash'terel still living is living on this world. Every talent we possess, developed over thousands of generations of practice and study, resides on a single planet. In a hundred years, the rift will open again, and more trained assassins than we've ever had to deal with before will come pouring through it. We'll need to meet the emperor's army of killers with a defensive one of our own, and that means weaponizing the talents of all of us so that some of us, at least, will survive."

Maldemaur lowered his chin, like a bull about to charge. "You know as well as I do that that kind of training takes time. In the meanwhile, once all those *hainbeka*—those talents, as you put it—start coming together in one place, the Yeng already on this world could very well decide that we pose a threat to *their* existence. And they won't wait a hundred years before doing something about it."

This was the problem with scientists, Shred reflected. They hypothesized too damned much.

"Well, before you jump down that rabbit hole, let me add another 'if' to this doomsday scenario you're building," Shred said. "It only comes to pass *if* the Council of the First Yeng learns about our plans for Middlevale. How do you suppose they'll do that? You and I certainly won't be telling them. And I seriously doubt whether any of our fellow Nash'terel, including Victoria Spears, will jeopardize a plan meant to keep them alive."

As hoped, Maury's expression lightened perceptibly.

"So, not to worry, Maldemaur," Shred continued. "We're going to make that miserable cheat an offer she can't refuse. And if she uses her *hainbek* to try to push us around, we'll just double-team her with light and heat."

The miserable cheat's office address was a storefront near the corner of an older block of businesses in a run-down neighbourhood of Vancouver.

This was Main Street? It was a misnomer, Shred mused as he steered the rental car into a parking spot at the curb.

The entire display window was covered on the inside by a red and gold sign proclaiming the name of The Church of Human Purification. The words formed a circle around the stylized image of a quasar wrapped inside a double helix of human DNA.

Maury and Shred stepped over the threshold and into a small, stuffy room. The desks, chairs, and tall, near-empty bookcase looked as though they had been picked up at five different yard sales. There wasn't a personal item anywhere in sight, and the only visible sign of technology—the only objects on either of the two desk tops, in fact—were a PC and a land line telephone. It was clearly a disused space, without even an identifying poster on the wall.

Maury had been right earlier, Shred thought grimly. This looked and felt like a trap. Only a fool would stay here, hoping to meet someone.

Before he could say so aloud, the door opened behind them and a melodic female voice declared, "Maldemaur and Gershred, I presume! You're finally here. Good! Now we can talk."

Turning in place, Shred saw a tall, willowy female with long auburn hair, a fair, flawless complexion, and mesmerizing green eyes.

"Vincaspera. You're Victoria Spears now?" he demanded. "And you've been expecting us?"

She closed the door and joined them in the centre of the room. "I am, and I have. Maldemaur set off a security alert when he called the number on the web site from his personal phone. I've been tracking your movements for a while."

Her lips curved in a gracious smile, revealing perfect white teeth.

"I live just a couple of floors up," she said. "If you'll follow me, I'll make you some tea and—"

"We can talk right here," Maury cut in. He pulled a chair out from behind one of the desks, then stood beside it, waiting with evident impatience.

Her smile faded. "You never did appreciate the niceties," she said with a sigh, and went to fetch a second chair. "All right, then. More biscuits for me. And can I assume that you came all the way out here to find me for a reason?" she added, as Shred pulled up a third chair and they all sat down.

"We're interested in Middlevale," said Maury. "Tell us about this experiment of yours."

"You mean the Church of Human Purification?"

"You know what I mean," he snapped. "I did some checking, Caspera, and it seems nothing has changed since RinYeng. You started up your 'cult' about three hundred and fifty years ago, shortly after I began trying to purify human essence. You learned what I was working on and just had to show me up, even if you had to cheat to do it."

She gave him a bewildered look. "*That's* what you thought I was about?" A moment later she added, "Of course. With our history, what else would you expect from me? I don't suppose you would believe me if I told you I had no idea what you were working on...?" His stony expression gave her the answer. "Very well, then. You don't trust me. I understand that. But the current situation is much larger than any differences we've had in the past, so I need you to set your feelings aside and listen to what I have to say. Can you do that?"

With obvious reluctance, Maury conceded, "All right, I'm listening."

"And you?" she asked, turning to Shred.

He nodded wordlessly.

"I don't know how current you are with what's been going on back on RinYeng," she began, "but—"

"You can spare us the info dump," Maury interrupted irritably.

"We know all about the emperor's purification campaign."

Her head jerked as though she'd just been slapped. "All right," she said, recomposing her features, "but know this as well: whatever you may think of me, Maldemaur, I'm Nash'terel too, and that makes me just as much a target for assassins as any other of our people on Earth."

"Any other adults, you mean. Or haven't you noticed how many of our Earthborn seem to die each time the rift opens?" Maury spat. "They're being targeted, Caspera. Specifically hunted down."

"Believe me, I'm painfully aware of that." Her expression hardened as she continued in a low, intense voice, "But my concern was for *all* the Nash'terel. When I learned how the emperor was using the rift, I realized that what we needed on this world was a safe haven, like our secluded valley back on RinYeng. I knew that it would have to be completely self-contained and self-sustaining, in order to keep its existence a secret. And I also knew that it would need an ironclad cover story to keep the segregated human food supply ignorant of their situation."

It made perfect sense—as carefully concocted stories tended to do, Shred reminded himself.

"You're not suggesting we believe that everything you've done for the past three hundred and fifty years has been altruistic, are you?" Maury said dryly. "Because we all know that would be a load of *shattra*. You may be familiar with the human expression about tigers not changing their stripes?"

"I suppose I had that coming as well," she remarked. "But a lot can change in a thousand years, Maldemaur, whether or not you choose to believe it's possible."

"Did the Council of the First contact you?" Maury demanded.

"No. Why would they?"

"Then how did you find out how the emperor was using the rift?" asked Shred, infusing the question with pleasant menace.

Her complexion darkened. "By interrogating the perpetrator of a failed assassination attempt. I don't appreciate being hunted, so I... pushed him around. He told me a great deal before I ended his pernicious existence."

That sounded more like the Vincaspera he and Maury had known in the past. Shred let himself relax just a little.

"By the way, I understand you have an apprentice, Maldemaur," she said chattily.

"I did," he replied.

"Well, I have one now, a most promising student. I would like you to meet her." Vincaspera took out her phone and hit a couple of buttons. After a moment, she said, "Lillandria? My guests are here. Come downstairs and say hello to them." Returning her attention to Maury and Shred, she continued, "My selective breeding project is supposed to be a secret. Aside from the question of how you found out about Middlevale, may I ask why you're so interested in it?"

"I want to buy it from you," said Maury.

At this, Vincaspera laughed out loud. "And you accuse *me* of cheating!" she declared. "Well, you can't present my experiment as your own, so you must have some other purpose in mind for it. Care to share with the class?"

Shred felt his jaw muscles tighten and had to consciously relax them. *Come on, Maury, say what needs to be said.*

"I think you misunderstand," he replied. "I want to buy all of Middlevale. The land, the human livestock, the facilities, everything. I plan to turn it into a training camp so we'll be ready to fight the next time the rift opens, spilling assassins onto this world."

"A boot camp for Nash'terel. How interesting," she said thoughtfully, adding, "And how ironic that you should come to me with this idea two centuries after I had it myself—and implemented it successfully, I might add."

When he could once more trust his voice, Shred demanded, "Are you telling us that for the past two hundred years you've been training an army? Without anyone finding out about it?"

"Don't be ridiculous! Of *course* they'd find out about an army. No, I've been training assassins. The rift can be travelled both ways. Next time it opens, the emperor and his advisors will be in for a very unpleasant surprise. As the humans like to say, sometimes the best defence is a strong offence."

Maury and Shred exchanged stunned glances. Then, hearing Vincaspera call out, "Ah, Lillandria! Come in, darling, don't be shy," they turned and saw what looked to be a human child about seven years old standing in front of the bookcase.

She was nowhere near a doorway, not one that they could see, at any rate. So how, Shred wondered, had she managed to enter the room undetected?

As the girl drew nearer, Maury declared, "She looks like a younger version of you."

"That's because Lilly isn't only my apprentice," she told him. "She's my Earthborn daughter."

"How long have you been training her?" he asked.

"Since her talent began emerging, shortly after her two hundredth birthday."

"She manifested early," Maury remarked, frowning.

"She's a prodigy," Vincaspera agreed. "Lilly has a most

uncommon *hainbek*, and I felt that it was wise to begin training it as soon as possible. So she can defend herself," she added pointedly.

"And what is her talent, if I may ask?" said Shred.

"Show them, darling. As we've been practising."

Lilly's features contracted, and for several seconds, she was the portrait of childish concentration. Then, Shred became aware that he was having trouble breathing. He couldn't seem to fill his lungs, no matter how quickly or deeply he inhaled. All at once his heart was pumping wildly, his vision and hearing fading...

In that instant, he understood: Lilly's talent was air. Vincaspera had weaponized it. And he was under attack.

Reflexively, he directed his essence to gather up the heat around him for a counterattack.

Vincaspera's eyes widened briefly. She'd probably felt the temperature drop in the room and realized what he was about to do. "That's enough, Lilly," she said. "Save your essence for when you feel threatened."

The child obeyed. Then, "Can I go back upstairs now?" she said impatiently. "I want to finish my hot chocolate."

"Yes, of course, darling."

His pulse still racing, Shred watched her approach the bookcase and touch something at the back of a shelf. The unit promptly pivoted ninety degrees, revealing a narrow opening in the wall.

Of course, it did. Nash'terel traps always came with emergency escape routes.

As the bookcase swung closed again, Shred's respiration and heart rate returned to normal, only to quicken once more at the thought of what had almost happened.

He turned reproachful eyes on Vincaspera. "I could have killed her."

"Never mind that," Maury put in. "She could have killed *us*. But all she cared about was not letting her drink get cold. This is why we don't teach young children to project their essence. Or am I the only one who sees how dangerous you've made her?"

"I wouldn't have let her kill you. For now, I'm teaching her defensive skills only. She'll be the youngest Nash'terel ever to wear the bloodstone."

This discussion was veering perilously off track. "Let's get back to business, shall we?" Shred cut in. "Maldemaur has expressed an interest in buying Middlevale. What is your response?"

Vincaspera rearranged her features and settled back into her chair. "Middlevale is not for sale. However, under the right conditions, I might be amenable to leasing you part of the compound as a training camp. I know you don't think of me as a team player, and maybe you're right. Nonetheless, we do have similar goals—or at least, compatible ones—so an arrangement would certainly be worth exploring. I'd want to see a detailed proposal, of course."

"Partners need to be able to trust each other," Shred pointed out.

She pursed her lips for a moment. "Quite true. Therefore, I will expect to see your terms for a truce included in the proposal. You'll need time to prepare it. Why don't we meet again at one o'clock tomorrow afternoon, to continue our negotiations?"

Shred and Maury exchanged looks. She was being remarkably fair-minded... or appearing to be. In any case, perhaps they could find some common ground after all.

"We'll see you then," said Shred.

Wordlessly, Maury stood up and preceded him out the door.

*   *   *

"There is no way I'll enter into a sharing arrangement with Vincaspera. I wouldn't do it on RinYeng, and I refuse to do it now," Maury declared, dropping with a scowl onto the wheat-coloured sofa in the living room of their hotel suite. "Besides," he added, "she won't sell us Middlevale, and without Middlevale, your grand scheme is dead in the water."

"But she's willing to negotiate terms with us," Shred pointed out. "And maybe all we need is *access* to Middlevale. This is going to be a process, Maury. Let's not give up on it before it's even begun."

The other being uttered a rude syllable.

Undeterred, Shred continued, "I understand your reasons for hating her, and they're valid. I've been telling you that for nearly two thousand years. She ruined your scientific career back on RinYeng, destroyed your reputation, got you kicked out of the Guild. All terrible, unforgivable wrongs. I also understand her reasons for establishing Middlevale, and in my opinion, they're valid too. But she's just as paranoid as you are, my friend, and I'm getting the feeling that she's like an automobile with no brakes, one bump in the road away from going completely out of control."

"And this is our problem because...?"

"Bilyash is like a son to us, and Lilly is Vincaspera's daughter. Look at how differently they've been trained. If she's willing to turn her own offspring into a lethal weapon at such a tender age, what do you suppose she's been doing in Middlevale for the past couple of centuries? What kind of Nash'terel assassins has she been turning out?"

He paused to let Maury digest this, then concluded tautly, "I'm not saying you should forgive and forget. Far from it. I'm only asking you to remember the greater purpose behind my 'grand scheme', as you put it, and continue to negotiate with her. The sooner we can get her seeing things our way, the sooner we can replace her program with ours and begin teaching the Earthborn how to survive."

"All right, then," Maury said with a sigh, "you win. Let's draw up a proposal and see what she says."

Chapter Two

The following afternoon, they walked through the front door of the storefront and found Victoria Spears waiting for them. She was sitting behind one of the desks, with a royal blue file folder at her right hand and a plate of oatmeal cookies to her left.

"We're prepared to negotiate in good faith," Maury said stiffly as he sat down across from her and placed his own, bright red folder on the desk top in front of him.

She looked relieved. "So am I. If you've brought hard copy, why don't we begin by trading folders and reading over each other's terms?"

"That works for me," he told her.

Shred remained standing today, carefully watching Vincaspera's reactions as her gaze swept back and forth across each page of the document that he and Maury had spent the past twenty hours framing. Any little snag had the potential to send the entire proceedings flying off the rails. He tensed as she stopped reading and straightened her shoulders.

"What's this?" she asked. "You want my assurance that none of the humans in Middlevale will be killed and eaten?"

"I have a reason for that stipulation," he replied.

"I'd love to hear it." She crossed her arms on the desk top and leaned forward on them expectantly.

Shred's spine went rigid. There were things that couldn't be revealed until after the deal was concluded, and this was one of them. He placed a warning hand on Maury's shoulder. Maury shrugged it off and opened his mouth to reply, just as…

…a brain-scalding scream erupted overhead, freezing all three of them in place for a moment.

Vincaspera's eyes widened with horror. "Lilly," she whispered. She jumped up and raced over to the bookcase, with Maury and Shred close behind her.

The three Nash'terel barrelled through the secret door, around the foot of the stairs, and up two flights, spilling breathlessly onto a landing where the sight and smell of blood brought them to an immediate, quivering halt.

It was perfectly quiet. Battlefield quiet, Shred called it, the kind of utter stillness that always settled over the carnage left behind by intense and decisive combat. He'd experienced it many times while fighting in human wars. Now, as then, it was making his fangs itch. Savagely, he stifled the primal response. If the blood that had been spilled here was Nash'terel, then it was forbidden to drink. Nash'terel did not consume other Nash'terel.

Shred broke away from the group and followed a trail of bloody footprints down a short hallway to an open window, where a yellow and white curtain had been hastily shoved aside and now lay draped over the sill. Outside, a wrought-iron fire escape zigzagged down to an empty alleyway.

From the apartment behind him came an anguished howl, followed by a series of crashes. Then, abruptly, the demolition noises ceased and a death wail took their place. A loud, keening moan that sliced straight into Shred's heart, it confirmed every Nash'terel's worst fear.

For a long-lived race like theirs, birth and death occurred very seldom, and for that reason were highly anticipated and extremely emotional events. Death coming naturally at the end of an individual's life was sad but inevitable. The loss of a child from disease or misadventure was tragic but had to be borne. However, the deliberate murder of a child by anyone and for any reason was an atrocity that cried out for blood vengeance.

Pausing a second more to brace himself, Shred walked through the apartment doorway and into a scene of chaos.

Every bit of furniture in the living room was lying or leaning against one of the walls, and everything else—books, figurines, candy dishes, lamps—now lay scattered in pieces atop the pile like sprinkles on a doughnut. Maury was standing in the middle of the room, a helpless witness, as Vincaspera knelt in a spreading pool of blood, cradling the dead body of her daughter in her arms.

At the sight of them, Shred's thoughts began to race. The child had been torn nearly in half—while still alive, judging from the amount of blood on the floor. The Nash'terel didn't do this to their prey. Wild animals did. And the Yeng did, when they were feeding on flesh. But Lilly's murderer must have known there were adults just two floors below, providing barely enough time for an escape once they heard her scream. So, it wasn't a meal this lone Yeng hunter had been after, just an easy kill.

At Shred's entrance, Vincaspera had gone ominously silent. Now she turned, her lips pressed tightly together, her face shiny with tears, and levelled an icy stare at him and Maury.

"Whoever did this knew that she would be alone up here. Who did you talk to? Who did you tell about our meeting today?" she demanded hoarsely.

"No one," declared Shred.

"Whoever did this also knew the layout of the building and had probably been here before," Maury cut in sternly. "Who did *you* talk to, Vincaspera?"

She shrank away from him. "Only one person. But he didn't do this. He couldn't!" she said with a sob, and hugged Lilly's corpse even harder. "He's her father."

Shred bent to put his face at her eye level and pointed out gently, "He might have shared the information. We need to talk to him and find out. Who is he, Vincaspera?"

She was rocking back and forth now and humming to herself, as if soothing a fretful child.

"Vincaspera, listen to me," he urged. "Lilly's father needs to be told about her. What is his name?"

"His name is Barron," she murmured bleakly. "He's in charge of the training program at Middlevale."

Shred had to bite back the curse that leaped onto his tongue. "Is he there now?"

She shook her head. "I asked him to come into the city today." Her tears spilled over again, thickening her voice. "He'll be here soon."

Maury and Shred shared a worried look. "He needs to be warned, Vincaspera," Shred told her. "He can't just walk in here unprepared. He'll—" Pulling out his phone, he said, "Tell me his number. I'll break the news to him before he arrives."

Barron's voice when he answered the call was hard and flat and struck Shred like a hammer blow to the head. He had hoped never to have to deal with this particular Nash'terel again. They'd trained and served together in human combat off and on for centuries. Barron had been known for his quick temper. On the battlefield, his behaviour had been described as "trigger happy". Now, his silence while Shred gave him condolences over the phone was deeply troubling. It didn't bode well for how Lilly's father would react the first time he saw her body.

"He'll be here in about an hour," Shred announced, ending the call. To Maury, he murmured, "Find the sofa and set it upright."

After a great deal of coaxing, they finally managed to pry Vincaspera away from Lilly's corpse and sit her down between them on the damaged couch. The front of her was covered with blood and the apartment reeked with it. It took all of Shred's self-control to keep his fangs from descending.

"Does he know?" she said dully, her gaze fixed on something across the room.

"He knows. I told him," Shred assured her.

"He'll find them. He'll make them suffer. He's good at that," she muttered, making it sound like an incantation.

Yes, I'll just bet he is, he thought.

"Vincaspera, we're going to avenge your daughter's death, I promise, but we'll need your help to eliminate suspects," Shred told her. "Tell me, are any of your trainees Yeng?"

That got her attention. She turned indignant eyes on his face and replied, "Absolutely not! Barron knew how important it was to keep the Yeng from finding out about our operation. He would have ended any spy who even *tried* to infiltrate the program."

"How many assassins have you graduated so far?"

"Um... seventeen in the first two cohorts. There were eighteen accepted, but one washed out a few years into the training."

A shiver trickled down the heat lord's spine. In his experience, washouts often carried grudges against those who'd forced them to leave.

"What happened to the one who washed out?"

No response. She'd resumed rocking back and forth, blank-faced, with her arms crossed as though she were holding an infant.

"I guess you'll have to ask Barron about that," Maury ventured.

"I guess." He paused briefly. "So, there are seventeen trained Nash'terel assassins here on Earth that not even the Nash'terel know about, waiting for the next opening of the rift. And doing what in the meanwhile? Living in Middlevale?"

He'd been talking to himself, but the question had apparently penetrated Vincaspera's mental fog. She stopped rocking and replied, "No, after graduation, they were—" Her face fell, then firmed up again. "They were ordered to go home and resume their normal lives until they were contacted again. You don't think one of them could have—?"

"Inadvertently given away information about Lilly to a Yeng? I don't know. I need to discuss it with Barron."

Her shoulders sagged as she sank once again into her thoughts. "He'll find out," she muttered darkly to herself. "He'll make them pay. He's good at that."

One hour after speaking to Barron on the phone, Shred heard heavy footsteps coming up the stairs. A moment later, the door was flung open and Lilly's father burst into the room.

He looked just the way Shred remembered him, right down to the camouflage fatigues and high-topped boots he'd worn the last time they'd served together—tall, heavily muscled, and with the same cruel twist to his mouth. He stopped short at the sight of

Lilly's bloodied body, and for just an instant he froze. The tough facade appeared to lose resolution. Then it hardened again, and he turned Nash'terel eyes flashing with hatred on the two males on the sofa and snarled, "If either one of you was behind this—!"

His left hand was shimmering. Belatedly, Shred recalled that Barron was a heat lord like himself. In his current state of mind, he could easily turn this building into his daughter's funeral pyre.

Maury and Shred sprang to their feet, both *hainbeka* at the ready. "We had nothing to do with it, Barney," Shred told him, addressing him by the other being's *nom de guerre*. "We were downstairs with Vincaspera when it happened. Look, we can burn each other up, or we can burn the building down, or we can cool off and work together to figure out who's responsible and make them pay."

Barron thought for a moment. "As long as I get to make the avenging kill."

"Yes. That pleasure will be entirely yours."

Barron's hand stopped shimmering. "Fair enough," he said, and rubbed his palm on the side of his pants leg. Then, as though suddenly remembering that he wasn't the only bereaved parent in the room, he dropped onto the sofa and gathered Vincaspera into his arms. They sat quietly like that for several minutes before Barron spoke again, in a dull and distant voice. "We can't involve the police. We'll have to use our own resources."

"I know," Shred agreed. "And I need to pick up a few things from our hotel room. When do you want to meet?"

Barron glanced around at the shambles Vincaspera had made of the living room, letting his gaze rest for a long moment on his daughter's cooling corpse. "I have some calls to make and a few items to gather as well. Meet me in the storefront in three hours."

*   *   *

Barron looked Shred up and down as he strode through the doorway.

"That should be camo, not denim," he commented.

"Sorry, I got rid of my uniforms when I was demobbed," Shred told him.

"That's right—your last tour was with the Brits. Shapeshifting, I heard. Lots of attention but no medals."

Shred shrugged. "I saved Field Marshal Montgomery's ass on a couple of occasions. It wasn't a complete waste of my time. How's Vincaspera holding up?"

Barron's expression sobered. "Vicky wants blood, the sooner the better. She says you were asking whether any of our trainees were Yeng. I never told her this, but one of them was."

"The one who washed out?"

Barron leaned back against the nearest desk top with a rueful sigh. "He didn't wash out. He got away. I figure he must have killed the Nash'terel recruit who'd been accepted into the program, then reblooded their *dashkra* and reported for training in their place."

"He wore a bloodstone?"

"Yeah. Produced it every day for inspection, just like all the other trainees. If his essence had been modified, I would have known what he was right away. Instead, it took a couple of years for me to put a bunch of little pieces together. I was going to disappear him during a training exercise, but he dropped out of sight before the exercise began. The rest of the cohort joined me on the hunt for him... something I had just taught them all how to elude. If that was his final exam, he aced it. No one was able to track him down."

"Why did you tell Vincaspera he'd washed out?"

"She'd put everything she had into this project. I just didn't have the heart…" He raised pain-filled eyes to Shred's face. "She trusted me, Gordie, and I let her down. I should have acted the moment I knew. But I tried to be tricky, and it backfired."

"Was that the only attempt to infiltrate the program?"

"There was a second, shortly after the first Yeng went missing, but this one had altered his essence. I sniffed him out immediately and incinerated him on the spot."

"How long ago was this?"

He paused to think. "The first plant came in with our most recent cohort to graduate, so that makes it thirty years ago. The second attempt was about eight years after that. What are you thinking, Gordie?"

"First, that if someone sent these agents to infiltrate your operation, then it isn't as secret as you believe it is. And second, I'm wondering how thoroughly you screen your recruits."

"Vicky does that. She performs deep background checks and keeps the paperwork updated on every one of our trainees."

"Then she should still have a file on the recruit the first Yeng infiltrator was impersonating. When you were hunting the Yeng, did you think to look for the Nash'terel he'd replaced as well?"

"No. I assumed it would be a waste of time since he had to be dead," Barron said, frowning.

"Then let's begin by testing that assumption. If it turns out he's alive, he may be able to give us a lead on the Yeng who took his spot in the program. Unless you can think of a better way to start…?"

"Track him down using Vicky's file? That was decades ago. He could have changed identities several times by now." Barron paused, looking skeptical. "But I guess it's worth a try."

"Timotazu," Gershred read aloud from the printed sheet in front of him. He frowned, adding, "That's the name he gave as his emergency contact on the application form. A Yeng planning to pose as an Earthborn Nash'terel recruit would have befriended him first, cultivated a relationship in order to gain his trust..."

"...and gotten him to drop his guard? That would have made killing him a lot easier, for sure."

"Agreed. And who would a young Nash'terel with no immediate family appoint as his emergency contact but his very best friend in the world?" Shred said. "They might even have been roommates. Or I could be completely wrong and Timotazu could be another Nash'terel."

"Either way, it's a lead, and we need to follow it." Barron stared over Gershred's shoulder. "That address is in the 'burbs. I doubt whether Timotazu would still be living there after all this time, but maybe the neighbours can point us in the right direction. Are you up for conducting a little street survey, Gordie?"

A couple of hours later, clipboards in hand and hopeful smiles on their fresh, earnest faces, the two Nash'terel had donned business suits and were going door to door, Shred on the north side and Barron on the south, on an established street in a development of townhouses and parkettes. The "survey", ostensibly gathering data that would paint a picture of the changing neighbourhood, included questions about playground use, shopping and transportation habits, and the residence history of each dwelling.

At every intersection, they met up to compare notes. After the second block, Barron announced, "Pay dirt! A female I just interviewed is the neighbourhood nosy body. She remembers a man named Thomas Reilly leaving that end unit about thirty years ago, and a Tim O'Tare moving in. Far as she knows, he still lives there." He pointed a thumb over his shoulder to the building on the corner behind him. "And she's certain he must have either bought or rented the place fully furnished, because there was no moving van. Everything Reilly took away with him and everything O'Tare brought with him fit into their respective cars."

Shred nodded sagely. "Been there, done that. So, it appears we've found Timotazu. Question is, is he Yeng, or is he Nash'terel?"

"There's just one way to find out, isn't there?"

Chapter Three

I t was three o'clock in the morning. They'd been parked across the intersection from O'Tare's two-storey townhouse for the past eight hours. There were no lights showing in any of the windows, and things were becoming blurry. Shred blinked hard, then realized that a light rain had been falling, and it was the windscreen of the car, not his vision, that needed clearing. He turned the defogger on and the wipers for good measure, putting them on a five second delay.

"I don't think he's coming back out to hunt," Shred remarked, glancing at his watch with Nash'terel eyes. "In fact, anyone who didn't know better would think he was a human, getting a good night's sleep."

"Uh-huh," Barron grunted. "Let's play my favourite game: 'What Are the Odds'."

"Okay. What are the odds that he realized we were onto him and he's already escaped out the back door, leaving us to watch an empty house?"

"I've got a better one," said Barron sourly. "What are the odds that he was impersonating Timotazu when he befriended my recruit and we've been looking for the wrong person all along?"

"Sneaky move," murmured Shred. "But it's a good one. I would say that if he knew to do that, the odds are he'd already been trained in evasion techniques before he came to you posing as a Nash'terel."

"So, what now? Do we really want to waste another minute sitting here?"

"No. I think it's time we went inside and discovered just who we're dealing with."

With that, Gershred got out of the car and walked across the road, with Barron close on his heels. The rain was unexpectedly cold and coming down much harder now. Shred hunched his shoulders, glad to be a heat lord at a time like this; but even a heat lord couldn't keep his feet dry in a downpour. If he and Barron took the time to reconnoitre before breaking into the house, the ground could be saturated, making it impossible not to leave wet footprints inside.

They paused beside the tall hedge that ran along the property line to the street. It provided no shelter at all. "What do you teach your trainees to do in a situation like this?" Shred asked over his shoulder.

"A situation like ours, you mean? Or like the target's?"

"Both."

"Okay, Taking Out the Target 101." Barron counted off on his fingers as he recited, "Always approach undetected. Scout the perimeter for traps and for ways the target might escape, and block them ahead of time if you can. Cut off alarm systems and land lines before entering the kill zone. Have your chosen weapon out and ready. Enter silently and unseen. Kill silently, from a distance if possible. Police and exit the area promptly, unseen. Leave no evidence behind."

"And if it's raining?"

Barron shrugged. "This is Vancouver. If we waited for perfect weather, nothing would ever get done."

"All right, then. What if you're the one being stalked and you know it?"

That was a different list. "Arrange a confrontation. Set a trap if you can. Meanwhile, be unpredictable, always have an escape plan, and be prepared to use your *hainbek* to kill your attacker. Remember that a shape-shifting assassin could look like anyone, including a friend, a colleague—" He halted abruptly.

Shred had had the same disturbing thought. "—a parent?"

Silence.

"Was there any sign of forced entry?" Shred asked.

"None. I checked. And Lilly knew better than to open the door to a stranger."

"Then he must have shaped himself into someone she would feel safe letting into the apartment."

"And turning her back on. Someone like Vicky." Barron's tone of voice made it sound like a curse.

"Or you. The empty apartment on the second floor would have given him the privacy he needed for a full body transformation. Did you tell your students about those guest quarters?"

"Yeah," Barron said with a rueful sigh. "We made them available to recruits who came into town on weekend passes. *Shattra*!"

"So, the assassin could have concealed himself there days earlier and simply waited until the child was alone."

More silence. Then, sounding quite earnest, "I really need to kill someone, Gordie. If I can't tell Vicky I spilled some blood tonight—"

"We have a deal, remember?" Shred reminded him. "First we confirm that he's a Yeng. Then we wring as much useful information as possible out of him. Then he's all yours."

"I know, I know," he said impatiently. "Let's scout the perimeter. You take the front and side. I'll take the back. Just like old times."

Yes, Shred thought. In fact, it was too much like old times. While he was carefully inspecting the front of the building for traps, Barron would probably deke inside through a rear entrance and make the kill by himself, as he'd done so often in the past, regardless of the actual parameters of the mission.

"All right," Shred said pleasantly. As soon as the other heat lord was out of sight around the corner of the house, he stepped carefully onto the darkened front porch, pulled his zipper case of lock picks out of his pants pocket, and in less than twenty seconds was standing inside the hallway, checking for security keypads. There were none.

Barron came through the back door a moment later, unsurprised to see Shred waiting for him at the bottom of the staircase.

"We go up together," Shred warned him softly. "And I question him first."

Barron stepped back and waved him upstairs.

As he stepped onto the landing, Shred heard a sputtering noise that reminded him of a chainsaw running out of gas. It was coming from a half-open doorway to his right, at the end of the hall.

The heat lords exchanged bemused looks.

They hesitated just long enough to make sure all the other upstairs rooms were empty. Then, silently entering the last bedroom, they found the source of the sound. A being with rumpled dark hair lay sound asleep in the bed, his arms and legs sprawling in all four directions. And from his open mouth came the annoying racket they'd heard in the hall.

"Human?" Shred wondered aloud.

"I'll check." Barron strode to the side of the bed. He grabbed a fistful of the tousled hair and planted his mouth over the sleeper's lips, instantly waking him. Ignoring his muffled screams and flailing limbs, Barron sucked a sample of essence out of him and swallowed it. "Human," he confirmed. Then he released the man and took a step back, his Nash'terel eyes glowing.

Shred had taken up a position on the other side of the bed.

"Who are you people?" the prey shrilled. He scrambled backward and pressed himself against the headboard, his terrified gaze swivelling back and forth. "What do you want?"

"We're looking for Tim. Or whatever he's calling himself these days," said Shred.

"Tim's not here. He's out of town and I'm house-sitting. Look, if he owes you money, my wallet and credit cards are on the dresser. Take them!"

"He's out of town?" Shred repeated. "Where did he go? And when did he leave? I want the truth, human!"

All at once there was a peculiar smell in the air. A washroom smell. Shred sighed inwardly.

Pulling the infra-red goggles out of his pocket, he said, "Turn on the light."

"I don't think I want to do that," the man stammered.

"Well, I do." And he bent and switched on the lamp beside the bed.

As expected, the man looked surprised by his and Barron's

human appearance. Surprised, but no less frightened.

"You called me 'human'," he declared with a shudder, "and your eyes were glowing!" Wordlessly, Shred showed him the goggles. "And he kissed me!"

"It was part of the script," Shred told him, casting a significant glance across the bed. Barron just shrugged helplessly.

"The script?" The man's face lit up with sudden comprehension. "You're actors? Did Tim put you up to this? Honestly, that guy with his practical jokes... he's going to be the death of me!"

Now Barron was openly grinning.

"Actually," said Shred, "someone else put us up to it. This prank was supposed to be on Tim. Where is he?"

"He left for the airport yesterday afternoon. He's in Toronto by now, getting ready for his big meeting."

With steely self-control, Shred asked conversationally, "Toronto, eh? Where is this meeting? Do you know?"

"Yeah. He mentioned some exclusive gentlemen's club downtown there."

Shred stiffened. "Is it the Riftgate Club, by any chance?"

"Yeah, that's the one. Listen, guys, I'm sorry that you wasted your time, and I'm sorry about... this," he said, indicating his soggy pyjama bottoms. "If you'll give me a few minutes to clean up, the least I can do is make you some coffee before you have to go back out into the rain."

"We appreciate the offer, but it really won't be necessary," said Shred. And, with a nod at Barron that said, *All yours,* he turned and walked out of the room.

"Are you feeling better now?" Shred inquired as Barron joined him inside the car.

The rain was letting up. Around the corner and across the road meanwhile, smoke was beginning to billow from the windows of the townhouse.

"A little," he allowed. "If we don't hear sirens approaching in the next fifteen minutes, I'm going to call 9-1-1 myself." After a pause, he added, "The prey was a vegan."

Shred sat back and gave him a look. "You can know that from the taste of his essence?"

"It's Vancouver. What can I tell you?" He broke into a grin. "Plus, I looked in the fridge before I lit the place up. Organic everything. I wish they all ate like that."

They sat in silence for another few minutes, watching for lights to come on in the adjoining and neighbouring residences. There was no sense in burning down an entire block of homes to cover a single kill. As soon as they knew the fire department had been alerted, they would leave before the street could fill up with vehicles and spectators.

"So now we're waiting for Tim the Yeng assassin to return from Toronto," said Barron.

"From his meeting with the Council of the First at the Riftgate Club," Shred confirmed. "It's their home base. I was there a while ago, with Maury." He paused for a breath before continuing, "The Council had apparently known how to contact all the elemental masters from Halifax to Winnipeg and invite us to a strategy meeting."

Barron's eyebrows rose. "Really! How interesting. Was anyone foolish enough to attend?"

"In person, you mean? Just the two of us, to confirm a suspicion. Because we found it interesting as well that the emperor's assassins have been remarkably good at hunting down our Earthborn offspring. It's as if they're coming through the rift already knowing who and where their targets are. "

"You figured somebody had to be tipping them off?"

"Yes, and now we're certain of it. At that meeting, the First told us that they have agents back on RinYeng, feeding them information about the emperor's plans each time the rift opens. Considering who's involved, it's got to be a quid pro quo, with intel travelling both ways. The Council is trading information about us, to make sure the assassins come after us and not them. No other explanation makes sense. They've probably been gathering and storing our data for centuries, for just that purpose."

"Wouldn't surprise me a bit. They're all a bunch of criminals. Sounds like it's high time someone put a stop to them," Barron said, a calculating smile trickling across his face.

Someone like us. The words hung unspoken in the air between them. Shred didn't object to the implication. He'd been feeling the same way for a long while.

"If my theory is correct, there will be a database located somewhere inside the Riftgate Club," he said.

"Mm-hmm. Backups as well, in digital or hard copy and most likely off-site," Barron reminded him. "Not even the Yeng are stupid enough to keep all their ill-gained intel in one place. The First have had time to rise to positions of wealth and power on this planet. And prominence. We'll need to penetrate their defences and neutralize them all at once, so that none of them have a chance to figure out what's happening and raise the alarm. Not an easy mission, but it's doable, and I know just the right operatives to carry it out."

In the distance, a siren's squeal pierced the night air.

"You're talking about a massive stealth operation, Barney," Shred pointed out. "It would have to be planned down to the smallest detail. Just laying the foundation for it could tie up all of your graduate assassins for months. Don't get me wrong. I'm in if you decide to go ahead with this, but I have to ask: are you absolutely certain we have the resources to pull it off?"

"Sure as I'll ever be, Gordie," came the grim response. "A snake murdered my Lilly, and the way to kill a snake is to cut off its head. But first we need to deal with Timotazu. Any ideas?"

"A couple. We'll need Maury's help. Let's go break the news to him."

As a hook and ladder truck rounded the corner, Shred put the car in drive and headed away from the scene.

"I'm beginning to understand why our females don't give birth more often. My centre of gravity is having an out-of-body experience, and I feel like a fucking beached whale," grumbled Maury, staring down disgustedly at his burgeoning belly. "Are you sure there weren't two heads on that coin we tossed?"

"Patience, my friend," Shred advised him. "You lost fair and square. Besides," he added, steering the rental car smoothly into a spot in the hotel's below-ground parking garage and turning off the ignition, "you're a menace behind the wheel. We'd die in a traffic accident before he could even get to us."

Maury said nothing, just let out a gusty breath.

This trap had been set and baited for three days now. Maury's associate, Pyotren, had used his connections in the human underworld to identify and locate Timotazu, aka Tim O'Tare, ostensibly a private investigator based on the west coast. Sometimes he did "special assignments" for "highly placed interests" in other parts of the country. As far as Pyotren had been able to determine, O'Tare's skills were general rather than specialized, and he preferred to work alone.

Knowing that, Pyotren had approached him, posing as a Yeng assassin looking for a third for a triad. The target was an Earthborn Nash'terel he'd recently found out about who'd fled to Vancouver with his pregnant mate and all their savings, converted into diamonds. It would be an easy double kill, since they were both just apprentices, and the diamonds could be split up three ways afterwards.

The Yeng were a greedy bunch. As anticipated, O'Tare had heard Pyotren out, declined to join his triad, then changed his flight reservation to one that would land him on the west coast two days earlier than originally planned. Safe to say, he had no intention of sharing those diamonds.

"Let's get the groceries upstairs," said Shred. "Then we can watch something banal on the television for a couple of hours. If no one's talked their way into the room and tried to kill us by the time we finish our meal, we'll take a walk in the park."

Maury gave him a look.

"What?" said Shred.

"I have a bad feeling about this plan of yours."

"You think he's twigged to the fact that it's a trap?"

"I think we've made it much too inviting for him and he knows it. He should have moved on us by now. He's probably been watching us go through this charade and laughing up his sleeve the whole damned time."

"Well," said Shred patiently, "maybe he's just waiting to catch me alone. I'll try walking by myself this evening and see what happens. In any case, we can't sit here all day." He opened the driver's side door and stepped out onto the pavement. "Come on, 'Free Willie', I'll help you out of the car."

As he was rounding the rear end of the vehicle, he caught a flash at the corner of his eye. Shred whirled, heat bomb in hand, but Maury's light shield was quicker. Shred was treated to the sight of a thrown knife stopping only centimetres from his chest, then dropping to the ground, as a voice rang out: "*Esstateh'mesh ma Nash'terel!*" It had come from behind one of the numbered cylindrical pillars.

Finally!

A heartbeat later, the assassin—a beefy man wearing jeans and a grey hooded sweatshirt—raced away, off to Shred's right, swearing loudly as it dawned on him that he'd been set up. These were not apprentices. Being without backup, he didn't stand a chance against them. All he could do was try to escape.

Without hesitation, both Nash'terel launched themselves after him. Shred went in direct pursuit. Meanwhile, Maury cut across a double row of cars and ran a parallel path, creating a wall of darkness with his *hainbek* to keep the Yeng on course.

They couldn't let him duck into hiding amidst the parked cars and concrete columns. They had to keep Timotazu on his feet and running toward the street exit.

It would have been easy to simply end him, but that was not part of the plan. Retribution for Lilly's death was not theirs to exact.

As he neared the door, the Yeng halted abruptly, then flew backwards as though picked up and flung by an invisible hand. His arms and legs flailing, he slammed with bone-shattering force into one of the pillars, where he remained pinned nearly a metre off the ground, wide-eyed and struggling to breathe. A moment later, a familiar female shape stepped out of a shadow. She had a hand raised in front of her as though about to wave to someone.

"Hello, Tim," she said, addressing the Yeng. "Remember me?"

"Vincaspera," Shred greeted her. "This is an unexpected pleasure. We thought Barron would be the one joining us."

"He's here, but I couldn't let the boys have all the fun," she replied, staring balefully at the captive assassin. She slowly turned her upraised hand ninety degrees, pulling an agonized scream from his lips and bringing a cruelly satisfied smile to her own.

As they watched, his human face seemed to melt away, revealing a protruding jaw with upward-thrusting lower fangs and a crown of toothlike protuberances that encircled the top of his head.

"Wait a second," Shred told her. "He's definitely Yeng, and his essence is unaltered, but let me question him to make sure we've caught the right one."

"Not a problem," she said, speaking through gritted teeth. "Ask away."

"Answer me quickly, Yeng," he commanded. "Is your name really Timotazu?"

Tears of pain were streaming down his bulbous cheeks. "Yes," he moaned.

"Did you murder my daughter, Yeng filth?" Her eyes glowing, she thrust each razor-sharp word at him as though it were a dagger.

He wouldn't last long. A trickle of red bubbled from the corner of his mouth as he wordlessly dipped his head.

Shred cut in urgently, "Did the Council send you to infiltrate the assassins' training program?"

The Yeng raised his head and gave them a look of pure contempt. "*Esstateh'mesh...*" Then he went completely limp.

"Heard enough?" Vincaspera snapped.

She didn't wait for his reply. Lilly's mother took her revenge.

She worked slowly, breaking every bone into fragments, pulping every bit of soft tissue, squeezing fluid from the Yeng's body like juice from an orange. Completely and utterly destroying him. When she finally stepped back, she was trembling in every limb and gasping for breath. Maury escorted her to her and Barron's car, while the heat lords set about cremating the remains and removing the ashes.

At the end, all that was left of Timotazu was a dark smudge at the base of the pillar and a scorch mark on the floor beside it.

"Thank you, Gordie," said Barron, extending his hand for shaking. "We owe you one."

"And once we're all back in Toronto, I plan to collect," Shred assured him. "But for now, let's focus on the bigger picture."

"The black op. Right. Once she's calmed down, I'll ask Vicky to make our plane reservations."

"Sounds good to me."

"Wait a minute. You're flying?" Maury piped up.

"We're *all* flying, Maury," Shred replied.

"But—"

"It *is* the fastest way to get to the staging location," Barron pointed out. "I'd like to be there before my operatives arrive."

"I understand that, but—"

"No buts, Maury," Shred warned, urging him toward their car. "If you think I'm going to send my pregnant mate all the way across the country by herself—"

"Not funny, Gershred!" Maldemaur sputtered.

"I mean, look at you! What if your water breaks while you're en route?"

As Shred pushed him into the front passenger's seat, Maury let out a guttural cry of frustration.

Barron's uproarious laughter followed them all the way out of the garage.

Part Two

2024

...And Sixteen
Years After It

Chapter Four

Every town in Canada has a hockey rink. It's mandatory in some communities, *de rigueur* in others, depending on which official language predominates. Some rinks are seasonal pop-ups, created outdoors and managed by volunteers. Other rinks are housed in arenas and used year-round, like the one where Maldemaur and Gershred found themselves on a cold and sunny Saturday morning in January.

It wasn't an open-air installation, but as far as Maury was concerned it might as well have been. The arena had an upper viewing deck—a glassed-in extension of the snack bar, actually— with the thermostat set to comfortable, and movable furniture rather than stationary seating, and even a wall-mounted screen fed by the closed-circuit cameras that encircled the ice surface. So civilized! However, Travis was accustomed to seeing them close by, watching him play. So, lower level was where they sat, as usual.

Fortunately, Gershred was a heat lord, able to make the air around them just warm enough for bare hands and unzipped jackets. He had to be careful, though, not to raise the temperature too much. Stripping down to shirt sleeves would undoubtedly draw the attention of the other players' family members, who sat hunched on their own royal blue fold-down seats elsewhere in the stands, bundled up and earmuffed and clutching jumbo-sized paper cups of steaming beverage.

"She's smiling and waving at us again," Maury muttered. "The orange-haired female wearing animal pelts."

"It's fake fur," Shred remarked mildly. "And she's just being friendly."

"Really? Are you sure she understands—?"

"That we're a couple? Yes, I made it quite clear to her when she hit on me earlier that you and I are in a long-time committed relationship."

"Then why is she staring at us like that?"

"Perhaps it's because one of us bears a strong resemblance to Robert Wagner, and she's been a lifelong fan of his work."

"She said that?" Maury cast him a long-suffering look. "I *told* you not to base your shape on a movie star. I warned you we might have to wear these forms for a very long time."

Shred waved off this attempt at reproof. "Says the being who could be the twin of Peter Capaldi."

"You keep repeating that name. Who is Peter Capaldi?" Maury demanded.

"Actually, it's Peter Capaldi was Who. But never mind. I've made sure the fake fur lady understands that we're nobody famous. We're just Travis's grandfathers, cheering him on at his hockey games."

"And yet, she's still staring," Maury persisted, "as if she can see right through us. You're certain she's human, not Yeng?"

"I'm pretty sure."

Maury levelled an accusing gaze at him. "You're *pretty* sure?"

"I got close enough for a sniff, and she doesn't have the smell on her. So, even if she *is* a Yeng, her essence hasn't been chemically altered. That means she's Earthborn, and probably not an assassin."

"Probably? Lovely," he grumbled.

He was talking to himself. Shred's attention was now focused on the play unfolding in the visitors' defensive zone. Excitedly, he elbow-nudged Maury. "You should watch this." In a hushed imitation of a sports announcer, Shred went on, "Travis has the puck. He's on a breakaway, his *hainbek* sweeping the way clear to the net. He moves in. He shoots. He scores! And the crowd goes wild."

"If they ever figure out that he's using his mind and not his stick to propel the puck into the net, they really will go wild, you know," Maury pointed out. "Maybe it's time—"

"—to cut him off from the sport he loves and ship him back to his parents in British Columbia to become one more weapon in the Nash'terel arsenal? He's a fifteen-year-old male. The front of his brain isn't connected yet and he's fuelled by hormones. You don't really believe he's going to go along with something like that, do you?"

"First of all, he may look human and be aging at the normal human rate, but his DNA is half Nash'terel. And second, we made Bilyash and Angie a promise."

"Yes, and we broke it months ago, when we decided not to notify them about their son's emerging talent. What will a few more days or weeks matter?"

"You mean when *you* decided not to tell them, and I decided not to argue with you. But that was then, and now the time has come,"

Maury insisted in a harsh whisper. "Travis's *hainbek* is uncontrolled. He's using it to score hockey goals, and we have no idea how many Yeng are sitting in the stands right now, taking notice. If he's not trained, he'll be defenceless when the rift opens again and the emperor's assassins come through it from RinYeng."

"Which won't be happening for another eighty-four years," Shred reminded him. "For a human, that's a lifetime. Travis may not even last that long."

"Regardless! He needs to learn what he is and who his enemies are, preferably before they have a chance to take him out."

A whistle shrilled twice, then a third time, drawing Shred and Maury to their feet. An altercation had broken out between Travis and one of the opposing players, directly in front of where the two Nash'terel had been sitting. Gloves dropped to the ice. In short order, and with a sudden flailing of limbs, so did the opponent who'd worn them. Travis hadn't laid a finger on him.

"I'd say he's already made a good start on his own," Shred commented evenly as they sat back down.

"No," Maury insisted. "He still doesn't realize the full extent of what he's got and what it makes him capable of. First comes awareness. Then, control. Ideally, it should be taught to him by someone with the same type of *hainbek*."

"Someone like his godmother, Vicky Spears?"

"She's the natural choice, I'm afraid. And she lives on the west coast, along with his parents. I'm tired of lying to them, Shred, even if it is only by omission."

Gershred sighed inwardly. He hated to admit it, but Maury was right.

Travis Fiore was a hybrid, the son of Bilyash—an Earthborn Nash'terel now going by the name Kenneth Smart—and Angelina

Fiore, a genetically-modified human. Maldemaur had taken Bilyash on as an apprentice after rescuing the youngster from a fire that had killed his entire family. Their *hainbeka* were vastly different—Maury's was light and Bilyash's was magnetism—a fact that had made training this Earthborn more challenging than usual.

However, for the past fifteen years, Ken had been out in British Columbia, establishing his new identity and receiving instruction from someone with the same talent as his own. With a mate and a child to protect, he was highly motivated to learn. He would soon complete the basic program and be granted the rank of initiate-adept. Like his father, Travis deserved to develop to his full Nash'terel potential, and that meant spending years in dedicated study and practice. It wouldn't be an easy sell...

All at once, Shred caught a whiff of a familiar, unpleasant aroma. A Yeng from RinYeng was somewhere nearby, carrying a chemical in their body that made their blood and their essence poisonous for Nash'terel to drink.

It had originally been a preventative measure, back on their home world—a vaccine against the "blood sickness" spread by the Nash'terel when they fed. That it also killed the vampire carrying the disease had been a bonus. Now the emperor was using it as a passive weapon, turning every exile and assassin he sent through the rift into poisoned bait... but also handing his enemy a huge advantage, since, unbeknownst to the Yeng, their modified essence gave off a sour, fishy odour that only the Nash'terel and certain Earth animals were able to detect.

Shred sat bolt upright, his eyes narrowing as he scanned the arena.

"You're smelling something rotten too?" Maury murmured beside him.

"It may not be an assassin. It may just be one of the exiles. Excuse me while I find out."

"Try not to leave a mess."

Shred shot him a look. Then he made his way to the aisle, sniffing the air periodically as he followed the scent down to ice level and across the front of the stands, headed toward the foyer. Disconcertingly, Fake Fur Lady's eyes remained on him the whole time. Maury was paranoid, but sometimes he was right. Perhaps he was right about *her*.

Shred filed that thought away, to be considered later.

At the corner of the seating section nearest the exit, he halted. The source of the fishy odour was just inside the door. The Nash'terel turned and gazed in that direction... and met the eyes of a man with a tentative smile on his face and way too much product in his hair. He'd been talking to a couple of spectators. He handed them his business card, then, still smiling, walked directly over to where Shred stood.

The stench as the Yeng approached was enough to turn Shred's stomach, but he forced his expression to remain neutral.

"Excuse me," the other being said pleasantly, "but I couldn't help noticing that you were sitting next to that other gentleman over there." He gestured in Maury's direction. "Do you know him?"

This was a new approach. Shred paused for a beat before replying, "As it happens, I do. We're life partners. Why do you ask?"

"Oh." He looked uncomfortable for a moment. Then the smile trickled back across his face. "My name is Mike Bryant. I'm a scout for the Soo Angels Junior A team," he said firmly, as though to convince himself of his own cover story. "I've been watching these boys play, and I have to say, I'm quite impressed with a few of them. Are you two scouting as well?"

"No. We're just here as spectators."

"Come to enjoy the tournament, eh? Support these kids as they play our national sport?"

Shred's only response was a toothy grin and a wordless nod.

Visibly unnerved, Bryant took a step backward. "Well, there's someone I need to track down," he stammered. "To talk to. About hockey. You and your life partner have a good day." And he spun and walked briskly toward the exit.

Shred glanced behind him, into the stands. He met Maury's inquiring stare and answered it with a shrug.

Bryant clearly knew he'd been speaking with a Nash'terel who'd identified him as a Yeng, but the question still remained: was he an assassin? If he was, and if his target was inside the arena, he wouldn't waste another minute now. He'd lost the element of surprise. He would go in for the kill and hope that speed alone could ensure his escape. If he wasn't an assassin, just a hockey scout who happened to be a Yeng, he might simply go about his business. However, if he had a gram of intelligence, he would not stick around to become prey for Nash'terel hunters. He would leave the building and get as far away as possible.

Unhurriedly, the heat lord followed the Yeng out of the rink and into the foyer, where adult humans clad in colourful toques and scarves and warm winter jackets stood in clusters, chatting animatedly. Meanwhile, their young offspring slalomed back and forth among them, occasionally bouncing off one of the yellow-painted cinder block walls. Carefully remaining out of Bryant's sight, Shred deked around a corner and observed.

In his experience, Yeng assassins—the trained ones—always

came in threes. As he watched, Bryant paused to exchange words with the man who'd been servicing the quartet of vending machines. The repairman immediately packed up his tools and headed for the side exit. Meanwhile, Bryant entered the corridor leading to the team dressing rooms.

There were no parents there. He must be going in for the kill. But that made only two assassins. Where was the third member of the triad?

Shred thought for a moment about following Bryant, then changed his mind. He'd been in similar situations before. The passageway was a dead end, and he already knew the dressing room doors would be locked. This had to be a trap, with Bryant as the bait and the other two Yeng lying in wait to spring it. Cautiously, he scanned the crowd again, but saw nothing that set off his mental alarms.

Well, there were three ways to deal with a trap: he could fall into it, avoid it, or turn it to his own advantage. Shred chose the third alternative. Keeping watch on the arena's front and side doors, he shifted his features, trading Robert Wagner's affable expression for a much craggier, more immediately threatening appearance. Then he waited.

Sure enough, the repairman returned, entering the foyer through the front door this time. He was wearing a different outer garment than before. It was longer, and bulkier on one side, most likely concealing a weapon that he'd gone outside to fetch after Bryant had told him that a Nash'terel was onto them.

Different clothes but the same face? Even a rookie assassin ought to know better than that...

Shred watched the man unzip his coat and stroll casually around the perimeter of the room.

...and he's trying far too hard to look uninterested in his surroundings. Next, he'll be whistling to himself. Definitely not the brightest light in the chandelier, this one... unless he's a decoy, meant to distract me while the other two take up their positions...?

He was an Earthborn Yeng. The odour coming from him, while unpleasant, wasn't even half as strong as what Bryant had given off. As soon as the repairman was close enough to be grabbed, Shred slipped up behind him. He clamped one hand on the man's arm and the other over his mouth and yanked him around the corner, out of sight.

Slamming the Yeng face first against the wall, Shred leaned in close and whispered, "I'm a heat lord. I can incinerate you from the inside out or flash-freeze you solid, and I will if you don't do exactly as I say."

"*Esstateh'mesh ma Nash'terel!*" hissed the man, reaching inside his coat as he twisted violently around.

He was quick, but Shred was quicker. He'd already gathered heat into his right hand. Now he pressed it to the other being's chest, pinning the Yeng to the wall and the concealed weapon in place, and poured that pent-up heat into both of them. The smells of seared flesh and scorched wool were soon rising into the air.

Shred cast a glance into the foyer to assure himself that no one else had noticed, then returned his attention to his prey.

"You can curse me all you like, but my ignoble death will have to wait," Gershred told him quietly, thrusting each word like a dagger at the assassin's contorting face. "Let go of whatever you've got in there and I'll cool you off before your clothing ignites. Or you can hang onto it and burst into flame. Your choice."

Gasping with pain, the Yeng withdrew a burnt and blistering hand from his coat front.

"Wise decision," Shred murmured. He reached in and relieved the would-be killer of his gun. Then, tucking the alien-made firearm into his own inside coat pocket, he continued, "Now, we're going to cross over to that corridor. Just walk in front of me, keep your hands in your pockets, and don't say another word."

They moved together, the Yeng as though he were negotiating a minefield, into the dimly-lit passageway. Once concealed from human view, Shred reverted his eyes to their Nash'terel form and scanned the space around him. The shadows were empty. No one was following him, and there was no Bryant ahead of him, not that he could see.

Keeping Maury comfortable in the stands for a solid hour and a half had made Shred a bit peckish, but he didn't dare drink this Yeng's essence. So, instead of draining the life of his defeated enemy in the time-honoured way of a warrior, Shred had to settle for pulling every bit of heat out of him and directing it through a vent into the air duct, then snapping the failed killer's neck. Instantly, the sour fish smell was obliterated by another kind of odour, this one detectable by humans.

One down, two to go. The entire process had taken no more than ten minutes. Shred paused, all his senses on high alert. Seconds later, a cheer went up inside the rink. Apparently, another goal had just been scored. However, the corridor he was in remained silent and empty, raising disquieting questions in his mind. Bryant should have made his move as soon as Shred disposed of his living shield. Where was he?

There were several closed doors set deeply into the cinder block walls of the hallway. They led to two team dressing rooms, a cleaning supply closet, the officials' office, and the ice rink. Moving forward cautiously, Shred tested the handle on the door labelled 'Maintenance'. It was unlocked. Weapon in hand, he burst through the doorway... and found himself in a small room lined with metal shelving. No Bryant here, but he did find an industrial-sized canvas laundry hamper on wheels. And half a dozen spray cans of air freshener.

Perfect.

Shred worked quickly. Keeping an eye on the passageway, he dragged the dead Yeng inside, pocketed the other being's car keys, then stuffed the corpse into the hamper, spritzed them both liberally with deodorizer, and pulled some towels off an overhead shelf to spread as a covering. Incineration was the best way to dispose of a Yeng body, but there was no time for that right now. Not while there were two more assassins out there, stalking their next target.

He hoped it was himself, not least because the Earthborn were easy kills, too young and untrained to defend themselves—the main reason that the Yeng kept going after them—but rather because Shred was now spoiling for a fight.

His fangs itching, he returned to the corridor and tested the air. Bryant had definitely gone down this hallway. Unless he had stolen past Shred while his back was turned—which was unlikely, since it would have meant passing up a perfect killing opportunity—the bogus hockey scout had to be lurking behind one of the other doors.

As expected, the dressing rooms were locked up tight. So was the officials' office. That left just one possibility: the passage leading to the rink, used by players to enter and exit the ice. He sniffed again. Bryant's scent was strongest here.

Shred cursed under his breath. While he'd been dealing with the repairman, Mike Bryant had positioned himself to close in for the kill. His target was most likely one of the players in the current game. Bryant could approach the Earthborn on his way back to the dressing room, flash a business card, and take the youngster aside on the pretext of discussing his future prospects in pro hockey. It was a near-perfect plan. Now Shred had to figure out a way to thwart it without drawing unwelcome human attention to himself. It wouldn't be easy...

...or then again, maybe it would. The rink door chose that moment to open, spilling a pair of angry voices into the corridor. Shred recognized their owners and smiled inwardly. Bryant was already being thwarted, by Travis's coach.

"You don't understand. I have permission to wait here. I'm a scout for the Angels."

"Yes, I do understand. No, you don't have permission. And I don't give a damn who you say you are, you're leaving."

Full-on grinning now, Shred took the Yeng gun out of his pocket and tucked himself into the recess of the door to the officials' office. With luck, Bryant's first thought would be to make sure the path to the foyer was clear, not to check behind him.

"But—"

"Now! Or would you prefer we carry you out of here bodily?"

Shred was quite familiar with the weapon he was holding. It was ion-based and designed for close quarters. It killed quickly, cleanly, and all but noiselessly. So much more practical in these surroundings than using his heat *hainbek*. Not nearly as satisfying, though.

Shred waited until Bryant was in the hallway and the door to the rink had closed. Then he activated the beam of the gun. Bryant stiffened and tried to turn around, but it was too late. Shred sliced downwards, cutting the Yeng in two without spilling a drop of his blood, before the other being could so much as let out a squeak.

Two down, one left to go.

According to the four-sided electronic scoreboard suspended like a chandelier over centre ice, the game was tied 4-4 and in sudden death overtime when Shred returned to his seat in the stands.

"Well?" said Maury.

"You were right. He was an assassin. I've disposed of two of the triad. No idea how they managed to graduate from training, if they got any at all. They were the most incompetent killers I've ever seen. The third one is not inside the arena—I checked. So, he's out there somewhere, probably watching the building exits and waiting for updates."

A pause, then, "Two are dead. Does that mean there's cleaning up to do?"

"In a way. There's a rather full laundry hamper that I need to empty before anyone else finds it," Shred replied. "Meanwhile, the third assassin will eventually be forced to realize that he's on his own and dealing with at least one Nash'terel with a *hainbek*, who's now on high alert. The smartest thing for any Yeng at this point would be to withdraw. The second smartest thing would be to take us out from a distance, preferably when we're surrounded by humans so he can make his escape in the ensuing commotion. The question is, is he smart enough to do either one of them?"

"Firing on us in a crowd, from a distance?" said Maury, scowling. "That's not really a Yeng assassin's style, is it?"

"It's a human strategy," Shred agreed, "crude but effective. Of course, it also means he doesn't get to yell that stupid curse at us, and I think that's half the fun for them."

"Well, you're the military mind in the family. What do you

recommend we do in this situation?"

For an experienced assassin-hunter like Shred, the answer was obvious. "We take him out by drawing him in and deceiving him into dropping his guard. How quickly can you get your friend Pyotren here?"

"About an hour if he's coming from home. I'll make the call," said Maury. "Should he bring Armin with him, in case they've done something to our car as well?"

"It probably wouldn't hurt. Now, about Travis..." he added reluctantly. "I've changed my mind. You're right. We can't keep his hybrid nature a secret much longer. He's safer on the west coast."

"I'm glad we're finally in agreement. I've been carrying his prepared *dashkra* around in my pocket for weeks."

Shred frowned. "A bloodstone? That's a little premature, don't you think? He's not even an initiate apprentice yet."

"He's aging at a human rate and may not have time to reach that skill level," Maury reminded him. "The sooner we can break the news to him and perform the ritual of passage, the happier I'll be."

"So when do you want—?"

"Right after the game," Maury told him, in a tone of voice that warned him not to argue.

Predictably, Travis Fiore's alien talent helped him score the winning goal, giving the Georgian Bay Rockets a berth in the tournament semi-finals the following day. Maury and Shred waited by the dressing room door to congratulate him.

Travis was tall both on and off his skates. Today, he was also the star of the game, and the easiest player to pick out of the river of blue and gold jerseys crossing the corridor from the rink. When he saw Maury and Shred, Travis's face lit up. He gave them a broad grin and a thumbs-up sign. Then the current carried him into the dressing room with the rest of his team.

Coach Brandeis was heavy-set, with a naturally scowling face that reminded Shred of nearly every gangster movie he'd ever seen. At this moment, however, he was grinning. "Your grandson did really well today, Dr. de Maur. You should be proud.

"We're going to stay and watch the next game, because we're playing the winners of it tomorrow morning. Then I was planning to treat the boys to lunch before our practice this afternoon."

"We'd like to tag along as well, if that's okay," Shred told him. "We'll pay our own way, of course."

"Not a problem! I'm certain other family members will be joining us as well," Brandeis said cheerfully.

"Would you just let Travis know we'd like to have a private word with him in the dressing room before he joins his teammates in the stands?" Maury chimed in.

"Sure." A pause, then, "You're not giving him bad news or anything, are you?"

Actually, Shred thought, that depended on how the youngster took it.

"No, no, not at all," said Maury, showing the coach a reassuring smile.

When they were once more alone in the corridor, Shred murmured, "Travis looks so much like his mother."

"And what part of his father would you like him to present to the world?" Maury growled. "The extra joints in his limbs? The scales? Maybe the skull ridges? He's much better off this way. What if he'd been born looking Nash'terel but not able to shift into human form? That would have marked him as a monster. We both know how humans react to monsters. And Angie wouldn't have been able to love him in spite of that because she probably wouldn't have survived giving birth to him."

"But it didn't happen that way. And now he's got his heart set on being a professional hockey player," Shred said with a sigh, "and that's not going to happen either. I'm afraid he'll react badly to finding out why."

"You said it yourself, we can't wait any longer. He may not be in danger yet, but he soon will be. And we *promised* them."

Gershred's shoulders sagged. "I know. You don't have to remind me. It's just that—"

"I know. I'll miss him too."

Nodding his agreement, Shred added, "And there's something else I'll miss. Having Travis around and being forced to engage with the human world for the past ten years has been good for you, Maury. It's eased some of your rampant paranoia. Taken most of the profanity out of your voicemail greetings, at any rate. And you can't deny that it's mellowed you."

"Right. Making the three of us a lot easier to identify and attack," Maury grumped.

Batting away his comment, Shred continued, "In fact, when Travis leaves us, as he inevitably will, one way or another, I think we ought to get a pet."

Maury tossed him a jaundiced look. "Really? Since when do Nash'terel warriors keep animals, except for transportation or emergency rations?"

"If Bilyash could bond with both a human and a dog, there must be something you and I could bond with. How about—"

"How about a flying pig?"

Shred responded to this challenge without missing a beat. "Okay. Wings or propellers?"

"Gravity *hainbek*."

"Hmm." Shred pretended to ponder. "That sort of genetic experimentation is more Vicky Spears' department than mine, but I'll see what I can do."

Chapter Five

It took half an hour for the Rockets to shower and change, then pack up their gear. Toting bulky zippered bags and carrying hockey sticks as though they were walking sticks, they filed out of the dressing room, politely acknowledging the two older gentlemen who stood patiently in the hallway.

Coach Brandeis was the last one to leave. "All yours now. Travis is waiting for you inside," he told them, handing Maury a key hanging off one end of a long wooden fob. "Just lock up when you're done and drop this through the slot in the manager's office door."

The dressing room, like the rest of the arena, had a poured concrete floor and cinder block walls painted in shades of yellow and orange. The colours were warm and cheery. When empty, however, this space felt far from welcoming. The air held a pervasive chill, and a slight echo seemed to hollow out every sound, giving it an ominous turn. For just an instant, it seemed to Shred as though the room itself was questioning Maury's decision to rush the bloodstone ritual.

Standing in the middle of the floor, Travis had his hockey bag at his feet, two sticks in his hand, and a look of puzzlement on his face.

"Coach says you need to talk to me. Is something wrong?"

"No," Shred assured him. "Have a seat, kiddo. You're not in any trouble. Not from us, anyway."

As the teen laid down his sticks and sank uncertainly onto a bench, Maury threw Shred a reproving look. Then, sitting down as well, Maury pulled the *dashkra* out of his pocket and dangled it on its chain in front of Travis's face. "This is what we need to talk to you about, Grandson."

The teardrop-shaped stone was polished and pristine, its milky surface broken only by the startling whiteness of its veins and whorls.

Travis began to reach for it, then changed his mind. "It's pretty, whatever it is."

"And it's precious. In the old language, this mineral is called *dashkra*. It means 'bloodstone'," Shred explained. "It's extremely rare. It made our people what we are, and now it defines and symbolizes us."

"Bloodstones are handed down from generation to generation," Maury said. "This one was worn by your late great-grandmother. I've been keeping it for you."

Unexpectedly, Travis frowned. "And you're showing it to me *now*? I mean, don't get me wrong, I think it's dope, but you never told me about this before. If it's some kind of secret—"

"Actually, it's more like a coming of age emblem," Maury replied. "Every adult who can trace their bloodline back to our—" Briefly interrupted by the sound of Shred clearing his throat, he set his jaw and continued, "—our *homeland* is eligible to receive one."

"We know you're not an adult yet," said Shred, "and originally, we were going to wait another few years to do this, but there's been a change of plans."

Travis swivelled his gaze from one to the other of them. "A change of plans? I don't understand."

"The Yeng may have found out about you," Maury said impatiently, "because of your special talent."

The kid's face lit up. "An Asian team wants me to play for them?"

"No, I'm afraid not," Shred replied. "The Yeng are our mortal enemies. They want to kill all of us, including you."

Travis's eyes went saucer-wide. "We're at war with the Chinese?"

Maury let out an exasperated syllable. "No! The Yeng are a different group. They're—"

"—extremists," Shred cut in. "From our homeland."

"And they want to kill *me*? Why?"

"Because they're them and you're one of us," Maury snapped, "and that's all the reason they need."

"So this is some kind of old country vendetta?" Travis exclaimed, his voice rising on the last word.

"Much worse than that, Trav," said Shred. "It's a genocide. It's the reason we're here and not back there. And now the Yeng have come here too, looking for us and determined to wipe us out."

"Whoa! Hold on!" Travis leaped to his feet and turned to confront them. "So the Yeng are not Chinese, that's just the name they've given themselves? And if I look them up online...?"

"You won't find them," Shred told him. "They're a secret organization. Nobody besides our people knows about them, or knows why they want us dead. We didn't tell you about them because we were hoping you would never have to—"

"Your parents are in B.C., preparing to fight them," Maury cut in, casting a defiant glance in Shred's direction. "They sent you to live with us because you were safer that way. But that isn't the case anymore."

A shadow crossed the adolescent features. "Why? Because the Yeng are among us? Because they might have seen how good I am at playing hockey?" he demanded.

"Not just 'might have', Travis," Shred replied, putting an edge on each word. "They're here today, in the arena. I've seen them. I've alread—" He caught himself just in time. "I've learned how to identify them."

A pause. Then, in a more subdued voice, "And my parents are learning how to fight them. Is it so they can protect me?"

"Yes, of course," Shred replied.

"Do *you* know how to fight them?" Travis asked.

"We couldn't have kept you safe for the last ten years if we didn't," Maury assured him, "and we'll continue doing it until—"

"Until my mother and father can join us?"

Alarms went off at the back of Shred's brain. There was a trap concealed in that seemingly innocent question. Moving quickly to avoid it, he replied, "Until we're all together again, yes, but that's not what's important right now." To Maury, he said quietly, "The ritual can wait. Agreed?"

With evident reluctance, the other Nash'terel said, "Agreed," and tucked the bloodstone back into his pocket.

"You have an unusual talent, Travis," Shred went on, "one that marks you as Nash'terel. That's our name in the old language. Think about all the impossible hockey goals you've scored lately. Your coach says it's as though the puck has eyes. You may not have realized it, but you've actually been using your mind to steer the puck around the goalie's stick and pads."

Excitement illuminated the youngster's expression. "Wow! I've been visualizing it while playing like Coach told us to, but I thought it was happening because—Wait a minute. Are you telling me I'm good at hockey because I have a super power? And you've got super powers too?"

Maury expelled a martyred breath. "You and your comic book heroes, Shred... you've been a bad influence on him. Yes, Grandson, every Nash'terel has a talent. We call it a *hainbek*. But we don't show it off, because we don't want to tip off the Yeng and get ourselves killed."

Travis's gaze became troubled once more. "And because I've been using mine, that's how they found me?"

"Unfortunately, yes," Shred replied. "When a puck takes an unexpected bounce on the ice, those are the breaks. But when it happens in mid-air, repeatedly, someone is bound to notice."

"I wasn't doing it on purpose, Grandpa G."

"I know. But it happened, and now that the Yeng are most likely aware of you, there's going to be a bull's-eye on your back. That's why, sooner rather than later, you're going to have to learn how to defend yourself against them."

Travis's chin came up. "I can fight. You've seen me fight."

"Yes. You're a big strong kid, and you can knock people off their feet without touching them," Maury allowed. "That's all well and good when you're up against an enemy you can see and confront. Not as effective when he's a sneaky bastard who'll wear disguises to get close to you so he can set you up for an ambush. The Yeng fight dirty, Travis."

"They do that because they realize they're at a disadvantage,"

Shred hastened to explain. "They don't have 'super powers', as you put it. But they'll come after you anyway, just for being Nash'terel. The best way to defend against them is to weaponize your talent, the way we've done with ours. That takes a lot of training, though. It doesn't happen overnight."

"In the meanwhile, no more using your *hainbek* to score hockey goals, young man," Maury told him sternly. "From now on, you have to appear to propel that puck with your stick, like everyone else. If you can't rein in your talent, then purposely miss the net occasionally, or aim your shot for the goalie's pads. You may not be a star player anymore, but you won't be advertising yourself as a target for assassins either, and that's all we care about. Understood?"

"Understood, Grandpa M."

The crestfallen look on the boy's face tugged at Shred's heart. "Listen," he said, "you did an outstanding job on the ice this morning. Your team is in the semi-finals because of you. We're proud of you, and so is your coach. And your teammates are over the moon. Enjoy that recognition, Travis. You've earned it."

"But avoid drawing attention to myself because the Yeng are out to get me," he recited in a sing-song voice. "Right."

"Just act normal, Travis," Maury advised him. "We'll discuss this some more at home tonight. Now, go join your teammates. Watch the game and talk about hockey, about food, about girls... about anything but the Yeng. We have something to take care of and will see you when it's over."

His smile now pinned back in place, Travis hoisted the carry-strap of his hockey bag over his shoulder, picked up his sticks, and hurried out the door.

Maury and Shred weren't fooled for one second.

"You lied to him," Maury observed evenly, "about his parents coming here to join us."

Shred stiffened. "No, I didn't. I just gave him a purposely ambiguous response."

"Uh-huh. And he saw through it quite handily."

"I know. But it wasn't a good time to have that discussion." Shred let out a weary sigh. Privately, he doubted whether there *could* be a right time to snatch away a youngster's hopes for the future.

Meanwhile, Maury was consulting his wristwatch. "Pyotren and Armin will be arriving soon. Let's lock up here. While we're waiting for them in the foyer, you can tell me how we're going to entrap the third assassin."

Fifteen minutes later, a man who was average-looking in every way walked through the arena's front doors. Of medium height and build, and possessing a set of utterly forgettable features, he wore blue denim jeans, a bluish-greenish winter jacket, and a scarf and matching toque that might once have been white but never would be again. He paused for a moment, then headed directly to where Maury and Shred stood near the row of vending machines.

"Hi," he said, pulling from his pocket a key fob with a multi-coloured stone set into it and flashing it like a badge. "I'm Pete Ryan. I understand you're in need of some automotive assistance."

"That's a new shape for you, Pyotren," Maury remarked.

"It's a burner. Armin's wearing one too. He's outside with the tow truck. Show me the problem."

Shred glanced around to confirm that the corridor to the dressing rooms was empty. "This way," he said, and led the others to the maintenance closet.

Pyotren and his cousin Armin were elemental masters with a

very useful *hainbek*, especially in the current circumstances. In addition to shapeshifting themselves, they could rearrange matter to alter the outward appearance of other beings' bodies, and change the forms of inanimate objects as well. Now, gazing down into the laundry hamper, Pyotren scowled and told them, "I hope you're not expecting me to put him back together. I'm good, but I'm not *that* good."

"We want you to help us look like them, and then make them look like someone else," said Shred.

"There may be a third assassin out there. We're setting a trap," Maury explained.

Pyotren gave them a broad grin. "And the first two are the bait? Brilliant!"

Twenty minutes later, it was done. The side door leading to the parking lot swung open into bright sunlight, and the laundry hamper emerged. It was push-pulled with difficulty along the snow-covered pavement by two beings who hoped the last member of the triad, if he was out there, would recognize the clothing they were wearing and come closer out of curiosity. They wrangled the hamper to the middle of the lot and stopped. Then, Shred-as-Bryant shaded his eyes with one hand and waved the other above his head while turning slowly to scan the rolling terrain around the arena.

"There!" exclaimed Maury-as-the-repairman, tapping him on the shoulder and pointing to a distant, well-padded figure who'd broken cover and was now galloping across a field toward them with what appeared to be a rifle slung over his shoulder.

"That Yeng does not look happy," Shred remarked. "Let's hope Pyotren did a bang-up job on us. Otherwise, this could get messy."

"You two... are in a lot... of trouble," the third assassin scolded them, panting. Judging from the shape he'd chosen, he hadn't expected to do any running today. "Why did you go silent?" he demanded once he'd caught his breath. "And what the hell are you doing out here?"

"We were setting up an ambush," Maury replied, gesturing at the laundry hamper. "And by the way, it worked. We got both of them."

He'd spoken in his own voice.

Shred forced himself not to react. As he watched the assassin for any sign of realization that something was wrong, he brought his own hand closer to his pocket, ready to draw the captured gun if necessary.

Fortunately, he didn't have to.

"Both of who?" the Yeng demanded impatiently. "You idiots had a single target—the kid—and he'd damn well better be in there."

Shred adjusted his own vocal cords and explained in a fair imitation of Bryant's oily tenor tones, "He's still inside the arena. We couldn't get to him, and his parents recognized what we were, so we had to take them out instead."

"Really? Am I supposed to believe that you bumblers actually got the drop on a pair of adult Nash'terel who'd already seen through your disguises?"

Shred shrugged. "We were lucky. They overestimated us and we were able to surprise them."

Still looking unconvinced, the assassin extended a beefy hand and pulled back the top layer of towels in the hamper. Then he let out a disgusted syllable. "Apparently, *I* overestimated you too. Cutting one of them in half? After I specifically told you we were going to make it look like an accident? No investigator, human *or*

Nash'terel, is going to fall for that now. *Ruffeh!*"

This Yeng expletive always reminded Shred of a sneeze. Each time he heard it, he had to stifle the urge to say, "Bless you!"

"Look, we need to get the hamper back inside before someone misses it," said Maury. "We can burn the corpses, just not here. Would you give us a hand...?"

"How did I end up with a couple of *ristima* like you?" demanded the Yeng. "All right, then. As long as we hurry. Pop the trunk of one of their cars. You did grab their keys, right? And their bloodstones, so we can get paid?"

Their bloodstones? These assassins are collecting bounties?

Shred nodded mutely, then shared a significant look with Maury. Someone had evidently put a price on Nash'terel heads. This smacked of vengeance.

Gershred reached into his pocket for the correct car key fob and pressed the trunk release button. Then he pretended to search for the source of the muted *thunk* that followed.

"That one," said Maury, pointing to where they'd parked earlier.

Together, they pushed the hamper over to the car. Shred lifted the trunk lid the rest of the way. Then, continuing to impersonate the screw-ups their handler obviously believed they were, they made a series of abortive attempts to transfer the first half of Bryant's body from the hamper to the trunk, arguing nonstop about the best way to do it.

As expected, the third assassin finally couldn't stand watching them fumble around anymore. Cursing them for incompetence, he leaned his rifle against the rear fender of the car. He elbowed Shred aside and took his place, then set about moving the hamper as close as possible to the mid-point of the bumper. After ordering Maury to lift the shoulder of the half-corpse, the Yeng grabbed hold of its leg, and together they swung and dropped it into the trunk of Maury's vehicle.

The assassin was upbraiding the two *ristima* the whole time, not paying attention to what was happening behind him. He leaned into the trunk.

Shred had been waiting for this moment. He took out the ion pistol and burned a tunnel with it, deep into the Yeng's brain. A shove from the side sent this third dead body the rest of the way in, wearing a startled expression on its face.

Shred glanced around the parking lot. No humans appeared to have witnessed his kill. Not that it would matter, of course, once he and Maury had returned to their own forms. Finally, he threw the rifle into the trunk and went through the third Yeng's clothing, searching for car keys.

At the bottom of a pants pocket, his questing fingers closed on something they recognized even before he pulled it out to show Maury—a bloodstone pendant. The clasp was broken. This *dashkra* had been ripped from someone's neck.

Maury cursed softly at the sight of it. "From a recent kill. The colours are still bright."

They wouldn't stay that way. A *dashkra* reflected and fed on the unique life essence shed by the being whose blood it had most recently drunk, but only if that being kept it on their person. Separated from its wearer, the stone would fade over time, returning to its original milky white appearance as it waited for a new food source to come along.

Shred took out his phone and snapped a photo of the colours that imbued the pendant currently in his hand, to preserve them for future reference. "Do you recognize the bloodline?" he asked Maury.

"Of course. But with all the interbreeding among the families, we'll need more information to narrow the search down to an individual."

"That was very nicely done." Pyotren appeared at Shred's elbow, stopping short when he saw what was in the other being's hand. "We've lost another one." It wasn't a question. "The Guild will need to be notified, so they can update the database."

"With what? We don't know whose bloodstone this is," Maury told him, "not yet, anyway, and the members of the Guild are trained as killers and protectors, not investigators. If we hand them a mystery, they'll just hand it back to us. Meanwhile, potentially valuable time will have been lost." After a pause, he added, "Are you still in contact with your Earthborn researcher friend? Seldon something..."

"Seldon Pratt. That was eighty years ago. Now he's shifted to selling real estate in the form of a woman named Stella Parr," Pyotren replied, holding out his hand. "Seldon could find a specific snowflake in a blizzard. Stella can track down whoever owned this."

Shred gave him the pendant. Pyotren slipped it into his inner coat pocket before continuing, "And now, let's take out the trash, shall we?"

Working rapidly, they finished unloading the laundry hamper into the trunk. Then Shred used the key fobs he'd removed from the dead Yengs' pockets to locate the assassins' three vehicles: a white sports van with a company name and logo on its side, a mid-sized metallic-green hybrid sedan, and a large black pickup truck with oversized tires. They would all have to be driven out of the lot if the narrative of Shred's plan was to hold together.

As Armin set to work hooking Maury's car up to the tow truck,

Maury, Shred, and Pyotren each took a fob.

"Okay," Shred announced. "There's an abandoned rock quarry about ten klicks west of here, just off the main road. We'll meet up there."

The Nash'terel were hunters with extraordinary night vision. Shred had noticed the quarry a week earlier, when they'd been driving to the arena in the hour before dawn. The sheer drop to the bottom of the pit on the side farthest from the road had appeared to be at least twenty metres. It was the ideal place to crash and burn a hybrid automobile with two bodies in the front seat and a third body in the trunk. Shred was a heat lord. After starting the car fire, he could focus its heat at will in order to totally destroy the vehicle and reduce the three Yeng corpses inside it to unidentifiable ashes.

The pickup and the van would later be abandoned in two separate, isolated locations, Armin and Pyotren would go their own way in the tow truck, and Maury and Shred would return to the arena in their own forms, driving their own vehicle. On roads that were clear and dry, with minimal traffic, they could zip along at a hundred klicks per hour both ways and arrive back in plenty of time to have lunch with Travis's team.

It was a perfect plan. What could possibly go wrong?

Chapter Six

Pyotren stood watching as the tow truck, the van, and the hybrid sedan lined up to make the turn out of the parking lot. Then he got to work pushing the hamper back to where they'd found it.

Work was the right word for it, he reflected darkly. Between the snow on the ground that kept grabbing the wheels and the heavy slab of door that wanted desperately to stay closed, he had the devil's own time returning the unwieldy hamper inside the building. By the time they'd both crossed the threshold, he was swearing under his breath in every human language he'd ever learned.

Then a voice barked out, "You!"

Startled, Pyotren nearly shifted spontaneously. "What?!" he yelped.

"Where did you get that?"

The man stalking toward him was built like a brick tool shed. He had the words "Rink Maintenance" embroidered on the front of his pale blue shirt, and accusation stamped on his full-moon face.

In response, Pyotren adopted an expression of confused innocence. "You mean the laundry hamper? I found it outside and was just bringing it in."

"Where outside?" demanded the man.

"On the walkway, near the parking lot."

"Those damn towel thieves!" The man leaned into the hamper and began rifling through its contents. "They must think this is a freakin' hotel. I've been losing a dozen large towels a month. Look at this!" He pulled up a fistful of terrycloth and shook it in the air. "These were never used. Half of them are still folded from being on the shelf. You're certain you didn't see anyone hanging around the hamper before you found it?"

"Positive. It was just sitting there, half-empty."

The man put a hand on the metal frame. Before leaving, Shred had warmed it up so that no one would realize the hamper had been outside in the wintry air. Of course, that only worked if Pyotren wasn't caught returning it.

Oops!

The maintenance man's doughy features kneaded themselves into a portrait of suspicion as he leaned closer and demanded, "Are you sure you weren't headed out that door instead of coming in?"

Only then did Pyotren catch the faintest whiff of Yeng in the air.

He forced himself to smile and gestured downward. "Would there be snow melting off the wheels if I were?" he said, purposely putting an edge of impatience on his voice. "Listen, I'm sorry you've been losing towels, but I'm not the one who's been taking them. In any case, I'm missing my nephew's game right now, so if you don't mind…?"

Grudgingly, the man pulled back and waved him toward the

rink entrance.

Pyotren located Travis, sitting with his team in the section of seats adjacent to one of the blue lines, and climbed to a spot several rows above them. Then he took out his phone and texted Maury: *Can't come now. Another Yeng at the arena. Am staying to keep an eye on things until you return.*

"*Shattra!*" Maury spat. "Pyotren's back there on his own, and we've got all the weapons!"

Armin was busy releasing Maury's car from the towing rod. "He's not helpless, you know," he called over his shoulder. Like his cousin, he was wearing a shape that would be difficult to describe, other than to say that he resembled any of a hundred other average-sized, middle-aged men. "Pete can change the boy's appearance and smuggle him out to the pickup truck."

"No," Shred said with a sigh, "we warned him today about the Yeng, and how they might try to deceive him. He won't recognize Pyotren in any of his forms, and even if he did, he wouldn't trust him. One of us will have to go back for the kid. And in case he really is in danger, I think it should be me."

"Really? You think I can't defend him?" Maury bristled. "You have a short memory, my friend."

"Oh, for *shattra*'s sake," muttered Armin. "Stop wasting time arguing. Flip a coin, or draw straws, but one of you go inside the van and shapeshift back to normal. I'll take care of the rest."

"Your *hainbek* is needed here, for the cremation," Maury pointed out to Shred. "If there's a situation at the rink, I'll find a way to get Travis out safely, without attracting attention, and I'll text you when I've done it so you won't have to worry. Okay?"

"Sure. Fine," Shred replied, biting off each word.

Fifteen minutes later, himself once more, Maury slid the van's door aside and stepped down to the ground. He paused at the sight of the other two Nash'terel standing there, apparently gazing approvingly at him.

"What?" he demanded, about to add, "You've never seen a full body transformation before?" The words died on his tongue when Shred and Armin high-fived each other, and he realized what they'd actually been admiring: the van.

While Maury had been inside it, Armin had turned its exterior black and shiny, adorning each side with the image of a wizard riding a dragon in flight. The colours were bold, the message crystal clear: this was the chariot of a powerful being.

So much for not attracting attention.

"What the hell—?!"

"It's your loaner vehicle," Armin explained. "It supports your story about having a car problem, and if you have to flee, the dragon is the detail that will stick in people's memories, making everything else fuzzy. Shred and I can handle things at this end. You go get your boy. I'll let Pyotren know that you're on your way."

From his perch halfway up the stands, Pyotren kept one eye on the back of Travis's head and the other on the pudgy-faced maintenance man. Seen from a distance and minus his earlier angry scowl, he looked a lot younger in human years than Pyotren would originally have guessed.

The Yeng had been wandering around the rink, carrying a broom and a long-handled dustpan but not doing much with either one of them. He did, however, keep checking his phone and visually scanning the crowd, as though searching for someone whose picture appeared on the screen.

That was curious behaviour.

Three times the Yeng had swung his gaze along the row where Travis and his teammates were sitting, and three times he'd frowned at his phone before directing his attention elsewhere.

Hmm.

Pyotren surveyed the arena and saw a hundred or so human spectators, all intently watching the quarter-final match in its last couple of minutes. None of them were paying the Yeng the slightest attention.

Now Pyotren *really* wanted to know what was on that phone.

The word *nash'terel* meant "secluded ones". The Nash'terel had isolated themselves from the rest of society for a reason, and most of them still remained that way, even on Earth. They adopted various human forms in order to blend in, then made themselves virtually invisible. The ones who didn't, who practised professions and ran businesses, were secretive and vigilant to the point of paranoia. They often wouldn't even identify themselves to other Nash'terel if they could avoid it, and they taught their Earthborn offspring to be just as careful.

Sixteen years earlier, after learning that the Yeng exiles to Earth who made up the Council of the First had been putting targets on Nash'terel backs for the emperor's assassins, the "secluded ones" had unleashed assassins of their own. Every member of the Council had been eliminated. That should have been the end of it. And yet, the Nash'terel Earthborn were still being tracked down and murdered by Yeng triads, apparently with ease...

A loud cheer erupted, startling Pyotren back to the moment. A tying goal had just been scored with seconds left to play. A countdown chant began. *Three... two... one...* A buzzer sounded, ending regulation time. Now the game would go into overtime. People stood up to stretch their legs. A gate opened at one end of the rink and volunteers poured onto the ice to remove the goal nets before the Zamboni rolled in to clear and smooth the playing surface.

Pyotren glanced at the Yeng. Still frowning, the maintenance man slipped his phone into the front pocket of his khaki trousers, then turned and joined the stream of spectators headed to the foyer. With luck, he was only satisfying an urge to count his towels.

As he exited the rink, Maury entered it and began threading his way through the stands.

Pyotren waited for Maury to make eye contact with him, then touched a forefinger to his chest and jutted his chin in the direction of the main exit.

Maury nodded in response.

Pyotren descended to ice level and headed out, pausing in a shadowed alcove to morph his facial features and shift the colours of his clothing before he entered the foyer. A red toque, a dark blue windbreaker and scarf, and he was ready. Shape lords like himself and Armin made excellent pickpockets. They could melt into a crowd in a matter of seconds.

The maintenance man was strolling, alone, down the corridor leading to the dressing rooms. Pyotren cursed silently. He had to get the Yeng back to the foyer where people were milling about, so that he could be jostled from more than one direction.

"Hey, buddy? Excuse me? *Yo, mac!*"

The Yeng came to a halt. His shoulders sagged. Then he turned around, wearing a polite but insincere smile. "Can I help you, sir?"

"I hope so. It's the main washroom on the other side of the foyer. I think someone's having a problem in there."

"What makes you think that?"

"The door is locked, and I heard what sounded like sobbing. Before we call 9-1-1, could you come and have a look? You've got keys to all the rooms, right? You could unlock the door, at least, and find out what's going on…?"

The Yeng replied wearily, "Okay, I'll check it out."

Picking just the right moment to pretend he'd been pushed sideways by someone, Pyotren bumped the maintenance man into someone else. The resulting distraction gave his light fingers access to the pocket he'd targeted.

"Hey, watch it!" he said as though speaking to someone behind him, then, "Sorry about that, buddy."

"Not a problem," the other man replied. "And my name is Alvin, not Buddy."

"And I need to find my wife, Alvin, so if you'll excuse me…?"

"Sure."

Pyotren hurried back into the nearly empty rink, melting into a shadow to return to his earlier appearance before resuming his seat.

At last, overtime was about to begin. The stands were filling up with spectators once more. Maury had stationed himself one section away, keeping Travis in sight. Now he wandered across the aisle and sat down at the end of Pyotren's row.

When everyone's attention was once more riveted on the action on the ice, Maury moved over as though trying to get a better view and murmured, "Well?"

"Alvin the maintenance man is a Yeng, and this is his phone. At least, I *think* it's a phone. He kept referring to it while he was scanning the crowd. Let's see what he's got on here."

Keeping the device on his lap, Pyotren pressed the power button. A plain blue screen came up, and a second later five yellow dots appeared, two of them moving.

"Oh, fuck," Maury said softly. "This is not a phone, Pete."

He was right. What they were looking at was the visual display of a tracking device. Only one thing would a Yeng assassin be interested in locating this way: Nash'terel prey.

A frisson crossing his shoulders, Pyotren let out his breath through his teeth. "The three stationary dots have to be you, me, and Travis," he whispered. "The other two..."

"There, behind the Coyotes' bench," said Maury. "Their coach is pacing. His movements match the fourth dot."

"And the fifth must be one of the players on the ice... Wait, I see him. The Coyotes' number 14." Sharing a look with Maury, he added, "Alvin smells like a Yeng, but I don't think he's an assassin. If he had one of these, then I suspect his job is to identify targets for the various triads, now that the First aren't around to do it for them anymore."

"If the Yeng have developed a technology that can identify us from a distance, then the only advantage we have over them is our *hainbeka*. I think it's time someone had a long, private chat with your friend Alvin."

Maury pulled out his phone and texted Shred an update. Less than a minute later, he received Shred's reply. "He's on his way," Maury said, replacing his phone in his inside jacket pocket. "Now we watch and we wait."

The overtime period was hard-fought and end to end, but one of the Coyotes—not number 14, Pyotren noted—eventually found an opening and flipped the puck past the goalie's glove to win the game.

As the final buzzer sounded, Coach Brandeis got to his feet. "Gentlemen, it looks like we've got our work cut out for us if we're going to beat the Thornbury Coyotes first thing tomorrow morning. I've reserved practice time at our home rink this afternoon, but first, who's up for some lunch?"

The boys were hungry. They let out a cheer.

"Dr. de Maur? Will you and Mr. Gershred still be joining us?" Brandeis called up to him.

Maury hesitated before answering. "Yes, but I'm afraid we'll be a little late. Gershred has something to attend to first, and he has our car, so—"

"Transportation's not a problem, sir. There's plenty of room on the team bus. You can ride to the restaurant with us and he can follow as soon as he's able. Unless you'd rather not...?"

"Actually, that works just fine. Thank you." As the Rockets began making their way down to ice level, Maury leaned toward Pyotren and said softly, "When Shred gets here—"

"We'll handle everything," Pyotren assured him. "And try not to be a spoilsport on the bus, okay? Travis is just a kid. Let him have his fun for now. He'll need some good memories to carry him through the bad times that we both know are coming."

A couple of minutes later, Pyotren's full attention was on the screen of the device in his lap. The tracker apparently had a short range. The dots representing the two Coyotes had slid off to the side and disappeared. The ones representing Maury and Travis were on the move, headed for the exit to the parking lot. That left—

"What did I miss?"

Pyotren glanced up and saw Shred standing at the end of his row. But there was still only one yellow dot on the screen.

"You look confused," Shred remarked.

"I am. This is supposed to detect Nash'terel, but you don't

register on it at all."

"That's odd." Shred sat down beside him and peered at the display.

Pyotren squared his shoulders. "Or maybe it's not. Maybe you're a Yeng who's shapeshifted into Gershred's form," he said.

"A Yeng with a *hainbek* would *really* be odd," Shred declared, holding out his left hand, palm upward. A moment later, a heat bomb appeared in the air immediately above it.

"Okay, you're you. But that still doesn't solve the mystery. What sets you apart from all the other Nash'terel, Gershred?"

Inhaling audibly, Shred pulled himself erect and said, "I know what it is, and I know how to prove it. Give me the *dashkra* pendant from your pocket." Pyotren stared a question at him. "I stopped wearing mine centuries ago. That's why—Give it here and I'll show you."

Holding the pendant in his hand, Shred descended the stairs to ice level and turned to face him. Sure enough, a second yellow dot had appeared on the screen.

"Damn!" Pyotren exclaimed. "This thing is a bloodstone detector."

Shred returned and handed the pendant back to Pyotren. "The triad that we took out earlier weren't just Yeng thugs doing the emperor a favour. They were being paid by someone on Earth for bringing in *dashkra*. As for this maintenance man of yours... Let's find him and see if we can shake some answers out of him."

Chapter Seven

Alvin was sitting on one of the lower rows at the far side of the rink, enjoying a foot-long meatball sandwich from Submarine Heaven.

Shred and Pyotren split up to flank him. They plopped themselves down on either side of him at the same time, startling him. Alvin must have known he was in trouble. When his gaze met Pyotren's, there was a *click* of recognition behind the Yeng's eyes. And something more.

"Is there anything I can help you with?" he asked warily, swivelling his head back and forth between them.

Pyotren had changed the colour of the bloodstone tracker's casing from brown to burnt orange. Now he waved the device in front of Alvin's face. "Does this ring a bell?" he demanded. "I'll give you a clue. It only *appears* to be a smartphone."

"I saw one earlier. It—" The maintenance man's shoulders sagged. Then the floodgates opened and words came pouring out of him. "It was yours, wasn't it? I wasn't going to keep it, I swear! I found it in the bottom of the laundry hamper after you returned it.

I was going to come and ask you about it, but it turned on all by itself when I picked it up, and it looked like some sort of game, so I was curious and tried to play it, but then it wouldn't work, and I was afraid you would think I was the one who'd—So I—But then it was gone suddenly and I—I didn't know where I could have—" His lower lip was wobbling. He looked about to wet his pants.

"I'm sorry," he blurted. "I'll find a way to replace it, I promise. Just don't tell my boss about this. Please! Mr. Harcroft is already mad about the missing towels. If he thinks I've stolen something from a visitor, he'll fire me for sure, and I really need this job."

Hmm. Frowning, Pyotren slipped the tracker back into his pocket. Alvin might smell faintly like a Yeng, but he wasn't behaving like one. Not like one who knew what he'd been playing with, anyway. On the other hand, the Yeng were shapeshifters, skilled at dissembling, so Alvin could just be putting on an act to avoid being killed by two Nash'terel.

Or to get them to drop their guard so another Yeng could surprise them...?

Pyotren's mental alarms began to shrill. He cast surreptitious glances around the rink, mapping escape routes in case of an attack. Meanwhile, to his annoyance, Gershred was smiling at Alvin and engaging him in pleasant conversation.

"How long have you been working at the arena, Alvin?" Shred asked.

"About ten years. I'd been hanging out here since practically forever, so Mr. Harcroft decided if I wasn't going to finish high school I might as well make myself useful. That's what he said when he offered me the job."

"How old were you then? Sixteen? Seventeen?"

Alvin nodded.

"When you say you hung out… you were really hiding out, weren't you?"

Alvin's eyes widened. "How did you know that?"

Shred patted him on the shoulder. "I'm just one of those people who know things. Don't worry about the video game, Alvin. It was already broken. If you find it, you can throw it out. And we're not going to say a word to Mr. Harcroft. In fact, this conversation never happened." He made eye contact with Pyotren and jerked his head toward the exit, and both Nash'terel got to their feet.

"Hey, thanks, guys," said Alvin, saluting them with his sandwich. His gratitude, if genuine, was pitiable.

By now the arena was pretty much deserted. Shred led the way to the foyer, pausing beside the nearest vending machine.

"What the hell was that just now?" Pyotren demanded.

"I could be wrong, but I believe Alvin is being truthful, about the tracking device, at least. I don't think he knows what it's for."

Pyotren narrowed his gaze. "And you're basing this belief on…?"

"The fact that he let you keep it. No Yeng assassin would have let us walk away with it."

No, he wouldn't, not unless he knew the other members of the triad could spring an ambush and retrieve it. He would have to alert them right away, of course. And that meant…

Pyotren put a silencing finger to his lips, then led the way back to the rink's main entrance. With Shred close behind him, he leaned carefully around the door jamb to see what Alvin was doing.

The maintenance man was precisely where they had left him, radiating unconcern as he polished off the last of his sandwich and took several swallows of something from a jumbo-sized paper cup. He gave a wave and a broad, open smile to the volunteer who'd come to open the gate for the Zamboni. Then he crumpled the sandwich wrapper, wiped his mouth with a serviette, and dropped wrapper and serviette into the brown paper bag beside him on the bench. As the Zamboni lumbered noisily onto the ice, Alvin greeted the driver, then leaned forward on his elbows to watch the rink being refreshed for the first of the afternoon games.

Shred was right. This was not the behaviour of an assassin worried about retrieving a piece of technology.

Damn! "Well, the smell is really faint on him, but it's definitely there," Pyotren declared, "and it's telling me that he's Yeng."

"I'm not disagreeing with you," Shred said. "But I think we've grown so accustomed to every Yeng we meet being a potential assassin that when we do run into one who's just minding his own business, like Alvin, it takes us by surprise." A pause, then, "If he's a hybrid with no shapeshifting ability, he may not even realize he's a Yeng, only that he's different. Hiding out, dropping out, plagued by strange and frightening urges that he doesn't dare let anyone know he has..."

"You've seen this before," Pyotren remarked.

"Not often, but yes, over the years it sometimes happened. Yeng mother, human father. In more primitive eras, the hybrid offspring didn't last long. The first time the villagers caught him quenching his blood thirst, they would kill him, then drive a stake through his heart and burn his mother as a witch for good measure."

Pyotren had taken up a position beside the rink door, with his back to the wall and both arena entrances in sight. He stole precautionary glances down both corridors, then pulled out the tracking device and stared at it for a moment. "This must have fallen from the pocket of one of the assassins you stuffed into the hamper." He pursed and unpursed his lips. "The Guild needs to be informed about it. I realize Maury wants to hold off—"

"Maury worries about a lot of things. He knows there are traditionalists on the Guild who would declare a hybrid like Travis to be an abomination and order him destroyed. It's one of the reasons we live as far away from Toronto as we do—to keep the kid off their radar screen. However, this device is a threat of much greater magnitude, and it has to take precedence. You're right, Pyotren. We have no choice. For the safety of every one of us who carries the bloodstone, a general warning must be issued, and only the Guild has the ability to do that."

"Just out of curiosity, what made you stop wearing your *dashkra*?"

Gershred gave him a thin smile. "What made you put yours on a key fob?" he countered.

Pyotren returned the smile. "Point taken. Of the two of us, you've got the better chance of convincing the Guild to cooperate," he added, handing Shred the *dashkra* seeker. "Here. Show them what the Yeng have been up to lately. Now, if you no longer have need of my services, Armin can tow the wizardmobile away and I can finally drive that honkin' big pickup truck out of the parking lot."

"And I get to join the Georgian Bay Rockets for a lovely, essence-polluting lunch. Lucky me!"

One hour later, Maury and Shred were standing beside their car, forcing themselves to smile and wave as they watched the Rockets' bright yellow bus pull away from the restaurant's parking lot. They'd made the right decision, letting Travis return to the team's home arena with his friends, Shred thought. The kid wasn't carrying a bloodstone, but even if he were, the odds of a Yeng assassin flagging down and boarding the bus while it was en route were negligible.

Travis sat in one of the rearmost seats, engaged in animated conversation with his teammates. Shred swallowed a sigh. Their next discussion with him was likely to be difficult.

As soon as the bus was out of sight, Maury scowled and announced, "Well, *that* was an experience I'd sooner forget." Shred watched him fling open the front passenger door of their vehicle, drop onto the seat, and slam the door shut again.

"Really? I wouldn't have guessed it," Shred said, tongue firmly in cheek as he slid in on the driver's side and turned the key in the ignition. "What didn't you like about it, Maury? The scintillating conversation with the goalie's parents? Or was it the banquet burger I watched you scarf down? What the hell were you thinking, ordering that? You know what humans do to their meat. They ruin it with fire, then bury it under other foods to give it a semblance of taste. Not even Bilyash at his most ravenous stage of growth would have devoured such a thing. And you know what?" he added as he made the turn onto the main road. "When you're in the washroom later, *harruffing*, don't expect any sympathy from me."

"Are you done?" Maury asked wearily. "First of all, I didn't order it. Travis did, before you arrived. He's convinced I don't consume enough, apparently, and he wanted to make sure I wouldn't faint from hunger while watching him on the ice this afternoon. I only ate the damn thing to avoid embarrassing him in front of his team. And second, I won't be spending any further time this afternoon *harruffing* in the washroom. I slipped away and emptied my gorge-pouch into the toilet in the restaurant while you were conversing with Brandeis and the assistant coach."

"Uh-huh," Shred commented. "I take it you're still hungry,

then. Well, it's too early to hunt, so how about we go home first so you can eat something from the fridge?"

"Good idea. I've been saving a piece of liver for a snack. It will tide me over until Travis is asleep and we can relax our shapes and feed properly without his seeing us." Maury let out an audible breath. "Life would be a lot simpler right now if we'd already told him the whole truth about us."

Shred threw him a sidelong look. "About his grandparents and his father being essence vampires from another world, you mean? About the Yeng and some Nash'terel liking the taste of human blood as well? It would have given him nightmares. He would have called us monsters and run away, just as Angie's family did from Vicky Spears' cult in Middlevale when she was his age. That's why she made us promise to keep him ignorant of our true nature—"

"—until a talent emerged that set him apart from other human offspring, which is exactly what has happened," Maury pointed out. "And now he needs to know about us, about what it means to be Nash'terel."

"But he doesn't need to know *everything*, Maury. Not all at once, anyway, and certainly not here. Once he's with his parents in British Columbia, they can find a way to explain things to him so they make sense. We only need to tell him enough to make him want to go there. In the meanwhile, Pyotren and I have discovered how the Yeng gadget really works."

Keeping his eyes on the road, Shred fished the *dashkra* seeker out of his pocket and dropped the device onto Maury's lap.

"Wait a minute. There's only one blip on the screen," he said after a pause.

"That would be you, because I don't wear a bloodstone," Shred explained, then had to wait for Maury to stop cursing before he could continue. "The mythos that our people have constructed around *dashkra* now makes it an existential threat. That's why, first thing Monday morning, I'll be paying a visit to the Riftgate Club. Don't worry, I'll keep Travis out of the discussion. But the Guild needs to be told about this technology, in person, so that they can send a warning to all the founding families."

Maury said nothing, just huffed out a breath.

"What?" Shred prompted him.

"There were three static blips on the screen back at the arena. Pyotren and I were sitting behind the Rockets at the time. We assumed the third blip was Travis, but he doesn't have a *dashkra*. So that can mean only one thing."

"There's another Nash'terel on the hockey team," Shred murmured. "He must have been the target of the triad we took out this morning."

"Not necessarily. There were also two moving blips—the coach and one of the players on the Thornbury Coyotes."

Multiple targets in one place. It was no wonder a Yeng triad had shown up at the arena. Where else were Nash'terel Earthborn tending to congregate? Wherever it was, they were in peril.

Shred drove the rest of the way home in silence, letting dark thoughts and old knowledge fill his mind.

It wasn't only the parasitic nature of *dashkra* that had made it dangerous. It was the terrible price the mineral exacted for the benefits it bestowed. Along with a greatly extended lifespan and the ability to shapeshift had come an obscene and unnatural thirst for the life essence of other beings.

Nothing could be done about the dust that had already infected RinYeng, but the Nash'terel had taken steps to prevent any more of the "blood sickness" from spreading. Divided up for safekeeping among the twenty-three founding families, the raw *dashkra* was zealously guarded and carefully handled. Scientists like Maury were permitted to experiment with some of it under controlled conditions, while the rest enabled the Nash'terel to preserve their culture in exile.

And now it had become a beacon, enabling an old enemy to identify and annihilate their entire race.

Convincing every family to give up millennia-old customs and rituals involving the stone could well be impossible, but if it preserved even one bloodline, the effort would be repaid.

Maury and Shred arrived at the rink one hour later for practice and found the parking lot beside the building rapidly filling up. Evidently, they weren't the only family members who liked to keep close watch on their young ones.

Fake Fur Lady was already there, sitting alone and drinking something from a thermos bottle. She beamed at them as they entered the stands. Shred pinned a pleasant smile on his face and waved politely to her.

"Just one more day," he murmured to Maury. "Then this tournament is over, Travis goes to B.C., and we can get off the grandparenting merry-go-round and choose never to look at any of these people again."

"Especially her," Maury muttered, "except as prey, perhaps."

Perhaps. Shred took out the tracking device and turned it on. "Let's see if we can identify Travis's Nash'terel teammate... and his parents, if they're here. Maybe give them a heads-up."

"And by revealing ourselves as Nash'terel give away Travis's secret as well? Not a good idea, Gershred."

Shred was too busy to respond. He was staring alternately at the screen and at the ice, trying to find the skater whose movements matched those of the yellow blip sliding around the display. One by one, every player on the team was eliminated. Several moments later, Shred sat back and said, half to himself, "Huh! That explains it."

"Explains what?"

"The other Nash'terel is Coach Brandeis. That explains why he was in the passageway this morning instead of behind the bench, and it also explains the way he turfed Bryant out into the hall. Brandeis smelled a Yeng and was reacting to it, just as we did."

"And are you going to warn him about the new technology?" Maury asked quietly.

Reluctantly, Shred replied, "Not yet. The tournament ends tomorrow, and then I'll be visiting the Guild. I can't imagine they'll turn me down, not when it's something like this. But if they do..."

That was the downside of being one of the "secluded ones". You always knew who your enemies were, but could never be sure whom to trust as a friend.

Chapter Eight

At Travis's request, they stopped to pick up a large pizza on the way home. It was his favourite—a meat lover's special with triple cheese. Just the sight of it was enough to make Maury's gorge-pouch pucker. Fortunately, he didn't have to look at it for very long. Hockey practice had given the kid an appetite. In less than an hour, their star forward had wolfed down the entire pie.

"We need to talk, kiddo," Shred told him. "About what happened in the dressing room this morning. About your *hainbek.*"

Travis halted in the midst of wiping his mouth with a paper serviette. "I was careful, Grandpa G," he protested. "I didn't use it once during practice."

"We know. This isn't about that. It's about your origin story."

"My origin story?" His eyebrows shot up. "Really? I mean, I know you love the old comic books, Grandpa, but—"

"—this is the real world. I know. But there's nothing comic book about our special abilities. They're real too, and they had to begin somewhere."

"Like in a radioactive meteorite crater?" Travis joked.

The kid was trying Shred's patience. "Hey! We didn't just wake up one morning able to move things with our minds. You need to know where your talent came from. You don't want to call it an origin story? Fine by me. But I've been mentally rehearsing it all afternoon, and you're going to sit there and listen while I tell it to you. Got that?"

Obviously humouring him, Travis replied, "Okay, sure. Tell me a story."

Maury just rolled his eyes.

Shred threw him a look before continuing, "Many thousands of years ago, a group of beings decided to devote their lives to understanding the natural forces. You've been studying some of them in school. They're called sciences.

"But these beings didn't want to be disturbed by worldly concerns while doing it, so they found themselves an isolated valley, far away from every town and village. It was a fertile place, full of life, and it was surrounded by mountains, with only one way in or out. Everything they needed was in that valley.

"They closed off the entrance, and for a very long time, they studied, and practised, and experimented, each of them focusing on a particular element of the natural world, and each generation preparing the next one to continue the work. They called themselves the Nash'terel, which in our first language means 'secluded ones'."

"I've seen this movie, Grandpa," Travis piped up. "*Lost Horizon*. They showed it to us at school as part of a film studies unit. The valley was called Shangri-La."

Maury's shoulders were shaking with repressed laughter.

Shred paused to rein in his temper and reminded himself: the movie was based on a novel by an Earthborn going by the name James Hilton, who'd thought it would be fun (not to mention lucrative) to loosely fictionalize the Nash'terel on RinYeng. Loosely was putting it mildly. Even though both book and movie bore very little resemblance to the truth when they were released, their existence had still created a furor among the twenty-three founding families. It had taken decades for their outrage to subside.

"The movie was a fantasy," Shred went on doggedly. "What I'm telling you now is factual. After many generations of work and study, there was a remarkable development. Well, two developments, actually.

"First, the Nash'terel gained an understanding of the way things worked that was so deep and complete that they actually learned how to control the natural elements they'd been studying. Grandpa M's specialty—his *hainbek*—is light. Mine is heat. We can summon them to us, move them from one place to another, change their state, and basically use them as tools."

"Or to defend ourselves," Maury added.

"Of course. Any tool can become a weapon when necessary," Shred conceded. "The second remarkable thing was that the Nash'terel's special abilities became imprinted on their genetic material, enabling them to pass their *hainbeka* from one generation to the next."

Travis sat up ramrod straight, his eyes wide. "Wait a second. I inherited this from my *parents*?"

"Yes," Maury said. "As I told you earlier, every Nash'terel has a talent, including your father. Your *hainbek* is in your genes. But it's far from unique. In fact, pressure *hainbeka* are pretty common among the Nash'terel."

"Are you done?" Shred demanded before the conversation could wander any further off track.

"For now," came the unrepentant reply. "You may continue."

Shred blew out a long-suffering breath before going on. "The Nash'terel could not remain secluded forever, unfortunately. When the Yeng found out what we were capable of, they saw us as a threat... and that was the trigger for the genocide. The emperor's army stormed into the valley, but by then we had already escaped to this world—"

"To this world? You mean Earth? You're telling me you guys are space aliens? No way!"

The kid was laughing. It was infuriating.

"Yes way!" Shred snapped. "Now let me finish."

But Travis wasn't listening. "Where's the comic book this came from, Grandpa G?" he blurted between fits of giggling. "I want to read it."

Shred's impatience was growing. He stared a prompt at his partner, and Maury ended the youngster's hilarity in a split-second, by pulling all the light away from where he was sitting.

A silent black bubble now occupied the space across the table from them.

Shred counted the seconds. *One... two...*

"What—what just happened?" Travis's voice teetered on the edge of panic. "Where are you, Grandpa? Grandpa G? Grandpa M? I can't see you! Oh, shit, I'm blind!"

"We're here, Grandson," Maury replied evenly, "waiting for you to take us seriously. What you're experiencing right now is a demonstration of the powers of a light lord from the planet RinYeng."

...thirteen... fourteen...

"All right, I believe you!" he yelped. "You're from outer space. Now turn the light back on. Please!"

Maury complied.

Blinking hard while his eyes readjusted to the brightness, a much-subdued Travis said, "So it's true? You and the other Nash'terel came here from another world? How?"

"We crossed over by way of a portal, called 'the rift'. It was inside one of the caves in the mountains surrounding our valley, so we hoped the Yeng would not find it. Unfortunately, they did," said Maury.

"You couldn't close it behind you?" Travis asked.

"No. We didn't create the rift, and we couldn't control it. All we could do was study it. We discovered that it opened for three days, once every hundred years. Eventually, the Yeng figured that out as well, and came after us to Earth, to hunt us down and kill us."

"So they're aliens as well," Travis said thoughtfully. "I don't understand something, Grandpa G. If all the Nash'terel had these special powers, why did they run? Why not simply use their talents to stand off the emperor's army back on the other planet?"

There was a long answer to that question, involving codes of conduct and existential philosophies. But it was a topic for a later discussion, so Shred gave him the short answer instead. "The elemental masters were relatively small in number. Our *hainbeka* gave us the means to win a battle, but the Nash'terel were not yet ready to win an all-out war against the Yeng. We're still not ready, not until every last one of us is fully trained and able to fight."

Travis's features contracted into a frown. "So you came here to hide. And when you're finally ready to take them on, Earth will become your battlefield," he summed up in a hard, flat voice.

"Only because they followed us here. And it won't be just us taking them on, Grandson," Maury reminded him. "You can trace your bloodline back to RinYeng. That puts you in the middle of the conflict as well."

"What if I don't believe you?" he demanded sullenly, crossing his arms over his chest and pressing himself against the back of his chair. "What if I just want to keep playing hockey and going to school and pretending to be a normal kid?"

This history lesson was going off the rails, and Shred was reaching the end of his patience. Time for drastic measures.

"Maury," he said, "bring out his *dashkra*."

The other Nash'terel levelled astonished eyes on his face. "His—? But now that we know about the Yeng device—"

"A bloodstone will demonstrate beyond doubt that he's one of us. And you know he won't be accepted into the program without it. Get it now, please."

A pause, then a surrendering, "All right." Maury stood up and left the room.

While he was gone, Shred told the youngster, "You may think life is like a big hockey game, but you're wrong. There's a lot more to reality than that. Life is complicated and at times messy, and some of it is downright unpleasant. We've protected you from the worst parts, but there comes a time when you need to know the truth, about yourself, and your parents, and us, and why we have to be on high alert, all the time."

"I hope you know what the hell you're doing," murmured Maury as he resumed his seat at the table.

"Just perform the ritual," Shred snapped.

With a look that clearly said he was complying with this order under protest, Maury placed the bloodstone on the table in front of Travis. Then, producing a lancet from his pants pocket, he said, "Give me your index finger."

Warily, Travis obeyed. "What are you going to do?"

"If you are truly Nash'terel, this stone will absorb your blood and change colour to show you your family line."

"Wait. My blood?" he yelped.

"Now, Maury!" Shred commanded him.

Maldemaur pricked the tip of Travis's finger, then held it over the *dashkra* and squeezed out a drop of blood. As the three of them watched, it landed on the stone, shrank rapidly, and disappeared. A moment later, a deep crimson blush filled the veins and whorls of the bloodstone, then overflowed into the remaining mineral, erupting like fireworks into splashes of bright turquoise, orange, and pale olive green. The colours spread and overlapped until not a trace of milkiness remained.

Travis stared wordlessly at the result.

"I suppose you want him wearing it as well, despite the danger?" Maury inquired wearily.

"Just until he gets to B.C.," Shred replied.

That snagged the kid's attention. "I'm going out west? But you said—"

"Did I?" he returned grimly. "I assured you that our family would be reunited. I didn't say where."

"But—"

To short-circuit any further protest, Maury placed the chain around Travis's neck, dropping the multicoloured stone inside the front of his T-shirt. "Listen carefully, Travis, because your life may quite literally depend on following these instructions. Wear this pendant concealed and next to your skin at all times."

"Including on the ice? And in the shower, after a game?"

Maury and Shred traded looks. The Rockets would be playing two more matches that weekend. Travis would be showering in the dressing room after at least one of them, and common sense had to prevail.

Gershred hemmed and hawed, then made an executive decision. "You'll hand it over to us before entering the dressing room to suit up for your first game tomorrow, and we'll give it back to you in the car on the way home. After that, it stays around your neck all the way to B.C."

Shred saw pained confusion in the youngster's eyes and had to armour himself against it. "Yes, you heard right—carrying this stone on your person puts you in even more danger than before. Hopefully, that knowledge will get your adrenalin flowing and sharpen your senses. It's not our first choice, but words don't seem to be getting through to you, kid. You are literally in a life or death situation right now, and you need to take it seriously. You need to understand that going to B.C. and training your *hainbek* is not just a life choice that we're making for you—it's an imperative, if you're to survive at all."

"But why do I have to be the one to go there?" he demanded. "Why can't my parents join us here?"

"Travis, we've talked about this—" Maury began.

"No, you've lied about it. First you told me that my father was working on the pipeline and my mother had to go overseas."

"You were six years old. You wouldn't have underst—"

"Then you said they were spies, on a top secret undercover operation. The last time we video-chatted, my father was wearing camo. I asked if he was still working in intelligence, and he didn't know what I was talking about. This morning the story changed again. You claimed that they're learning how to fight the Yeng so they can protect me. How can I believe anything you say now when everything you've told me about them for the past ten years has been a lie?"

Maury cast a glance filled with *I told you so* in Shred's direction. The two Nash'terel had been debating off and on about this very thing since Travis's seventh birthday.

"Do I even *have* a mother and father?" the youngster demanded shrilly. "Or did you hire actors to pretend to be my parents on all those video calls?"

"That's enough!" Shred thundered, getting to his feet and looming over the table to emphasize his point. "Yes, when you were very young we lied to you. And continuing to do so as you grew older was obviously a mistake. But we're not lying to you now. Your parents are real. The danger we all face is *very* real and always has been. The safest place for you to be is together with your mother and father, in British Columbia. So that's where you're going, right after this tournament is over, whether you like it or not."

Shred sank back onto his chair, not trusting himself to say another word. Meanwhile, finger-stroking the bump his pendant made beneath the fabric of his T-shirt, Travis was glaring at the tabletop. His lips were compressed into a hyphen. Shred knew what was going through his own mind at that moment. He could only imagine what was going through Travis's.

Fortunately, Maury stepped in, speaking softly and with a look of sympathy in his eyes.

"You're a hybrid, Travis," he said. "The offspring of a Nash'terel father and a human mother, but not just any human mother. She has a unique genetic mutation, one that attracts Yeng like a magnet and makes it dangerous for her to be anywhere except where she is right now. That's why she can't come here to you. You'll have to go to her."

The youngster's gaze remained riveted on the dining room table. "Why should I?" he muttered. "She sent me away."

"Like you, she had no choice," Maury told him patiently. "When you were born, none of us knew which parent you would take after, or where you would fit in. Would you be human, or would you be Nash'terel?

"After five years, it appeared that you were perfectly human, so your parents asked us to bring you back here to live a normal human life. We promised to provide one for you, and I think you'll agree that we've succeeded. Regrettably, it meant we had to keep you unaware of certain things—but we made sure you knew your parents and had regular contact with them. Whatever else we may have told you about them, they love you, Travis, and they wanted you to be safe. That was always the truth."

Anger building like a darkening cloud across his features, Travis raised his chin defiantly. "So they had to send me away? Why? What was so dangerous about me living a normal human life in British Columbia?"

Because in a Nash'terel community, a normal-appearing human would have been seen as prey. Shred swallowed that response the second it dropped onto his tongue.

"You would have been surrounded by Nash'terel. It simply wouldn't have been possible," Maury replied.

"How do you know that?" Travis demanded. "You're Nash'terel, and I've been living with you for as long as I can remember. How could you even know whether your definition of a normal human life would be the right one?"

Apparently out of answers, Maury turned helpless eyes on his partner.

Shred's jaw muscles were working. Ten years earlier, he and Maury had taken on an enormous and very important responsibility. It had put them both on a steep learning curve as they found themselves negotiating a dense tangle of human social systems—health care, education, and child welfare among them—in their efforts to ensure the normalcy and well-being of the offspring who'd been entrusted to their care.

At times, Shred had felt as though he and Maury were in danger of losing themselves in their grandfatherly roles, of being trapped in a never-ending procession of birthday parties, parent-teacher interviews, and after-school sports. And then had come the hockey, with its heavy schedule of games and practices and tournaments. Despite all that, they'd persevered, for Ken and Angie's sake, and for the trust they'd placed in Maury and Shred to raise Travis, all the way from happy childhood to healthy human adulthood, if necessary.

And now, this selfish outburst, this petulant display of ingratitude... it was almost too much.

Almost.

Shred hardened his expression. Then he hardened his voice. "Listen up, kid, because I'm done sugar-coating the truth for you. The normal life you've been living is the one your mother chose for you. She gave us a list, and we've been checking things off it. If you'd stayed with her, she would have had to keep you hidden. That means never leaving the house. No technology that can be traced, so no phone, no internet, no television, no social media. No school and no visitors, so no friends or social activities at all... and definitely no hockey.

"Compare that with the life you've had up until now. Which

one would you thank your mother for choosing for you? Because, trust me, everything that has happened to, for, and around you for the past ten years has been in accordance with *her* wishes." *Not ours.* The words were implied but not spoken aloud.

Travis leaped to his feet, his fists clenched at his sides. "It's *my* life!" he shouted, his voice breaking on a sob. "I should live it the way *I* want!"

And with that, his face a portrait of adolescent outrage, he raced into his bedroom and slammed the door shut.

For several heartbeats, it felt as though all the air had been sucked out of the room. Then Shred exhaled gustily, turned to Maury, and said, "Isn't it your turn to hunt tonight?"

Maury stared at him in shock. "You really think I'm going to leave the two of you alone together in this house before you're on speaking terms again? Have you forgotten what it was like raising Bilyash?"

"No, I haven't," he replied, not bothering to keep the weariness out of his voice. "I remember what he was like before you made him your apprentice. The mood swings, and those powerful magnetic fields he threw up every time he lost his temper. I just thought raising a human boy would somehow be different. Simpler."

"There's nothing simple about adolescence, for humans *or* Nash'terel. In any case, you laid it on a lot thicker than necessary just now."

"Well, I was angry."

Maury threw him another reproachful look. "I could see that. Still, you didn't have to come down on him so hard. Travis has every right to be upset. He's been blindsided—Surprise! You're a chimera!—and now his life is about to turn upside down whether he wants it to or not. I think you're pissed because you've finally been forced to realize that I was right not to want to keep secrets from him all these years. Admit it," he needled. "It annoys the hell out of you, doesn't it?"

Leaning back in his chair, Shred replied with a sigh, "Yeah. A little."

"No. A lot," Maury corrected him tartly. "It *was* my turn to hunt, but you cremated those Yeng this morning, so you'd better go out tonight. With luck, Travis will wake up in a more forgiving frame of mind tomorrow." A pause, then, "I couldn't help noticing... on his bloodstone..."

"The turquoise? It was hard to miss. When Vicky Spears injected her own DNA into her grand genetic experiment in Middlevale, she expanded her bloodline to include every human in her cult. Now Travis is part of it as well, by way of Angie, who was born there... which probably explains why Vicky and Travis share the same *hainbek*."

Maury cursed inwardly. He wouldn't have minded Vicky and her mate Barron being Travis's godparents, if they'd been Ken and Angie's choice for the job. But they weren't. Vicky had simply stepped into the role of godmother on the day the youngster was born, and no one had had the energy—or the courage, to be perfectly honest—to recast the part.

Maury had always suspected that she saw Travis as a replacement for her daughter Lilly, and that when the time came, Vicky would simply adopt a new role, making the boy her apprentice. The problem was, Vincaspera routinely took shortcuts. She'd done it in Middlevale and she'd done it while training Lilly. If she trained Travis the same way, he would be weaponized before he had full control of his *hainbek*, making him a danger to himself as well as to others.

There had to be a way to prevent that from happening. Maury just needed to find it.

Travis remained in stubborn solitude in his bedroom all evening—like a true Nash'terel, Maury mused ironically. Shred waited to leave until the slit of light beneath the youngster's door had winked out. Then he bundled up for show, shifted his facial features, and went out to hunt in the cold night air.

Maury sat in the living room meanwhile, pretending to read a book as he listened for sounds of movement. He'd lived this scene many times before, while raising Bilyash, and knew the script backward and forward.

A door creaked open. Padding footsteps grew nearer. Maury's lips curved in a faint smile.

"I'm sorry, Grandpa M."

He lifted his gaze and saw Travis standing in the doorway, an expression of utter misery stamped on his young face. Maury closed his book and patted the seat beside him. "Come sit down. Let's talk."

Fifteen was an awkward age in more ways than one. On ice skates, Travis flew with the unerring purpose of a missile. Off them, however...

A bundle of arms and legs crossed the room and flopped down onto the sofa.

"What are you sorry for, Trav?"

"For losing it. I didn't mean to make Grandpa G angry. I just—I'm so—" He looked about to cry. "If I ask you a question, will you tell me the truth?"

"Of course. You can ask me anything."

"Does anyone really want me? Besides Coach Brandeis on the hockey team, I mean."

Maury could guess where this was coming from. "Travis, Nash'terel birth control is a hundred percent effective, so trust me, if your parents hadn't wanted you, you would not have been conceived, let alone born. Your mother worked hard to give birth to you, and your parents and godparents loved you and spoiled you rotten for the first five years of your life. When they get you back, they're going to be thrilled to have you."

"Because I have a *hainbek* now, like them?"

That would be Vicky's reason, for sure, Maury reflected sourly. But—

"Wait a minute. You think your parents handed you off to us because you were different from them?"

He shrugged uncomfortably. "Like you said earlier, I didn't fit in there. And now that I've changed, you're afraid I won't fit in here, either."

"It's not just a matter of fitting in, Travis, it's a question of your safety, and there's safety in numbers. When we thought your human side was all there was, it made sense to merge you into human society. And while there's certainly human society in British Columbia, your parents and godparents aren't part of it, not the way Grandpa G and I are, here in Ontario."

"They're part of a Nash'terel society?"

"Yes, and now that that side of you has manifested itself and the Yeng are aware of you, it's much safer for you to be part of it as well, out there with them."

The youngster buried his gaze in his lap. "What if I'd never changed?" he said softly. "What if I'd turned out to be just human?"

Abruptly, Maury realized what this was really all about.

"There's no expiry date on belonging to a family, Travis, and you were born into ours. *Hainbek* or no *hainbek*, you are our grandson, and we will always love you, and watch over you, and support you as you follow your dream, wherever it takes you. Nothing can ever change that."

"Even if I'm a pain to be around? Even if I make Grandpa G lose his temper?"

"I'll be honest with you, Travis—we're not as young as we used to be, and keeping up with you during the last ten years has taken a lot out of us. Grandpa G can be a grouch when he's tired—and even when he's not tired, truth be told—and that sometimes makes him say things he doesn't really mean. But deep down he's just as proud of you as I am."

The youngster raised eyes welling with tears to Maury's face. "Then don't send me away. Please! I won't use my *hainbek*. I'll take off my bloodstone. Everyone thinks you and Grandpa G are just regular people. They'll think I'm a regular person too."

"What about your parents, Travis? They love you and are proud of you also, and you have no idea how much they've missed having you in their lives."

"You're right. I have no idea. What I've got is a life here with you and Grandpa G. I've got friends, and classmates, and teammates... I've got an identity, Grandpa. What would I be if I went out there?"

He'd be a target for Yeng assassins, just like every other Nash'terel at the training camp. But now was not the time to point that out.

Mentally crossing his fingers, Maury replied, "You would be the new kid in the class, until you made some friends. And once you'd completed your training, you would be whatever you decided to make of yourself. The Nash'terel are a very private people, Travis. We're used to keeping secrets, even from other Nash'terel. Nobody you met outside of our family would ever need to know that you're half-human."

"What you're telling me is that no matter whether I go or stay, I'll have to keep secrets and pretend to be normal. So, doesn't it make more sense for me to stay here, where I already know what's normal, than to drop me into a situation where I have to learn what's normal, so I can pretend to be that way?"

He was like a dog with a bone. He wasn't going to let it go. Maury sagged backwards into the sofa. "I understand what you're saying, Travis. No promises, but I'll think about it. In the meanwhile, you've got an important game to play tomorrow morning, and the two of us to protect you, so you'd better get some sleep."

Chapter Nine

The following morning, Maury and Shred drove Travis to the rink for the Rockets' semi-final game and accompanied him to the dressing room. The atmosphere in this windowless space was charged to the point of sparking with anticipation. Nervous chatter and the sour tang of sweat filled the air as young players padded their bodies and laced up their skates.

Shred felt a stirring in his blood. This scene was calling forth memories, of shields and armour and sharpened blades... and trenches and yellow gas and flames like a dragon's breath. Nearly all his time on Earth had been spent gearing up for one war or another. These adolescents were going into battle too, although their blades were on the bottoms of their boots and at the end of a stick rather than attached to a rifle, and no one was supposed to die.

Coach Brandeis greeted Maury and Shred as they walked through the door, adding, "Is there something you need to discuss?"

"I just have a question," Maury replied. "Do you happen to

know the man who's coaching the Coyotes?"

"Bruce Dagomir? I've spoken to him a couple of times at regional meetings, but we've never sat down over a beer or anything. Why?"

"He looks familiar. I think I may have known his family, years ago. Is his son on the team, by any chance?"

Brandeis's lips quirked briefly into a smile. "Yes. I believe his name is Leo."

"I thought so. The resemblance is hard to miss. Thank you, Coach. After the game, I may go say hello to them."

Was Brandeis aware that the Dagomirs were Nash'terel? Maury's interest in them had clearly piqued the other being's curiosity. Shred could practically feel the coach's eyes boring into his back as he and Maury left the room.

Shred waited until the door had closed behind them, then whispered tautly, "I thought we'd agreed to wait until after I've spoken to the Guild before alerting anyone about the Yeng device."

"That's not what I'm planning to talk to Dagomir about," Maury replied in a hushed voice. "If I'm successful, Travis will have a friend from home training with him in British Columbia. A fellow hockey player."

"Huh." Shred's eyebrows rose in surprise. "You're going to recruit Leo for Barron's program?"

"And his father. At least, I'm going to try. Something the third assassin said to us yesterday stuck in my mind. He told us Bryant and the repairman had had a single target—'the kid'. Since it couldn't have been Travis, it had to be Leo. Now that he's been identified as prey for Yeng assassins, his parents may be open to the idea of relocating to the west coast. And if Travis and Leo become close..."

"...you figure he's more likely to resist Vicky's influence over him," Shred supplied, adding, "She won't let that stop her, you know. She'll find a way to interfere with their relationship."

"Of course, she will. And while she's tying herself in knots to break up Travis and Leo, Ken and Angie will have time to bond with their son."

So, in strategic terms, Leo was a diversion, allowing defences to be put in place. Shred smiled inwardly. He had obviously been a positive influence in this scientist's life. However...

Sobering, he nudged Maury into a shadow near the end of the corridor to continue the conversation. "I think you've forgotten something. There's more to the Dagomir family than just Bruce and Leo, and what you're about to ask them to do—pack up their lives and move across the country to keep Travis company...? It's a lot. What if the answer is no? When you bought into Vicky and Barron's operation out there and the three of you set up the military training camp for Nash'terel, didn't you all agree that it had to remain a secret?"

"Its location, yes, and so far it still is. We always knew that word would get out about its existence. We hoped the information would stay contained within the twenty-three founding families. But the Yeng are such devious bastards that I wouldn't be surprised if they were aware of the program as well." A pause, then, "Tracking down and killing triads of assassins has become a fact of life for us, but earlier, you mentioned an all-out war against the Yeng. Do you honestly believe things could go that far?"

Shred thought for a moment, then was forced to admit, "Eventually, yes, I believe they will."

"In that case, we need to be actively recruiting every Nash'terel on the planet to join the program and defend it, and I'm beginning with Bruce and Leo Dagomir, right after the game."

Once he and Maury were seated inside the rink, Shred leaned over and said, just loudly enough for Maury to hear, "Make the train reservations for you and Travis. Tomorrow morning, after I've briefed the Guild, they may try to drag me into planning and executing an operation to flush out whoever put the bounty on our *dashkra*."

"And how will you answer them?"

Shred stopped to consider his reply. "I'm willing to help them plan. As to the rest...? I honestly don't know. Regardless, I'll keep you in the loop, and I'll fly out west and join you as soon as I can."

Maury nodded.

Despite the early start time, there weren't many empty spots in the stands. This was the final day of the tournament. All but the top four teams had been eliminated, and their rankings would be determined by the outcomes of the last four games. The first one was promising to be an exciting semi-final match between the Rockets and the Coyotes.

Both teams were on the ice now, warming up. Shred looked for Travis in the whirl of helmets and padded uniforms, and found him slowly returning to the bench.

"What's the matter, kiddo?" Shred muttered, sitting up straight for a better look. He nudged Maury with his elbow. "Am I imagining things, or is he limping?"

Maury narrowed his gaze. "He appears to be having a problem with his left skate. You don't suppose..."

"...that he's got his father's big scaly feet? And bad timing to go with them? I'm not sure," Shred returned tensely. "Shapeshifting generally manifests earlier than this, but he's a hybrid, so anything's possible. Let's go find out."

The two Nash'terel wasted no more time. They burst into the team dressing room to find Travis lying on his back on the bench, tears of agony trickling from the corners of his eyes, and Coach Brandeis leaning over him with a pocket knife in his hand.

Brandeis glanced toward them as Maury and Shred entered. Then, still holding the knife, he straightened up and said, "I'm not supposed to do this, but I'm about to cut the laces. It's the fastest way to ease some of the pressure, and, hopefully, reduce his pain. Normally, I would have my assistant call 9-1-1 and request paramedical help, but I've got the feeling that won't be necessary here."

"I'm pretty sure you *know* it won't be," said Shred. "Thankfully, you're Nash'terel. Otherwise, there could be unpleasant consequences."

"Yeah. I've coached a lot of teams and seen a lot of sports injuries over the years, but this is definitely a first for me," he told them, gritting his teeth as he bent once more and began yanking the blade through the ladder of lacing, two rungs at a time. "On the off-chance that we're all guessing wrong and this is just a bad sprain, I have to ask: did you notice him having any problems with his foot after the practice yesterday? Was he complaining of any discomfort?"

"Truthfully, no and no," Shred replied.

As the sides of the boot sprang apart, Travis uttered a groan of relief... and Shred glimpsed something other than human skin through a tear in the youngster's sock. Maury had seen it too, and reached in to adjust Travis's legging. No matter how grotesque its shape, a swollen human foot could be explained away. The same could not be said for an armour-like layer of iridescent scales.

Brandeis folded his knife and put it away in a pants pocket. "So, he's begun shapeshifting. Is this his first manifestation?"

"Yes," Maury replied.

"Well, it couldn't have picked a worse time to happen," said the coach with a sigh, "but I guess there's nothing we can do about it here and now." Addressing Travis, he went on, "I'm afraid you won't be playing in the semi-final or final games, Trav. That's the bad news. The good news is that you still get to share in whatever success we have today, since you're one of the reasons we've made it this far, and everyone on the team knows it."

To Shred's relief, the kid managed to muster a brave smile of acknowledgement.

"Okay," Brandeis said briskly, speaking to Maury and Shred once more. "You need to take him home. I'll tell everyone that he sprained his foot during practice, said nothing because he was determined to finish the tournament, and ended up aggravating the injury. After you've signed the necessary indemnifications," he added, reaching into a file folder sticking out of his zipper bag, "I'll release him into your care, and you will take responsibility for getting him the appropriate medical attention."

Which, by tacit agreement, would be no medical attention at all.

Brandeis handed Shred two forms and a pen for filling them out.

"Out of curiosity," Shred remarked conversationally, "how long have you known about Travis?"

"I spotted his *hainbek* a while ago. I realized it was emerging and figured you would inform me if and when things became an issue," said the coach.

"And no one else on the team suspects...?"

"No. I've made sure of it."

Meanwhile, Maury was busily removing the skate from Travis's still human-appearing right foot, then stuffing it into a snow boot.

Once the official formalities were out of the way, Brandeis helped Shred pack up Travis's hockey bag while Maury went to bring the car around. Shred slid a guard onto the blade of Travis's left skate and draped the kid's jacket and scarf over his shoulders. Then the grandfather and the coach worked together to move boy and bag out to the foyer—mercifully empty of humans—where Maury was waiting to assist Travis into the back seat of the car.

Taking charge of the hockey bag and sticks, Shred paused to thank Brandeis for his help, adding, "Please convey Travis's regrets to his teammates, along with our best wishes for success in the tournament."

"I will. And you can tell him that we'll be dedicating the last two games to him," Brandeis replied.

Maury was already behind the wheel. He popped the trunk. Once Travis's gear was safely stowed and Shred was settled in the front passenger's seat, they were on their way.

"What's wrong with my foot?" Travis blurted anxiously. "Why did it do that?"

"It's nothing to be alarmed about, kiddo," Shred told him, "just another Nash'terel talent making its presence known." He threw a grin into the back seat and added, "We're taking you home, where you can transform in private."

"Transform? I'm changing? Into what?" he demanded. "I'm not turning into some comic book monster, am I?"

Seeing the dismayed expression on the youngster's face, Shred hastened to assure him, "Not at the moment, you're not. The Nash'terel are shapeshifters. That's our second special power. We only look like monsters when it suits us to do so. And we'll explain everything to you once we're all in the house, behind closed doors."

*   *   *

Fortunately, Maury and Shred's home in Collingwood was a detached bungalow on a quiet, tree-lined street, and Travis's Nash'terel foot was completely concealed from view. Now they just had to get the youngster inside before anyone noticed what he was wearing on it.

"Side door, and cover," Shred instructed as Maury backed the car into the driveway.

Nodding once, Maury aligned the rear passenger door with the side entrance to the house, then stopped. As he and Shred helped Travis inside, they used the car and their own bodies to block any casual view of him from the street. Then it was a matter of getting him up the four steps to the main level of the house and into his bedroom.

Travis's room left no doubt about his main preoccupation in life. The walls were well postered with autographed images of his favourite pro hockey stars, and every horizontal surface displayed trophies he'd earned while working his way up from house league to U-16 level in the minors. The kid had a real gift for the game, as well as a passion, Shred reflected as he and Maury assisted Travis over to his bed and pulled the boot and the skate off his feet. If he'd remained completely human, he might have made it all the way to the NHL. Now he was done, and that was a shame.

The youngster swung his legs up onto the bedcovers and sat still. Sidney Crosby and Auston Matthews looked down on him from one wall and Alex Ovechkin and Connor McDavid watched from another as Maury took a pair of scissors to the remains of Travis's left sock. Moments later, the Nash'terel appendage was revealed in all its scaly, green-skinned glory.

Shred recognized it immediately. Travis Fiore was definitely his father's son.

"That is not the foot of a human being," Travis declared shrilly, a flush darkening his cheeks.

"And we wouldn't expect it to be," Maury remarked in a matter-of-fact voice, "since you are, after all, half-alien."

"But—But is the rest of me going to—?"

"Hard to say, kiddo," Shred told him. "There are no other hybrids like you that we're aware of, so it could stop with the foot. Or, you could be capable of a full-body transformation. We won't know until it happens."

"And until then?"

"We wait," said Maury. "These changes take their own time."

The silence that followed his words seemed to suck the essence right out of Travis. His gaze dropped to his lap. His head drooped forward. His shoulders rose in a shrug, then sagged dispiritedly.

Seeing him this way made Shred's heart ache. A warrior, he knew exactly how the youngster was feeling. Gershred had been wounded in combat many times over the years, and no matter how painful his injuries had been at the time—or how quickly he knew he could recover from them—being ordered off the battlefield had always hurt a lot more. Travis may not have been physically injured, but he was definitely out of action. Soon he would be left behind as well, and nothing Shred did or said was going to put a happy face on that.

Maury, however, was evidently determined to try. "I'm going to make our train reservations," he said, taking out his phone. "As soon as I can arrange it, we're heading west, young man. No arguments!" Then he left the room.

Meanwhile, Travis had swung his legs off the bed and was staring at his foot again. The scales on his skin were iridescent, changing colour as the light played over them. While Shred watched, the youngster rotated his ankle, pointed what should have been his toes, and yawed his foot from side to side. The more Travis experimented, the deeper his frown became. Then he blinked hard and murmured brokenly, "I'm turning into a fucking reptile," and Shred couldn't be silent anymore.

He had not been looking forward to this moment, but the moment didn't care, and the words needed to be said. "Do you remember us telling you that your *hainbek* was in your genes? That you'd inherited it from a Nash'terel ancestor?"

Travis nodded, seemingly unable to tear his gaze away from the end of his leg.

"Well, it appears that there's something else you inherited from your father—his true Nash'terel form."

"His—his *true* form?" Now the kid's eyes came up. Wide and horror-filled, they locked with Shred's. For a long moment, his mouth was working but no sound came out. Finally, Travis said in a choked voice, "My father is a reptile?"

Reminding himself that Travis was only reacting this way because he'd been living in ignorance, like every other "normal human" on the planet, Shred forced himself to speak conversationally. "No, he's not. First of all, reptiles are native to Earth, and the Nash'terel aren't. Second, even in our true form, in our wide variety of shapes and sizes, we are humanoid. We took human form when we arrived on this world centuries ago, in order to fit in. Now, it has become our habitual shape, and, as I told you earlier, we only resemble the human image of monsters when we choose to."

The youngster's brow furrowed in concentration as he struggled to digest this. "So you and Grandpa M are only *pretending* to look human? And when you're not, you look like...?"

"We're from two different families, and your father was adopted from a third, so we've inherited different Nash'terel shapes."

No longer horrified, the kid's expression was becoming curious. "What does *your* true form look like? Do you have scales too?"

"No." Shred hesitated briefly. "You've seen images of Sasquatch?"

"You're Bigfoot?" he hooted, then immediately sobered. "No, you're not. You're just messing with me."

"Maybe. One day I'll show you and you can decide for yourself."

Just then, the phone rang in the living room, and Shred stepped away to answer it.

A few minutes later, he met up with Maury in the dining room.

"I had to call in a favour, but I've reserved a private compartment all the way to Vancouver. Departure time from Union Station is 10:00 a.m. on Friday," Maury reported. "Who was that on the land line?"

"Coach Brandeis. He wanted us to know that the Rockets just won their semi-final game by a score of 4 to 2, so the only question to be settled is whether their medals will be gold or silver. However things end up, the awards ceremony won't be over until sometime around six o'clock this evening. He says he can't stop by tonight, but he'll collect Travis's medal and drop it off to him one day this coming week."

"Okay, that works."

Suppressing a smile, Shred went on, "I also mentioned how much you regretted not being able to reconnect with your old acquaintances, the Dagomirs, as you'd planned to do before we had to rush out."

Maury frowned. "And...?"

"Brandeis is going to give Bruce Dagomir our land line number. We should be hearing from him later on today."

"We? Does that mean you'll be staying home instead of driving down to the city to brief the Guild?" said Maury, the hopeful note in his voice matching the expression on his face.

"The Guild can wait one more day," Shred told him. "Travis just took a body blow and will probably need both of us for support, so yes, I intend to be here for him."

Turning together, they saw that Travis had closed his bedroom door.

"He wants privacy," Maury remarked.

Shred nodded soberly. He knew from experience what it meant when a warrior went quiet after being cheated of a battle. The Nash'terel had many words for silence. The one that came closest to describing Travis's situation was *trekhtamasuir*—"anger burning within". Until the fire inside him had died down, disturbing his solitude could only make things worse.

So, while Maury puttered in the kitchen, Shred took up a post in the living room, picking the seat that gave him the broadest view of the rest of the house. Keeping one eye on the hallway and the other on his newspaper, he watched and he waited.

Eventually, the kid came out of his room, wearing an expression that fairly broadcast a warning not to talk to him. Clomping along on his big, scaly Nash'terel foot, Travis paused at the top of the stairs to the basement. Then, slowly, grimacing as though it gave him physical pain, he tackled them one step at a time.

Shred knew where Travis was going. The laundry room was in the basement. That was where his hockey gear lived. After each game, it was the youngster's own responsibility to wash and dry his jersey, towel, cup holder, and leggings, and put them back into his bag, ready for the next match.

Today would be different, though. More than just a tournament was over for this player. Travis was done for the year, maybe even for good.

Shred listened, alert to any sound from downstairs that might indicate the kid was using his *hainbek* to vent his feelings. Frustration and an untrained talent were a dangerous combination, but other than a couple of hard door slams, it was surprisingly quiet down there.

As the time passed, he imagined Travis emptying his bag, turning it inside out and arranging his cup, shin pads, elbow guards, gloves, and shoulder padding on the cement floor to air out. By the end of a season, those items tended to be quite aromatic. Skate blades needed to be cleaned, dried, and smeared with gel to prevent rust. Hockey pants were hung on a clothesline overnight. All of this was a ritual of closure.

When Travis reemerged from the basement, he was clutching a pile of folded laundry to his chest. Wordlessly, he carried it into his room and firmly closed the door. He came back out for lunch, hardly speaking a word as he cleaned his plate, then excused himself and disappeared into his bedroom again.

Shred exchanged worried looks with Maury. The youngster was obviously suffering, but there was nothing they could do for him. When a dream died, its loss needed to be grieved.

In mid-afternoon, Travis finally broke his silence.

Clomping into the living room where Shred sat pretending to watch a movie on TV, he plopped himself down on the other end of the sofa and said, "So, my *hainbek* is pressure."

Shred reached for the remote control and blanked the screen.

With an inward sigh of relief, he half-turned to face the youngster and replied, "That's right, and once it's trained, you'll have control of it."

Travis frowned. "But I can control it now."

"Can you? All we've seen you do so far is push things away."

"I only do it when I want to."

"Yes, and that's a very good beginning. But with complete control of your talent you should be able to exert pressure on an object from any direction you choose, with any amount of weight that you choose, using only your mind."

Shred glanced up and saw Maury standing in the doorway, slowly shaking his head.

"How do you know I can't do that already?" Travis challenged.

Maury was right to be concerned. Coming on the heels of this morning's disappointment, another failure would be devastating for the kid. But the expression on his young face said that he wasn't going to let this go.

"How do you know you *can*?" Shred returned. "Have you tried?"

Travis's chin went up. "Test me."

Maury rolled his eyes and retreated into the kitchen.

"Okay, then," Shred said.

Selecting three objects from the living room, he set them down in a row on the glass-topped coffee table. From lightest to heaviest, they were an empty plastic water bottle, a carved wooden scale model of a totem pole (purchased in B.C. during their last trip out west), and a wrought iron statuette depicting a faceless figure with limbs that resembled pulled taffy.

"This is going to be about controlling the weight you apply. Pick any one of these items and push it as close as you can to the edge of the table, without letting it fall to the floor."

Travis narrowed his eyes and stared at the water bottle. A second later, it took off as though it had been thrown. It described a shallow arc in the air and bounced off the wall beside the door jamb. The kid sagged backward into the sofa, his lips pressed into a hyphen.

"Hey, it's okay. A light touch takes practice to develop," Shred assured him. "As I said before, you'll need years of training."

"In British Columbia. I heard you." Heaving himself forward again, Travis declared, "I want to try another one."

Shred swallowed a sigh. "Okay. This time, imagine yourself extending an invisible hand and pushing gently at the base of the object with your fingertips."

His shoulders hunched, Travis gazed intently at the metal statuette. For several moments nothing happened. Then it lurched into motion. Remaining upright, it scudded away from him, ran off the edge of the glass, and landed with a *bang* on the hardwood floor.

Travis huffed out a frustrated breath. Shred glanced sideways at him. The kid was blinking back tears.

Forcing himself to smile, Shred gave him a comforting pat on the shoulder. "Don't fret, kiddo. Every Nash'terel had to start out somewhere, including me and Grandpa M. We had to work hard to get to where we are now. It'll happen for you too."

Travis glared at the totem pole as though willing it to burst into flame. "Yeah. After years of training," he muttered sullenly.

All right, Shred decided, he'd had enough of this pity party. "Listen, the ability to play U-16 level hockey didn't come to you overnight. You had to build your strength and hone your skills. That took time and practice. Put in the same kind of effort with your *hainbek* and it will pay off in the end. You'll see."

Travis said nothing, just heaved a discontented sigh.

The land line rang while they were eating dinner, and Maury excused himself to go answer it.

Maury was only a passable cook—his oft-stated aim was to fill up a growing human boy, not create works of culinary art—but this evening's meal was pretty good, Shred thought. Besides the rib steaks (broiled medium-rare for Travis, *bleu* rare for himself and Shred), the main course included pan-grilled mushrooms and peppers, a generous tossed salad, and a large bowl of mashed potatoes.

He'd made considerable progress in the past ten years. Of course, the other way to look at this was that it had taken him ten long years to get here, on a journey that consisted largely of learning as many different ways as possible to combine meat, carbs, and vegetables into casseroles. It was cookery, as opposed to anything that could be called cuisine. Thankfully, Travis had never been a picky eater. He always consumed whatever Maury put in front of him—raw, burnt, whatever—and never left a scrap of food behind on his plate. That (along with his fondness for meat lovers' pizza with triple cheese) probably explained why he was so tall and broad for his age.

"That call was from Bruce Dagomir. He's just leaving the rink and is on his way to have a talk with us," Maury reported, returning to the table. "He estimates he'll be here in about an hour." As he sat down, he cast a glance under the table where Travis's foot, unchanged since that morning's transformation, was taking up much of the space.

Meanwhile, it never ceased to amaze Shred how influential a full belly could be when the mood of an adolescent male needed lightening. The hockey gear and the dream that it represented were apparently out of sight and out of mind. British Columbia was somewhere in the foggy future. Now, if only Travis's left foot could be shut away and forgotten about as well!

"If I'm a shapeshifter, why can't I just put it back the way it was?" the youngster demanded. "And where does the extra part go when that happens?"

Shred stifled a groan. *Here we go again.*

"The extra part returns to wherever it was before your foot shifted," he said, with effort keeping his tone conversational. "As for your first question… The Nash'terel gained control over all the natural elements, including the energy inside our bodies. We call that energy 'essence', and it exists inside every living creature. Nash'terel essence is what rearranges our bodies into different shapes, but it's a tool, and like any other tool, it's not going to obey you until you understand how it works. Getting to that level will take time and training."

"*More* time and training?" he moaned. "So you're telling me I'm stuck with this."

Travis stared morosely down the length of his leg.

"Only temporarily," Maury assured him. "Basic shapeshifting is the first thing a Nash'terel youngster is taught to do. I'll begin your instruction tomorrow morning. You should be back to yourself by the time we reach Vancouver. Until then, if necessary, we can bandage your foot to make it appear that you're wearing a walking cast. That will get you through the crowd and onto the train platform without attracting undue attention."

"Did you have to teach my father to shapeshift?"

"No, he already had that ability when he came to us," said Shred, adding, "Don't be discouraged if it takes you longer than expected to nail this, Travis. You're a hybrid, remember, and there's a lot of your mother in you."

"Yeah," he replied darkly. "Everywhere except my left foot."

Chapter Ten

Installed on the sofa with his Nash'terel foot on full, ugly display, Travis waited for the sound of the doorbell. He would have preferred to go to his bedroom after dinner, but Grandpa M had insisted that he stay out here and say hello to the Coyotes' coach when he arrived.

The Dagomirs were Nash'terel. So was Coach Brandeis. There seemed to be a lot more shapeshifting aliens in U-16 hockey than anyone suspected. This opened some interesting possibilities. Did it mean Travis was already part of a Nash'terel community, right here in the middle of Ontario?

A loud chime yanked him back to the moment and launched Grandpa M toward the door. He opened it and spoke to someone. Travis couldn't see who was standing on the front porch, but the visitor's voice pulled an image out of his memory, of a tall, stern-faced man, clutching a pair of eyeglasses in one gesticulating hand as he protested the penalty that an official had just handed down to one of his players.

"I hope you don't mind, Dr. de Maur. We're on our way home

and there are Yeng abroad, so I wasn't about to leave him in the car."

"Completely understandable." Grandpa M swung the door wide and stepped aside to admit two beings into the house. Travis watched as they left their coats and boots in the hall and stepped into the living room. The younger visitor Travis recognized immediately, having faced off against him many times in the past few years.

"Travis," said Grandpa M, "this is Coach Dagomir."

"And this is my son, Leo," Dagomir added, urging him forward.

Travis got to his feet to reply, "I'm pleased to meet you."

"No, you're not," Leo said with a lopsided smile. "But it's okay. I still remember how *I* felt when I started shapeshifting."

"I think we all do." Leo's father was nodding his head. "You were angry as hell. Slammed a few doors right off their hinges." Turning to Grandpa M, he added softly, "Pressure *hainbek*. Something else they have in common."

"Gershred's waiting in the kitchen with a pot of Arabica," said Grandpa M. "Why don't we talk in there and let the boys get better acquainted?"

As the two older Nash'terel disappeared through the doorway, Travis locked eyes with Leo and commented, "You're a lot skinnier off the ice."

"So are you. And we're both a few inches shorter," Leo returned, his eyes twinkling with good humour. "Sort of like knights without their armour. So," he added, gesturing downward, "it started in your foot, eh?"

"Yeah," Travis acknowledged. He kept his chin up, refusing to look where the other boy was pointing.

"With me it was my hands. Mom kept me in the house for a

week until I got them under control. After that, shifting became a lot easier. Word of warning, though: changing back to human form…? It's going to hurt. It'll feel like there's ice cubes moving around under your skin. And not just the first time. It's that way every time you shift. The pain doesn't get any less—you just eventually get used to it. At least, that's what my dad keeps telling me will happen. I'm still waiting for it."

Travis returned to the sofa, inviting Leo with a wave to sit down on the adjacent easy chair. "Thanks. Pain isn't a big deal for me, but it helps to know what to expect." After a brief pause, he said with forced casualness, "So, have you been training your…?"

"…my *hainbek*? Yeah, for a while now. It's the same as my dad's, so he's taken me on as his apprentice." Leo grinned. "We've had you pegged for Nash'terel since the first game of the season. Some of the goals you scored this year must have blown the officials' minds. There are a lot of us in hockey, you know. And curling. It's great for practising pressure skills. My dad and I golf a lot too, and he's teaching me chess. What sports have you been doing?"

Travis swallowed hard. "Right now, hockey."

Looking a little confused, Leo cocked his head. "Just hockey? Nothing else?"

"I played some after-school baseball and basketball in elementary school, but once I got into hockey, it was all I wanted to do. Until this happened, I really thought I had a chance of qualifying for one of the Junior teams," he concluded, breathing a wistful sigh.

"Wait. You go to a human school?" Leo remarked. "The same school each year?"

Now it was Travis's turn to be confused. "Yeah. Well, two of them, actually. Grades 1 to 8 at one school and grades 9 and 10 at another. Why?"

The other boy shook his head as though to rid himself of an unwanted thought. "It's just that every Nash'terel we know is home-schooled, that's all."

Travis leaned forward and narrowed his gaze. "Well, I'm not like every Nash'terel you know," he said, sharply enunciating each word, "and this is the life my mother wanted for me, so it's the one I've been living."

"Hey, chill out!" said Leo, raising his hands in a gesture of appeasement. "I'm not saying there's anything wrong with it. In fact, it kind of makes sense. A human school is the last place a Yeng would expect to find one of us."

Travis relaxed back into the sofa and asked, "How did the Coyotes finish up, by the way?"

"We took bronze," Leo replied. "And the Rockets won silver. A tip-in found the back of the net in overtime. No way your goalie was going to stop it. Final score was 2 to 1."

I should have been there. It would have been gold if I'd played...

"Silver," Travis muttered darkly. "The only medal you get by losing."

"They played their hearts out, Travis." Coach Dagomir's disapproving voice broke into his thoughts. "They left everything on the ice. When you don't have a *hainbek*, that counts for something." The coach had entered the room unnoticed while they were talking. Now he came to stand beside the coffee table, wearing a key ring on one index finger and cradling the keys in his palm. "Time to go, Leo. Your mother and I have a lot to discuss."

Throwing Travis a sympathetic smile, the younger Dagomir got to his feet. "It was good meeting you, Rocket Man," he said.

Travis stood up as well and replied sincerely, "You too, Coyote.

Take care."

Leo went to the front door, where Grandpa G stood waiting with a winter coat draped over each arm.

Meanwhile, "All the best to you, Travis," said Coach Dagomir, looking him up and down as though deciding whether to let him off the bench. "I hope to see you again soon."

Unsure how to respond to that, Travis just said, "Thank you, sir."

A few moments later, both visitors were gone. Grandpa M and Grandpa G stood by the window until the sound of Dagomir's car had faded in the distance. Then they traded looks.

"What do you think, Maury? Will they do it?"

"I think there's a good chance, but I'm not going to hold my breath," came the reply. "As you said earlier, it's a lot to ask."

Curious, Travis piped up, "A good chance of what, Grandpa M?"

Grandpa G responded, "We're betting that the Dagomir family will be moving to the west coast in the very near future, and that you and Leo will be able to spend a lot more time together out there."

Not that Travis would mind that, necessarily, but, "What makes you think he'll *want* to hang out with someone like me?" he asked.

"Because you'll have a lot in common," Grandpa M replied.

Travis considered for a moment. What they had in common—really, *all* they had in common besides their *hainbek*—was currently airing out in the basement laundry room. Fingers crossed, he remarked conversationally, "I'll bet Coach Dagomir makes sure Leo takes all his hockey gear with him."

Grandpa M's face fell. "We're going to have a lot of luggage to carry, Travis," he pointed out. "I don't know how—"

"If he has all his stuff and I don't even have a pair of skates to wear, how much time do you think we'll be spending together? You want us to be friends, right?"

Grandpa M's face tried on a series of expressions, from worried to chagrined to something like pleading. Travis could imagine what was going through his mind. He was probably visualizing himself or Grandpa G having to lug that bulky hockey bag around.

"I'm strong, Grandpa. Even if I'm on crutches, I can manage the bag so you won't have to do it."

"Without trying to use your *hainbek*?" Grandpa G asked sternly.

Travis raised his hand as though swearing an oath on the bible. "I promise!"

"Well, Maury? Up to you."

Grandpa M's features settled into a thoughtful expression. "Okay, Grandson, you win," he said at last. "We'll just have to find a way."

Yes!

It was Maury's turn to go out that night. He took an essence receptacle with him. Knowing that he would have no safe opportunities to drink from live prey while on the train, he planned to gather and store enough human essence to last him all the way to Vancouver. A single flask ought to do it, he figured, holding contributions from two or three nights of hunting. That was in addition to the couple of long swallows he needed each time, to stave off a feeding lust.

An hour before sunrise, he returned to find Shred prowling the house, muttering to himself as he rehearsed what he was going to say to the Guild.

"I don't remember the last time you were this edgy," Maury

commented, frowning as he tucked the flask away at the back of a cupboard, "and my memory goes back a long way."

Shred halted and blew out a breath. "That's because you haven't seen me in the moments before a battle. The Guild and I didn't exactly part on the best of terms before, so I want to make sure I get this right. What I'm about to ask them to do is unprecedented. What if Monicandra turns me down flat?"

Shred had made coffee. Maury stopped in the midst of pouring strong Arabica into a mug and spun to face his partner. "Then we have Barron and his staff and trainees as a fallback. And we have you. You'll think of something, I'm sure. After all, you said it yourself only yesterday: when the rift opens again, it will take more than the Guild to protect us. Every Nash'terel on the planet will need to be able to fight."

He finished filling the mug, then handed it to Shred, waiting until the other Nash'terel had begun to drink before pouring a second coffee for himself.

As Maury was lifting the cup to his lips, he noticed the calendar thumbtacked to the bulletin board beside the fridge. Today was Monday. Yesterday had been the last day of the winter break. He'd forgotten about that. Maury would have to contact the attendance secretary at the high school. And then...

A one-day absence could be handled with a simple phone message, but Travis would be going away for good. The problem was, he was part of the humans' educational system, too young to simply stop attending school without a good reason. Any lie Maury told them was certain to be checked out by the authorities. And he was for *damn* sure not going to tell them the truth.

There was only one quiet and practical solution to this problem: Travis would have to be switched over to home-schooling before he and Maury departed for B.C. on Friday. Of course, that meant more paperwork to fill out, and precious time wasted in some bureaucrat's office being briefed about a pack of useless provincial curriculum requirements. The humans revelled in this sort of thing.

Maury sighed inwardly. It was what it was, just another part of the charade. Nonetheless...

Shattra!

Two hours later, filled with grim determination fuelled by three cups of extra-strong coffee, Shred said goodbye to Travis and Maury and headed out the front door. Maury had left a plausible excuse on the school's answering machine, and the kid had just tucked away a breakfast of multigrain cereal with milk, scrambled eggs, sausages, whole wheat toast with jam, and a tall glass of orange juice.

After putting his dishes into the dishwasher, Travis stomped into the living room. He sank onto one end of the sofa, stuck his left foot out in front of him, and stared balefully at it for several long moments. Nothing about the foot had changed overnight. Maury wasn't surprised by this. Travis, however, leaned back with a disappointed groan.

"I hate my body!" he declared, slamming his hand down on the seat cushion beside him.

"I can see that," Maury remarked mildly. "And maybe I'm wasting my breath, preaching patience to a fifteen-year-old, but it's all I have for you right now." He settled himself onto the easy chair. "That and perhaps some answers to your questions...?" he added, elevating one knowing eyebrow. "After the Dagomirs' visit, I'm sure you've got a few. What did you and Leo talk about?"

"Shapeshifting, mainly. Leo told me it started in his hands. Does that mean he was born looking human too?"

"Yes. Every Nash'terel offspring begins life in the gender and shape that are chosen for it by its parents. On Earth, for obvious reasons, that shape is human. At some point, however, the shapeshifting gene switches on, and the true form begins to emerge, whatever it happens to be. Yours is the same as your father's, because your mother is not a shapeshifter. But if both your parents were Nash'terel—"

"Whoa, wait a minute!" Travis sat bolt upright, his expression quizzical. "Back up a bit. Nash'terel parents are able to shape their baby before it's born?"

"The mother does, yes. The developing offspring is part of her body, and shapeshifting means having total control over every part of your body. So, naturally, she can give birth to whatever she wants. Or at least, whatever she and the father have agreed on."

"But later, when the child becomes able to shapeshift their own body...?"

"After learning that kind of control, they can choose the form they wish. Within reasonable limits, of course."

Maury watched emotions parade across Travis's face as he digested this information.

Finally, the youngster said, "So, if it turns out that I can change my whole body... I could become a girl?"

"Outwardly, yes. You could adopt any appearance you desired, and maintain it for as long as you wanted."

"Does that mean you and Grandpa G could pretend to be women?"

"Of course, if we wanted to. And if there were some advantage to it."

"Could you look like a little girl?"

"Actually, she would have to be a very large one. We can't change the amount of matter that makes up our bodies, you see… although why any adult would want to—"

But Travis was already racing ahead. "Okay, so, while pretending to be a woman, could you get pregnant?"

For several heartbeats, Maury was speechless. Then he blurted, "No! Why? Is that something *you* would want to experience?"

"No. But you said you would answer my questions, and that's one of them."

He was testing boundaries. Like father, like son. Maury expelled a martyred breath. This wasn't the kind of talk he'd planned to have with Travis today, but there seemed no way to avoid it. So, with fingers mentally crossed, he dived into an explanation.

"As with humans, a Nash'terel's reproductive cells are formed in the womb," he said with deliberate patience. "Depending on the mother's preference, an offspring will be born with either *holladima* or *sussadima*. In human terms, they would be sperm or eggs. We call this choice by the mother a birth gender, and it never changes, regardless of how an individual might choose to appear to others."

"Why not?"

Maury hesitated. Nash'terel scientists had been wrestling with this very question for thousands of years, and there was still no answer in sight.

"We don't know," he replied at last. "We're shapeshifters, so we ought to be able to change a *holladim* to a *sussadim*, but we can't. Within the body, they can only be awakened from dormancy or put back to sleep. Outside the body, they quickly lose their essence and die."

Travis paused again before asking, "So there are only two Nash'terel birth genders?"

"That's correct, Grandson. And, just as with humans, it takes one of each to reproduce biologically, regardless of who one's romantic partner might be."

That much of their original identity, at least, had survived all the changes wrought by the bloodstone, Maury reminded himself. The Nash'terel would still have something of themselves to cling to once the *dashkra* had been set aside. *If* it were set aside, he corrected himself. Common sense was no guarantee of success.

Travis was staring thoughtfully at his alien foot. "One of each. So, are you and Grandpa G really both male, or is one of you just pretending to be?"

"Our birth genders are identical, Grandson, and we stopped pretending otherwise years ago." And Fake Fur Lady thought they made an adorable couple. Wanted them to *think* she did, was more like it. The memory of her cloyingly indulgent smile was enough to make him cringe inside. One day, Maury promised himself, he was going to track that woman down and drink her dry.

"Now, it's time we move on to something else," Maury said briskly, addressing himself as well as Travis. "Like learning how to change that foot back to a human appearance. Shall we?"

His expression brightening, Travis nodded energetically.

"All right. Imagine that your brain is a giant warehouse full of shelving. One of the shelves is labelled 'Shapes'. On that shelf sits a row of cardboard boxes, each with a tightly fitting lid. The first box contains the blueprint for your human shape, and the lid is open because you're wearing that shape right now. The second box contains the genetic blueprint for your true form, however much of it you've inherited from your father. Its lid should be closed, but one corner has worked its way loose. Hence, the foot.

"When you shift from one shape to another, you're mentally instructing your essence to switch over from the blueprint in one box to the blueprint in the other. Your father once described this to me as giving permission to his essence to change his form."

"So all I need to do is... what? Visualize myself shutting the lid of that second box?"

"Eventually, but not yet. First, your Nash'terel essence has to be fed the details of each blueprint you want it to follow—programmed, if you will, like a computer. And, like a computer, it needs your commands to be so specific that they cannot be misinterpreted. That means you have to thoroughly understand the makeup and composition of all the parts of your human body, beginning with your left foot, since that's the main issue right now."

Maury went to his carry bag in the front hall and brought back an e-reader. "I've downloaded some books on human anatomy that you need to study. That second box is going to jog itself open more than once before you're in full control."

"Leo told me that Nash'terel are usually home-schooled. Is this the reason why?"

"If you mean because advanced human anatomy isn't taught in grades 1 through 10, then yes. The Nash'terel curriculum is very different from the one you've been exposed to so far." *And each grade level takes thirty Earth years to complete,* he wanted to add but thought better of it.

Stick to the basics, Maury...

...because he'd been right earlier. If Travis was aging at the normal human rate, there wouldn't be time to train him at higher than fundamental levels. The past ten years represented ten percent of his life—the equivalent of about six hundred years for a Nash'terel.

"So Leo is way ahead of me because he's been learning this stuff all along?" Travis persisted.

"Stop comparing yourself to Leo Dagomir," Maury ordered him. "He's a full-blooded Nash'terel, not a hybrid like you, and he's a lot older in Earth years than he looks."

It had slipped out in a moment of vexation. There was no taking it back.

Fuck!

In a frighteningly quiet voice, Travis asked, "So he's only pretending to be like me?"

Cursing himself inwardly, Maury paused, choosing his next words carefully. "He *is* like you, Travis. That isn't an act. In terms of emotional maturity, you're both adolescents. But because Nash'terel age much more slowly than humans, it's taken him longer to reach that stage of his development."

"That still means I have a lot of catching up to do, because he's had longer to practise his special talents." Travis tossed the e-reader onto the seat cushion, following it with a resentful glance.

"What did I just tell you?" Maury scolded him. "This isn't a competition. You and Leo may both *look* human, but you're genetically quite different from each other. Your only job is to focus on developing your own potential by applying your best effort during whatever time lies ahead of you."

"And how long is that, Grandpa?"

"I don't know," he exclaimed, throwing up his hands in exasperation. "No one does, because you're the first and only human-Nash'terel hybrid. But you've been aging at the normal human rate so far, so it's probably safe to assume that your lifespan will be closer to your mother's than to your father's."

The youngster's chin rose to a stubborn angle. "What if I took my father's true form? Would that give me more time to learn how to do this?"

Maury stared sadly into his face. "I'm afraid it would shorten your time, Grandson. Humans would see you as a monster, and the human response to monsters is to cage them or destroy them. Every Nash'terel family has lost loved ones this way. Grandpa G and I will kill if necessary to prevent it from happening to you."

Chapter Eleven

Travis spent most of Monday tracing illustrations of a dissected human left foot from the anatomy textbooks, beginning with the bones and cartilage and then adding one layer at a time of soft tissue, including the nerves and blood vessels. The final drawing depicted the outer dermal surface, with toenails.

By late afternoon, Maury couldn't help noticing that the youngster's attention was wandering. Perhaps this would be a good time for a practical test of his knowledge so far.

Maury scanned the series of drawings with a critical eye. Young Bilyash had had a flair for this sort of thing. Evidently, he hadn't passed it along to his son. Well, the reproductions weren't perfect, but they would serve as a starting point, the older Nash'terel decided.

"Now, you're going to mentally program your essence to rebuild your original left foot from the inside out. Bones first, just the way you've drawn them, then everything else in the same order that you've studied. Close your eyes. It will help you concentrate. You need to visualize this process happening inside the foot you're currently wearing. You'll know it's working when—"

"—when it feels like there are ice cubes sliding around under my skin. I know. Leo warned me. He said it would be painful."

"That sensation is your Nash'terel essence following orders. The good news is that essence never forgets what it's been taught. The next time you need it to transform your foot back to human, all you'll have to do is think the command, and it will know what to do and simply do it."

In response, the youngster shut his eyes and grimaced. "Ow!"

"It's started. Good. Your bones are reshaping themselves. Don't open your eyes yet," Maury instructed him. "Just focus your mind on the structures you've been studying. Remember them in detail, one layer at a time. When your essence settles down again, you should have your human-appearing foot back. Then you can close that second box and relax. Theoretically, at any rate."

"Theoretically?!"

"Ssh! I can see the skin undulating. You're almost there. Stay focused."

As Maury watched, the alien appendage shrank, settling into the familiar contours and proportions of heel, ankle, arch, instep, and toes. Finally, the armour of scales dissolved, leaving a smooth, tight casing of skin around everything.

He heard Travis groan and glanced up to find him staring in dismay at his no-longer-Nash'terel foot.

"It's still green, Grandpa. And my toes... it looks like I'm wearing a sock."

"But it's the right size and shape," Maury pointed out encouragingly. "Not bad for a first try."

Travis's gaze remained riveted on the end of his leg. "But it's green!" he insisted.

Maury bit back the remark that dropped onto his tongue, saying instead, "Not what you were hoping for. I understand. But I made you a promise, Grandson, and I intend to keep it. In four days, we'll be getting on a train. Three days and a bit after that, it will be pulling into the station in Vancouver, and you're going to step onto that railway platform on a perfectly normal-looking human left foot. And do you know why? Because you're going to spend the rest of this week educating your essence. Once it has learned all the details of your human shape, that will be your default form, the one your body will revert to automatically at a single command."

"Does every Nash'terel have to go through this?" Travis wondered plaintively.

"Yes, for each new shape we adopt. Every additional box on the shelf needs to contain a detailed blueprint of the form it represents, and most of us have had to reinvent ourselves many times over the years."

Just then, Gershred stepped through the front door. He did not look happy.

"I've had to book a flight to Vancouver. The earliest one available departs Wednesday morning. Can you get Travis and yourself to the railway station without me on Friday?"

"We'll manage. I gather this has something to do with your meeting earlier today?"

He nodded curtly. "You might say that. And no, I don't want to talk about it."

Maury understood: this was not for young ears to hear. "All right, then. While our grandson is showing you his new and improved foot, I'll get dinner ready."

*   *   *

Maury received his briefing that night, after Travis had fallen asleep.

"So, Monicandra took the bloodstone seeker from you for analysis and countermeasures, and then turned down your request to put out a warning about it to all the families?" Maury summed up. "Why?"

"According to the members of her team, it would have been a waste of time and resources. Apparently, they've already asked the twenty-three families to surrender their raw *dashkra* to the Guild for safekeeping and have been told by every last one of them that hell will freeze over before they give up their bloodstone to a bunch of assassins. Any further warning from the Guild would most probably be seen as an attempt to manipulate the elders and would be rejected out of hand."

"Sad to say, I'm not really surprised," Maury said with a sigh. "Not by the reactions of the family elders and not by the attitude of the Guild." A pause, then, "So what now, Gershred? I've booked a compartment large enough for three. Are you sure you don't want to come with us on the train?"

He shook his head. "This can't wait another week, I'm afraid. If I could leave right now, I would." Reluctantly, he added, "We need to find out who the *dashkra* collector is, and the sooner I can get Vicky and Barron involved... Listen, I hate to ask this, but... we may have to bait a trap."

"With *dashkra*?"

"Yes. My first choice is to borrow some of Vicky's, but in case she refuses..."

"Don't worry. I'm not about to leave anything behind that can be located with one of those damned tracking devices. If Vicky won't loan you any of her bloodstone, you can dip into what's left of mine. But I don't have much, so consider it only as a last resort."

Early Tuesday morning, as Shred was hanging up his coat after returning from the night's hunt, he heard an anguished wail coming from Travis's bedroom.

Both Nash'terel ran to investigate. The youngster was sitting up in bed, his eyes wide, his covers kicked off. His lips were moving, but no words were coming out. Instead, he was jabbing an urgent index finger in the direction of what should have been his right foot but was now, quite literally, the twin of his left one.

"Lovely," Maury remarked dryly.

Travis was gulping air and struggling to speak.

"I—I woke up and—it was—was like—scales and all green and—"

Maury and Shred shared a knowing look.

"—and you told your essence to make both your feet the same," Maury supplied.

"Yes!"

"And it followed your orders, exactly as you gave them."

"No!" Travis railed. "I mean—I didn't mean—not like *that*!" With a guttural cry of frustration, he grabbed his pillow and hurled it against the wall, right at the smiling face of Connor McDavid.

Maury breathed a weary sigh. "Grandson, do you remember me telling you that essence is like a computer, and you need to be very specific with your instructions or they might be misinterpreted?" He pointed to the errant right foot. "This is why."

"Nash'terel essence is more than a computer, Trav," said Gershred as he moved to stand beside the bed. "It's a highly intelligent tool, like an AI. It learns and it remembers."

"But it's only capable of doing what you've trained it to do," Maury chimed in, "and that's just one thing so far."

"Giving me a foot that looks like that," the kid muttered disgustedly.

"Stop beating yourself up, kiddo," Shred advised him. "You've been at this for one day. I know it may not feel like it right now, but you're already making progress."

"We're going to keep working on it," Maury assured him. "To continue the computer analogy, you're going to fill your mental directory with executable files, as many and as detailed as possible. That way, if you wake up one morning with a Nash'terel hand, or a Nash'terel face, you can simply visualize what you want instead, and your essence will put it back the way it was. The way you will have programmed it to do."

"And it will close up the box in my brain?"

Maury smiled. "Yes. And you'll find that the more you interact with your essence, the more you teach it about your human body, the tighter that lid will become. Eventually, like other Nash'terel, you'll only change shape when you choose to, and only become what you want."

"But it will always be painful."

"I'm afraid so, Grandson. Change is never easy. Be grateful that all you've had to contend with so far is two left feet."

Part Three

Gershred Goes West

Chapter Twelve

In the predawn darkness of Wednesday morning, as Shred sped south from Collingwood to Pearson International Airport, he was mulling over how to convince Vicky Spears to help him capture a Yeng assassin *and* keep them alive for questioning. Her record for this so far was not good. Sixteen years after her daughter's murder, Vincaspera was still out for Yeng blood.

Her never-ending thirst for vengeance was bound to be a liability. However, if this operation was to remain beyond the reach and ken of the Guild, Barron and his people were Shred's best and only hope. He knew Barron would not keep anything secret from his mate, so it would be futile to try to exclude her from the mission.

By the time Gershred had gone through luggage inspection and found his departure gate, he knew a simple trap wouldn't do. This would have to be far more subtle, a con that entangled Vicky as well as the mark. In the air, en route to Vancouver, he recalled and rejected several types of stings that had worked for him in the past.

Then, as the Boeing 737 touched down on the ground once more, he came up with one that should not only induce a Yeng fly to walk into a Nash'terel spider's parlour, but also give both Shred and the spider what they wanted.

Normally, it wouldn't have taken an experienced military strategist like Gershred an entire cross-country trip to come up with a workable plan. However, this hadn't been a normal or comfortable flight for him.

Being responsible for a human child—and, in particular, keeping that child unaware of his and Maury's true nature—had complicated their lives in ways neither of them had anticipated. For one thing, it reduced their hunting and feeding hours to overnight, when Travis was sleeping. As he grew older and stayed awake longer, their roaming range became progressively more restricted. In winter especially, hunting close to home was problematic. They lived in a small town, where the prey selection was limited to begin with, and it dwindled even further in the dark and cold of a January night.

The other thing was, they couldn't always drink their fill anymore. A large, populous city generally had an abundance of dangerous places, where immoral people engaged in questionable activities. In Toronto, for example, there had never been a problem finding adult prey whose loss, while perhaps regrettable, would not cause much of a stir and—what was equally important—could also be otherwise explained. In a small town, however, no human death went unnoticed, and he and Maury couldn't afford to do anything that might make headlines in the local newspaper. When they couldn't drive down to the city to hunt, they settled for local essence, drinking just enough every couple of days to take the edge off their thirst.

Shred's hunt the previous night had been even more unsatisfying than usual. Finding no likely prospects at either of the two pubs in town, he'd headed up a side street, where he discovered a man apparently passed out drunk in a parking lot. Nothing about this felt right (it was like scavenging road kill) but his thirst was becoming strident, so he took as much of the human's essence as he dared, leaving him alive and propped up against the side of a car.

As expected, the essence was polluted with whatever substance the prey was on, but Shred had been drinking human blood and essence for centuries and figured his system could handle it. In this case, he'd figured wrong. Up to and during the five-hour flight, nothing he tried was able to ease the chills and achiness that played in every part of his body.

At around 11:00 a.m. local time, he and the other passengers deplaned at Vancouver International Airport. By now his internal organs had had a chance to filter out and collect the impurities he'd ingested, and the cramping in his midsection was warning him that he'd better find a washroom before he attempted to do anything else. Then Shred walked out into the Arrivals area and spotted a familiar individual waiting for him.

Barron's preferred human shape was that of a battle-hardened soldier. Square-jawed, stony-faced, and covered neck to heels in pocket-studded camo and lace-up military boots, he stood at ease, watching Shred cut through the crowd and cross the concourse toward him.

"I wasn't expecting you to meet me here, Barney," Shred observed.

"I was in the city when I received your text message. It sounded urgent, so I came straightaway. What's up, Gordie? And why are you travelling alone? You're not bringing bad news, are you?"

Shred shook his head and instantly regretted it as a tide of nausea rose in his throat. Clapping a hand over his mouth, he replied through his fingers, "I'll tell you everything in the car. But first—"

Barron pointed to the washroom sign. "Drop your bag. I'll stand guard out here."

A short while later, Shred emerged from the men's room, feeling both much better and much worse than before.

Barron hadn't moved from his post. As they turned and strolled together toward the parking lot, he remarked, "The airline food was that bad?"

Shred gestured dismissively. "I drank some polluted essence last night. I mean, *really* polluted. I don't know what street drug that human was on, but it took its own sweet time going through me."

"Uh-huh. Speaking of hunting, has Travis shown any signs of the thirst?"

"Not yet. In fact, he still has no idea we're essence drinkers. We've kept that knowledge from him, in case he turned out to be completely human."

"But he's not. According to your text, he has a strong *hainbek*, and he's begun to shapeshift. That means he's been expending essence in nonhuman ways. Have you checked to see whether he's developing fangs?"

"There's no need to. Trust me, that sort of itching would not go unnoticed, by him or by us. So far, he's been replenishing his essence by digesting food. And he's still growing, which means he's eating enough for five humans right now. The bloodstone we hung around his neck last weekend may give him a more Nash'terel-like appetite. We'll just have to wait and see."

Barron's vehicle of choice was also the most distinctive one in the lot—a pickup truck, displaying a winter camouflage pattern. Some things never changed, Shred mused as he climbed into the passenger's seat. From the moment they'd met, on the battlefield at Stamford Bridge in Yorkshire in 1066, Barron had always struck Shred as having the soul of a Viking warrior. He was ever ready for combat, certain that the next opportunity for glory was just around the corner.

"Enough for five, eh? I'll warn Vicky to stock up the fridge," Barron said, turning the key in the ignition. "I gather Travis is not producing essence as overflowingly as his mother does?"

"Not that we've been able to detect. Once he's reached adulthood, that could change. If it does, he's safer in Middlevale than anywhere else on the planet. And... there's something else I need to discuss with you and Vicky before Maury arrives."

"Okay. But I'm not driving you anywhere in your current condition. There's a flask of pure essence in the glove box. It should settle your stomach and tide you over. Drink up, Gordie. The last thing we need is for you to fall into a feeding lust while we're en route and attack a pedestrian on the street in broad daylight."

Barron let Shred out in front of Vicky's building on the ironically-named Main Street, then drove around the corner to put the truck away.

From the outside, the storefront hadn't changed since Maury and Shred's last visit, ten years earlier. The display window was still covered by a large red and gold sign proclaiming the name of The Church of Human Purification. The quasar-and-DNA logo was the same as well.

For the past three hundred and some years, this cult had been the cover for Vicky's grand experiment on Earth. She'd been selectively breeding humans in order to create a source of pollution-free essence, and the isolated town of Middlevale had been her laboratory.

Victoria Spears hadn't changed her outward appearance either since the last time they'd met. She was still the same willowy female with green eyes and long auburn hair that Shred remembered. However, the interior of the storefront had undergone a major makeover.

All the furniture now matched, for one thing—two identical smallish steel desks, each topped with a woodgrain-veneered slab of composite and paired with a black faux leather chair. There was also a work table holding an array of office-appropriate technology, bookended by two more chairs. The walls looked freshly painted in a pale beige colour, and the floor appeared to have been recently refinished. So did the tall wooden shelving unit in the corner. Now holding a variety of printed material, it had been stained to match the desk tops.

As Shred paused on the threshold, taking it all in, Vicky rose from her seat and stepped to the middle of the room. "Do you like what you see?" she said, smiling.

"It's quite an improvement. I gather you picked out the décor, since there's no camo visible," he teased her.

"That's because this is my work space, not his. Barron's work space... Well, you'll see it for yourself when he takes you out tomorrow morning to tour the camp. He wanted to drive up there this afternoon, but I talked him out of it. Depending on the road conditions, it can take up to five hours in the truck, and I figured that after your long plane ride, you would probably have had your fill of travelling for the day."

"You figured correctly, so thank you for that."

She smiled and nodded a gracious, *You're welcome.*

"You're going to love our new facilities, Gordie," Barron announced. He'd parked in the alleyway and entered through the back. Now he stood in front of the shelving unit as it pivoted shut once more, closing off the concealed route to the stairwell next door. "It's perfectly camouflaged. Unless they're using infrared satellite imaging, the installation is invisible from the air."

Shred sighed inwardly. "I'm afraid the Yeng no longer need human imaging systems to find Nash'terel prey, Barney. They're using a different kind of technology now, one that detects *dashkra*."

A leaden silence dropped over the room.

Vicky was the first to speak. "You've seen it in operation?" she said tautly.

"The short range version, yes. Seen it, captured it, verified it, and turned it over to the Guild. And there's more."

"Worse than what you've just told us?" said Barron.

"It appears that someone is paying Yeng assassins for the bloodstones from the bodies of their victims. We don't know who it is, or precisely why they're collecting *dashkra*. Not yet, anyway."

Vicky raised a suspicious eyebrow. "We? As in you, working with the Guild?" *Again?* The unspoken word hung in the air.

He brushed the question aside. "Monicandra wants to set a trap and bait it with raw *dashkra*."

Now her eyes were flashing. "Uh-huh. Let me guess. None of the family elders are willing to provide this bait, so now she's casting her eyes on the scientific community. Have you asked your partner to loan them his supply, since, unlike mine, it won't have to be transported across the whole damn *country* to them?" The last few words landed like slaps across Shred's face.

Dragging in a lungful of air, he replied, "Actually, I've come up with a plan of my own to capture the mystery collector and shake out some answers. It's a sting, not a trap. But it would involve you and some of your *dashkra*."

"Does it also involve the Guild?"

"No. The whole thing would take place out here, without their knowledge. If it's successful, we can present it to them as a *fait accompli*. If it's not..." He ended the thought with a shrug.

Frowning, Barron opened his mouth to say something, but Vicky beat him to it. "Keep talking."

"First, we convince the collector that there's a competitor out here who has to be dealt with. We do that by using social media to advertise a chunk of *dashkra* for sale. All that's needed is an image, not the stone itself. Then we rig the auction so that the bloodstone doesn't actually get sold, except to our own backstopped 'collector'."

"So *we're* the competition, selling it to ourselves."

"Right. After all the times we've had to reinvent ourselves on this world, creating a fake identity shouldn't pose any problems. It will probably take several bogus auctions on different platforms to demonstrate that our collector is a serious buyer."

"Then what?"

"Then I'm hoping the mystery collector will be curious enough to contact us and arrange a meeting with one of their representatives."

Barron was still frowning. "A meeting? That's it?"

"That's just the beginning. Remember how we purged the Council of the First? We're shapeshifters. We kill the representative and send back an impersonator, a Nash'terel spy assigned to glean intel about the collector and their organization. It's a necessary step. The scenario for the sting will have to be convincing and the bait irresistible, and we can't be sure of either one without more information about the mark."

"I remember the Purge," said Barron, his frown deepening into a scowl. "But do *you* remember how long it took for each operative to learn enough about the target simply to make the impersonation credible? From what you've told us, time is of the essence right now. How many of our Earthborn will be lost while this mole is fitting into their role and *then* gathering data that may or may not be useful in the end?"

Shred remained silent, his fingers mentally crossed.

"And what's to prevent the mystery collector from sending their rep on a mission to find out about us so they can set up their own sting and take *us* out of the picture?" Barron went on.

"Not a thing, which is why whoever replaces that person will have to be especially careful not to reveal anything that could be used against us." Shred leaned forward and said earnestly, "Listen, if I believed the collector were Nash'terel, I wouldn't even be suggesting this. We're experts when it comes to traps. The Yeng and the humans, not so much. As long as we're not wearing *dashkra* we can easily pass for either one."

"Our mole would be improvising. Any number of things could fly sideways," Barron pointed out.

"It's intel gathering, Barney. That goes with the territory. Come on! In the past, we've adlibbed our way through entire reconnaissance ops."

"Yeah, in wartime, backed up by an army and with an extraction team waiting in case we got into trouble. But this—! What you're proposing is an off-the-books operation, Gordie, without a safety net. We created the Guild to *prevent* stuff like this from happening. Now you, of all people, want to go rogue?"

"I have a good reason for doing it this way. And it's funny, but I don't recall you being this cautious before, Barney. Makes me wonder whether there's something I should know."

Barron and Vicky exchanged a freighted look.

"I can't tell you," he replied. "I'll have to show you, tomorrow."

"I'm curious," said Vicky. "Have you shared this proposal with Maldemaur?"

"Haven't had a chance," Shred replied. "I came up with it during the flight from Toronto and wanted to run it past you first, since you'll be making the largest investment in its success."

"You want my honest opinion?" Barron said.

No, I want hers, Shred thought. But he kept silent, and Barron continued, "I think that bad essence you drank has interfered with your thinking process, because I could drive a whole convoy of tanks through the holes in this scheme of yours."

At last, Vicky weighed in. "It's flawed, that's true, but I believe the basic concept has merit. Why don't you leave it with me, and I'll see what I can do with it."

Shred nodded, somehow managing to conceal his satisfaction behind an expression that was at once chastened and hopeful.

He'd known Vincaspera when she was Maury's assistant-turned-scientific-rival back on RinYeng. She'd always preferred to do things her own way—insisted on it, in fact. Sure, Shred could have worked out every detail and plugged every hole in his plan, but that would have made it a hard sell, and he wanted Vicky on board. So, he'd dangled something half-baked in front of her, which pretty much guaranteed that she would pounce on it, develop it, then push to implement it, claiming the idea had been her own from the get-go.

She couldn't help herself. This had been her *modus operandi* back on RinYeng. It was practically written into her DNA. And—a bonus—if the sting he'd envisioned on the plane worked, it would give her an opportunity to spill Yeng blood in the name of her murdered daughter.

An angry, grieving mother was a force of nature. Victoria Spears was that and much more: she was a Nash'terel elemental master, a pressure lord, able to kill from a distance with a twitch of her hand. This mysterious collector and their minions, whoever and whatever they were, wouldn't stand a chance against her.

Chapter Thirteen

◆

Shred had drunk the entire contents of the flask in Barron's truck. Between that and the late lunch of raw pork loin, steamed sweet corn, and grilled asparagus that Vicky had prepared, he wouldn't need to eat or feed for another fifteen hours, at least. As he texted Maury an update, Shred smiled to himself. Being able to eat when he was actually hungry instead of following a human schedule of three meals per day... it felt so liberating!

Barron and Vicky lived in the apartment two storeys above the storefront. Thanking his hostess for lunch, Shred excused himself and went downstairs to the second-floor flat reserved for guests. He'd been looking forward to enjoying some long-delayed R and R. Unfortunately, his mind had other plans. Memories kept running laps inside his head, and his thoughts wouldn't let him relax.

Ten years. That was how long it had been since Travis and grandfatherhood had taken over his life and Maury's. Swallowed them whole, it felt like. Time was such a funny thing. It seemed to shapeshift like the Nash'terel, passing quickly for some, more slowly for others. Mathematically, the last ten years represented a tiny one-fifth of one percent of Shred's life so far; and yet, those years had loomed so much larger, dragging themselves out until together they felt even longer and more taxing than the five hundred years it had taken to raise Bilyash from childhood to adolescence.

Were human youngsters that much more demanding of time and energy than Nash'terel offspring? Or were Maury and Shred just getting old? And what would life be like once Travis had been handed off to his parents? Shred recalled his time with Maury before Bilyash and Travis as though it were a dream, dissolving like mist in his waking mind, never to be whole and present again.

There were books and magazines in the apartment. Shred tried to read, but a restlessness had invaded the core of his being. Nash'terel warriors were familiar with this sensation. They called it "battle itch". It made them hyper-vigilant, and, like a rush of human adrenalin just before a charge into combat, it compelled them to expend their essence. What had triggered this imperative in himself, Shred could not say, but he knew better than to try to deny it.

He prowled the apartment until nightfall. Then he went out and prowled the dark and mostly empty streets. None of the prey he saw aroused his thirst, so he stole past them, invisible in the shadows, driven to keep moving until muscle fatigue forced him to break off the hunt. With an ache in his bones that told him yes, he was getting old, he climbed the stairs to the second floor, where he dozed off sitting up on the sofa.

Shred slept until Barron knocked on the door, come to invite him upstairs for breakfast.

*   *   *

The road north was clear and dry, and the day was crisp and sunny. As they left Vancouver farther behind them, the six-lane highway shrank down to four lanes and then two, the die-straight county road eventually plunging into a dense growth of evergreen forest. Barron drove the way he always did, as though traversing a battlefield while under fire—a habit acquired from taking vehicles through combat zones in at least three wars that Shred knew of—and reached the turnoff to Middlevale in less than three and a half hours.

The right turn put them on one of those rutted dirt trails that sidled off the main route and disappeared into the woods, its location marked by a No Trespassing sign nailed to the trunk of a tree. At this snow-covered time of year, only the sign was visible. Travelling alone, Shred mused, he would have driven right past it. But that was probably the whole idea.

As with everything Nash'terel-owned, the way to the human community of Middlevale was heavily protected. Barron steered the truck carefully through the trees, pointing out surveillance cameras strategically concealed overhead, and tripwires at ground level that triggered noisy alarms or swung barriers into place. Shred also glimpsed what looked like the business ends of weapons peeking out of the shrubbery.

"Maldemaur helped us set the tripwires last time he was here," Barron explained.

Of *course* he had. Maury was careful to the point of paranoia. He'd established a defensive perimeter around every home they'd ever had on this world and was especially fond of traps.

"Killing or disappearing every outsider who chances to wander onto our property is a sure-fire way to draw police attention to ourselves," Barron continued, "and that's the last thing we want. So first, we try to scare off intruders. If that doesn't work, we scramble and *head* them off. Surround and challenge. Every trainee knows the drill. Humans are escorted back to the main road and released with a stern warning. Yeng spies are executed on the spot. Either way, no one gets within sight of Middlevale who isn't authorized to be there."

Shred nodded his approval. "This is military-grade security."

"As it should be. We're running a top secret military training facility," Barron pointed out. "We were a lot more vulnerable to infiltration before Maldemaur became a partner. He helped us tighten things up considerably, and since then we've had no attempted breaches at all."

"Not even one? What about the press? Human reporters can be extremely inquisitive."

"Human curiosity hasn't been a problem for us. Not since you made headlines by streaking a campsite in your Nash'terel form, about a hundred years ago. In all the excitement over Bigfoot sightings, we dropped off the grid entirely as far as the humans were concerned. And that's pretty much where we've remained. Like Area 51. Occasionally, someone will speculate online about a secret military installation somewhere in the Canadian wilderness, but no one has actually come looking for us."

"Not even the Yeng? It doesn't sound like them to have simply forgotten about you, Barney."

"I agree. It's never good when the enemy goes quiet. That's why our defences stay up and we remain vigilant. If they're planning a major offensive, we'll be ready for them. In the meanwhile, once or twice a year a lost hiker stumbles onto the property and has to be dealt with, and that's about as far as it goes for now."

"Uh-huh, but with all the new technology that's being developed, you know it's just a matter of time," Shred pointed out.

Barron let out a sigh. "Yeah. Middlevale can't stay a secret forever, and eventually, just disguising ourselves won't be enough. Vicky has been talking about finding better ways to assimilate into the human population. She hasn't ruled out the possibility of interbreeding. That's partly why she's so excited about having Travis join us out here. He's a hybrid, living evidence that it can be done."

"The hybrid is your godson, Barney," Shred said, bristling, "and trust me, the last thing he wants right now is to be seen as an interesting scientific specimen."

At that moment, the truck emerged from the woods. Barron pulled to a stop on the crest of a ridge overlooking a scene that might have inspired a Currier and Ives print. In a broad basin formed by long white slopes sat a large collection of detached houses and low-rise buildings with snow-covered rooftops, all lined up along streets that radiated outwards from a central town square. Smoke drifted lazily from chimneys. In many yards, snowmen stood guard. Elsewhere, snow forts were being vigorously attacked and defended. In a fenced area adjacent to one of the buildings, about twenty small children played, under the watchful eyes of four adults. On the far side of town, older children were riding sleds and toboggans down a hill, while others skated back and forth on the frozen surface of what might have been a pond.

"This is the latest iteration of Middlevale," Barron said with evident pride. "Population six thousand. Inbred as hell, but in every other respect a damn near typical Canadian small town. There aren't any franchises or big box stores, but it has almost everything else that a being could want. It's a far cry from the genetics laboratory Vicky set up in the wilderness all those years ago."

"And yet, it's apparently still an experiment," Shred remarked, "only no longer isolated, since there's access from the highway... and that raises an interesting security question."

"How come they're all still living here, instead of leaving to explore the outside world, you mean?"

"I presume the answer has to do with the surveillance and protective measures you've set up along the path to the main road. Are you disappearing humans who try to break away from the cult?"

Barron gave him a broad grin. "There's no reason to. The residents of Middlevale are staying put because they've got everything they need right here, including the internet, filtered through a server in the training compound. Vicky knew she couldn't keep them backward and ignorant forever, so she gave them a powerful incentive not to leave. It was brilliant, really.

"As soon as she realized that she'd achieved what she'd set out to do, she called a town meeting. She announced that she had had a divine revelation—which, in a way, was the truth—and that the residents of Middlevale had finally arrived at a state of grace. Their essence was pure and abundant. They were the chosen ones. In a world rife with soul-polluting evil and corruption, they had a new, ongoing mission: to keep themselves and their essence untainted so that they could inherit the planet after everyone else had been consumed by their own iniquity."

She'd painted them a picture of a planet wracked by sin, Shred mused. And the filtered internet feed would then have reinforced that impression, showing them nothing but wars, poverty, the cruelty of criminals in positions of power... and online trolls, shaming and bullying without restraint. Vicky had said that her dream was to create a safe haven for Nash'terel on Earth. Making Middlevale a sanctuary for humans was evidently a vital first step in her plan. And Barron was right—she'd chosen the perfect way to keep them where she wanted them.

"Is this why you're being so cautious lately?" Shred remarked.

"Middlevale is her life's work, her only child right now. I won't do anything to compromise or endanger it, especially if there's a risk the Yeng might rediscover us and come knocking."

Barron shrugged as though to rid himself of his darkening mood. "After Maldemaur shared his process with Vicky for creating receptacles, she was able to change the way she drew off and stored human essence. That was when Middlevale really began to flourish. They've even elected a mayor—he's more of a liaison, actually, between Vicky and her flock, but it makes the humans feel that they're running things. Depending on how the rest of the weekend progresses, you might get to meet him. In the meanwhile, our destination is the training compound, about a klick north of here."

So saying, Barron put the truck in gear and continued driving along the rim of the basin, back toward the woods. A couple of minutes later, they emerged again, into a clearing with a large, flat-roofed structure in the middle of it. Unlike the buildings in the human settlement, this one had camo-patterned stucco walls. It also sported a large sign: POLLEY'S DINER AND SPA.

Really? Shred stared a question at his driver.

"This is our motor pool and admin-slash-rec centre," came the answer. "Polley's expecting you."

"And Polley is...?"

"My second in command. The best weapons instructor on the

base and one of the toughest soldiers I've ever served with—next to you, of course. Polley bounces back and forth between male and female shapes and claims not to have a birth gender. Sound familiar?" Barron tossed him a grin. "Anyway, once we've dropped the truck off and you're signed in as my guest, I'll give you a quick tour. After that, we'll go the rest of the way on foot. Of the thirty-six students in the compound right now, sixteen are adepts receiving military training. The other twenty are Earthborn apprentices, learning defensive skills from half a dozen specialist instructors with different *hainbeka*. We can watch them work for a while before I introduce you to them."

"Introduce me as what?" Shred asked warily.

The grin widened. "You'll see."

Shred leaned back in his seat, disquieting possibilities milling around inside his head. This was supposed to be a simple visit, a way for him to see how Bilyash—now known as Ken—was doing, while also satisfying his curiosity about how the training camp was set up. Now, however, Barron's reticence was raising red flags in his mind.

Gershred felt a pinch across his shoulders and rotated them to relax his tightening muscles.

Barron drove around the corner of the building and parked the truck in front of an unmarked bottle-glass door. Then he led the way inside, through a second glass door and into a spartanly-furnished outer office divided in half by a gated waist-high counter. The brown-skinned woman who glanced up at them from behind her computer screen had a no-nonsense cast to her features and was dressed in camo quite literally from head to toe. Even the wide elastic band that fastened her tightly curled hair into a ponytail was mottled brown, tan, and olive drab. She stood up and walked toward them, a smile sneaking across her face.

"You must be the redoubtable Gordie Sharp," she said.

"And I take it you're Polley?" he returned.

"Every bit of me. Sign in, please." She slid a clipboard with pen attached across the counter to Shred. Addressing Barron, she added, "Want your truck sheltered, sir?"

Wordlessly, he handed over his key fob. Then he turned to face his guest. "Follow me, Gordie, and prepare to be amazed."

Uh-huh. Amazed and then introduced. He was being led into an ambush, all right.

They went through another door, into the motor pool. It contained more than a dozen assorted vehicles, ranging from motorcycles to panel trucks, all wearing winter camo. This was thanks to someone named Yanni who answered to two titles: chief mechanic and resident shape lord. Shred surveyed the area, noting that it looked spacious enough to take up most of the interior of the building. Then Barron ushered him onto an elevator car, and Shred realized with a start that this single-storey structure was actually the top floor of an underground facility.

Okay, he was amazed. Shred had known from his last visit that the place was under renovation, but this was far more extensive than he could have imagined.

On the first sub-level, Barron showed him the kitchen and dining area, the games/video room, and the gym. All were well-equipped and appeared initially to have been modelled on the standard human-run military base. Only on closer inspection did one notice certain discrepancies, such as the types of meat and many items with "blood" in their names listed on the daily menus, and some extra markings on the walls and ceiling of the gym.

"You've got gravity *hainbeka* in this cohort?" said Shred.

"A couple," Barron replied with a grin. "They've invented a variation on basketball that you aren't going to believe."

As the door hummed open on the second sub-level, Shred sensed a familiar chill in the air. Barron crossed the hallway to a large metal door, hauled it open, and, with a sweeping gesture, invited him to enter...

...a hockey rink. It was similar in size and layout to the one that the Georgian Bay Rockets called home, but with a single three-tiered section of bench seating on each of the four sides of the ice. A three-on-three game was in progress. *Awfully quiet for a hockey match,* Shred thought. Then he took a second look and realized why.

"No sticks."

"It's a Nash'terel version of the sport," Barron explained. "I've modified the rules for players with two types of talent: pressure and gravity. Everyone on the ice is both a forward and a goaltender, and they're all moving or blocking the puck with their minds." As though on cue, the puck rose into the air, lurched back and forth a couple of times, then shot like a missile into one of the nets. "It's an exercise in teamwork," he added. "And focusing one's attention."

Shred narrowed his gaze. "How long have you had—?"

"A rink in the compound? Long time, actually," came the prompt reply. "The first ones were above ground, improvised during the winter months, just like the pond rink in Middlevale, and strictly for recreation. So, the games were all shinny, played using human gear and according to human rules. However, as part of the major upgrade of the facilities, I decided to bring the rink indoors and incorporate hockey and curling into the program. Yanni can convert this ice surface into a curling sheet in a matter of minutes."

"You never even mentioned it the last time we were out here."

Barron shrugged. "It was need to know, and you didn't need to know."

"But now I do?"

The other Nash'terel just smiled and said, "Let's go back up top. There's still the rest of the compound to visit, and we'll want to return here by dinnertime. Chef is preparing a special dish this evening, in your honour."

In his *honour*? As they walked back to the elevator, Shred eyed his guide suspiciously. "Barney, what have you been telling people about me?"

"Nothing that isn't true," he maintained.

"Really! Such as?"

"That you're one of a small number of original refugees from RinYeng who have managed to hide in plain sight among the humans for going on sixteen centuries. That you did it by completely reinventing yourself over and over. And that your experience at fitting into the various pockets of human society makes you the closest thing we have to an expert on the subject. You've got a wealth of first-hand knowledge to share, Gordie. In fact," he added, escorting Shred into the car and selecting G on the wall-mounted keypad beside the sliding door, "around here you're something of a legend."

Shred swore silently. Aloud, he grated, "So the trainees all know about me."

"Yes, and they're eager to meet you and learn from you. Hey, you know the score out there. The Nash'terel are being hunted. As we both agreed on our way up here, it won't be long before simply taking human shape won't be enough to protect us from the triads. Tell me, can the tracking technology detect the *dashkra* in our blood?"

Shred recalled the device's failure to identify him at the arena the previous weekend and replied, "No."

Barron made a sour face. "You mean not yet. Give them time. The previous cohorts, the adepts I've trained specifically to be assassins—they're going to be all right," he continued. "But the others, the apprentices who know they're soft targets and just want to be able to protect themselves against a Yeng attack...? They'll need to perfect their camouflage skills if they're to survive until the next opening of the rift."

Barron and Shred were both heat lords, able to keep themselves warm without outer clothing, even in the depths of a Canadian winter. However, as though to provide a teaching example of what passing for human looked like, they paused to zip up their jackets and don hats and scarves before stepping outside into the chill January air.

"The parts of the compound are actually linked by underground passageways," Barron explained. The vapour of his breath streamed alongside his face as he set off at a brisk pace in the direction of the trees. "We're taking this route so I can show you something."

"You came to Earth at the same time as I did and have been passing successfully for just as long," Shred reminded him. "Why can't *you* teach them?"

"You already know the answer to that. Being a soldier is all I've ever wanted to do, on both planets. Fighting and teaching others how to fight, that's pretty much my repertoire, and the trainees know it. I can teach them how to submerge themselves into an already-existing military culture. You, on the other hand... On RinYeng, you followed the philosophy of Sidu'Hama, training as both a warrior and a scholar. On Earth, you've been everything from a farmhand to a priest. There's simply no comparison between us, Gordie. You're the best instructor for this they could have. Will you at least consider it?"

As they hiked across the snow-covered ground, Shred subsided into his thoughts. He'd never seen Barron like this. First, he'd pulled back from a risk in order to protect Middlevale. Now he was admitting his own shortcoming and giving his trainees "the best instructor they could have". It was a dramatic change from the arrogant berserker Shred had served with in so many human wars. And, perhaps as planned, it had aroused his curiosity.

"All right," he finally replied with a sigh. "No promises, but I'll think about it."

"Good."

Shred paused to savour the crisp, clean air. There was a cathedral-like quality to the forest here, not only in the silence that graced it, but also in its architecture. Douglas fir trees and Lodgepole pines stood shoulder to shoulder, their massive trunks stretching high into the air, while the broad spreading branches of poplars and birch intertwined overhead. They formed a vaulted ceiling that broke up the afternoon light, dappling the forest floor with gold. Some places could be described as magical. This one evoked a deeper, more introspective reaction, Shred thought...

...until he noticed the orange 'X's that someone had spray-painted on several of the tree trunks. Barron wouldn't have permitted a logging operation this close to the compound, so what the hell was this?

He watched as Barron positioned himself beside one X in particular, then continued forward slowly, counting his steps aloud. After six paces, he dropped to a knee and dug his hand into the mixture of snow and leafy debris on the ground. Then he grasped something and pulled it upward with effort to reveal a large square opening.

"There are several of these trap doors scattered throughout the complex," Barron explained, "but this is the only one that's marked above ground. It's here in case any of us are cut off from Polley's Diner by enemy action and need to drop out of sight quickly. The others are escape routes. Or we can use them to outflank an invading force in the unlikely event that a foe has breached our defensive perimeter."

Following Barron down a flight of noisy metal stairs, Shred asked, "Where's Ken right now?"

"At this hour, he'll be in the ops centre, working one-on-one with an instructor. He spends his free time with Angie in a cottage not far from here."

"There's a cottage nearby? That's convenient."

Barron threw an amused glance over his shoulder. "Actually, it was necessary. Angie and Vicky seemed to get along fine as long as they had an infant to care for. After a couple of years, though, it was clear that the offspring was aging at a human rate, and the friction between mother and godmother was growing almost as quickly as he was. So, I put some of the trainees to work on a construction project. Fortunately, it was sufficiently completed to let Angie and Travis move into it before Vicky's patience completely ran out. Otherwise..." He blew out a breath. "You've seen her on a rampage. It wouldn't have been pretty."

The stairwell opened out into a circular hub with minimal lighting. Narrow corridors led away in four different directions.

"Which ones are the decoys?" Shred asked.

"They all are. The barracks and training complex are one level down."

In the closet of darkness behind the staircase, a metal slab in the wall turned out to be the entrance to another staircase, accessed by means of a concealed keypad.

"Listen, I understand why you couldn't bring Angie inside the compound, but—"

"They're still inside the security net, Gordie," Barron assured him. "My original plan was to house them below ground as well, in an apartment connected to the complex by a tunnel, but Angie wouldn't go for it. She said she wasn't raising her son in a bunker. So, we did the next best thing—surrounded the cottage with proximity alarms and closed circuit cameras, wired each room for emergency communications, and gave her a cellar linked to the compound by a concealed underground passageway. At the first sign of trouble, whoever's inside the building can alert the command centre, then disappear to safety.

"So far, we haven't *had* any trouble, but I attribute that to luck. And Yanni keeps the building camouflaged, so it's virtually invisible from any angle, at all times of the year. In short, Ken and his family are as protected as I can make them without bubble-wrapping them and locking them in a closet."

"Maybe. Maybe not. Is Angie still wearing the bloodstone pendant Maury gave her when she and Bilyash mated?"

"Yeah, there's that, isn't there?" Barron said thoughtfully. They'd reached the lower level. As he keyed in the code to open another slab of door, he added over his shoulder, "I'm afraid you'll have to ask *her* about it. Truth is, I haven't spoken to Angie more than a couple of times since she came to the city to hand her child over to you and Maldemaur, ten years ago."

Ten years was a long time for a human. Angie was spirited, not the sort to put up with being sequestered in a cabin. So, Shred wondered, what could she have been doing in the meanwhile?

"These are the barracks," said Barron, breaking into his thoughts.

They walked out into another large circular area, this one evidently designed to serve as a common recreation room. It was wood-panelled, softly lit, and comfortably furnished with overstuffed chairs and loveseats. Hard copy books lined its shelves, and games were stacked on several low tables, but Shred saw no televisions, computers, or anything else with a screen. He paused for a moment to observe two trainees playing chess. The pieces were moving as though nudged by invisible fingers.

"First the hockey, now this," he remarked. "You seem to have a lot of pressure *hainbeka* in the program this time around."

"It's one of the most common talents, but you're right about this cohort in particular. Ten of the trainees are gifted that way, and two more will soon be arriving. A father and son. You may know them, since Maldemaur was the one who pointed them in my direction."

"You're talking about the Dagomirs?"

Barron nodded in response.

"Travis knows them too, from hockey," said Shred. "The father is a coach."

Barron chuckled. "It figures. Your partner is a wily old *cavanga*, my friend. You'd better practise ducking, because when Vicky finds out about this, she is going to be pissed."

Pretending ignorance, Shred inquired, "Oh? Why?"

"Because she'll see him as competition for training her godson. She was always planning to do it herself."

Recalling his conversation with Maury outside the Rockets' dressing room door, Shred smiled inwardly. They made a good team, taking turns at predicting Vicky's behaviour and thwarting her intentions. With luck, they would be able to keep doing it until Ken and Angie's family was whole once more.

On the barracks level, as on the one above it, corridors radiated away from the common area in four different directions. The difference here, Shred surmised, was that the doors in each hallway opened into sleeping quarters, not traps for an invading enemy to fall into.

"Strategy room is that way," said Barron, pointing left. "But I'm guessing you'd rather have a peek at the ops centre first."

Shred followed him along one of the corridors to its end, where they made a right turn into an alcove containing two entrances. The one straight ahead was a double door with the word "OPERATIONS" stencilled above it. The unmarked door to the right was the one Barron opened. It took them into a small, sparsely furnished room lined with large screens, each subdivided into four to six different images.

"Each trainee has been assigned a separate practice area in this part of the complex," Barron explained. "Closed circuit video has proven to be the best way to keep an eye on all of them at the same time." He went to a keyboard and punched in a series of characters, and one of the images expanded to fill its screen. "Ken on the left you know. Jarrent on the right is his instructor."

Ken Smart was one of a series of identities that Bilyash had created for himself over the centuries. He'd been forced to change his shape as well as his handle some sixteen years earlier, when he'd been "killed" in a car crash to shake off the Yeng assassins targeting him.

Like Shred, the kid had been a fan of old movies. He'd even worked in the industry as a special effects makeup artist. So, it was only natural that he would draw inspiration from film classics whenever he reinvented himself. How else to explain why Ken Smart's face reminded Shred by turns of James Dean and James Coburn?

James Dean was best known as a rebel without a cause. Clearly, the kid had been making a statement to go with his "great escape".

Shred stared at this younger- and tougher-looking edition of his and Maury's son for a moment, then said, "What's with the spoons?"

"His *hainbek* is magnetism. He's mastered control of his ability to create magnetic fields and has moved on to projecting his essence into metal objects beyond his grasp, turning them into magnets as well. He's been able to increase his range to several metres in every direction. Lately, he's been practising attracting metal objects toward him from a distance.

"He's fine with large things that he can catch two-handed, like garbage can lids. Single-handed capture can be tricky, though, and in the case of something sharp, he still needs to fine-tune his control so as not to injure himself. That's why Jarrent is having him work with something harmless. Once he's mastered spoons, he'll graduate to butter knives. I expect that will be soon. He's a very motivated student."

They watched in silence for several more minutes. Shred counted ten flying spoons, only two caught by their handles, the rest by their bowls. Then Barron minimized the screen again and he and Shred headed back toward the common area.

"I have to admit, Barney, I am both amazed and impressed," Shred commented. "A large complex like this, fully functioning, completely underground... Whether you built it first or built it later, just excavating the hole to plant it in must have been an enormous undertaking. And with all that heavy digging machinery coming and going, I'm surprised you were able to keep the process a secret."

A pause, then, "It wasn't as difficult or as much work as you think, Gordie. In fact, other than a small fleet of dump trucks to carry away the loose soil, we didn't have to use any heavy equipment at all."

Shred came to an abrupt halt at the entrance to the hub. "What do you mean?" he demanded, whirling to face his guide. "Is there a new *hainbek* that nobody knows about?"

Barron glanced around the common room. Shred did as well, noting that the chess game was over and the players gone. "In a way. You know how the old stories say that the bloodstone was first discovered inside a cave? Well, it turns out that *dashkra* may have been the reason there was a cave there in the first place."

"I don't understand. Are you telling me this mineral created its own cave?"

"Yes. It burrows to escape ultraviolet light. Vicky found that out by accident and conducted some experiments to confirm her observations. Drop a chunk of raw *dashkra* on the ground out in the open, leave it there for a day, and when you go back, it'll be hiding in a shadow at the bottom of a hole."

"A hole." Shred spread his arms to indicate the space they were in. "Large enough for something like this?"

"Not all at once. If you distribute a sufficient amount of *dashkra* over an area, it will dig you something deep enough to serve as a crawl space. After that, it's just a matter of repeatedly rearranging the stones and keeping them in daylight, until you have the excavation you need."

"But what about all the ritual jewellery that Nash'terel have been wearing for thousands of years? Pregnant females wear it on the outside of their clothing where it's exposed to UV rays. Wouldn't someone have noticed if their brooch or pendant came to life and tried to burrow through the material?"

"The cut and polished stones don't behave that way. They're inert." Barron paused, his expression uncertain, then visibly made up his mind. "Just between us, Vicky's theory is that *dashkra* is like coral, made up of millions of tiny creatures stuck together, and that by processing the stones, we may actually be killing some of them. Needless to say, she's decided to keep this theory to herself. But it's the reason she's tucked her remaining stash of bloodstone away in a dark and secret place while she figures out what to do with it."

Sacrificing another life form as part of a Nash'terel ceremony? That had a primitive feel to it. And how ironic it would be, Shred reflected, if it turned out that the primary targets of the Yeng emperor's purification campaign had unwittingly been conducting a slow genocide of their own. No, that was the wrong word. Genocide applied to sapient beings. *Dashkra* was...

A sudden thought sent a shiver down his spine. "Barney, does Vicky have reason to believe that the bloodstone may be intelligent?"

"Not so far. Why? Are you afraid that if we put all the raw *dashkra* in one place it will rise up and wreak its vengeance on us?"

With a growing sense of urgency, Shred told him, "There are Earth plants that release chemical irritants to punish predators. What if all the changes that *dashkra* dust has made to the bodies of the Nash'terel are the bloodstone's way of punishing us for killing some of them?"

"Then I would say it's already done its worst, and we have nothing more to fear."

"Are you sure? Until today, I had no idea that *dashkra* could burrow. That makes me wonder what else we don't know about it."

A shadow briefly crossed Barron's expression, and Shred decided to press his point.

"When the Guild suggested putting all the *dashkra* in one safe place, every family elder turned them down. What if the reason for that was that, like Vicky, other Nash'terel scientists had discovered something troubling about the bloodstone and chosen to keep the information to themselves?"

Silence.

"Listen, we both know how deeply isolation and seclusion are ingrained into the Nash'terel consciousness," Shred went on earnestly. "The Science Guild was dissolved when we fled to this world, and the families have made it clear how they feel about the existence of an Assassins' Guild. But this new information emerging about the bloodstone is too disturbing not to share with other Nash'terel. We need a way for learned knowledge to be pooled. Maybe that means reestablishing the Science Guild. I don't know. What I do know is that someone needs to start the process rolling by finding and contacting all the family elders, sooner rather than later."

Barron's face had acquired a faint, mirthless smile. "And by someone, you mean us," he said. "This is payback for telling the trainees about you, isn't it?"

"No, it's not. As warriors, we have a duty to ensure the continuation of the Nash'terel race, in whatever form it may take. And we're elemental masters as well, two out of a number that gets smaller with each passing century. You told me earlier today that we shouldn't keep what we know to ourselves. And you're right. In this case, it would be a betrayal."

Tight-lipped, Barron was shaking his head. "I don't know, Gordie. The elders have been in hiding for nearly sixteen hundred years, scattered all over the planet. Even if we located them all *and* they agreed to talk to us, getting them to open up to one another would be a whole other challenge. And where would you suggest we begin? It's been a couple of millennia since I last spoke to anyone in my family, even longer in your case."

Shred winced inwardly. His parents had disowned him back on RinYeng. Distant though it was, the memory was still painful. "True. But we have to try. Someone out there is buying up *dashkra* taken from the bodies of dead Nash'terel. We need to access every resource we've got and find out why. What does the shadowy collector know about the bloodstone that we don't?"

A heavy pause, then, "The Guild is in charge of protecting Nash'terel personal data," said Barron. "They can tell us the current location of every family elder. But we would have to give them a compelling reason to hand the information over, something more than what you've already told them, and I don't think 'this mineral can burrow' is going to cut it."

"That will be a problem," Shred agreed. "Monicandra and her team basically shut me down and tossed me out when I tried to convince them to talk to the family elders about the bloodstone."

"So, their minds are closed, and we'll have to pry them back open. Okay. It won't be the first time. But we'll do it together, Gordie. Once Travis is settled in, I'll come east and we'll make our request to the Guild in person. Deal?"

"Deal."

"Polley's had quarters prepared for you in the instructors' wing of the barracks. You don't have to make any formal presentations.

Just spend the weekend on site. I'll give you the long tour. We can talk about old times while the trainees follow us around and listen in, and you can answer questions as they come up."

Shred expelled an audible breath. "You're not going to take no for an answer, are you?"

"Nope."

Part Four

Family Matters

Chapter Fourteen

Listening to the metronomic muttering of train wheels on track, Maury sat watch in the darkened compartment.

It was Friday, the first night of their journey and the end of a day filled with firsts for Maldemaur. It was the first time he'd undertaken a long trip without feeding the night before. It was also the first time he had opted for privacy during a train ride. Generally, Maury preferred not to hand that advantage to any Yeng assassin who might happen to come aboard. He especially hated having to do it now, knowing that the pendants around his and Travis's necks were like beacons identifying them as prey for Yeng on the hunt. But he'd made the youngster a promise, and this was the only way he could keep it without drawing unwanted human attention.

Like nearly everything else in life, there was a trade-off. The fact that Travis needed to sleep for several hours every night meant that Maury got a periodic respite from the stress of giving a hybrid adolescent a crash course on the Nash'terel skill of shapeshifting (yet another first). It let him focus instead on the constant stress of keeping his young charge safe in what Maury had never stopped seeing as a dangerous world.

Shred had been wrong earlier. Caring for Travis hadn't decreased Maury's paranoia—it had just driven it deep inside him. Now that the new technology had come to light, others were being forced to realize something that he'd been aware of all along. Their acknowledgement should have given him a feeling of satisfaction, or vindication, at least. Instead, all it did was sharpen his sense of foreboding.

As the youngster slept peacefully on the adjacent lower berth, Maury sat in a corner of the compartment, staring with Nash'terel eyes at both the darkness outside the window and the darkness within. All at once he jerked upright, his gaze riveted on Travis's blanket. It looked as though something was moving around beneath the covers in the vicinity of the youngster's feet.

Maury leaned forward and flipped up the bottom of the bedcover. Then he sank backward again, his jaw sagging in stunned disbelief.

There was a sledgehammer at the end of Travis's left leg. Not an actual hammer, of course. Harnessed essence could do only so much with the organic material that made up a body. So, while it *appeared* that the foot had transformed into something usually made of iron and wood, it was still just a flesh-and-bone facsimile.

"*Shattra!*" Maury hissed under his breath.

"Grandpa?" Travis was sitting up now, blinking hard as he located Maury in the dark. "I just had the strangest dream. I dreamed that my foot was turning into—"

"Don't look down, Travis."

So, of course, that was precisely what he did.

Travis let out a yelp.

Maury let out a sigh.

"Why did it do that?" Travis demanded.

"Because the part of your brain that controls your shapeshifting ability never sleeps, and it mistook your dream for an instruction. Teaching it to tell the difference will be the next stage in your training."

Travis sucked in a calming breath. "It's still just my feet." He sounded strangely disappointed.

"Trav, it's been less than a week since your first manifestation. Give it time. In the meanwhile, you need your rest. Go back to sleep. We'll deal with this in the morning."

A pause, then, "Your eyes are glowing, Grandpa. Does that mean—?"

"—that we see in the dark? Yes."

"And will I—?"

"Maybe."

"Night vision would be a great super power."

Yes, it would... as long as he had it in both eyes for depth perception... and it only switched on when he told it to... and he lived long enough to learn that kind of control...

Maury replied wearily, "Go to sleep, Travis. We'll talk later."

Chapter Fifteen

By late Monday afternoon, Ken had already signed out a vehicle from the motor pool, and he and Angie were on their way down to the city to join Shred, Barron, and Vicky for dinner. Barron and Shred would be leaving right after dessert to pick up Maury and Travis from the railway station and bring them back to the apartment above the storefront. After that, the plan was for Maury and Shred to spend the night at a hotel while Angie, Ken, and Travis took the guest quarters one floor below Barron and Vicky's place.

Vincaspera was the one who had proposed the family meal—had insisted on it, really. This was suspiciously out of character for her, Gershred thought, but Barron had been eager to please her, so he'd gone along with the idea.

However, as he watched Vicky stalk around her kitchen, flinging fridge and pantry doors open, pillaging their shelves, then banging her loot down on the countertop, Shred was having second thoughts. She wasn't using her *hainbek* yet, but it was just a matter of time. Perhaps it would be wiser to put some distance between her and the others by installing Travis and his parents in the hotel room while he and Maury stayed in the spare flat.

As though she'd just read his mind, Vicky's spine stiffened. With one venomous glance, she slammed a cupboard door shut with ear-ringing force on the far side of the kitchen.

Shred shared a look with Barron, who had nothing left to give him at this point but a helpless shrug.

Vincaspera hadn't been this way when they'd returned from the compound the previous day. She'd prepared a late evening meal for them and sat listening attentively as they discussed a variety of topics, including Shred's successful foray into instructorhood over the weekend and the planned visit to the Guild. Somehow, she'd morphed overnight into a tense and irritable version of herself, brusque and silent by turns. They'd been trying all day to get her to open up about what was bothering her, but to no avail. The only hint she'd dropped was an off-handed remark about nothing working properly that could have referred to anything or anyone, including her extended family.

That it was dysfunctional, there could be no doubt. Vicky and Angie hadn't exchanged so much as a friendly greeting for the past ten years. Travis was being forced to cross the country by a genetic inheritance he'd never wanted, to be returned to parents he didn't know.

Barron's gentle suggestion that Vicky might want to postpone this dinner until she was feeling better had been met with an icy stare. Now she was at the kitchen counter, vigorously ripping packaging apart and giving Gershred a very bad feeling. There was enough tinder already waiting to combust this evening without the addition of whatever was currently buzzing around inside this volatile female's head.

So, Shred made an executive decision. Coming to stand in the kitchen doorway, he cleared his throat and said, in as mild and placating a voice as he could manage, "Vincaspera, we're concerned. If you're upset about something we did, or something we didn't do, we need to know what it is, so we can make things right again."

She paused for the length of a breath. "It's not you," she replied hoarsely. "It's me."

"Are you nervous about this evening, *dallim*?" Barron asked softly.

The endearment was wasted. Her lips compressed into a hyphen, she gave her head a violent shake no.

"Then is it something we talked about earlier? Something we *plan* to do?" he persisted. "It can't be the Guild. Last night you supported our approaching them to ask for the elders' contact information."

Silence. It gave Shred a space in which to glimpse a further possibility. "Is there some reason for us not to contact the elder of your family, Vincaspera?"

More silence. Then, in a voice coming from so far back in her throat that he scarcely recognized it, she replied, "If it's to ask for their bloodstone, there's no need. I am in possession of all the *dashkra* that was entrusted to my family when we came through the rift from RinYeng."

"You're the eldest member of your family?"

"No." Visibly bracing herself, she turned to face him and continued, "I stole the bloodstone from my older brother. I needed some for my experiments. He refused to give me any because he disapproved of my work. So, I learned where he was keeping it and I paid him back by removing all of it—except for what was being worn at the time—to a secret location of my own. Then I went into hiding. Long story short, none of the other members of my family have been able to prepare a fresh *dashkra* for ritual use in more than a thousand years, which means none of our Earthborn offspring have been able to blood one."

Except for Angie, whose blood contained enough of Vicky's DNA to turn a pendant turquoise, and Travis, who inherited Vicky's talent through his mother. Keeping that thought to himself, Shred said instead, "That's how you had enough to excavate the cavity for the compound."

"Yes, in its raw form, and then I used a large portion of it to create essence receptacles. Maldemaur told me his method for doing it, and I found a way to accelerate the process for mass production." She raised her chin and continued stiffly, "As your partner pointed out shortly after we'd negotiated our deal, I'd made all the humans in Middlevale part Nash'terel, and we don't hunt or consume our own. Stealing their spare essence and making it available in flasks to the staff and trainees in the compound was the only practical alternative. Now, if you'll excuse me..."

With that, she wheeled in place and returned to attacking dinner.

Shred swallowed a curse. And he'd thought tracking down his own family was going to raise difficult issues!

"Vincaspera, you said you used a large portion of the *dashkra* for receptacles. How much is left?" he asked her.

She was standing at the sink, washing a head of romaine lettuce. As her shoulders squared in response to his question, Shred glimpsed Barron's hand very wisely reaching out to remove the chopping knife from the cutting board beside her.

Vicky slammed the lettuce onto the counter, couldn't find the knife, and set about ripping the leaves to pieces with her fingers instead.

"To make a peace offering with, you mean?" she said, biting off each word. "None. I've been wearing the pendant I prepared for Lilly before she was taken from us, along with the one I was given by my parents back on RinYeng, but that's all I have here. The rest is hidden in a remote location, and that's where it will stay. And by the way," she added, "one thing my brother has always been good at is holding grudges. So if and when you find him, just make damn sure he can't find me back."

So... vindictiveness was a family trait. Good to know.

Ken and Angie arrived at the door of Vicky and Barron's apartment right on time for dinner. Angie had baked a hostess gift of cookies—something sweet, she explained as she handed them to Vicky, to symbolize a long-awaited family reunion. And of course, she added, they'd also been Travis's favourite kind when he was much younger.

Both the gift and the gesture were very human, Shred mused. A hostess gift generally signified gratitude and appreciation. Unfortunately, the body language that accompanied this offering was giving it a whole other meaning.

Angie's lips were curved in a polite, pro forma smile, but her back was as rigid as a rifle-mounted bayonet. Vicky's spine as she accepted the plastic container was just as straight, and her expression just as strained. Evidently, she saw this "gift" for what it was—a reminder of whom she was dealing with, and a warning not to insert herself between the human mother and her offspring.

"Oh, you shouldn't have," Vicky purred.

There were two ways to interpret her words. Neither one put

Shred at ease.

Barron stepped over, ostensibly to help Ken and Angie hang up their coats, but mainly, Shred suspected, to break the tension of the moment. Barron had clearly understated the animosity between Travis's mother and godmother earlier. No matter how little time passed on the clock, it was bound to be a long and stressful evening.

The dining room table had been set for five, with a centrepiece consisting of artfully arranged (and presumably filled) essence flasks. Since everyone was now present, Vicky invited her guests to take their seats, then headed for the kitchen with the cookies. Shred remained on his feet meanwhile, determined to greet Ken and Angie in person before the main event began.

Tall and curvy, and still practically oozing essence from her pores, Angie appeared not to have aged a minute since the first time Shred had laid eyes on her. Only her hairdo had changed, the dark ponytail giving way to a much shorter style. Like Vicky's, her smile was a little too bright for the occasion, he noted, but there was steel in her expression as well. She was on a mission to reclaim her child, and if that meant making nice with the vampire godmother for a few hours, then that was what she would do.

Knowing how Travis already felt about his parents, Shred amended his earlier thought: it was going to be a long and *exhausting* evening.

Ken strode over to stand beside his mate. His posture was protective and he was clearly on alert, his narrowed gaze sweeping the room. Ken was assessing the threat level. That was good. It was one of the skills he had come out here to learn. And yet, there was something disquieting about the way shades seemed to come down over the light in Angie's brown eyes each time she looked at him.

The tension between them was like a static charge in the air. Shred made a mental note to take Angie aside later. Whatever was going on, Ken would probably not want to talk about it. He was becoming a warrior, and warriors tended to be stoical.

This was quite a change from the rebellious adolescent Bilyash had been fifteen years earlier. For Shred, seeing the kid the way he was now brought out mixed feelings.

Ken was still several hundred years away from achieving the level of adeptness with his *hainbek* that would normally be a requirement for parenting an offspring. However, the love of his life wouldn't have lasted that long, so he had jumped the gun. In terms of maturity, he now had a mate who was twice his emotional age, and a half-human son who was only slightly younger than himself. Fitting those pieces together into a family could prove to be a challenge, one that Shred hoped would not be overwhelming.

"It's good to see you again, Gershred," said Angie. She walked over and gave him a brief hug, then stepped aside as Ken came forward to greet him too.

"Are you two all right?" Shred asked in a hushed voice.

"We're fine," Ken replied. "Just being careful." Without moving his head, he cast a sideways glance at the kitchen door.

Meanwhile, Angie stood with her lips pressed together, as though to hold back a different response. When she did speak, it was to ask, "How is Travis? Is he looking forward to joining us?"

The short answer was no, he wasn't, but Shred wasn't about to tell them that. He led the way to the dining table and waited until everyone was seated before replying, "Travis is fifteen human years old. He's the star forward on a U-16 hockey team that just medalled in a regional tournament, and for now, he's both loving and hating being half Nash'terel."

"For now," Ken echoed, frowning. "Meaning, until he gets here and decides how he *really* feels about it."

"He's not keen on moving west, is he?" Angie said with a sigh. "He'd rather stay in familiar surroundings."

"Yes, but we couldn't give him that choice," Shred replied, "not after he began shapeshifting on the ice, in front of all those spectators."

Eyes widening, Ken leaned forward in his chair. "He's begun shapeshifting too? How much of him?"

"When I left for the airport last Wednesday, it was just his feet."

"And he was on skates at the time, you said?" Ken grimaced. "That must have been painful."

Just then Vicky emerged from the kitchen, carrying a plank heaped with Ken's favourite dish, steak tartare. She set it down in the middle of the table, then added a large basket of gourmet breads and fancy crackers. A huge wooden bowl of Caesar salad took up most of the remaining space. Finally, looking like something that had gotten lost on its way to an entirely different meal, a bread and butter dish full of cold cuts appeared next to Angie's place setting.

This had to be Vicky's response to the cookies. The three male Nash'terel watched to see what Angie's reaction would be.

Smiling with a warmth that didn't reach her eyes, she said, "Thank you, Victoria." Then she picked up her spoon, plucked half a roll from the bread basket, and scooped some of the steak tartare onto it before putting it deliberately onto her plate.

All eyes now turned to Vicky, who had also chosen to smile. "I thought you would prefer cooked meat."

"And I appreciate the thought. But Ken introduced me to tartare years ago, and I rather like it. So, unless you only made enough for four...?"

Everyone in the room heard that gauntlet figuratively hit the floor. As Shred and Barron exchanged concerned looks, Vicky drew herself up and refreshed her expression.

"You ought to know by now that I always make more than enough, my dear. By all means, help yourself."

It would have been a hospitable invitation had it not been offered through gritted teeth.

Attention ping-ponged back to Angie. With a gracious nod of acknowledgement, the only human at the table brought her tartare-laden roll to her mouth and bit into it with obvious enjoyment.

Shred noticed movement behind Vicky's upper lip and realized that her fangs had to be itching. She was massaging them with her tongue.

He was definitely going to give his and Maury's hotel room to Travis and his parents.

"You were talking about Travis beginning to shapeshift, Gershred?" said Vicky, once more the good hostess making dinner conversation.

Shred resumed telling the group about the incident at the hockey rink. "Fortunately," he said, pausing with spoon and bread in hand, "Travis likes having a pressure *hainbek*. He calls it his super power. He can suppress it, but that's all the control he has over it at the moment. What's *really* interesting is that when we blooded his *dashkra*, there was a lot of bright turquoise in it," he added, purposely locking eyes with Vicky.

Her brows shot up, then plummeted into a scowl. "You believe he got his *hainbek* from *my* bloodline? That's not possible," she declared. "It must have come from Ken's side."

"No," Ken said in response, and counted off on his fingers. "Magnetism, sound, gravity, and heat. My parents kept records going back for a hundred millennia. There's never been a pressure *bainbek* in any generation of my family."

Vicky sank slowly back into her chair, a calculating air settling over her features. "Well, well. How fascinating! That gene must have lain dormant for two hundred and fifty years, then activated with the reintroduction of Nash'terel DNA. If it's a reproducible phenomenon..."

Angie snapped to attention in her seat. "My son will not be part of your next experiment, Vicky," she said, bristling.

Determined to head off round two, Shred cleared his throat to get everyone's attention and pointed out, "We're talking about a fifteen-year-old male hybrid who will be arriving with a wild talent, two shapeshifting feet, and probably a lot of attitude. Travis is at a pivotal point in his emotional development. If he's mishandled, we'll very likely lose him. So, it's essential that he be instructed by someone with experience at reaching and teaching human adolescents."

A glance in Angie's direction showed him that her attention had been captured. Shred met Barron's gaze and flicked it that way as well.

Picking up on the cue, the other being announced, "As it happens, I've got someone coming into the program who fits that bill perfectly. Gordie, you mentioned that Travis plays hockey, right?"

Shred nodded.

"Well, this Nash'terel adept that I'm expecting has been coaching a minor league hockey team in the under-16 division," said Barron.

Angie's shoulders relaxed. That was encouraging, but they weren't out of the woods yet.

"Is this the one Maldemaur referred to you?" Vicky demanded frostily, her expression darkening. "Right after he decided to bring Travis back here?"

Vincaspera and Maldemaur made good business partners, but they had a much longer history of being rivals and adversaries... and, as Maury was so fond of saying, leopards didn't change their spots. Not overnight, anyway.

"It's perfect timing, you know," Barron said, breezing right past Vicky's question. "With two more players and a coach, we can finally have two teams playing proper games on that rink. All we'd be missing would be a crowd of spectators to cheer them on."

He leaned back and gave her a broad smile. Meanwhile, Shred could practically hear the wheels turning in Vicky's head.

There were already live spectators inside the compound, just not many of them. If Barron wanted more, they would have to come from Middlevale. But letting humans into the rec facility would create an entire array of problems... unless they were hybrids passing as Nash'terel, like Travis.

Barron had earlier suggested that Vicky would love to have more hybrids to study. The problem was, she couldn't create them by simply making an excuse to siphon off *holladima* from the male birth-gendered trainees and then using them to covertly inseminate human females. Deception wouldn't work because, unlike with humans, Nash'terel reproductive cells only switched on when the beings carrying them consciously intended to make a baby.

That meant trainees and Middlevalers would have to have sex, which would only happen if they were permitted to socialize, which in turn was explicitly against the rules for a couple of damned good reasons. Not the least of them was the feeding lust that would surely be triggered by putting a Nash'terel in close proximity to an overflowing source of pure essence.

Vicky knew all that. Nonetheless, she was far too impatient to let nature take its course. She would find a shortcut, and a way to implement it.

Shred didn't even want to imagine what that might be.

Chapter Sixteen

———◆———

Two hours later, Shred and Barron stood on the mezzanine, shaking their heads in disbelief as they watched Maury and Travis cross the stone-tiled main concourse of Vancouver Central Station.

Shred had almost forgotten how majestic this building was. On arriving with Barron and seeing the high-ceilinged foyer with its angled, golden-coloured skylights and its double rows of die-straight supporting columns, he'd been reminded once again of an ancient temple.

There had been many of those proud buildings on Earth when the Nash'terel had first come through the rift. On feast days, the "secluded ones" would observe covertly as humans gathered from places near and far to honour their various gods. The worshippers were tired and dusty from their travel, but also glad to see one another and boisterous with anticipation of the celebration to come. This evening, the Trans-Canada train had completed its journey west, and Shred could sense a similar excitement percolating through the throng of disembarking passengers.

Then Maury and Travis appeared, forcing Shred to amend his comparison.

The kid was cutting across the room like a car through a cornfield, mowing himself a path using his *hainbek*, just as he'd done on the ice rink back home. But this wasn't a hockey game, and these travellers weren't on skates. As they felt themselves being shoved aside and watched their belongings mysteriously topple and slide, they looked around for the cause of the disturbance.

"He's attracting some angry stares," Barron commented. "I thought you said he could repress his talent."

"He can," Shred replied. "But I don't think he wants to right now."

"Come on," Barron urged, striding forward. "We'd better go down there and meet them before he totally blows his cover."

Maury's evident relief at seeing them only seemed to amplify Travis's sullenness.

"Welcome to Vancouver, Travis," Barron said heartily.

Declining to make eye contact, the youngster shrugged off his godfather's welcome. "Yeah, whatever."

Maury shot him a look, then turned away, shaking his head.

"Rough trip?" Shred inquired.

"You might say so. He hasn't slept properly in two days, and he's pissed because his sledgehammer doesn't want to stay inside its box."

"I won't even pretend I understand that," Barron said.

"You don't have to," Maury grumbled. "Just be glad he's wearing his shoes on the correct feet for now, and let's get him the hell out of here."

The drive back to the apartment was oppressive, like the unnatural calm preceding a thunderstorm. Each time Shred glanced into the back seat of the car, Travis was staring downward, as though daring his feet to shift, while Maury kept his thoughts to himself and his gaze directed out the window.

Barron pulled to a stop off the alleyway behind the building, next to a door with a single yellow light shining bravely above it. "I'll go up first," he told them. "Reconnaissance."

It seemed wise.

The three of them sat quietly in the dark for what seemed a long time. At last, the driver's side door opened and they heard Barron's strained voice, telling them, "Ken and Angie are in the guest apartment. Take Travis there while I try to settle Vicky down. Something set her off. Now she's using her *hainbek* to sling the furniture around."

Shred had been afraid of this.

"They had a disagreement?" Maury ventured.

"It's an ongoing thing," Barron told him. "I'll let you know when it's safe to come upstairs."

He ushered them through the back door and up to the second floor guest quarters, then knocked on the door and left. A moment later, it swung open, revealing Ken standing in the small front hall and Angie waiting expectantly in the living room.

Nudged through the doorway by Maury, Travis stomped inside and shrugged off his coat, then turned to face Ken. They were the same height, and nearly the same build. For several long seconds they sized each other up while the others stood silently by, hardly daring to move. Angie was biting her lower lip and casting anxious glances at Maury and Shred. The tension in the room was thick enough to spread on one of Vicky's fancy crackers.

To break it, Shred spoke first. "Travis, say hello to your parents. These are the people you've been video-chatting with regularly since you were five years old."

"H'lo," Travis said, without expression, like a trained animal obeying a command.

Shred wanted to smack him. As though reading his mind, Maury put a restraining hand on his shoulder.

"Hello, Travis," said Ken. "We've been waiting a long time for this moment."

"You're not gonna try to hug me or anything, are you?"

Straight-faced, Ken replied, "I wouldn't dream of it." A pause, then, "But your mom is probably itching to put her arms around you right now," he added, gesturing toward Angie.

Travis turned his head to look at her. She smiled and gave him a timid wave.

"Hmph," he said, and returned his attention to his father's face.

In an instant, the hopeful joy that had lit up Angie's expression at the sight of her son went dim.

So, in spite of everything they'd explained to him, Travis still felt wronged by his mother and was paying her back with rejection. Now Shred *really* wanted to smack the kid.

"We hear you've begun to shape-shift," Ken remarked.

"Yeah. Grandpa G keeps telling me I have your feet."

Ken's lips curved in a sympathetic smile. "Well, you've come to the right place to learn how to control that ability. And how to control your *hainbek* as well. Apparently, it's strong enough to qualify as a super power." A pause, then, "We also hear that you're a better than average hockey player. Good enough to help your team get into the semi-finals. Congratulations on that."

Travis responded with a shrug, then dropped his gaze.

"He's overtired," Maury hastened to explain. "And upset because he had to miss the last two games of the tournament."

"Yeah," Ken said with a nod. "That would tick me off too. However, he'll get to play plenty more hockey out here."

That snagged the kid's attention. "I will?" he said, raising startled eyes to meet his father's.

"You did bring your skates with you, I hope?" Ken already knew the answer to that. He tossed Shred a significant look before continuing, "Because we've got a team that needs to fill its roster."

"A minor league team?"

"Not quite. It's a Nash'terel team. But they're in the same age range as you, relatively speaking, and their talent is pressure, like yours. They'll help you to keep developing your skills while you're getting your *hainbek* and your shapeshifting under control. And after that, who knows?"

A pause, then, "I'll need new skate laces."

"Not a problem."

"And sticks. Grandpa M wouldn't let me bring mine."

"Oh, you won't need them. Our players use their *hainbeka* to move the puck."

Travis's eyes sprang wide. "It's super hockey?"

"Nash'terel hockey," Ken corrected him.

"That... sounds interesting." Then, raising his chin and narrowing his gaze, the kid added, "Are you on the team?"

"No, my talent is magnetism. But I can sit in the stands and shout encouragement... and maybe use my super power to pull the net off its pins at strategic moments...?" he added with a sly grin.

Travis's lips were twitching. They clearly wanted to smile, but they were having a hard time overcoming his adolescent determination to be grumpy.

No matter, Shred decided, letting out the breath he'd been holding—it was the thought that counted. Common ground was a beautiful thing.

And rejection was painful. Angie had been looking on, tears welling in her eyes. Safe to say, those weren't tears of happiness. Shred's heart ached for her. But perhaps it was better in the long run if she and Travis didn't become too attached to each other.

After all, first to develop was the *hainbek*. Then came the ability to shapeshift. And finally, the thirst for essence. Travis's thirst hadn't emerged yet, but if the first two traits were present, the third was very likely to follow. And then, aroused by her presence, by the abundance of essence she emanated uncontrollably, his thirst would force Travis out of their cottage and into the compound with the other trainees, thus separating Angie from her son once again.

Ken walked over to join Shred and Maury. "We want to thank you for everything you've done for him, both of you. We appreciate the sacrifices you must have made. You've done a great job."

"And you're welcome. But now it's your turn," Maury agreed, "yours and Angie's."

"Don't expect it to be easy," Shred advised.

"Nothing worthwhile ever is... Grandpa G," Ken returned with a smile. "But thanks to you, he's got a passion. At the very least, it will motivate him to learn to control his *hainbek*. He'll want to be as good without a stick as he's been so far with one. And what's more important, he'll be part of a team again."

"But not if he doesn't get some sleep," Maury pointed out. "He was cranky as hell on the train. Every time he dozed off, his foot shifted, waking him up again."

Ken shuddered visibly. "I remember those days. He really *does* have my feet, doesn't he?"

A knock at the door signalled Barron's return. "I'm afraid Travis is going to have to wait to meet his godmother," he announced from the threshold. "Both she and the apartment are in no condition to receive company this evening."

As silence dropped into place behind his words, the assembled group became aware of the noises filtering through the ceiling. It sounded as though a demolition was in progress upstairs.

Shred stared a question at Ken, who replied with a shrug, "She wanted to train Travis herself. We explained why we thought that wouldn't be a good idea. Then we came down here."

...leaving her alone to concoct a conspiracy theory involving Maury, Ken, and Angie and then trash the place in anger. Wonderful.

To Barron, Shred said, "Just to be on the safe side, perhaps those of us who aren't Nash'terel masters should spend the night elsewhere. I booked a hotel room earlier."

"Good idea, Gordie. Come on, then—let's get the three of them squared away."

In short order, bags and bodies were spirited out to the appropriate vehicle, driving directions were given, and Shred, Barron, and Maury found themselves alone together on the second floor, listening to the mayhem going on overhead.

"What's the hunting like around here?" Maury wanted to know.

"Locally, the quality isn't that great," Barron replied. "Pollution levels are high. However, if you're hungry..." He crossed to the kitchen and flung open the fridge and cupboards. They were stocked with enough to feed an army—or one fifteen-year-old male human. "Vicky was expecting Travis to be here for a couple of days."

Maury pointed at the half-dozen metal flasks lined up on one of the cupboard shelves. "Are those...?"

"Yep. We keep some here in case of unexpected company." Barron snatched one up and tossed it to him, then took two more and led the way back to the living room.

Something went *crash* on the third floor. None of them flinched or glanced up.

"Is it wise to leave her alone when she's like this?" Maury asked.

"When she's lethally dangerous, you mean? Absolutely," he declared, dropping onto an easy chair and taking a swallow of essence from one of the flasks. "Don't worry. Eventually she'll run out of steam. Then I'll go upstairs and give you two some privacy, something I expect you haven't enjoyed much in the past ten years."

But romance was the furthest thing from Shred's mind at that moment. "Were you serious earlier about wanting to have spectators at trainee hockey games, or did you just say that to distract Vicky from what Maury had done?"

"I've actually been thinking about it for some time," Barron told him. "Watching the Middlevalers take possession of their town and add amenities to it, like the library and the recreational programming, made me realize how useful that could be for our own training purposes. And how badly some of the kids in the current cohort need to be exposed to those human environments. You heard their questions on the weekend. Too many of our Earthborn have been leading sheltered lives. Some of them have never even been inside a human department store. Ken is an exception, because of who raised him, but the others..."

Shred couldn't disagree with that. He'd known Bilyash's biological parents. If they'd survived the fire that burned down their cottage, they would probably have locked their offspring in a tower, like Rapunzel in the fairy tale, to keep him insulated from un-Nash'terel influences.

"That's why you were so insistent that I talk to them?"

Barron nodded sadly. "They think just looking human will protect them, but I'm afraid their lack of experience at *acting* human is going to get them killed, Gordie, even before the rift opens. They need to practise it safely, under controlled conditions. Learning how to behave in public without drawing attention to themselves would be a good place to start."

"For example, being among the human spectators at a sports competition," Maury put in. "But not inside the compound, surely!"

"Of course not. There's plenty of open space between the base and the town. We could set up an outdoor rink, with bleachers. Maybe even organize a few games, our team against one from Middlevale."

"The trainees wouldn't be able to use their *hainbeka*."

"And that would be the whole point," Barron confirmed. "Perfectly counterfeiting human behaviour, both on the ice and in the stands."

"What about the thirst?" said Maury. "How do you propose to deal with *that* problem?"

"I don't," Barron told him. He took another long swallow from his flask. "I'll let Vicky figure it out. She's already working on a way for us to create more hybrids."

"Via mass production, no doubt," Maury muttered, only half to himself.

"Listen!" Barron hissed, signalling the other two to be quiet. He pointed upward.

The sounds of destruction from overhead had ceased.

"That's my cue," he said, getting to his feet. "The cleanup will probably take all night, so make yourselves at home, and I'll see you in the morning." A moment later, he was out the door, leaving Maury and Shred alone together in the apartment.

They locked eyes across the living room, both wondering the same thing.

"We should call them," said Maury.

"No," Shred decided. "They need this time for themselves."

"But what if things are going badly? What if Travis is having a meltdown and needs to hear a familiar voice?"

As Shred was opening his mouth to reply, his phone chimed to tell him a new text had hit his inbox. He raised a hand to pause their conversation, then opened the message. It was from Ken.

Just so you know, T fell onto the bed and went to sleep as soon as we arrived. A is dozing on the sofa, worn out from all the drama. And I'm polluting my essence with something from the bar fridge and thinking about next steps. Didn't want you two to worry. See you in the a.m.

He read the text aloud to Maury, who remarked, "He thought we'd be worried. Were you worried?"

Shred gestured dismissively. "Nah. You?"

"Not a bit," Maury declared, smiling. "Not about them, at least."

"What's that supposed to mean?"

"I meant to tell you earlier, but we got sidetracked. Pyotren messaged me on Friday, shortly after the train pulled out of Union Station. He believes that his realtor friend, Stella Parr, may have been killed. He'd been trying for days to arrange a meeting with her, but she wasn't returning his calls or texts, not even the coded ones they'd agreed to send if either of them was in trouble. So, he drove into the city to locate her. Spoke to all their mutual acquaintances. Tracked down some of her current clients. No one had seen or heard from her in over a week."

"And there's no chance at all that she's simply—?"

"Pyotren says no. Even when she's shifted and dropped off the grid, she's always let him know how to reach her. He's going to keep searching, but he's pretty sure she's gone."

Shred uttered a heartfelt curse. It gave him some release, but it didn't make the loss of yet another bright young Nash'terel any easier to bear.

Maury opened his flask and took a long swallow from it, then continued, "Would you like some more news? Something closer to home?"

"Such as?"

"The body of a male human was discovered early Wednesday morning in a parking lot in Collingwood. Could that have been the one you drank from just before you left for the airport?"

Shred's frown deepened into a scowl. "It could be. But I didn't kill him."

"I know. Apparently, he'd been poisoned earlier in the day."

"Ah! That explains why I felt sick all the way here on the plane."

"Of *course* you did. And that, boys and girls, is why we never scavenge essence from unconscious prey."

"Well, whatever the poison was, I managed to *harruf* it up before leaving the airport with Barney, so I'm all right now."

"Yes, and I'm glad you are. Meanwhile, the local police have opened a criminal investigation, and the wisest thing for us to do is be good Nash'terel, keep our heads down, and stay as far away from them as we can. Agreed?"

"Agreed."

Chapter Seventeen

— ◆ —

The drama upstairs didn't survive the night. At nine o'clock the following morning, Shred answered a knock at the apartment door and found Barron standing out on the landing.

"Vicky wants to know whether you'll be joining us for breakfast. It'll be just the four of us," he hastened to add. "Ken texted me overnight to say that he and Angie had some errands to run. They'll bring Travis by for a visit after lunch, then head back up north straightaway."

"Playing it safe?" Maury remarked.

"I would do the same," said Barron. "Ken understated what happened last night. It appears some incendiary accusations were levelled while we were fetching you and Travis from the train station. Ken was caught in the crossfire and very prudently retreated from the battlefield, dragging his mate with him."

"And Vicky couldn't attack another Nash'terel, so she trashed the apartment instead," Maury remarked. "That much, at least, makes sense. But why—?"

"Angie refuses to acknowledge this, but Vicky takes her godmother role very seriously," Barron explained. "She bonded with Travis when he was still here. Then he was gone. Lilly's death just about sent her over the edge. And now Travis is back, but she feels as if she's losing him for a second time."

"Because they want someone else to train him?" said Maury. "That's the reason?"

Barron shrugged. "It may or may not have been triggered by a single event. In any case, the friction between them began around the time Angie received the first book shipments for the Middlevale library. While she was up there, stocking the shelves, she left Travis with Vicky down here. He was a busy toddler, curious about everything, so Vicky was teaching him some Nash'terel words. Nothing inappropriate. Just greetings, and names of some common objects, and how to ask for things. Stuff like that. He picked it up right away."

"There has to be more to the story than that," Maury insisted. "I can't see Angie getting angry about her offspring learning a bit of the Nash'terel language. She knows what we are. She's seen Ken's true form."

"I'm sure you're right, but at the moment, Vicky is the only one willing to talk about it." With that, Barron turned and led the way upstairs.

Breakfast was blood sausage and fried potatoes, washed down with coffee strong enough to have a *hainbek* of its own. Peering at Vicky over the rim of his mug, Shred couldn't help noticing a certain whiteness around her knuckles as she held her fork, and a tension around her lips when she spoke.

"I imagine the two of you must be feeling some relief at getting back to living an unencumbered Nash'terel life," she remarked stiffly.

Maury and Shred shared a freighted look.

"Actually," Shred told her, "we were thinking this would be the perfect time to figure out what to do about the bloodstone collector. Have you had any thoughts about the plan that I proposed earlier?"

Vicky leaned back thoughtfully in her chair. "In fact, I have. A series of fake auctions would get the collector's attention, to be sure, and the operative we send to impersonate the underling might be able to fool them long enough to gather some useful information, but that still leaves us at square one where the sting itself is concerned. Unless it gives us a sure-fire way to bring the mark to us, all that preparation time will have basically been wasted, and in this case, time spent translates to Nash'terel lives placed in jeopardy."

"What would you suggest as an alternative, then?" Maury asked.

Her lips curved in a wicked smile. "That's easy. We don't wait for the collector to come to us—we take the sting to them. But first, we need to do some collecting of our own, by setting a trap for Yeng assassins who are carrying *dashkra* detectors on their person. We kill the Yeng scum and keep the detectors."

Shred noted that her knuckles weren't white anymore. Apparently, just the thought of spilling Yeng blood was enough to relieve her tension.

"Brilliant!" Maury dropped his bloodstone pendant in the middle of the table, startling everyone. "And we can use these as bait. Cut and polished *dashkra* is what the detector will be seeking out. The more of it we can put in one place, the better our chances of attracting the desired prey."

Vicky evidently agreed. Wordlessly, she removed both her own and Lilly's pendants from her neck and placed them with Maury's. A moment later, Barron's bloodstone raised the total to four.

The spider was spinning her web, exactly as Shred had hoped she would.

"Barney, what about the staff and trainees at the compound? You told me earlier that you plan to advise them not to wear their stones anymore. Now is as good a time as any, and we can put their *dashkra* to good use."

Nodding, Barron pulled out his phone. "Good idea. I'll have Polley collect as many as possible and bring them to us."

"Yeng assassins come in threes," Shred pointed out. "If one member of a triad gets away, the word will spread that it's a trap and we'll have to come up with something different. It's imperative that we take all of them out at once."

"I'm certainly up for that," said Vicky, her spine straightening as though a thread had been pulled at the nape of her neck.

Shred turned to Barron, who was busily texting, and added, "Tell Polley we'll need weapons as well."

"My *hainbek* is lethal," Vicky reminded him sharply. "So is yours. So why—?"

"It's in case we decide to pose as Yeng," he told her. "They don't have *hainbeka*."

Narrowing her gaze, she allowed, "All right. That could be useful. And is there anything else relevant to the operation that you'd like to share with the class?"

Shred drew a long breath. "As a matter of fact, there is. The tracking technology being used by the Yeng was developed by the Yeng defector, Pritchard, with our help."

Instantly focused, Barron snapped, "How the hell did you come to that—?"

"Monicandra told me, the last time I visited the Guild. As soon as she saw the device we'd captured, she recognized it as his. She is now firmly of the opinion that Pritchard was a spy all along, that he lied about defecting to trick the Guild into giving him what he needed to complete his work, and that once he had it, the other Yeng must have faked his death in order to extract him."

"Which, as I recall, was precisely what you suspected had happened and tried to warn them about at the time," Barron pointed out. "When you last spoke to her, did she apologize for refusing to listen to you earlier?"

Shred uttered a derisive syllable. "No. I think she's still waiting for *me* to apologize for calling them a bunch of useless *ristima* and storming out of the Club that day."

"You're saying Pritchard may be out there, alive and well and overseeing the production of a device that gets Nash'terel killed," Maury spat. "*Shattra*! This just gets better and better."

"So, on a scale from one to ten, where one means abysmal failure and ten signifies success beyond our wildest dreams, how do you think this plan will end up?" said Maury when he and Shred were alone downstairs once more.

"From whose viewpoint?" Shred asked. "Vicky's happy with any excuse to kill Yeng. Whatever takes away some of the pain of losing Lilly will be a win, as far as she's concerned."

"And Barron?"

"He covers it well, but he misses the excitement of the battlefield. I hope I'm wrong about this, but when it finally comes down to a confrontation between us and the Yeng, I'm betting he'll revert to the berserker I fought beside in the Boer War."

A pause. Then, in a softer voice, "And you?"

Shred expelled a breath and leaned back thoughtfully in his seat. "Sidu'Hama teaches us to place value on every life, including that of the enemy, and to reject blind revenge in favour of just and measured retribution."

"That's not an answer."

Shred shrugged uncomfortably. "I don't have one for you. When you're a warrior, your way is clearly marked. Defeat the enemy. Defend the helpless. Fight combatants. Spare those who surrender. I didn't think I would ever be a parent, let alone a grandparent, and yet, here we are, and the path ahead is no longer that well-defined for me."

"You were never really comfortable in the grandfather role," said Maury. "I could tell. Every time it chafed, you got cranky. And yet, nothing could keep you away from his hockey games. That was the saving grace in your relationship with him, I think. You didn't miss a single one."

"Of course not." Shred smiled, half to himself. "He was going into battle. As a fellow warrior, I had to support him. As for your original question," he added, "every sting and every trap has the potential to backfire, this one more than most. Yeng assassins are known quantities. We can generally predict how they'll behave. However, we know nothing about our ultimate target, the *dashkra* collector. If that doesn't change, then on a scale of one to ten, I'd place our chances of success somewhere between four and five—optimistically speaking."

Shortly after 1:00 p.m., a tattoo of footsteps on the stairs and some hushed conversation out in the hall signalled the arrival of visitors. Maury glanced up from the book he'd been reading and saw Shred already opening the apartment door.

"Can we come in?" said Ken's voice. He sounded worried.

"Of course." Shred stepped aside to admit them. "Is something wrong?"

"No! It's very right, actually, just... unexpected." Ken heel-toed out of his boots and went to the dining table to set down the pizza carton he was holding.

As Travis came through the doorway, he locked eyes with Maury and crowed, "I used my super power, Grandpa M! Boarded a bad guy, good and proper!"

"We don't think anyone saw him do it," Ken assured them, "other than the Yeng that he pushed into the wall. But..." He bounced a harried look between Maury's face and Shred's. "Have either of you explained to him how nasty things become whenever the police get involved?"

"Whoa!" Shred exclaimed. He paused in the act of helping Angie off with her coat. "Start at the beginning. What happened?"

"Travis wanted pizza for lunch, so we took him to the place Angie and I used to frequent when she was still living in the city. I thought it would be safe," said Ken.

"But...?" Maury set aside his book and got to his feet.

"After we began eating, someone walked in and took a seat. He didn't order anything, just sat watching us from another table. He definitely had the thirst in his eyes. I pointed him out to Angie and Travis. Then we cut short our meal and left the restaurant."

"Okay. I gather he followed you out?"

"We led him around the corner and into a laneway, where I could deploy my *hainbek* unseen," Ken replied. "However—"

"Travis beat him to it," Angie cut in. "He sent the Yeng flying backward against the wall. I was afraid there would be a smear of blood on the bricks when he slid to the ground."

"And...?" Shred prompted.

"There was no blood. He was just knocked senseless," Ken said. "I finished him cleanly. Then we got the hell out of there."

"Did he yell anything at you when he charged?" Maury wanted to know.

"Like that dumb-assed curse of theirs, you mean? No," Ken replied.

"He might have been trying to," Angie allowed, "but he hardly had time to open his mouth before Travis let loose."

"Assassin or not, the Yeng was acting alone, I'm sure of it," Ken said. "We wouldn't have come here if I'd thought he was part of a triad. I would have put up shields and called for backup."

"In the meanwhile," Angie added, "Travis needs to finish eating and settle down before Victoria meets him. I hope you don't mind if he does it here. We'd already checked out of the hotel and didn't know where else to bring him."

Maury cast a glance in Travis's direction. The youngster was beaming, his elation both heartwarming and disturbing to see.

Maldemaur was beginning to understand why the pressure *hainbek* had become so commonplace among the Earthborn Nash'terel, and why Vicky had insisted on beginning Lilly's training at such a young age. Untrained offspring with talents other than pressure were the easiest targets for assassins.

"It's not a problem," Shred assured them. His hearty voice pulled Maury back to the moment.

"No problem at all," Maury echoed. "When Travis is ready to visit her, we'll go up there with you."

Maury carried the pizza carton into the kitchen, transferred the last four slices onto a large plate, then slid the plate into the microwave oven. The pizza looked very familiar when it came out again a couple of minutes later.

"Let me guess," said Shred. "Meat lover's special with triple cheese?"

"Yep," Ken replied with a grin. "The pizzeria owner could tell whose idea it was. He looked Travis up and down when we placed the order, then chuckled to himself as he was filling it."

Travis dropped onto a chair facing the open plan living room and set to work devouring the rest of his lunch. After swallowing his third mouthful, he paused to stare at the adults who were all seated on the chairs and sofa, quietly conversing.

"What's the thirst?" he asked them.

His words seemed to drive the power of speech out of everyone's brain.

"You said he had the thirst in his eyes," Travis persisted. "What was he thirsty *for*?"

Worried glances crisscrossed the room.

Finally, Shred cleared his throat and said, "The thirst is an overwhelming desire to kill, Travis. Do you remember the talk we had about a week ago, when Grandpa M explained why your mother couldn't come east with you when you were five years old?"

"The genetic mutation?" the youngster replied.

"That's right. It makes her give off something that arouses the thirst of any Yeng nearby. That's what happened at the pizza place."

"Oh." Then, just as Shred was relaxing in his seat, wearing a self-congratulating smile, Travis asked, "Do Nash'terel get the thirst?"

"Yes," Maury said firmly, heading off any further half-truths. He knew they were just trying to ease a young person into an unpleasant fact, but Travis was almost an adult in human years, and the time for avoidance was over.

A pause. Then, in a very small, very young voice, "Will *I*?"

Throwing a reproachful glance at his partner, Shred replied, "We don't know. You're only half Nash'terel, so you may not have inherited that particular gene. We'll just have to wait and see."

Travis gazed anxiously around the room. "How will I know—?"

"When human food is no longer enough," said Maury. "Each time you deploy your *hainbek*, each time you shapeshift, you use up some of your body's essence. It needs to be replenished. The human way is with food and drink. When the day comes—*if* it comes—that your body cries out for something more, what it will need is the essence of other living beings, stolen directly from their bodies. That is the thirst, and despite what Grandpa G just told you, you *can* satisfy it without killing, as long as you don't wait too long to quench it."

"But that isn't necessarily going to happen, Travis," Ken pointed out. "You're half human too, and if you take after your mother, then you'll never develop the thirst because your own body will produce all the essence you need, more even than you can possibly use."

If that was meant to reassure him, it failed. The youngster's features paled and puckered as though he was fighting not to throw up. "So," he finally managed to say, "I'm either going to turn into a vampire or become food for vampires." Levelling an accusing stare at Maury, he added, "You told me I would be safe here, Grandpa."

"Oh, for heaven's sake!" Angie sprang to her feet and crossed to the dining table. "Here's what they're not telling you," she said, dropping onto the chair across from his. "Every human in Middlevale is part Nash'terel, including me. Many of them have the same genetic mutation as I do, and it's forbidden for Nash'terel to feed on other Nash'terel. So Grandpa M wasn't lying to you. Once we get you home with us, you'll be in the safest place you could possibly be."

Looking only slightly less upset, he demanded, "But what if I—?"

"—grow fangs? Start speaking with a Transylvanian accent?" Ken teased him.

"—get the thirst around *you*?" Travis persisted, addressing Angie. "What then?"

"All you need to know for now," Ken replied, "is that there are ways to prevent a thirst, and you'll learn them when the time comes. Whichever one of us you take after, you're going to do just fine, son, that's a promise. Now, please," he added, "finish up that pizza before it gets cold again. We've got one more thing to take care of, and then a long drive home ahead of us."

Travis sucked in a deep breath and let it out in a quavery sigh. So did everyone else in the room.

"Travis, this is Victoria Spears," Shred said. "Her Nash'terel name is Vincaspera, and she and Barron are your godparents. You may not remember them, but they've been waiting a long time to see you again."

The room in which they were standing was oddly furnished, compared with the previous day. The dining chairs looked as though they belonged to three different sets. Both the easy chairs were covered by throw blankets. The original lamp stands had been replaced by tables and lamps from other rooms. Clearly, a major rearrangement had had to take place in order to prepare the apartment for company. Shred also saw dings and dark scrapes on every wall, mute testimony of Vicky's angry rampage. And she wasn't done yet. The threat of another storm hung in the air, stiffening everything from Angie's spine to Vicky's features.

Shred felt his shoulders rising and consciously relaxed them. Under the circumstances, it felt appropriate to wait for an invitation to sit down. Instead of issuing it, however, their hostess stepped forward and gazed with wondering eyes into Travis's face.

"You've grown so tall," she murmured. "The last time you were in this room, you'd just turned three years old. I used to watch over you whenever your mother had to go out somewhere. We spent a lot of time together, you and I."

Angie's lips were pursing. This wasn't a good sign. She didn't have a *hainbek*. Still...

Evidently sensing the need for preemptive action, Ken stepped up and put his arm around Angie's shoulders.

"...and we're grateful for the care that every family member has given him," he announced to the room. "Together, you've helped him grow into a fine young human. Now it's up to us to support him, and Barron's program to train him and add the finishing touches, and he'll be a fine young Nash'terel as well."

The breath that Vicky released then would have been a sign that she was relaxing, were it not for the glint of resentment that remained in her eyes. "And does 'us' include *both* of Travis's godparents?" she inquired in a dangerously soft voice.

"No one is cutting you out of his life, Vincaspera," Shred assured her. "I'm certain there will be visits back and forth."

"Visits," she echoed bitterly. "Whenever you happen to be in the neighbourhood, I suppose."

"*Sh'tamah regniu asharra,*" said Travis. These unexpected Nash'terel words hit pause on whatever Vicky had been about to do or say. For a moment, she could only stare speechlessly into his face.

I would like to see you again, Shred translated. Out of the mouths of babes...

"You remembered," Vicky said in a choked voice. Her eyes shining now, she turned to Angie and told her, "Don't waste a minute that you have with him. You don't know how many there will be."

There were two ways to take that, one friendly, the other not. Angie didn't say anything, but the sudden upward tilt of her chin told Shred which interpretation she was leaning toward.

Ken had caught her reaction as well. Offering as an excuse the distance they had to travel, he cut the visit short. Barron stayed with Vicky on the third floor landing, watching Maury and Shred follow the other three downstairs to the guest apartment, where they'd left their boots and coats.

As Ken and Travis were dressing to go outside, Shred nudged Angie into the living room and said in a hushed voice, "I couldn't help noticing that there's a little bit of awkwardness between you and Ken. Is everything all right?"

She dragged in a breath and replied, "I think so, but..." Her brows knitted in an expression of pain.

Shred's heart constricted in response as he waited for her to complete her thought.

At last, the words tumbled out in a whispered rush. "I didn't fall in love with a soldier, Gershred. I fell in love with a funny, sexy, caring, creative guy. He once told me that no matter what his outward appearance might be, he would always be the same person inside. Now, after all his training... I'm not so sure he *is* that person anymore. We haven't laughed together in a very long while."

"Well, Maury and I will be sticking around to take care of a few things. If you need us for anything, you know how to reach us."

Ken was holding her coat open for her. She gave Shred a grateful smile and went to let her mate help her on with it.

"Are you okay driving those side roads after dark?" Maury asked. "Shred says they can be hard to find even in daylight."

"Not if you have Nash'terel eyes and a GPS," Ken replied. "I know you like to worry, but we'll be fine, Grandpa M, really."

Meanwhile, Travis was silent. He was putting on a brave face, but his eyes were pleading for rescue. Shred felt another tug at his heart and had to fortify himself against it.

After a round of hugs, Ken shepherded his little family out the door and down the remaining stairs. Maury and Shred came onto the landing to watch them go. The separation was apparently proving difficult for Maury as well. He stared after them, his lips pressed tightly together.

Sensing movement at the corner of his awareness, Shred looked up and saw Barron and Vicky leaning over the third-floor railing. He waved to capture their attention and called out, "We need to have a serious talk, Barney."

Barron nodded assent. "I'll make some tea," he called back. "Come up in ten."

Vicky and Barron were sitting at the table when Maury and Shred walked through the doorway to join them. Leaning on her elbows, Vicky stared ahead as though in a trance. She was holding her cup at the level of her chin, and she seemed to be inhaling the vapour rising from the liquid inside it. Shred's first thought on seeing her was that her "tea" had to be some sort of narcotic. Then, abruptly, she snapped out of her drowse. She turned to acknowledge the new arrivals with a nod and a smile before taking a careful sip and setting the cup down in front of her.

"You have questions," Barron said, greeting them. He got to his feet and poured three additional cups of steaming brew from the large, round-bellied pot on the trivet in the middle of the table. "We're ready to answer them."

Finally!

When all four Nash'terel had been served, Barron resumed his seat and said, "Gordie, you noticed a change in me earlier, and I know you weren't really satisfied with any of the reasons I gave you for it. I wanted to tell you the truth, but I couldn't, not until Vicky agreed. Some superstition or other about the first month..."

All eyes now turned to Vincaspera, whose face wore an expression of feline contentment.

Maury was the one who spoke its name aloud. "You're expecting. Congratulations!"

Now the changes in her behaviour made sense, Shred mused, along with Barron's apparent lack of concern about them. He'd been living with Vicky's raging hormones for weeks already. Fortunately, he was a seasoned veteran, accustomed to battlefields. Living in a war zone for the next five months shouldn't faze him in the least.

"You don't look very happy for us, Gordie," Barron observed, breaking into his thoughts. "Is there a problem?"

"No, of course not! I'm thrilled for you," he hastened to reply. "But I do have some further questions."

"It's a late pregnancy, we know, and the midwife warned us there could be complications," Vicky explained. "But a thousand and a half years gives us time to raise an Earthborn to full adulthood, and we wanted an heir, someone who can take over the

Middlevale project when we're gone. We've discussed it and decided that this offspring will be male birth-gendered."

...with Barron taking a much more active role in the rearing of his son than he'd done with Lilly, no doubt, perhaps even moving the Earthborn to the compound at a young age to oversee the training of his *hainbek*. As Shred recalled, Barney Ross had always admired the educational system of ancient Sparta.

"...make you uncomfortable, my dear," Maury was saying, "but it's rather obvious that all is not well between you and Travis's mother, and we can't help wondering what might have caused it."

Vicky exhaled audibly, then cast a glance at Barron. "Angie was a Middlevaler who'd peeked behind the curtain. She knew what we were and why the town existed, and as a result, she has never trusted me to have the best interests of any humans at heart, including her own and Travis's. Anything I did had to be for some nefarious ulterior motive. She wouldn't even accept a gift from me. Not even if it was for the child." She shook her head sadly. "I cared for him as though he were my own. She didn't like that. She wanted me to stay at arm's length."

"So, when you began teaching him to speak Nash'terel...?" Shred prompted her.

"She told me I was overstepping my bounds, that all a babysitter was supposed to do was keep the child safe. When I explained that I was simply giving him love, that just inflamed the situation. She decided I was calling her a bad mother and trying to take her place. After that, things spiralled. She would take exception to something I did, I would try to explain myself, she would interpret my words as criticism and take it badly..." She huffed out a breath. "After a while I gave up even trying to get along with her. All it did was make me angry and frustrated."

Vicky's cheeks were flushing. Evidently, just recalling the chain of events was enough to get her riled up.

"Hence, the cottage," Barron put in. "It wasn't a perfect solution, but it was the best I could come up with at the time. It reunited Ken and his family while putting some distance between Angie and Vicky."

"And neither of you saw Travis again after that until yesterday?" said Maury.

"I had business and rituals to conduct in Middlevale from time to time," Vicky said with a sigh. "I heard that Angie had hired someone in town to watch over him while she worked at the library. I kept my eyes open, hoping for a glimpse of him, but... no. And then he was five years old, and you came out for your visit, and we found out—after the fact—that Ken and Angie had sent Travis back east with you when you left. It hurt," she added, "and I was madder than hell for a long time after that... but I can't honestly say I was surprised."

"What about now?" Shred wanted to know. "Barron told me you had your heart set on training Travis's *hainbek*."

"Because I thought it was the only way I could become reacquainted with my godson," she replied, staring into her teacup as it turned to and fro on the tabletop, seemingly all by itself. Then she lifted her gaze and shared it with the others at the table. "However, it appears I was wrong. Travis remembered me. He knows I care about him. And since he's aging at the human rate, he'll be an adult soon enough, able to choose how he spends his time away from the compound. I've waited this long to get to know him. I can wait a little longer."

Part Five

Operation *Dashkra* Collector

Chapter Eighteen

◆

Polley arrived at midday on Wednesday, driving a black SUV with the Church's logo on its sides. Barron had been watching for it through a third-storey window. When he saw the vehicle go past, its turn signal flashing, he hurried down to unlock the rear door of the building.

Maury and Shred had been relaxing in the guest apartment. Shred heard the pounding of footsteps on the stairs and shared a look with Maury. Then both Nash'terel closed the books they were reading and headed out onto the landing to investigate. Peering down the stairwell, they observed chests being carried inside from the alley, bringing with them a current of cold air that could be felt all the way to the second floor.

Shred counted three boxes. "Weapons," he murmured.

Vicky passed behind them, on her way downstairs. "And a few more *hainbeka*, apparently," she remarked cheerfully. "Shall we go meet them?"

As Maury and Shred followed her around the corner at the bottom of the stairs, the last of three new arrivals came inside, and

Barron was finally able to close the back door.

Shred almost didn't recognize Polley without her camo. The weapons master was wearing black jeans and a grey, down-filled parka. As she pushed the hood back from her face, her barely-controlled ponytail twigged his memory.

"What have you brought us, Polley?" he asked.

"Mr. Sharp," she said, acknowledging him with a smile. "Handguns and rifles, with plenty of ammo. Didn't know whether you'd be needing human-made or captured Yeng ordnance, so we came with both. And these two grunts," she added with a wave in their direction, "are Mittitander and Froman. They're not elemental masters, but they're the best adepts we've got. They're also locals like myself, meaning we're familiar with the terrain, and I figured their *hainbeka* would prove handy when push came to shove. Froman is Yanni's trainee. Mittitander has been working with Jarrent."

"So, shaping and magnetism, respectively," Shred explained for Maury's benefit.

"And what is your special talent, my dear?" Maury asked her.

Her grin grew positively wicked. "Sound. I can use it to throw one person off their game or make a whole roomful nervous as hell."

Barron tapped Polley on the shoulder. "The pendants?" he asked.

Reaching inside her jacket, she produced a dark blue cloth bundle and dropped it onto his outstretched hand. "There are thirteen in there, in total. I picked our most trusted personnel and approached them individually. This is a black op. Didn't think you'd want me making a general announcement about it."

He uttered a satisfied syllable and pocketed the parcel.

"Now that they have been introduced, I think we should show these travellers some hospitality," Vicky declared. "They've had a long drive to get here, and there's tea and essence waiting upstairs. Once they've warmed up and relaxed, we can all talk about what to do next."

Froman had adopted the most unwarriorlike shape Shred had ever seen. Rail-thin and stoop-shouldered, wearing thick glasses that he kept having to push back up the bridge of his nose, he hardly looked capable of *lifting* a weapon, let alone firing it. "So, the primary objective is to capture as many of these *dashkra* detectors as possible with a single trap?" he said.

"While eliminating as many Yeng as possible, yes," Vicky confirmed.

"That's the first step. It shouldn't be difficult," Shred told them. "These are home-grown assassins. With few exceptions, they tend to be opportunistic thugs without much specialized training, and they're greedy. They would probably kill just for the thrill it gives them, but what's been motivating them to focus on killing Nash'-terel is the collector's bounty, combined with how easy it's become to identify us using that damned device. Put enough *dashkra* in one place and it should draw them like flies to a rotting corpse."

"So, we need to simulate a place where Nash'terel might gather," Mittitander said, a smile creeping across his angular, weathered face. "And I think I know just where we can do it. We can even spend the night there, without being interrupted by other Nash'terel." He paused, evidently for effect. "My uncle owns an art movie house, in an industrial mall downtown. It's not for profit. He keeps it dark most of the time. Once or twice a month, he opens it up for a mini-festival of student and amateur films.

Three times a year, though, he invites all the members of our family to gather for a special midnight showing. He keeps the date fluid and the marquee blank, and everyone enters by the back door because we know the Yeng are watching the front."

"So they're already surveilling the theatre, and the premises are dark right now?" Vicky's mental wheels were turning. Shred could see it in the glittering of her eyes. "That will work," she said, "but we're going to need some props. Some kind of humanlike figures, to start with, to fake an audience. We'll need a couple dozen of them. And clothing for them. And for us."

"I know of a mannequin storage warehouse that we can raid," Polley offered. "Froman and I can bring the audience to the movie house and meet you there. We can probably find a few used clothing drop boxes to scavenge as well. What kind of time line are we talking about?"

"I'll need a day or so to find my uncle and get the key from him," Mittitander replied.

"Since when does a master thief need a key to get past a door?" Froman said with a grin.

Mittitander had evidently been expecting to be teased. Without missing a beat he tossed back, "Since it belongs to a family that I would like to remain part of. First lesson my father taught me was what would happen if we ever stole from our own."

"So, Friday, then?" said Polley, cutting short their exchange of words.

"Friday night," Vicky declared, and heads bobbed in agreement all around the room.

"Uncle keeps a library of old movies in a vault in the basement of the building, and he showed me how to use the projector," Mittitander continued. "I'll choose a film that can cover the sound of weapons fire. And we'll need a lure to get the Yengs' attention. Perhaps something on the marquee?"

"No. Your uncle left it blank. We'll do the same," Vicky told him. "I've got a better idea for drawing in the prey."

The words "art movie house" had planted an image in Shred's mind of a small, out-of-the-way theatre, a little faded and shabby, like many others that he'd visited over the past century or so on at least three continents. As it turned out, however, even that expectation was too high. From the outside, this hole-in-the-wall cinema appeared to be taking its description quite literally.

For starters, the theatre had no name on display, or even the kind of illuminated advertising matrix that the word "marquee" generally implied. Instead, a largish square of weathered plywood sat above the double doors. It looked makeshift and temporary, like a file card pinned to a bulletin board. The front entrance was tucked in between a couple of wholesalers' clearance houses, which meant the complete lack of glass on the side facing the parking lot made it virtually invisible after dusk.

Around back, surrounded by loading docks, the dark grey metal door would have been invisible as well, except for the green symbol painted onto it—a large 'H' with a double crossbar, and a circle perched atop each of the uprights.

"It's the sigil of our family," Mittitander explained. "You need Nash'terel eyes to spot it at night, and no one unrelated to us would know what it means. Except the six of you now, of course."

"Don't worry, your family secret is safe with us," Barron assured him as Mittitander turned a key in the lock to let them enter.

"And your uncle is okay with us using this place for an ambush?" Polley asked.

"He wouldn't have given me the key if he weren't," Mittitander replied. "There's just one condition, though."

"Uh-oh," Froman said under his breath.

"He says we have to kill every Yeng who sets foot inside the building. I told him that wouldn't be a problem."

Once all the chests and props had been carried through the door, Mittitander locked it again. Meanwhile, Barron and Shred had done some reconnoitring and discovered the auditorium proper.

It was at least eighty years old, built first as a venue for live theatre, then retrofitted for showing films. Its screen was suspended like a window shade from the proscenium arch, in front of a patched burgundy curtain. Behind the curtain sat a well-trodden hardwood stage, the marks of many actors still visible as streaks of colour on the boards. In the wings, meanwhile, were hand-crank operated mechanisms for raising and lowering things onstage.

It had been a long time since the last live performance. Peering around, Shred made mental note of two dog-eared, water-damaged backdrops propped one atop the other against the rear wall, a handful of tattered tormentors, and a pair of long light bars overhead, their bulbs pulled like teeth, leaving empty sockets behind.

The audience area was just as worn and almost as neglected. Seven or eight rows of overstuffed blood red seats, many of them visibly mended, swept up and away from the stage on a slanted, carpeted floor. Shred did a rapid count and estimated the total house capacity to be no more than sixty. Thankfully, there were no boxes or balconies. Having everything on one level would make the trap much easier to close.

"I've found the electrical panel," Barron called from one of the wings. A moment later, the house lights came on. Wall-mounted sconces shaped like hands holding torches provided a dim illumination, perfect for Nash'terel purposes.

"All right, then," Vicky announced. "Let's get to work!"

By dusk, the ambush was ready. The house lights were dimmed, the projector was loaded up, and twenty-seven mannequins were in their seats, tastefully garbed and each supplied with a lifelike human face, courtesy of Froman's *hainbek*. Managing the audience was his assignment. Once cued that Yeng were about to enter the auditorium, he would position himself in the centre of it and make the mannequins' heads appear to be moving in reaction to what was on the screen.

Fourteen of these decoys—all sitting in the three front rows— were wearing *dashkra* pendants around their necks. That left three to create the lure that would get the Yeng assassins' attention and bring them into the trap.

Vicky had that part covered. Copying a strategy that had worked well against the Americans in the War of 1812, she, Maury, and Froman would make three Nash'terel appear to be many more by walking repeatedly around the outside of the building. They would shift their faces and change their clothes before each circuit, and would let themselves be seen entering singly and in pairs through the front doors, over and over again. Vicky had organized the ploy like a fashion show, with outfits on hangers hooked over exposed pipes near the back door.

Meanwhile, Barron, Shred, and Polley had already exited that way—equipped with networked phones and armed with captured Yeng pistols—and had taken roundabout routes to their assigned observation posts. They would be monitoring the parking lot in front of the building, watching for the arrival of the prey.

"I'm in position," Barron reported.

"Me too," said Polley. "No traffic yet."

"Be patient," Shred advised her. "The night is young, and we know the Yeng are watching. Just remember what we rehearsed."

"Hey, I'm an actor. I've done this kind of thing before," she informed him tartly.

"You really think we'll get useful intel on the first attempt, Gordie?"

"As long as we play it right, I'm sure we will," Shred replied. "Once our marks have led us to the collector, we can find out the truth and, at the very least, get rid of that damned bounty. And speaking of marks," he added, "heads up, people. I think we have our first lucky contestants."

A car had turned onto the side street, then doused its lights before entering the parking lot. It backed into a spot at the outer edge of the lot, facing the front doors of the theatre.

"Ooh, *that's* not suspicious at all," Polley remarked softly.

"How many in the vehicle?" Barron asked.

"Two that I can see," she replied. "And there are exhaust fumes. They're idling the engine, waiting for someone."

This had better not be a damn drug deal, Shred thought.

Barron had read his mind. "We need to know whether they're Yeng. You know what to do?"

"You betcha, boss."

Shred heard the smile in her voice. Polley was enjoying her time out of the office.

"Keep your line open so we'll know when to move," he advised her.

Polley strode briskly across the parking lot, setting a direct course for the car. The light was fading, but not yet gone. From his position (and with his human eyes), Shred could see the driver's side window slide down as she approached. The person behind the wheel was male, with features that looked as though they'd been violently rearranged more than once.

Polley stopped about a metre away and leaned down to peer into the front seat.

"You're late!" she declared, gesticulating impatiently with both her arms. "A dozen prey have gone through that door already. What did you do—detour through Kelowna?"

"Kelowna" was the word she was to use if she smelled Yeng.

"It's show time, Vicky," Barron's voice hissed.

"Copy that," came the terse reply.

Just then, a man who had been walking across the street broke into a run, headed toward Polley.

"And there's the third member of the triad," Shred muttered. "Let's move, Barney."

Both Nash'terel began jogging toward the car, coming from opposite sides of the parking lot.

Meanwhile, Polley had taken a step backward and pulled her Yeng pistol out from under her jacket. "You're not my crew. Who the hell are you and what are you doing here?" she demanded in a cold, flat voice.

"Relax, babe," said one of the Yeng in the car. He opened his coat, presumably to show her his own weapon. "We're here for the same reason you are. To rid the world of Nash'terel filth and make a few bucks doing it."

"Make a few bucks? What the fuck is that supposed to mean?" she bristled.

The third man had been reaching inside his jacket as he ran. When he was close enough to overhear her questions, he slowed to a walk and withdrew his hand. "You don't know?" he asked, giving her a disarming smile.

It failed to soften her mood. "You with them?" she snapped, gesturing at the two Yeng in the vehicle with the business end of her pistol.

"Yes, they're my crew," he replied, "and if you wouldn't mind pointing that somewhere else...?"

"Like at you?" she returned, aiming the gun at his midsection.

Barron and Shred arrived then and took up positions to either side of her.

"Who are these mooks, Ginna?" Barron asked.

Without taking her eyes off the third man's face, Polley said, "They think they're going to move in on us."

"We've had this place staked out for weeks," Shred spat. "What gives them the right to just—?"

"This does." Extending a placating hand, palm out, to signal that he wasn't drawing a weapon, the third man slipped his other hand into an inside coat pocket and pulled out a familiar-looking device.

Barron and Shred exchanged glances. The sting was working perfectly so far.

"A phone?" Polley scoffed. "Who have you got on speed dial? The Prime Minister?"

The Yeng smiled indulgently at her. "It's not a phone."

While the three Nash'terel remained patiently in character, he proceeded to demonstrate the tracker for them, concluding with, "There's a man in Toronto who's been making these and giving them out free to any triad that wants one, so if you're thinking of mugging us for this, trust me, it's not worth the trouble. You can get your own with a single call. Shipping takes less than three days."

He reached into a different pocket and pulled out a business card, then flipped it over to show what appeared to be an eleven-digit number already written on the back in ballpoint ink. "Make sure you mention my name when you place your order. I get a commission."

"A commission," Barron repeated skeptically. "On a freebie?"

"On each Nash'terel pendant you sell him. He'll explain how everything works when you contact him."

This was all Barron and Shred needed to hear. Now they just had to send the Yeng inside the theatre, so that Vicky could spring the trap and visit her vengeance on them.

Polley's last job before joining Barron's program had been as a supporting actor in a locally produced television series. Clearly feeling in her element, she plucked the card from the third man's hand.

"That's all well and good, and we thank you for the tip…" She consulted the card, squinting in what was rapidly becoming semi-darkness. "…Gerald. But what about tonight? This is our kill. We worked damn hard for it, and we're not giving it up."

"I think we can come to an equitable arrangement. The tracker shows seventeen pieces of bloodstone inside that movie theatre, all stationary. They'll be sitting in the dark, facing the screen with their backs to the entrance. We'll wait out here while you sneak in, make one kill each, grab their pendants, and get out again before they realize what's happening. Then you'll give me the pendants you collected as a quid pro quo for putting you in touch with the tracker supplier. Fair?"

Nope, Shred thought, not in the slightest. It was time to switch the focus and put things back on track.

"Wait a minute. You get paid for these pendants, you said?" said Shred.

"Yes. At a rate set by the end purchaser."

"And what's the going rate for pendants these days?" he persisted.

"Not something you need to concern yourself with." A note of impatience had crept into Gerald's voice.

"I disagree," Polley told him. "If you're getting a finder's fee for recruiting triads, it should come out of your purchaser's pocket, not ours."

Gerald heaved a disappointed sigh. "In that case, I must ask you to remain outside with me while my people do what we came here to do."

In an instant, three weapons were trained on the Nash'terel.

"After we've left, you can go in and pick up the scraps," he added scornfully.

Shred repressed a smile. Gerald was just as greedy as they'd hoped he would be.

"Step back, lay your guns on the ground, and kick them toward me," the Yeng instructed.

Sharing a look, the Nash'terel complied. As they straightened up, Barron and Shred each put one hand behind their backs. It took only seconds for heat bombs to form.

Meanwhile, Gerald had sent his crew racing toward the front entrance of the movie house. As soon as they disappeared inside...

Polley's hands were in motion. To an onlooker, she might have appeared to be washing them, but Shred knew what she was doing. She was deploying her *hainbek*, barraging the Yeng with low frequency sound waves. Almost immediately, Gerald began showing signs of unease. Soon he was casting anxious glances toward the marquee. The heat lords waited until he was looking away from them. Then they shifted their eyes to Nash'terel and struck together, aiming both their bombs at his head.

The Yeng never had a chance. When he dropped to the ground, his face a smoking ruin, Polley leaned over and emptied his pockets. Then Barron and Shred positioned him in the driver's seat of the car (taking care to fasten his seat belt) and proceeded to cremate the rest of Gerald's body from the inside out.

Just for fun, they left his clothing intact. (There hadn't been a spontaneous human combustion reported in Vancouver for some time, and Barron was certain the local police must be getting bored.)

All at once, a howl of misery and torment drifted from the speaker of Polley's phone, momentarily freezing the Nash'terel "triad" in place and reminding them: while they'd been busy disposing of Gerald in the parking lot, another violent drama had been unfolding inside the theatre. The trap they'd set earlier had been sprung. Two Yeng assassins had been ambushed. And now, judging from the incoherent noises emanating from the phone, it appeared Vicky was visiting a slow, torturous vengeance on the intruders. Soon, their agonized screams gave way to strangled gasps and pleading whimpers... and then all sounds of suffering ceased, and Froman's voice announced unnecessarily, "All clear. We got them both."

Shred looked at Barron and Polley in turn. "Shall we go assess the damage?" he invited them.

"After you," Barron replied with a wave of his hand.

Shred's first thought on entering the auditorium was that Mittitander's uncle would be pleased at how tidily everything had been done. Two Yeng bodies lay on the floor between the seats and the wall, looking like examples of shapeshifting gone wrong. Unfortunately, they'd managed to get off a couple of shots each before going down. Shred counted four holes, two burned into the wall beside the stage and two burned into the screen. Fortunately, the team included an adept with a matter-shaping *hainbek* who could patch them over.

Both would-be assassins were quite dead, but neither one was bleeding onto the carpet. Of course, their pants were full, and between that and the unpleasant odour that normally wafted off a Yeng with altered essence, the air in the room would probably take a while to freshen out. That was a separate issue.

His second thought was that Mittitander's choice of a war movie to serve as a backdrop to the action had been poetically appropriate.

"It was teamwork," Froman explained as the house lights came back up and Mittitander went to the projection booth to halt the screening. "Maldemaur blinded them, Mitt disarmed them, and Vincaspera slammed them down and crushed them. We can reset the trap and use it again if you want. These two never had a chance to warn anyone about it."

"I don't think it will be necessary," said Shred.

"Oh? Did you get what you needed?" Vicky asked, strolling up the aisle with a satisfied grin on her face.

"We got more than we expected," Barron told her.

Wordlessly, Polley showed her the device and the card.

Vicky's eyes widened. "So that's a *dashkra* seeker?"

"In good working order, apparently," Shred replied. "And the phone number on the card gets us the inventor and distributor of these things, and that individual, whoever they are, should lead us to the collector. All we have to do is continue playing our roles."

Chapter Nineteen

By mid-morning the next day, the trap had been dismantled. The two Yeng bodies had been cremated, leaving nothing but a layer of ashes inside a steel drum, and the drum had then been covered and left beside a dark blue metal dumpster behind the theatre. The mannequins had been returned to their warehouse. The clothing had been stuffed into garbage bags and dropped off at a nearby collection box. Finally, the interior of the movie house had been restored to the condition in which they'd found it, and Mittitander had phoned his uncle to thank him for the use of it.

Gerald's ashes, inside his clothing, would eventually be discovered in the parking lot by someone arriving to work in one of the adjacent buildings. The tabloids would be all over the story in no time.

By half past noon, seven Nash'terel were crowded around the dining table in the second-floor guest apartment, making short work of the food that Vicky had stockpiled there in advance of Travis's visit. It hadn't taken her and Maury long to turn most of it into a very large and tasty brunch consisting of scrambled eggs, cut-up raw fruit and vegetables, fried potatoes, sausages, and back bacon, all washed down with tea, strong black coffee, and essence.

When the dishes had been cleared away, Barron fetched the bag full of *dashkra* pendants and dumped them out onto the middle of the table. Then he sat down again, exhaling a thoughtful breath.

"That was awfully easy," he remarked. "Perhaps a little *too* easy."

"It's in our nature to distrust anything that comes from a Yeng under any circumstances," Shred reminded them. "In this case, however, I think we're safe. The humans have a saying: never look a gift horse in the mouth."

"They also warn one another that if something seems too good to be true, it's probably a con," Maury grumped.

"They're just a bundle of contradictions, aren't they?" Mittitander remarked with a grin.

Shred had been fingering one of Gerald's cards. He dropped it onto the table, then turned the card over so that the phone number was facing up. "Okay," he began, tapping it with an index finger. "Do we run with this, or do we find another venue, reset the trap, and see what a second triad gives us?"

"I think, first and foremost, that we need to proceed with caution," said Vicky, reaching for the card as she got up from the table. "Beginning with a reverse search on that phone number."

She was right. There was too much they didn't know, and too much at stake to risk a shot in the dark.

"Let's think this through logically," Shred suggested. "Put ourselves in the collector's shoes. We want to gather as much bloodstone as possible, as quickly as possible, so we turn the Yeng on Earth, some of whom are already hunting down Nash'terel, into our labour pool. We expand our active workforce by implementing a proven business model—a system of commissions and recruitment bonuses—and provide this phone number to be handed out to likely prospects."

"But I don't think it leads to the collector," Maury pointed out. "Not unless the collector and the distributor are one and the same. We're not dealing with a *ristim* here. The collector must have realized how freely this contact number would be circulated among the Yeng, so, to avoid being called up by every hunter wanting to make a more profitable side deal—"

"—there would be barriers erected between the hunters and the end purchaser of the *dashkra*," Shred concluded. "Maury's right. This collector is no fool."

"Well, if the collector is too intelligent to be a Yeng and we can't imagine them being Nash'terel, that leaves only the humans," Mittitander reasoned. "But no more than a handful of them even suspect that we exist."

"A handful would be all that's necessary," said Barron.

"A handful of humans who covet our *dashkra*?"

"...and who realize what we are," Polley added, "and what they are to us. That would explain why the collector is only interested in the cut and polished stones. Each one is evidence of a kill."

"It's a security company," Vicky announced, rejoining the group at the table and opening her laptop in front of her. "Eyes on the World Incorporated. I checked them out online. They develop and distribute tracking and surveillance equipment. Established twenty-two years ago by a man named Oliver Weisskopf, who passed away twelve years later and was replaced by then-Vice-President of Research and Development Glen Partridge. I have an address for their head office. It's in Vaughan Township, just north of Toronto."

"And what about this Mr. Montgomery who's mentioned on the card?" Shred asked her.

"There's a Eugene Montgomery listed as the VP of Sales," Vicky replied. "With the company since its launch, promoted to his current position seven years ago. How or why he's been so successful I have no idea, because on the web site he looks like a shifty-eyed weasel." She made a face. "Seriously. I would not buy anything from this man."

"Which may explain why he's giving the product away," Mittitander quipped.

"Gerald said the distributor was a man. He did not use the word 'Yeng'," said Barron.

"He knows all about the Yeng and has been dealing with them," Shred pointed out.

"Yes, but dealing with them at arm's length," Barron returned. "And Pritchard, the inventor of the device, came to Monicandra, *claiming* to be a Yeng, although he didn't smell like one."

"Remember Ellsworth's assistant, George?" Maury said, addressing Gershred. Then, in response to the questioning stares from around the table, he went on to explain, "George was a human working with the Yeng to kill Nash'terel, sixteen years ago. Before Bilyash ended him, he hinted that there were others like himself, who knew about the conflict and were taking an active part in it."

"But we figured the Council of the First must have been behind the recruitment effort, because there was no sign of human involvement following the Purge," Shred reminded him.

"Montgomery could be a Yeng, fronting for Pritchard. Or for Partridge, who is, after all, the one with the research and development background."

"Or maybe Pritchard and Partridge are one and the same?" Froman ventured. "Nash'terel aren't the only beings who can replace and impersonate, after all."

"What if this is a side hustle of Montgomery's that neither Pritchard nor Partridge knows anything about?" Polley pointed out.

"In which case, why would he give out the company's publicly listed phone number as a way to contact him?" Maury said. "It makes no sense."

All eyes now turned to rest on Gerald's card, returned by Vicky and once more sitting on the tabletop.

"Speculating about this isn't bringing us any closer to the truth," Shred decided aloud. "We need to try the phone number and see where it leads us."

As the phone rang twice, then three times at the other end of the line, Gershred put the call on speaker, mentally crossing his fingers that Gerald's "tip" was on the up-and-up.

"Eyes on the World, your surveillance tech solution," chirped a bright young female voice. "How may I direct your call?"

"I'm inquiring about..." He turned over the card and read aloud the bottom line of print, enclosed in quotation marks. "...'Mr. Montgomery's special unlimited offer'. Gerald told me about it."

"One moment, please."

There was dead air. Meanwhile, the six other Nash'terel were leaning in, taut as drawn bowstrings.

Finally, the receptionist came back on the line. "He's in a business meeting right now. If you'll give me a name and number, he'll call you back as soon as he's free."

Uncertain looks crisscrossed the table. Thankfully, no one

uttered a word.

"My name is Gordon," Shred told her, "but he won't be able to reach me. I'll have to call again later."

"Very well, Mr. Gordon. Give him a couple of hours. He'll be expecting to hear from you. Have a safe day."

A soft click, then silence.

"A couple of hours? That's enough time for a background check," said Mittitander.

"It's more likely to be a reference check," said Vicky. "Did any of you think to relieve Gerald of his phone before you roasted him?"

"Yep." Polley placed it on the table in front of her. "And I heard enough of his voice to imitate it if anyone calls him."

"Good."

Meanwhile, Maury slumped in the easy chair, his brows knitted with concern. This was why they made such a perfect couple, Shred reflected. Every warrior needed a worrier by his side, to temper his boldness with caution.

"What is it, Maldemaur?" Barron asked.

"I'm just remembering the stories Gershred told me about you and him in North Africa," he replied, "and I'm seeing some disturbing parallels here with the gunrunners you put out of business a century or so ago."

Barron sat up straight in his chair. "You're talking about the profiteers who played the different tribes off against one another. I remember those guys. They kept hostilities stoked high to maintain a steady demand for their product. That is, until we were ordered to take them out of the picture in the bluntest, bloodiest way possible, by a commanding officer with an obnoxiously strong moral compass."

Shred grimaced. He remembered the sergeant-major all too well, and morality had had nothing to do with the human's decisions.

"So, if the Yeng and the Nash'terel are the tribes, then who are the profiteers?" Polley asked, frowning. "It can't be Montgomery or the collector. The Yeng are getting these trackers free of charge and then being paid a bounty. That's money going out, not revenue. So where is it coming from, and who's making the profit?"

"What if it's Eyes on the World?" Maury suggested thoughtfully. Pieces were evidently falling into place inside his head.

Barron shot him a quizzical look. "Supplying the bounty money, you mean? Or making the profit?"

"Both. This company does not deal in weapons. It sells security systems."

"You think the collector is ramping up the conflict between the Yeng and the Nash'terel in order to sell their systems to both sides?" said Vicky, visibly trying the idea on for size.

"It's good business sense," Maury confirmed. "Demand for security gear increases, the price rises along with it, and the firm rakes in higher profits."

"That doesn't feel like something a Yeng could have come up with," Barron declared. "Not the ones that we know, at any rate. They're more the smash-and-grab type."

"I agree," said Shred. "However, if it fattens the company's bottom line, that could be a reason for its CEO to turn a blind eye to what Montgomery is doing, and it doesn't change our plan to identify the collector. We need to let the sting play out."

Exactly two hours after the first call, Gershred put his phone on speaker and punched up the distributor's number again.

"Hello, Mr. Gordon," said a deep answering voice.

"Mr. Montgomery, I presume?"

"You presume correctly. What can I do for you today?"

"I understand you're running a special unlimited offer. I would like to take advantage of it."

"You need a piece of technology?"

Something told Shred that Montgomery already knew the answer to that question. "I have the technology," he replied. "It's the rest of the offer that I'm interested in."

A pause, then, "I see. Can I assume that Mr. Gerald gave you more than my number, then?"

"You assume correctly. Gerald had no further use for the device, and I am now in possession of product that I would like to sell you."

Another pause. "Take me off speaker. Then we'll talk."

Shred complied.

"So, Gerald's out of the game?" Montgomery continued. "All right, then, what city are you calling from?"

"Vancouver, B.C."

"I have one representative out there. Write down the business address I'm about to give you."

Shred mimed writing, and pen and paper appeared on the table in front of him. As he used them to record the information, he was aware of necks craning and eyes straining all around him. When done, he repeated the address aloud, mainly for the benefit of the other Nash'terel in the room, and saw Mittitander's eyes widen with recognition.

"Anything else I need to do?" Shred asked the man on the other end of the line.

"Yes. Mention my name to the proprietor when you hand over the merchandise. You'll be paid on the spot, in cash. Then walk away."

If Montgomery had one representative in the Vancouver area, that meant he had more elsewhere. Seizing on the opportunity to pull more intel out of him, Shred said conversationally, "I have friends all across the country who would like in on this offer of yours. Are there other numbers they should be using?"

"No, just the toll-free one Gerald gave you. Be sure to tell your associates the code phrase as well. And when it's appropriate, I'll refer them to the nearest representative to redeem their product for cash."

A plan was taking shape in Gershred's mind.

Forcing his voice to remain calm, he said, "All right, then. A pleasure doing business with you, Mr. Montgomery."

The pause that followed was telling. "Perhaps. We'll see, Mr. Gordon."

The line went dead.

"I know that address," Mittitander declared. "It's a pawn shop, still run by a human who used to be an acquaintance of my dad."

"Did he know your family was Nash'terel?" Barron asked.

"No, just that we were regular customers."

"A pawn shop is a convenient way to fence stolen goods," Gershred remarked, nodding, "and it sounds like this Montgomery has a whole network of them. I think I know how we can use it against him, but we can't move too fast. He's suspicious about me. I heard it in his voice. We need to keep the sting rolling a little longer. Once we have the intel we need, Barron and I will go to Toronto and bring the Guild on board."

Vicky did not look happy about that.

Too bad.

Chapter Twenty

Maury and Vicky were scientists. Although it frustrated Barron to no end, they demanded proof of concept before the rest of the op could proceed.

At just past ten o'clock on Sunday morning, the pawn shop opened for business. Shred had been waiting outside. He knew he would be on camera the moment he entered the store. That was why he had shifted his face before setting out from the apartment, exiting the building by the back door. A Robert Wagner lookalike would be far too memorable. He reverted his features to the tough and whiskered mug he'd worn two days earlier, for the sting at the movie house.

Gran's Pot o' Gold was like an entire warehouse crammed into a single room. Separating the customers from the inventory sat a wooden countertop at waist height, atop a barrier formed of glass display cases. Beings could see but not touch the collections of cameras, jewellery, sports memorabilia, and various *objets d'art* inside them. Mounted on the walls were musical instruments, autographed posters, and artwork, all jockeying for space around shelves crowded with miscellaneous "finds". The place looked as though adding one more item might trigger an explosion, tossing its contents like a salad.

"Are you buying or selling?"

Pulled back to the moment by the bright and pleasant voice of the young woman behind the counter, Shred reflexively sniffed the air while pressing a hand to his front pants pocket, the one holding the specially prepared pendant.

She smelled of lilac. That didn't mean anything. Not every Yeng had altered essence.

"Mr. Montgomery said I would be dealing with the proprietor," he said stiffly. "Is that you?"

One of her hands slipped beneath the countertop, most likely preparing to press a silent alarm button. Or pull a gun. "And you are...?" she said with a smile.

He returned it. "Gordon."

The hand came back out, empty. "He's expecting you, Mr. Gordon." Never moving her gaze from his face, she gestured toward a door at the rear of the shop. "Through there. There's a gate at the end of the counter."

Of course. This would be a backroom deal, out of sight of the pesky security cameras.

He walked through the indicated door and found himself in a small, cluttered office, standing face to face with a bald-headed male (human, according to Mittitander) sporting the most outlandishly sculpted moustache Shred had ever seen.

Must be a Vancouver thing...

"It's for a competition," the man snapped, apparently expecting a question he'd already tired of answering. "For charity." He held out his hand. "Never mind. Just show me the stone."

Shred dug the pendant out of his pocket and lowered the *dashkra* by its chain onto the man's outstretched palm. With fingers mentally crossed, he watched the pawnbroker inspect the merchandise.

Vicky had taken over the op again, and she was fond of Trojan horses. At her insistence, Froman had used his *hainbek* to reshape the mineral around a micro GPS tracking chip she'd originally placed inside the computer in her office. Shred had expressed some reservations about this ploy. Montgomery's guard was already up. If the alteration to the stone were detected, he would double his defences and plan A would be scuppered. However, it wasn't the stone that the pawnbroker was finding interesting, but rather the clasp on the chain. It was intact.

Shred cursed silently as he recalled that the clasp of the pendant he'd found on the assassin at the arena had been broken. The chain had been ripped from a Nash'terel's neck—as had so many others, no doubt. Certain that his cover was blown, Shred glanced around, plotting his escape from the room.

"Is there a problem?" he asked tightly.

"No. It's just that I haven't seen a chain like this before," the pawnbroker remarked. He raised curious eyes to the Nash'terel's face, then slid his gaze up and to Shred's right without turning his head.

Shred understood the signal. Eyes on the World evidently had eyes on Montgomery's representatives as well. Mr. Gordon was playing to an audience. He would need to be both mindful and convincing.

"Is it worth something extra?" he asked, purposely gruffing up his voice.

"Perhaps."

"Then I'll be sure to bring you more of them."

Stepping behind his desk, the pawnbroker unlocked a drawer and extracted a single crisp fifty-dollar bill.

"This is the going rate?" said Shred as he reached out to accept the money.

"It's all I'm authorized to pay you. If you believe your merchandise is worth more, you're welcome to take it up with Mr. Montgomery. In the meanwhile, I suggest you exit the way you came in. Otherwise, there might be questions."

They were done. With a final nod goodbye, Shred walked out the door, through the gate, past the security cameras in the shop, and back onto the street.

By the time Shred had finished briefing the other Nash'terel about his visit to the pawn shop, the silence that dropped over the dining table in the third floor apartment could have given birth to an elephant.

Mittitander was the first to speak, in a voice brimming with barely-controlled rage. "Fifty dollars? That's all a Nash'terel life is worth to them?"

"It's what a Yeng gets for bringing in a pendant," Shred corrected him. "Yeng hunters are on the bottom rung of a ladder of business transactions. If the representative is paying out fifty dollars for each bloodstone, you can be sure he's collecting more than that from Montgomery. If Montgomery isn't the collector, then whoever sits directly above him on the ladder will be reimbursing him his costs plus a commission, and so on. And let's not forget that recruiters like Gerald get a bonus for each new hunter they bring on board. Totalled up, that's a lot of money going out. Either the collector has deep pockets—"

"—or he's not on the top rung of the ladder," Maury supplied dryly. "But let's try to think positively about this, shall we?"

"Does the pawnbroker realize where these stones are coming from?" Vicky demanded. "That people are being murdered for them?"

"I got the feeling that he does, but he thinks there's nothing he can do about it," Shred told her. "He knew from looking at the clasp that I wasn't there for the money, and he warned me about the surveillance in his office so I wouldn't blow my cover. I don't think he's doing this voluntarily. It wouldn't surprise me if none of them were."

"And so the legacy of the Council of the First lives on," Vicky said disgustedly, "only they're enslaving humans now as well as other Yeng."

"Last time I met with the Guild, Monicandra said she'd been expecting something like this, that a new generation of Yeng leaders would be stepping up to replace the ones we took out sixteen years ago, but they'd be cagier about how they conduct their business."

"Okay," said Polley. "So where do we go from here?"

"We remain in character and play our roles, appearing to do what Montgomery wants us to do—hand out his toll-free number to others across the country who are willing to sell him *dashkra*," Shred decided. "In the process, we slip as many baited pendants as possible into the pipeline and follow them as far as they'll take us. With luck, the GPS chips inside them won't be detected until they've led us to the collector."

"I know a good place to start," Maury declared, pulling out his phone. "Pyotren and Armin are shape lords, and Montgomery is bound to have representatives in the Toronto area."

"Unh-unh," Vicky cut in tartly. "The Guild is based in Toronto as well. The reason I bought into this operation was that it was supposed to take place on the west coast in order to avoid attracting their notice. Now Maldemaur is talking about running it practically under their noses."

"Pyotren has a stolen *dashkra* chewing a hole in his pocket," Maury returned. "I figured we may as well let him put it to good use. Besides, you know the Guild is going to find out what we're doing eventually."

"Yes," Shred told him, frowning, "but I was hoping it would take us longer to get to that point. I want to have Montgomery nailed down and an address for the collector before Barney and I pay our visit to the Riftgate Club." Addressing the rest of the group, he said, "We need to get our hands on a bunch more GPS chips, install them in the pendants we've collected, and find a way to sell the *dashkra* to Montgomery's representatives all across the country, without alerting our targets... or the Guild," he added with a reassuring look at Vicky.

"Sounds like a road trip to me," Polley remarked. "Two teams setting out, one from here and the other from down east, meeting up somewhere around Winnipeg."

"Ontario and Quebec have the largest populations," said Froman, "so whoever ends up heading west from the Maritimes will need to carry more of the stones."

"And they'll have to buy and use a different burner phone in each city, and change their appearance for each sale," Mittitander advised. "We have to assume Montgomery will be surveilling every one of his representatives."

"Meanwhile, I'll be monitoring the chips," said Vicky, brandishing her phone. "I originally downloaded the app so I could use GPS to track the whereabouts of our essence flasks. Bring me about a dozen and a half fresh chips. Once I've added them to this controlling device and Froman has implanted them, we'll be good to go."

And just like that, she was back in charge again.

It was half past three on Sunday afternoon. Mittitander and Froman had been sent out shopping for microchips small enough to fit inside a *dashkra* pendant. Barron, Vicky, and Polley were deep in discussion, pairing up operatives and plotting their cross-country itineraries. Maury and Shred excused themselves and went downstairs to make a private phone call.

Angie picked up on the third ring. She was alone in the cottage. Shred put her on speaker for Maury's benefit.

"You're late," she told them. "After the events of last Monday and Tuesday, I thought for sure we'd have heard from you days ago."

"Well, things have been a bit busy here, and we didn't want to intrude before Travis had settled in," Shred responded.

"How are you all getting along?" Maury asked.

There was a pause, long enough for Maury and Shred to exchange concerned glances.

"Okay, I think," she finally replied. "As you probably planned, Ken and Travis are bonding over hockey. They're at the rec centre of the compound right now, watching a practice, but I'm expecting them back soon."

"And you and Travis?" Shred wanted to know.

Angie let out a sigh. "Not so much, I'm afraid. I'm more like a taskmaster than a parent right now. And Ken's more like a friend. I hate having to crack the whip so much, but it really feels as though one of us has to, because we've lost ten years of his life and have a lot of catching up to do. Don't get me wrong—I'm not criticizing you. You did a wonderful job raising him. I just wish—"

"Wish what, Angie?"

"I wish he felt comfortable enough around me to call me 'Mom'. Or even 'Angie'. When we're together he doesn't call me anything at all."

Shred felt a tug at his heart. "It will happen. Give it time."

"I know," she assured him. "It's just—never mind. You're right. He's still settling into new surroundings."

"And how does he seem to be adjusting?" Maury asked.

"Well, he's taken ownership of his bedroom, and he's already friends with a couple of boys his age. He met one at the library in town, and the second one at the pond, apparently. Leo Dagomir. I understand they played hockey together back east...?"

"Yes, in the same league but not for the same team," Shred replied. "Leo's father is the hockey coach Barron mentioned at dinner last week, the new instructor who's going to help Travis gain full control of his *hainbek*."

"I think we met him yesterday. He ran the morning practice."

Ah, yes, those early morning hockey practices... Maury and Shred traded knowing smiles.

"So this coach is Nash'terel, and he's going to be teaching both Travis and Leo?" she asked. "Inside the compound?"

"Eventually. Like Travis, Leo is a bit underage," Shred told her. "It will be a while before they qualify for the full program."

Silence, growing heavier by the second.

"What's wrong, Angie?" said Maury, frowning.

She cleared her throat. "Nothing, I guess. I mean, I knew Travis would need special training. I just never thought of it as a full time thing. I assumed that it would be fitted in around his academic studies, because he hasn't even finished grade 10 yet and—"

"You want him to graduate from high school," Shred supplied. He sighed inwardly.

Despite all the evidence proving Travis was Nash'terel, Angie persisted in thinking of her son as human, needing to reach human milestones on a human timeline. Like getting a human education at the expense of what was essential knowledge to every Nash'terel. Shred searched his mind for something comforting to say and came up empty.

"And he *will* graduate," Maury chimed in, saving the moment. "Like any other elite athlete, he'll work with his coach, and together they'll find a way to make everything fit into a reasonable schedule. This doesn't all have to be on your shoulders, Angie. Coach Dagomir is a good teacher. He's been training human adolescents and interacting with their parents for many years. He knows what he's doing."

She let out a shuddering breath that they could hear through the speaker. "And will Travis continue to live with us in the cottage?"

"Whether he does or he doesn't, you're not going to lose your son to the Nash'terel. That's a promise," Shred declared.

A pause, then, "I have one more question. This may sound silly, but... Travis keeps waking up with strange feet. Should that be happening?"

Maury replied with a grin, "As long as he can put them right again, it's nothing to worry about, my dear."

Mittitander and Froman had spent the hours before and after noon on Sunday purchasing GPS microchips at five different stores. Vicky connected them to the app on her phone, and

Froman spent another hour reshaping the remaining pendants around them. Wherever these bloodstones went, they would be "calling home" to report their coordinates. Eventually they would gather at the same place, giving away either Montgomery's location or the collector's (or both, if they turned out to be the same person) and providing a target for a sanctioned strike by the Guild. Theoretically, anyway. Nothing was certain yet.

Meanwhile, teams 1 and 2 had been making preparations for their cross-country trips. Barron and Polley would be flying to St. John's, Newfoundland and working their way west. Mittitander and Shred would be renting a car in Vancouver and heading east. The two teams were going to rendezvous in Kenora, just inside the western border of Ontario, and hold position there, waiting for updates.

That evening, they gathered around Vicky and Barron's dining table for a meal and an essence top-up before their departures. Then Vicky brought out the box containing the baited pendants that they would be dropping off as they travelled, nine for the westbound team and six for the eastbound one. Smiling, she pulled the box flaps open and made to reach inside... and froze.

The colour drained from her face. Shred got to his feet, concerned that she might be about to faint.

Barron stood up as well. He stared into the box. His jaw sagged. "*Shattra!*" he spat, and dropped back onto his chair.

"What is it?" Polley demanded.

"See for yourself," he replied disgustedly. He tilted the box to show everyone the large, solid, milky white lump of *dashkra* inside, uniformly studded with dark metal bits that only hours earlier had been microchips, gold settings, and chains of varying thickness.

"They've all melted together," Froman observed. "How is that possible?"

Vicky had no words. She opened and closed her mouth a couple of times as though to reply, then had to wave the question away.

Shred and Barron shared a solemn look.

"So, in addition to ultraviolet light, it doesn't like human technology. You were right, Gordie," Barron told him. "The bloodstone *hasn't* shown us everything it can do." He cursed again, then fell silent.

"We're back to square one?" said Mittitander.

"Not quite," Shred said, staring at Vicky until she raised her eyes to meet his gaze. "We still have one pendant out there."

She found her phone and opened the app. Frowning at the screen, she informed him, "It's not registering anymore. These chips come with batteries built in. Either this one ran down because it was an older chip, or the *dashkra* killed it by absorbing all the remaining energy. Either way, it appears we're done."

"No, we're not," Shred decided. "Today is Sunday. The pawnbroker isn't going to simply drop something like that into a mailbox. He'll package it up tonight, then hand it to a courier tomorrow morning. Bear with me. I have an idea."

Chapter Twenty-One

When it came to obtaining intel, the old-fashioned ways were often the most reliable, as long as they were well-timed. In this case, timing would be critical, and the window of opportunity pencil-slim.

The reconnoitring team had reported back at 3:00 a.m. The pawn shop was protected by a security system that not even Mittitander had ever seen before, and he'd been a professional burglar, from a family of expert thieves, before joining the program. In his opinion, an overnight break-in was far too risky. Better to postpone the incursion until Monday morning, when alarms would be turned off.

Gran's Pot o' Gold opened for business at 9:00 a.m. sharp. The man who walked through the door ten seconds after that had a weathered face and callused hands, both reddened by the cold. His hair and beard were untrimmed, and he wore a fleece-lined green and amber plaid flannel shirt in place of a winter jacket. Shred slipped into this role easily. It was one he'd played many times in the past.

"Are you buying or selling?" The same chirpy-voiced girl was standing behind the counter.

"Neither," he rumbled. "Get the manager out here."

"Are you lodging a complaint, sir?" she asked.

"No. I just need to talk to the manager about a private matter," he explained patiently.

"O-o-kay. Wait here and I'll get him."

A moment later, the man with the sculpted moustache was standing behind the counter, wearing an expectant expression. Meanwhile, out on the street, a shapeshifted Polley was monitoring the scene through the storefront window while pretending to be waiting for a bus. She said something into her phone. Mittitander, now in the form of a grizzled old homeless man, had been pretending to pick through the dumpster in the alley behind the pawn shop, waiting for Polley's signal before setting to work on the locked back door.

Shred positioned himself so that he could both converse with the pawnbroker and see what Polley was doing without having to turn his head.

"If I asked you to find something special, could you do it?"

"It would depend. Can you describe the object?"

"It's a necklace. It used to belong to my wife before she died. A really pretty multicoloured stone on a gold chain. She'd inherited it from her grandmother and wanted it to go to our daughter, but when I looked for the necklace among her things, it wasn't there. It was her favourite piece of jewellery. She wore it all the time. I suspect it was stolen, either during the funeral or shortly afterward, but I didn't report it to the police because it would have meant an investigation into the family, and things are strained enough already between me and my wife's relatives. You understand?"

The other being nodded sagely. "Indeed, I do. I gather you want me to search discreetly for a replacement necklace identical to the original, so that no one will need to know there was a theft. Do you have an image of the piece?"

Shred pulled out his phone and called up the photo he'd snapped earlier of the pendant he'd found in Bryant's pocket after executing him at the arena.

"Can you zoom in on the stone?"

Shred obliged.

The pawnbroker stared at the image for a moment. Then, looking distinctly troubled, he asked, "Do you mind telling me how your wife passed away?"

Polley hadn't moved, so Shred hemmed and hawed, playing for time. What was taking their master burglar so damn long back there?

Finally, Gershred replied, "A drunk driver ran a red light and T-boned our car. Lola had insisted on driving because I'd been drinking. If I'd been behind the wheel, we would probably both have survived the crash, but I wasn't. She was pronounced dead at the scene. There's been bad blood between me and her family ever since."

"I'm so sorry."

No, he wasn't. The look in his eyes actually spoke of relief. And that answered Vicky's question—this human definitely knew how the bloodstones were being obtained.

"That looks to me like a black opal, or maybe a dark opal. Opals are rare, and extremely valuable," said the pawnbroker. "I'm not surprised it was a family heirloom. Tell me, is there a time limit on this search?"

"Not really. Her death was sudden, and it's going to take a while to put everything in order. No one but me even knows that the piece is missing. How much would you charge me for the necklace, assuming you're able to find a replacement?"

He considered for a moment, then handed Shred a business card with an email address on it. "Send me a copy of that picture. I have a friend who's a gemologist. She can give me some idea of what a piece of jewellery like this would be worth, and based on her estimate I'll be able to quote you a price. At the moment, though, I honestly have no idea what it might be."

Polley was pocketing her phone, her conversation apparently over.

Finally!

"Is there a fee for the search?" Shred asked.

"No. There's no charge for that."

Of course there wasn't, because this human believed he wouldn't have to go looking for a replacement pendant—it would be coming to *him*.

"I'll need your name and phone number as well," the pawnbroker was saying.

Polley had already walked out of view. Shred scrawled his assumed name and the number of his cell phone on a piece of paper. With any luck at all, the killing would stop before a "replacement stone" was found and he wouldn't have to deal with this mustachioed man again.

Then, tossing a "Thank you" over his shoulder, Shred walked back out onto the street.

Less than an hour later, the Nash'terel were all sitting around Vicky and Barron's table again, comparing notes.

"What the hell were you doing in there?" Shred demanded. "It was supposed to be in and out. You find the package, you snap a picture of the destination address, you leave."

Mittitander huffed out a breath. "Supposed to be. Right. Well, it wasn't," he said, bristling. "That office was a sty. Papers piled up everywhere. Bags and boxes covering every horizontal surface. And where was the package? Inside a fucking *safe*. Any idea how hard it is to crack a safe while maintaining an electromagnetic shield around yourself to foil surveillance cameras? You should try it sometime. It damn near gave my brain a charley horse."

"I'm sorry," said Shred. "I didn't see a safe when I was there the first time."

"That's because it wasn't in plain sight," Mittitander grumped. "I had to dig for it. Fortunately, it was one of the older models, with dials and tumblers, or I'd still be there, trying to break into the thing."

And if he hadn't had a *dashkra* tracker to aid in his search, he might never have located it at all.

Mittitander reached into his pocket, pulled out a phone, and tossed it across the table to Polley.

She pulled up the photo he'd taken. "It's going to a post office box in Richmond Hill, Ontario," she announced. "That means someone will have to stake out the post office until the package is picked up, then follow it, hopefully to Montgomery's actual location."

"Don't look at *me*," said Barron. "All the graduates of my assassins' program are now members of the Guild, and the current cohort of trainees are babes in the woods."

"I've got an agent for you," Maury told them. "Pyotren is extremely reliable. He also lives just north of Richmond Hill and knows the area well. It's where he hunts."

"Get him on the phone, then," Barron decided, "and let's push this op forward."

Chapter Twenty-Two

Tuesday was spent regrouping. Bags were packed or repacked. Travel plans and plane reservations were made. Barron and Shred would be returning to Toronto on the first available commercial flight, to be ready to meet with the Guild. Maury would stay behind in Vancouver to keep Vicky company until her mate returned. Polley, Froman, and Mittitander had fulfilled their roles in the sting and would go back to the compound, taking the truck and most of the weapons with them.

Barron contacted Yanni at the training camp and ordered him to collect all the remaining *dashkra* from the trainees and staff members. When Polley arrived, she was to conceal it somewhere outside the compound, under surveillance, in case any Yeng with bloodstone trackers came sniffing around.

Late Tuesday afternoon, Maury received a text from Pyotren, informing him that "Pete" was in position outside the post office in Richmond Hill. Pyotren had chatted up the clerk inside. No package fitting Maury's description had yet been delivered to the P.O. box in question, but she promised to keep an eye out for it and let him know when it arrived.

That evening, Gershred placed a video call to the cottage, keeping his fingers crossed that all three of the people he needed to talk to would be home and available to chat.

Angie responded on the third ring. Even allowing for poor lighting, he thought her face looked a little drawn.

"Gershred!" she said with audible relief. "Hello! Is there some news?"

"News?" he echoed, puzzled.

"Someone from the compound was just here, confiscating our pendants. When I asked why, they wouldn't tell me, and I couldn't help thinking—"

The worst. Of course.

"It's nothing you need to be concerned about," he assured her. "There's an operation in progress, and for safety, Barron has ordered the facility cleared of all *dashkra* until further notice. In the meanwhile, I have to fly back to Ontario tomorrow, and I promised Travis I wouldn't leave without saying goodbye."

"Grandpa G?" said a familiar voice off-screen. A moment later, the youngster came into view, bending to look over Angie's shoulder.

She handed him the phone.

Travis was smiling. He looked almost as happy as he'd been after the quarter-final match at the hockey tournament. Shred felt a sudden pang of loss. This *au revoir* was going to be more of an *adieu* than he'd anticipated.

"Hey, Grandson, how are you doing?" Shred asked, forcing his lips to return the kid's smile.

At once, the floodgates opened. Apparently, a lot had happened lately, all of it exciting.

Travis and Leo had found each other and a new friend from town besides, a boy named Oscar. Coach Dagomir had taken all of them under his wing and was going to be running hockey clinics and practices on the pond outside of Middlevale. Town kids were welcome to join. Their parents had begun coming out to watch, and so had Travis's. Leo and his father were going to help Travis get his *hainbek* under control. He was learning to play chess. And did Grandpa G know that Ken could ice skate?

Travis stumbled over his words, unable to get them out quickly enough and in the right order. It seemed that Maury's plan was working like a charm, and their grandson was exactly where he ought to be.

"I'm glad to hear that you're settling in, kiddo. I'm sorry to have to say goodbye this way, but there simply isn't enough time for me to do it in person. I hope you understand."

"Sure. But when you're back home we'll still stay in touch, right, Grandpa?"

It was growing harder and harder to keep a smile on his face. "Absolutely! We can chat anytime you like. Now, if you don't mind, I just need a private word or two with your parents."

"No problem. I've got some homework to do before lights out. Bye, Grandpa G. Take care of yourself. Love you."

That did it. Gershred had to turn away and wipe his eyes.

When he turned back again, Ken's face was filling the screen.

"I know that look. You're going into battle again, and you're not sure you'll be coming back," Ken said soberly.

"We're hoping it doesn't come to that. We're trying to take down someone who's playing the Yeng and Nash'terel off against each other on this world. We're ready to fight in case things get violent, but our objective is to defuse the situation. A war between our races will only weaken both sides and make us easy prey for the emperor's assassins."

"You sound like Lawrence of Arabia, uniting the tribes to fight the Turks."

Shred paused. "I guess I do," he said thoughtfully.

Dinner for four at Vicky and Barron's that night was a subdued, almost solemn affair, consisting of medallions of veal on a bed of wild rice, served with spinach and strawberry salad on the side and dark chocolate mousse for dessert. There was essence to drink, of course, along with a medium dry white wine.

"Excellent meal, Vicky," Maury declared. "Thank you."

Smiling, she acknowledged the compliment with a gracious nod.

"You've been awfully quiet, Gordie," Barron remarked. "Something on your mind?"

"About the op," Shred began, frowning.

"Oh?"

"I'm wondering whether we're going about this the right way."

Vicky froze in the midst of clearing the table. "Isn't it a little late to be having second thoughts?" she said.

"I'm not pulling out, if that's what you're thinking," he assured them. "Just listen to what I have to say."

"All right, we're listening," said Barron, leaning back and folding his arms across his chest. "Talk."

Under the expectant stares of three pairs of eyes, Shred continued, "If our target has been purposely feeding the conflict on Earth between the Yeng and the Nash'terel for his own profit, what more fitting way would there be to take him down than for the two adversaries from RinYeng to join forces against him?"

Barron's chin was rising. "You want to bring the Yeng onside?

This flies in the face of wisdom as well as tradition, Gordie."

"Which is why it would be perfect strategy," Maury commented, nodding. "He would never see it coming."

Meanwhile, Vicky's face had gone pale. It was not a good sign.

"Vincaspera?" Shred ventured.

With a gem-hard glint in her eyes and lips pressed tightly together, she deposited the plates she'd gathered back onto the table. "After all the murdered children, all the Earthborn they've taken from us," she said in a dangerously soft voice, "you think we should just forgive and forget?"

Shred leaned forward and replied in matching tones, "No, I don't. Too much blood has been spilled for there ever to be a lasting peace between us. But I also don't think we should let the collector get away with manipulating us and the Yeng into destroying each other. What I'm suggesting we offer to both sides is a truce, a temporary arrangement just long enough to let us put the collector out of business. Then we can return the situation to normal."

"I get that you want to share intel with them," said Barron. "But how are we supposed to do that? Corner one on the street and order them to take us to their leader? If there's a reconstituted Yeng Council, it's way underground. The Yeng would sooner die than reveal its location to a Nash'terel."

When Shred didn't respond immediately, Barron continued, notes of alarm seeping into his voice, "You're not about to suggest that we go undercover, posing as Yeng to get an audience with their leaders, are you?"

"No," he replied at last. "It won't be necessary, because we don't actually need to speak to the Yeng Council. We just need to find one powerful Yeng who will hear us out and then relay our proposal to the rest of them.”

“And what about the Guild?” Vicky reminded them. “They won’t look kindly on you making an independent deal with our sworn enemy.”

He threw her a wounded look. “Of course, they won’t. That’s why we need to talk to Monicandra first. But not until Montgomery’s parcel has arrived at his P.O. box,” he added. “His street address will be the key that gets us through the door of the Riftgate Club.”

The heat lords had reservations for a 10:00 a.m. flight to Toronto. After a light breakfast together, Barron and Shred tossed their bags into the back of the truck. Then Vicky and Maury drove them to the airport.

While they were waiting to board, Shred received a text message from Maury:

Pete reports package arrived at PO. Not picked up yet. Stay tuned.

“So, we might have to kill some time in Toronto,” Barron said, settling back in his seat with a sigh.

Or someone... Shred kept that thought to himself. There were humans around.

Instead, he reminded Barron, “It’s a five-hour flight. A lot can change while we’re in the air.”

The other Nash’terel had traded his beloved camo for solid olive drab and was clad in fatigues and a short, well-insulated jacket. Shred’s winter coat was longer, making it an armful to carry. Technically, neither heat lord had need of protection against the weather, but it was February, the coldest month of the year in Canada, and appearances mattered when one wished to pass unnoticed by humans.

"One more thing has occurred to me," Shred said, leaning in and lowering his voice. "We should interrogate Glen Partridge."

Barron glanced around, then leaned in as well. "To find out whether he's Pritchard? Or to find out whether he's Yeng?"

"Both, and to learn just how involved he is with Montgomery's cash-for-bloodstone business."

Barron gave him an appraising look. "As part of our current errand, you mean? Or are you suggesting we should go off on our own again, without telling the Guild?"

"It depends on the outcome of our meeting at the Riftgate Club."

Barron said nothing, just turned away and let out a sigh.

In fact, they both already knew what would happen once the Guild was read into the op. Monicandra would take it over, and whether or not she was receptive to the idea of a truce with the Yeng, neither Barron nor Shred would likely have much say in its running after that. They would need a plan B, and then plans C and D just in case.

Their flight landed in Toronto half an hour after sunset, local time. Since neither Nash'terel had any checked baggage to pick up from the carousels, they headed directly to the Arrivals area, and from there walked briskly to the exit doors leading to Long Term Parking.

When they reached his car, Shred was glad he'd paid extra to put it in a covered spot. There had been a couple of snow storms during his absence. The owners of the vehicles in the open-air lot would have a good deal of clearing and window-scraping to do before they could get on the road. A pair of heat lords would have made quick work of that, of course, provided there was no one around to see them do it. But this way was better. He and Barron were able to stow their travel bags on the back seat and set off immediately for the highway, without raising questions in any Yeng or human minds.

As he was merging with traffic on the 401 eastbound, Shred thought to ask his passenger, "Do you need to hunt before we check in at the motel?"

"Nah, I'm good." Barron shifted in his seat. "I won't need an essence top-up for another…" He frowned. "I don't know how long. I've been drinking the pure stuff from Middlevale on a regular basis, so it's been a while since I've felt the thirst. I guess we'll have to see."

Shred fell silent, sifting his mind for the last time he'd felt the urge to seek out prey, and came up with a memory: the battle itch, his first night in Vancouver. But that had been more of a restlessness than a thirst for essence. Since then, he'd felt nothing, not even around Angie.

Hmm. *That* was strange. Middlevalers practically exuded essence into the air. An unspoken invitation to feed, it hung around them like a mist, arousing the thirst of any Yeng and Nash'terel who happened to be nearby. That was what had prompted the incident at the pizza joint the previous week. Maury and Shred had felt the effect as well, quite strongly, the first time Bilyash had introduced them to Angie and every time they'd been around her after that, up to and including their visit out west ten years earlier. And now Shred was somehow immune to it?

Setting that puzzle on the back burners for the time being, he focused his attention on the highway traffic.

Gershred drove east to the Don Valley Parkway, then north to Steeles Avenue, where a three-storey motor hotel sat surrounded by ethnic restaurants. Korean, Indian, Mexican—whatever nationality visitors were in the mood for. While they were checking in, his phone chimed. A text message had arrived from Maury, consisting of a street address in Richmond Hill, followed on a new line by *Good luck*.

They had Montgomery's location.

Chapter Twenty-Three

The entrance to the Riftgate Club—formerly home to the Council of the First Yeng and now the headquarters of the Nash'terel Assassins' Guild—was an unmarked metal door situated near the end of an alleyway between two storefronts on an older block of College Street in Toronto. The surveillance camera directed at the doorway had been installed by the Guild, to provide an early warning of intruders.

This wasn't the original location of the Club. Since the purge that had replaced the entire Council with shapeshifted Nash'terel some sixteen years earlier, the Riftgate Club had become mobile. Its purpose was now more narrowly defined than before, making the definition of an intruder much broader and more flexible.

"Charming spot," Barron murmured dryly as they turned down the alley toward the metal slab of door. "Lots of ambience."

"Get ready to demonstrate your *hainbek*," Shred advised him. "There are security measures in place."

Bracing himself with a lungful of air, Gershred hauled the outer door open. Up a flight of stairs sat a second door, this one a little fancier and made of wood. There was also a second surveillance eye peering down from a corner. Visitors were few, but all were required at this point to prove that they were Nash'terel. One after the other, Barron and Shred identified themselves by producing heat bombs in the air, in view of the lens.

A couple of seconds later, they heard the *snick* of a latch unfastening. With a confirming nod to his companion, Shred led the way inside.

Back on RinYeng, outsiders who entered the valley of the Nash'terel in search of bloodstone disappeared, never to be seen or heard from again. On Earth, with its hyper-vigilant media systems and doggedly inquisitive law enforcement agencies, the Guild had been forced to adopt more subtle and creative methods of discouraging unwanted visitors.

On his previous visit, Shred had stepped through the doorway into what looked like the rather shabbily furnished anteroom of a casting office, complete with a gum-chewing, self-absorbed receptionist.

This time, the small room behind the wooden door resembled the cashier's desk and waiting area of an automotive repair shop. The guard on duty appeared to be a short, stout male wearing a stained grey uniform with a logo stitched to one side of its zipper closure and his name (Bert) embroidered on the other side. He had grease under his fingernails and even more of it in his hair.

"Are you dropping off or picking up?" he barked.

"They're kidding, right?" Barron said to Shred.

"Afraid not." To the guard, he said, "We're here to see Monicandra."

"What's the make, model, and year of your car?" the guard demanded.

Shred leaned across the desk toward him. "I see you've enhanced your security with a password since the last time I was here. That's nice. Now, assume that we don't give a damn and pass us through. We have important information that your boss is going to want to hear."

"And I see your manners haven't improved much since the last time we spoke, Gershred," said the guard, this time in Monicandra's voice. "Don't look so surprised. We rotate sentry duty, and it's my turn to take a shift. Now, pull up a couple of chairs and brief me."

Barron and Shred exchanged disbelieving looks. Then they complied.

"Is that important enough to put before the Guild?" Barron asked when they'd finished updating her.

"If it's all true, then yes. Let me make sure I understand this. You're telling me that the *dashkra* collector may be purposely provoking a Yeng-Nash'terel war in order to make a financial killing?"

"That's our strong suspicion, based on what our sting has uncovered," Shred confirmed. "The collector could be a single Yeng or a committee of them, all hiding in plain sight. Or we could be looking for a Yeng and a human, working together."

She stiffened. "It's highly unlikely that a human would survive such an arrangement."

"Not once it concluded, no," he agreed. "But this is ongoing and appears to be picking up momentum. The Yeng might not be the brightest bunch, but they wouldn't murder a dupe who could still be useful."

"Well, you're right about one thing," she said grimly. "Whatever the collector's motive might be, we definitely need to put a stop to any further trafficking in *dashkra*, and the supplier of all the detection devices is a good place to start. His name is Eugene Montgomery, you said. And you have his location?"

"We know where the package went that was addressed to him, and we believe he can be squeezed for information that will lead us in the right direction," Barron replied. "For obvious reasons, we would prefer to let the Guild take point for that. And then there's Glen Partridge."

"Uh-huh. Apart from the similarity of their names, what reason do you have to suspect he might be Pritchard?"

"Several, actually," Shred told her. "First, Pritchard was an inventor, and Partridge was in charge of research and development before his promotion to CEO. Second, Montgomery has to be conducting his business with Partridge's blessing, since he's given out Eyes on the World's toll free phone number to all the Yeng hunters. Third, the *dashkra* tracker that Montgomery is handing out to hunters was created by Pritchard, and Partridge stands to profit from whatever benefit it brings the company. Glen Partridge may not personally be at the centre of Montgomery's little enterprise, but I have a hunch that we'll find him damn close to it."

"And by 'we' you mean...?"

"Barron and me. It makes sense. If you're pulling sentry duty, it means the Guild is stretched thin. How many operatives do you currently have available?"

"You've made your point," she grumbled. "Move along."

"If we time the two visits so that we're interrogating him while you're simultaneously grilling Montgomery," he persisted, "neither one of them will have a chance to find out about the other and disappear. Naturally, we would share any gathered intel with the Guild, for possible future action."

"Problem is," Barron said with a sigh, "even once we've taken Montgomery out of the picture, it will be a while before the Yeng realize the 'unlimited offer' is no longer on the table. By the time that information filters down, a lot more of our people will have come under attack, and many of them could die."

"Unless, of course, all the Nash'terel stop wearing *dashkra*," Shred chimed in.

She blew out an impatient breath. "You're back to that? Be realistic, Gershred. If a families-wide warning is issued, two things are bound to happen. First, none of them will give up their bloodstone. And second, they'll all go to ground, believing that will protect them. If they do, it may be decades before we're able to locate them again."

"But a much shorter time before the Yeng find them, using whatever number of tracking devices are already in circulation," Shred pointed out, adding angrily, "So you're telling us we're screwed? Nothing can be done?"

Barron made his expression stern. "We formed the Guild specifically to prevent something like this from happening," he reminded her. "There has to be a way to get the word out, if not to the Nash'terel, then to the Yeng."

The grease monkey's eyes widened. It was disturbing to watch—he looked as though he'd just swallowed a bug—but only for a second.

"To the Yeng," she repeated slowly. "What a lovely idea! I don't suppose you have any of them on speed dial?"

"*We* don't," said Barron, "but I'm betting the Guild knows how to contact them. I trained you all, remember? Unless you've forgotten the parameters of the operation that put you in your current positions...?"

"Of course, we haven't. As per your instructions, we've been tracking the family members and close associates of all the First Yeng we purged, just in case one of them became suspicious and started digging. I can tell you that of the ten Earthborn Yeng who have attained the same level of wealth and power as their forebears, three have remained in the Greater Toronto Area. One of these owns a multi-media network and is well-positioned to 'get the word out', as you put it."

"Why do I sense a 'but' coming?"

Now the grease monkey was scowling. "Because first we would have to convince them that we're not the ones playing them. Given our past history with the Yeng, that's going to be damn near impossible to do."

"Not if we read that individual in and let them eavesdrop on Montgomery's interrogation. They would hear the damning words from his own mouth." Barron's steady gaze dared her to find fault with this plan.

As she leaned over the counter, digesting what he'd said, a wicked grin made its way across Monicandra's face. Shred decided he would never let anyone who smiled like that get under the hood of his car, ever.

"You know, I believe that might actually work," she said.

"How quickly can you access this Yeng?" Shred wanted to know. "We've had a team staking out Montgomery's residence for a couple of days already."

"One step at a time, Gershred," she said. "First I have to convene a quorum of the Guild to get the op sanctioned. Then I'll approach the Yeng media mogul. *Then* we pay a visit to Mr.

Eugene Montgomery. In the meanwhile, I am provisionally greenlighting the second part of your plan. While you wait for my signal to proceed, I suggest you spend your time figuring out the best way to get to Glen Partridge."

The hotel had free Wi-Fi, but it was a forty-five minute drive north of the downtown core, and Monicandra's parting advice had left Shred with a nameless sense of urgency. So, he and Barron walked along College Street instead. A couple of blocks from the Club, they found a café that would provide them a password in exchange for the purchase of a snack and a beverage each. With lattés and muffins in hand, they settled in side by side at a table in the most obscure corner of the shop. Then they logged on and began browsing the net for anything relating to Glen Partridge.

It didn't take them long to arrive at a couple of conclusions. First, if they wanted to delve into the CEO of Eyes on the World, they needed better hacking skills. The security around this being's personal information was tighter than Queen Victoria's corset.

Second, their best chance of surprising him was to show up unannounced at his office.

"And follow him home?" Barron added.

Gershred shook his head. "He'll be taking precautions. Think about it. If he's a Yeng, he's a shapeshifter. He could leave the building looking like Chuck from the mailroom and walk right past us."

"So, we'll have to catch him inside while he's still in his own shape. That raises a thorny question: Eyes on the World specializes in cutting edge security technology, and they're sure to have a lot of it installed around the executive suite at the company's head office. What's your brilliant plan for foiling all those measures and countermeasures?"

"It's simple," Gershred said with a grin. "We persuade Partridge to invite us into his sanctum for a very private meeting."

"Simple for you, maybe," Barron grumped.

"It's a carrot and stick manoeuvre. The dangling carrot is a *dashkra* pendant. If Partridge is the collector, not only will he want to get his hands on it, he'll also be very curious to find out how a couple of Yeng hunters—that would be us—managed to identify him. I'm betting this is not something he'll want to discuss with others present."

"And the stick? Ah!" Barron chuckled. "It's our *hainbeka*. Forget I asked."

Monicandra inspected her face in the visor-mounted mirror and gave her short, ash blonde hair a final finger-comb before stepping out of the car.

Justine Stoneman was coming home.

Monicandra had been one of fifteen Nash'terel assassins executing the operation nicknamed "The Purge", and the media baroness, a member of the Council of the First Yeng, had been her assigned target. Monicandra had insinuated herself into the Stoneman household wearing one face, and into Stoneman's head office wearing another. She had spent weeks observing, researching, and studying her as she conducted her life. She had watched Justine access her computer and thus learned the necessary passwords. Watched her open her safes and thus learned their combinations. Watched her arm and disarm her security system and thus learned its codes.

She had memorized how the target interacted with family, friends, employees, and servants. She had seen and memorized the target's true Yeng form.

In fact, she had practised assuming all the target's customary shapes and performing all her activities, save for one—the despicable way she treated her only child, a daughter. It wasn't part of her mission to befriend the girl, but Monicandra had done it anyway. The abuse, she'd decided, would not continue once Justine was gone. Cruelty to offspring was a line Monicandra refused to cross.

She had also learned when and how her target hunted, and what was preferred as prey.

One night, Justine had gone out to feed, and had not come back home. Instead, Monicandra had taken her place. Stepped into her life. Changed all the passwords and combinations and codes. And adopted her daughter.

When all fifteen Nash'terel assassins had eliminated and replaced their targets, taking possession of the information stored in their homes and at the Riftgate Club, the Council of the First had ceased to exist, except in name.

Over the next ten years, phase two had erased even that.

One by one, the members of this "shadow Council" had retired to distant shores and/or died (in a variety of carefully choreographed but natural-seeming ways), leaving their vacant seats to be filled, one by one, by the fifteen assassins, once more in shapes of their own choosing. By unanimous vote—and behind closed doors—the Council had then formally voted to disband, and had reconstituted itself as the Guild.

It had been five years since Monicandra had answered to the name Justine Stoneman. Five years since she'd last set foot inside the century-old house in Rosedale. Six bedrooms, a library, a front parlour, a downstairs apartment for the live-in help, all contained within a two-storey brick and fieldstone edifice sitting on a park-like, landscaped lot. When first built, it had been one of many prestigious residences located in a precinct of wealth and privilege. Now, despite being well cared for, the exterior of the house was aging. It bore its scars and stains with great dignity, as would a finely-wrought bone china tea service, or a set of heirloom embroidered linen napkins.

Monicandra tried her key in the lock. Not surprisingly, it no longer turned. She rang the doorbell.

The servant who opened the door recognized her immediately. He relieved her of her winter coat and welcomed her home, then waited for "Mum" to tell him she required nothing further before respectfully leaving her alone in the foyer.

As Monicandra entered the library, Laetitia Stoneman looked up from the document she'd been perusing. She removed her reading glasses and placed them beside it on the desk. Then she pressed herself backward into her chair and levelled cool grey eyes at this new arrival.

"You finally decided to pay me a visit. How nice," she said, wearing a faint smile. "I know you've been tracking me."

"Only out of curiosity. Like any mother, I'm interested in what you've been up to."

"But not interested enough to stick around and watch."

"We both know why I had to disappear, Tisha. I shouldn't even be here now."

"And yet, here you are. Because you found out that I've expanded my media holdings to include security and surveillance technology? Are you afraid I might have the means to keep track of *you*?"

"Would you really do that?"

The other woman's expression grew sober. "No. I forgave you your sins long ago. My biological mother was a monster. I don't know how you got rid of her, and I don't want to know, either. What I do know is that you were a better parent to me while impersonating her than she'd ever been. You cried tears when you had to leave me. I've never forgotten that." A pause. Then, narrowing her eyes, she said, "Answer my question, Mother. Why *are* you here, instead of on your island retreat? Bora Bora, is it? Or Roratonga?"

"It's neither. How much do you know about Eyes on the World Incorporated?"

"Quite a bit, in fact, since I now own thirty percent of the company. That's not common knowledge, by the way, so I'd appreciate it if you kept it to yourself."

"You have interest in two competing security firms? That's brilliant." *...and typically Yeng,* she added privately. When it came to business, Tisha really was her mother's daughter.

"Thank you. Are you looking for information about Eyes on the World?"

"Actually, I already know more than I care to about certain individuals in the company. That's why I've come here, to ask for your help in taking one of them down."

A speculative gleam ignited behind Laetitia's eyes. "You have a story for me?"

"An exclusive."

"And would it be about Glen Partridge, by any chance?" she said softly.

"Perhaps later, although he is on our radar. My primary target right now is Eugene Montgomery, the VP of Sales."

"Uh-huh." She nodded sagely. "I've suspected for some time

that Partridge and his protégé might be involved in something illegal. Why don't you have a seat, Mother, and bring me up to speed?"

Monicandra eased herself onto the dark green leather-upholstered guest chair in front of the desk and asked, "How would you like to have concrete evidence of Montgomery's malfeasance to show your fellow members of the reconstituted Yeng Council?"

"It depends. What makes you believe the Council would take the slightest bit of interest in it? Not that I would ever admit to a Nash'terel that such an organization exists, of course."

Of course.

Monicandra filled her lungs and replied, "We have reason to believe that Montgomery is up to his neck in a scheme to ignite open warfare between the Yeng and the Nash'terel on Earth, in order to increase Eyes on the World's bottom line. If we're right, he's put something in motion that can't be stopped simply by eliminating him. I plan to interrogate him to determine whether our theory is correct."

"And assuming it is, what would be the concrete evidence?"

"Closed circuit video of the interrogation, witnessed live by you so that you can authenticate the recording when it's presented to the Yeng Council..." She paused for a beat, then added with fingers mentally crossed, "...along with a proposal that the Yeng and Nash'terel on this planet form a temporary alliance to thwart his intentions."

The grey eyes were sparkling now, possibly with amusement. Monicandra couldn't tell.

"I doubt whether they'll go for it, Mother, but *I'm* certainly intrigued by the idea. What do you need from me?"

"Up-to-date spying and recording technology. We have people with the expertise to set it up. None of yours would have to be involved in the interrogation. You would be the only witness. And before you protest that your word alone might not be sufficient, you should know that I, at least, am aware of how much clout you personally wield in the Yeng community."

Laetitia leaned forward across her desk. "All right, then, draw up a list and you'll have it, on one condition. If the interview pans out, I get to broadcast it as an exposé. It will send our ratings through the roof."

The final destination of the parcel Pyotren had been tracking was a smallish, semi-detached bungalow on a quiet crescent. A bit of digging in public records had revealed that it was currently being rented by one E. Montgomery. That had been the signature on the lease, at any rate. According to the owner, everything had been done online, including a virtual tour of the premises and the digital signature.

Sure, Monicandra mused darkly. *Nothing suspicious or incriminating about that, right?*

Her partner on the mission, Daniell, was a tech specialist. Tisha had been promised a front row seat to the interview and had come along as well. All three of them had assumed nondescript male shapes, clad in Eyes on the World service uniforms. Before they entered the house, Daniell disconnected the alarm system. Then Monicandra texted Gershred to let him know the operation had launched, and Daniell positioned the recording gear around the room they'd selected for the interrogation. A chair was also selected and positioned, and outfitted with restraints.

After that, they simply had to wait for Montgomery (or his

designate) to come pick up his parcels. There were a number of them—small padded envelopes sitting in a cardboard box in the front hall closet. Each one represented a dead Nash'terel, most likely a child. Just looking at them pulled the taste of bile up the back of Monicandra's throat.

Interrogating this target wasn't going to be easy. Her fangs were already itching.

Meanwhile, Tisha had been wandering around the house. "I found a safe," she called from a back room. "After we're done with whoever walks through the door, we should crack it open. There may be evidence inside."

"You know," said Daniell, "Montgomery may be paying the rent on this place, but nobody's living here. All the cupboards are bare. There isn't even a toothbrush in the washroom."

And yet there was a safe. And a box full of pendants—no, of *packages*—in the front closet. This place was smelling more and more like a decoy. Or even a trap.

The *dashkra* detector was back at the Riftgate Club. However, there was another way to discover what was inside those envelopes. Monicandra opened the closet and slid the carton out into the front hall.

"I've got a bad feeling about this," she told Daniell. "Pull out your knife and let's find out if I'm right."

Chapter Twenty-Four

The head office of Eyes on the World took up the top three floors of a modern, medium-rise tower at one end of a large strip plaza on Dufferin Street. Barron and Shred had been sitting in their car in the parking lot for a little over two hours already, waiting to hear from Monicandra.

When at last the text arrived, it was brief and to the point: *green light*

"They've arrived at Montgomery's receiving address," said Shred. "Time for us to go inside as well."

As they walked toward the double glass doors at the main entrance of the building, Shred patted his pants pocket and felt the reassuring hardness of the *dashkra* pendant that Pyotren had dropped off to them earlier. Their *hainbeka* were the only weapons they'd brought with them today. With luck, the two Nash'terel would be able to achieve their goal and then withdraw without having to deploy them.

The blue-uniformed security guard in the lobby scanned them with practised thoroughness as they approached the reception desk. Behind it sat another guard, this one wearing an expectant smile.

Shred smiled back at him. "We're here to visit Mr. Partridge. He's the CEO of—"

"We know. Do you have an appointment, sir?"

"No, but he'll want to speak with us. Tell him Mr. Pritchard and Mr. Dashkra would appreciate a few minutes of his time."

The receptionist nodded and picked up the phone. After a brief, muttered conversation, he hung up and instructed them, "Take elevator number five to the top floor. You'll be met and escorted to Mr. Partridge's office."

Met by what, Shred couldn't help wondering, his warrior instincts on high alert as he stepped into the elevator car. Barron was thinking the same thing. No words were exchanged. However, in unison, the two Nash'terel each put a hand behind their back and began gathering energy for a heat bomb, just in case.

By the time the door slid open once more, the air temperature in the car had dropped several degrees Celsius.

In the hallway in front of them stood a youngish-looking man in a well-tailored grey business suit. "Mr. Pritchard? Mr. Dashkra?" he said in a lightly accented tenor voice. "I am Rosario, Mr. Partridge's executive assistant. This way, please."

They released the heat from their hands and followed him along the corridor, glancing backward by turns to ensure that no one could surprise them from the rear.

The wall at the end of the hall was transparent. Beside its door stood a heavy-set man wearing the same blue uniform as the two guards in the foyer of the building. He ran a critical eye over them as they filed past him into an anteroom furnished with armchairs and tall potted plants. Shred recognized the décor. Add a registration desk and it could have been the lobby of a five-star hotel.

"That's kind of old school security, isn't it?" Barron muttered to him. "Not what I'd expect from an outfit like Eyes on the World."

Their escort had excellent hearing. "That's because it is the building's security, not ours," he replied. "Company security is entirely technological and virtually invisible. You have already been scanned twice and found to be unarmed, with no police record or legal history. Trust me, gentlemen, if we had any reason to suspect either one of you posed a threat, you would not have been permitted to exit the elevator."

Not a threat, were they? Well, technology wasn't everything, Shred thought, smiling to himself.

Rosario crossed to a wide stainless steel door. He swung it open, stepped over the threshold, and said something to the occupant of the inner office.

"Thank you, Rosario," said an unseen male's voice. "This will be a private meeting, so I'm taking the room offline. Hold my calls until I tell you otherwise."

"Yes, sir." He bowed from the shoulders, then returned through the doorway. "You can go in now," he announced.

Partridge's sanctum was exactly what Shred had expected from the head of a company on the cutting edge. Nostalgia had no place here. Looking around, he saw plenty of clean, straight lines, an abundance of glass and metal, and the latest in space-age furniture design. Presiding over this high-tech fiefdom from behind a desk with a kidney-shaped smoked glass top was a gnome of a man with a sparse crop of hair and eyes bright as freshly minted coins.

Shred had seen Partridge's image on the company web site. Either it had been doctored for public consumption or the man in front of them was a second-rate Yeng imposter.

"For now, nothing that happens here will be monitored or recorded, so we can speak freely," he said in a voice that tweaked something at the back of Gershred's mind. "Which one of you claims to be Pritchard?"

"That would be me," said Shred. "Tell me, did you replace Partridge before his promotion to CEO, or after it?"

"Did you come here to talk, or just to waste my time?" he retorted.

Shred pulled the pendant out of his pocket and lowered it by its chain onto the desk top. The bloodstone no longer resembled a black opal. After several weeks, its colours had faded to pastel, as the stone slowly returned to its original milky white appearance. Keeping his voice under tight control, he said, "We came here to get some straight answers to direct questions. Are you the one who's been collecting these?"

The gnome stiffened in his chair. "What if I am?"

"We want to know why," Barron cut in, stepping forward. "Why are you trying to wipe out the Nash'terel?"

Now he was looking puzzled. "I'm not. The Yeng are, and have been for a long while."

"You're wrong. The Yeng and the Nash'terel were never friends, and at one time we were bitter enemies, but that didn't last. Until recently we had an unspoken truce that most of us kept," Shred told him. "We left them alone and they left us alone, and whenever assassins came through the rift, the Nash'terel hunted them down and killed them without interference from the Yeng on this side. Then you came along. You're paying Yeng to kill Nash'terel and steal their pendants, stirring up conflict that will weaken both our peoples and make us easy prey for the next wave of assassins from

RinYeng. Why? Is this strictly business for you? The almighty bottom line?"

"I had no other choice," Partridge said hotly. "I wanted to work with the Nash'terel, but they were already in thrall to the *krekh* and refused to give up their masters. Stoking the Yengs' underlying animus toward the Nash'terel was a poor alternative, but it was the only one available to me, so I took it. And this is not about business. It's about life and death. The scourge must be stopped before it overtakes another world."

"Wait a minute. What the hell is the *krekh*?" said Barron.

Partridge pointed to the pendant. "That creature," he replied, his lip curling with disgust. "That's the *krekh*. It's a colony consisting of millions of organisms. Break it apart and they scatter, becoming a parasitic infestation that takes control of every living entity it encounters. It poisons planets and destroys civilizations."

"And you believe the Nash'terel are... in *thrall* to it?" Shred said softly. "But not the Yeng. Why?"

"The Nash'terel protect the *krekh*. They nourish it. They cherish it. They wear it on their bodies and show it to one another like some badge of belonging. They freed the parasite to wreak havoc on the population of their home world. Then they brought it here with them so it could enslave another race of beings."

"Except it hasn't. The humans are unaffected by *dashkra*," Barron pointed out.

"So far," Partridge corrected him. "Eventually, they will succumb to it. And that is precisely why the *krekh* must be removed from this world, even if I'm forced to do it one pendant at a time."

Shred placed both hands on the desk top and leaned forward to add in menacing tones, "And one dead Nash'terel at a time?"

Partridge met his diamond-hard gaze and leaned forward as well. "They are a lost race, beyond saving," he said, enunciating sharply. "Once all its protectors have been eliminated, I'll find the rest of the *krekh* and take it away."

Before he could respond to this, Shred felt a restraining touch on his arm.

"Take it away?" said Barron. "Why not just destroy it here on Earth?"

"That's not possible. I've tried."

"I sincerely doubt that, Pritchard—or whatever your name really is—or you would know how it reacts to ultraviolet light and the electrical energy stored in human technology."

Partridge fell back against his chair. "And how would *you* know that?" he wondered aloud. "Unless..." Comprehension dawning in his eyes, he swallowed hard and said, "You're not Yeng. You're Nash'terel. Are you here for revenge?"

He was reaching slowly toward a keypad built into the rounded corner of his desk top.

"I wouldn't advise that," Barron warned, extending his hand palm up to show him the heat bomb hovering just above it.

Reluctantly, Partridge slid his own hand back to the centre of his desk.

"We didn't come here to kill you," said Shred, standing upright again. "We came to get answers to our questions, and to share with you what we'd found out about the bloodstone, but now I think what you really need is a history lesson.

"Despite what the Yeng might have told you about us, the Nash'terel didn't come through the rift voluntarily. We were driven through it when the Yeng emperor launched a genocide against us. We understood at that point how dangerous the bloodstone dust was, so we brought it with us not to keep the *dashkra* safe, but to protect others from its effects.

"We wear pieces of it as a symbol, that much is true. But the rest has been hidden away so that it can't turn anyone else into what it's made of us. Bottom line is, you're dead wrong about us, Pritchard. The Nash'terel are not *in thrall* to anything or anyone, and we're certainly not beyond saving."

The imp-like features twisted with indignation. "You think not? The changes to your genome are irreversible. You thirst for blood to nourish your body and are forced to steal living energy to feed the parasite inside you. Once it finds a host, not only is that being's fate sealed, but also the fate of their biological offspring. This I know with certainty. I was an explorer. I visited worlds where the *krekh* had gained a foothold. I saw the devastation it had caused. So trust me when I tell you that your race is doomed."

Shred shook his head. "Doomed, perhaps, but not dying, not if we have anything to say about it, and not for a good long while." Leaning forward on his hands once more, he fixed Partridge with a stern gaze and added, "And now I have another question for you: what kind of precautions have you been taking with the pendants that the Yeng have been sending you? Those polished pieces of *dashkra* may not give off dust, but they're alive and they thirst for blood *and* essence. This *I* know with certainty. Have you been as careful in your handling of them as we've been for the past fifteen or sixteen centuries on this world?"

Partridge's voice acquired an admonishing note as he replied, "Please! Give me some credit. I've been taking every precaution."

"Really! And has Montgomery?" Barron chimed in.

A glint came into the gnome's eyes then that told Shred whatever answer he heard would be a lie.

"Of course! He knows as well as I do how dangerous they can be."

"And he receives a handsome bonus for each one he forwards to you. Right?" said Shred.

The glint increased in brightness. "He is well rewarded, yes."

Shred and Barron shared a knowing look. They'd been dealing with humans for far too long not to realize what Pritchard's game had to be.

"You must have deep pockets," Barron remarked. "That is where Montgomery's bonus has been coming from, right? Or have you been paying him out of company funds, now that you're the CEO?"

"You have, haven't you?" Shred cut in. "And piggybacking a tidy extra payday for yourself onto it."

"Not for myself," he declared, spitting each word as though he wished it were a poisoned dart. "For the research. For the manufacture of the detectors. A project like mine needs a constant flow of revenue."

"Then why involve Montgomery at all?" Barron demanded. "Why not cut out the middle man and keep all the money for yourself?"

All at once the glint was gone, and Pritchard's lips were a tight, straight line. In that moment, the final puzzle piece fell into place in Shred's mind.

"There's never been a middle man," he murmured. "I knew I'd heard your voice before. You're the one I spoke to on the phone. Montgomery's not a front—he's a patsy. I'll bet he knows nothing about any of this."

The look on Pritchard's face confirmed everything Shred had just surmised.

"You're not a Yeng, and you look nothing like the body that was found at the safe house. Are you a shapeshifter?" Barron demanded.

"No. I used someone else's face in all my online dealings with your Guild, and a go-between for in-person meetings."

"So, you led them to believe the go-between was you, then killed him in order to fake your death."

"*Fuck*, no! I'm not a murderer!"

"That's a matter for some debate where I come from," Barron informed him in a voice fairly dripping with menace.

Shred smiled inwardly. "Why don't we show him where you come from?" he suggested. "Do you think Vicky would like to meet him?"

Barron's eyes widened. "I think... it would give her great pleasure to offer him her hospitality."

"Okay, here is the way it has to go," Shred said, addressing Partridge. "We know how to destroy *dashkra* and will gladly demonstrate it for you—"

"You're bluffing. If the Nash'terel knew that, they would have done it by now."

"I didn't say *all* the Nash'terel, I said *we* know how to do it. If you'd spent more time negotiating with the Guild, you would have learned how insular the various families are. Now, pay attention, Pritchard, because we're going to solve this problem to everyone's benefit."

...except yours.

"What's the catch?"

"You need to come with us to Vancouver," Shred told him.

"And if I refuse, what are you going to do? Drag me out of the building?"

Barron reached out swiftly and pressed the intercom button. In an excellent imitation of Pritchard's voice, he said, "Rosario, is Eugene Montgomery in his office right now?"

"He just returned from lunch, sir," came the response. "Do you need to speak with him?"

Fixing an inquiring gaze on Pritchard's rapidly blanching face, Barron mouthed the words, *Do we?*

The gnome's shoulders sagged in defeat. He shook his head.

"Not at this time," Barron replied, still in Pritchard's voice. "I have an emergency family matter to take care of. I'm not sure how long I'll be gone. Clear my calendar for the next ten business days, to be on the safe side."

"Very good, sir. Will you be travelling? I can book you a flight."

"That won't be necessary. I'll let you know if I need anything further."

"Yes, sir."

Click.

Pritchard swivelled his sullen stare from one Nash'terel face to the other. "What now?"

"Now we walk out of here together," said Shred. "You will accompany us to our car and get into the back seat, where you will buckle up and sit quietly while we drive you home to pack. After that, it's straight to the airport."

"And if I give you the slip at the airport and report my kidnapping to the police?" he challenged.

"You may not be a shapeshifter, but we are," Barron warned. "You won't know who to trust or avoid, and we will eventually find you. In the meanwhile, we will have told Eugene Montgomery about your plans for him, meaning that Eyes on the World will be looking for you as well, and not for a good reason."

"And don't even think about trying to take us out yourself," Shred added. "You may know the Yeng, but you clearly know nothing about the Nash'terel. Now, excuse me while I send a text."

"Cheer up, Pritchard," Barron told him. "You're going for an airplane ride."

Chapter Twenty-Five

efinitely not a Yeng, was Maury's first thought as he stood in Arrivals with Vicky, watching Barron and Shred escort a third being across the concourse toward them. *Not a self-respecting Yeng, anyway,* he amended, his gaze bouncing from the pointed chin to the button-bright eyes to the thinly distributed hair that rose to a peak at the top of this individual's head. Scaled down, he would have been a perfect addition to someone's garden. And yet, there was something very familiar about him.

Vicky had noticed it too. Maury heard her gasp and stage whisper, "I think that's Glen Partridge, unphotoshopped. What the hell are they doing, bringing him here?"

In fact, they were looking peculiarly self-satisfied, as though they'd won him in a contest.

"This is Mrs. Dashkra, my mate," said Barron, beginning the introductions. "She's the family emergency you just took personal leave to deal with. Darling," he added, turning to Vicky, "you've been saying how anxious you were to meet the collector...?"

Her eyes sprang wide and a predatory smile curved her lips. "So, you're the collector," she said in a honey-laden voice. "I have a lot of questions for you. Why don't we all go somewhere private so we can talk?"

Partridge shuddered visibly, his eyes filling with desperation. Maury recognized that look. The prey realized there was no escape, but was about to bolt anyway.

Then Shred's and Barron's hands landed on both of Partridge's shoulders at once, knocking the spirit right out of him. And so, flanked by Mr. and Mrs. Dashkra, the collector previously known as Pritchard let himself be shepherded out the exit to the parking lot.

Following close behind, Maury murmured to Shred, "You're certain he's the one who's been—?"

"So he says," came the reply.

"But you've got your doubts?"

Leaning in, Shred lowered his voice and replied, "Oh, Barron and I are both certain he's *a* collector. However, Eyes on the World is a multinational corporation with a dozen regional headquarters. Partridge may be the CEO of the company, with state of the art communications technology at his fingertips, but he's also just one being, in one head office, in one country, reachable by a single toll-free number. Meanwhile, we're being hunted all over the planet. What do *you* think?"

Maury muttered a curse under his breath. Shred was right: there was no way Partridge was working alone. "I think this snake has many heads, and we're going to have our work cut out for us to identify them and lop them all off. Did he tell you *why* they want the *dashkra*, at least?"

"Yes, and you're not going to believe it."

Vicky drove them to the building on Main Street, with Maury in the front passenger seat and Partridge behind them, sandwiched between Barron and Shred. He looked very small back there, small and hopeless and filled with dread. Vicky was enjoying this, Maury noted—each time she glanced in the rear view mirror, the sight of her "guest" on the verge of wetting his pants brought a satisfied smile to her lips.

Moving like a condemned prisoner on his way to the gallows, Partridge exited the vehicle and climbed the stairs to the third floor. He stared around him in puzzlement at being ushered into what appeared to be a rather ordinary (if spartanly furnished) apartment. Barron pushed him down onto one of the sofa cushions. Then Vicky offered him some tea and cookies.

The gnome's features composed and recomposed themselves as though he couldn't decide whether to be relieved or disappointed that all his earlier trepidation had been for nothing. In fact, it had been entirely justified. Anyone who knew what to look for could tell that Vicky was itching to sink her fangs into this prey.

"What?" she scolded him. "You don't like my hospitality? The tea is too hot? The cookies aren't your favourite kind? Or maybe you were expecting a torture chamber. An iron maiden, perhaps, or the rack? We're civilized beings, Mr. Partridge. This is plain orange pekoe tea, and those are store bought chocolate chip cook-ies, and all we want from you in return is some enlightening con-versation—and a promise to stop killing our children," she added, injecting a sinister note into her voice as she loomed over him.

Silence. As Maury watched, Partridge's whole body went rigid. His lips pressed tightly together, as though physically holding back information he'd rather not share.

Vicky shot Barron a significant glance. "He doesn't know, does he?"

"It never came up. Perhaps you should show him," her mate replied.

She walked to the middle of the living room and flipped up the corner of a green and grey area rug. "You see that stain on the floor? That's from the bleach we had to use to remove our daughter's blood from the surface of the wood. This is the very spot where she was savagely torn to pieces by a Yeng assassin. The Yeng are cowards, you see," she said, turning to rivet her guest to the sofa with a narrowing emerald gaze. "The odds are against them if they take on an adult who can defend against them, so they attack our Earthborn offspring instead. Every pendant you've received and paid for has been ripped from the neck of a murdered child."

Maury watched some of the colour drain from Partridge's face. His stubborn expression, however, did not change. "You can't blame me for the bad choices made by Yeng hunters."

"We can when your cash bounty is the reason they're hunting us in the first place," Shred pointed out, adding in a bitter voice, "not to mention the tracking device you invented that makes it so much easier for them to find us."

"You're responsible for this hunt," Barron grated. "And now, one way or another, you're going to cancel the bounty and end it."

"And what about *my* hunt?" Partridge reminded them. "You promised to show me how the *krekh* could be destroyed."

"The *krekh*?" Vicky echoed, pausing as she straightened the rug again.

"That's his word for *dashkra*," Barron replied. "Mr. Partridge here, formerly known to us as Pritchard, claims to be from another planet, one that was devastated by the bloodstone. Whether or not that's true, what he told us supports your theory about the mineral actually being a colony made up of billions of living organisms."

"Once the parasite gets into your blood, there's no saving you," Partridge declared with evangelical vehemence. "The infestation is total, claiming every part of your body. It's passed down from generation to generation, and it spreads like a disease each time you feed, dooming others to the same fate. I've seen it happen on many worlds, including RinYeng."

Vicky drew herself up, her eyes flashing dangerously. "You came here from RinYeng?" she said, deliberately enunciating each word. "Through the rift?"

"You mean the wormhole. No. I couldn't wait that long. I was getting nowhere with the emperor, so I followed the Nash'terel here in my ship, arriving about forty years ago."

He'd clearly missed the warning signs. Maury held his breath, watching for Vicky's reaction.

"Really! And how did you know where to come?" she demanded. "Who gave you the coordinates of this world?"

The pointed chin jutted defiantly. "I had a chart. I was an officer on an exploration vessel. One of the planets we discovered had been the home of an ancient race. They'd stored a wealth of information: star maps, diagrams, records of scientific experiments... and a chart of the wormhole system they'd set up. They'd been studying the evolution of life on other worlds. But evolution is a slow process—"

"—so they set up the rift to open just once every hundred years," Barron cut in. "Who are these people, Partridge? Can you contact them? Can they seal the rift?"

"You don't get it," the gnome snapped. "They can't help you. They can't help anyone anymore. They've been dead for centuries. Meanwhile, their wormholes have allowed the *krekh* to spread halfway across the galaxy, including to my home world, and yours. Wherever the parasite has gained a foothold, the infestation has spread to the entire population."

"Except here on Earth," Shred interjected quietly. "The Yeng and the Nash'terel have been feeding on the essence of humans for a thousand and a half years. In all that time, no human vampires have emerged. I've travelled the world, and from what I've seen, the entire human race appears to be immune to the blood sickness.

"So, I've been thinking—if the *krekh* are at a standstill on this world, confined to the Yeng and the Nash'terel, we've got it cornered. You told us back at your office that you're on a mission to rid Earth of the *krekh*. What if there were a way to kill the parasite without killing the host?" he said slowly.

Partridge frowned, clearly intrigued. "Without killing the host? How?"

"Before flying out here a few weeks ago, I unwittingly drank essence from a human who had been poisoned. I experienced only a few hours of discomfort, but the human I'd fed upon died. Human physiology may be compatible with ours in some ways, but it's different in others. What if the same can be said of our physiology and the *krekh*'s? What if there's something that kills them but only makes us ill, and all we have to do is find it?"

"We already know about two things that might fit that description," Barron said. "We just need to determine whether they're lethal."

Vicky fetched the cardboard box and opened it to show Partridge the hardened mass of bloodstone that had once been pendants on chains.

"We know that *dashkra* will burrow into the ground to escape the ultraviolet radiation from Earth's sun," she told him. Indicating the contents of the box, she continued, "This is what happens when an active GPS chip is implanted into the centre of a pendant. Originally, this was fifteen of them."

Partridge licked his lips. "All right, I'll grant you that feeding it the wrong kind of energy could possibly kill it when it's outside of your body, but what about the *krekh* that's already inside you? The blood sickness, you called it."

Everything fell into place in Maury's mind then, springing sharply into focus. "Yes, but the thirst isn't a disease. It's more like an addiction, and as the humans have demonstrated, while addictions cannot be generally cured, on a case-by-case basis they can be controlled."

"That's only provided the addict is both willing and strong enough to resist the urges of the addiction," Partridge reminded him. "Too many beings are neither. And there's something else you're forgetting: the *krekh* is an organism, not some feel-good chemical compound. Once it takes up residence in a living body, it can't simply be flushed out again.

"Believe me, my people tried everything to rid themselves of the parasite, and what they learned, they learned the hard way. Once you've been infested by it, it feeds continuously. If you stop eating, it will not starve. It will simply take its nourishment from your body. It will devour you from the inside out until there is nothing left of you."

"Exactly!" Maury crowed.

Partridge's eyebrows shot up. "I was right," he announced to the room. "You're all doomed."

"You don't understand," Maury told him with growing excitement. "The addiction to which I was referring is the *krekh*'s. It manifests itself as the thirst, but we're not the ones addicted to essence—*dashkra* is. That is the appetite that needs to be either killed or controlled."

Now the gnome's face was the portrait of skepticism. "And how do you propose to do that, pray tell?"

"Humans who are addicted to chemical substances develop a tolerance for pollution. Street drugs are routinely diluted or adulterated with other substances. To these beings, pure product taken in the quantity they're accustomed to is actually poisonous. It overdoses them and can kill them if they don't receive medical attention."

Vicky inhaled sharply. "And for the past fifteen hundred years, the Nash'terel have been feeding the *dashkra* in our bodies with polluted human essence... and since the addiction is the bloodstone's and not ours... Maldemaur! Are you suggesting what I think you are?"

The lilt in her voice planted red flags in Maury's mind, along with images of leopards and tigers.

Reluctantly, he replied, "Yes, Caspera, I am. It's entirely theoretical, and there's still a lot of work to do to prove its tenability. So before you start advertising any claims as fact—"

"I'm a scientist, Maldemaur. I'm quite familiar with the process," she told him.

"And you'll follow it?" he persisted. "Even if it takes longer than you want it to?"

"Of course. Once the product has been clinically tested, we'll know what we've got and how permanent the effect is. And then we'll have some business decisions to make together. Meanwhile," she added, waving a desultory hand in Partridge's direction, "what are we to do with this creature? We can't simply put him on a plane and send him back east. Not with all the blood of our offspring on his hands."

Partridge gulped audibly.

"You can't simply execute him, either, *dollim*," Barron pointed out reasonably. "We need him to cancel the bounty and call off the hunt."

"I disagree," she corrected him with a menacing edge on her voice. "We only need someone who looks and sounds like him to do it. And then disappear. Forever."

Before anyone could react, Vicky had used her *hainbek* to bounce Partridge off the sofa and pin him to the ceiling. He squirmed and wriggled up there for a good thirty seconds, making piteous sounds, before she relented and let him drop with a *thud* to the floor.

Barron yanked him back onto his feet and made a show of dusting him off.

Meanwhile, Maury cleared his throat and said, "If I may suggest a compromise?"

All eyes turned toward him as he continued, "Mr. Partridge has a great deal to answer for, it's true. However, he also has a great deal to offer us as a way of making amends. For example, as the inventor of the *dashkra* detector, he might begin by giving us a way to block or scramble that device. Then, with his background in research and development, he could be a valuable asset in the laboratory as we work to control the thirst. Once we have a successful product, his experience at running a large corporation might be useful in the marketing and distribution phase of the project. But he can't do any of those things unless we keep him alive."

Maury cast a significant look in Vicky's direction.

"And we'll want him to turn his ship over to us as well, to be hangared inside the compound," Barron added, displaying a toothy grin, "along with all the *dashkra* he's already collected. Can't let that fall into the wrong hands, now, can we?"

The gnome's expression darkened. He'd evidently been hoping they'd forgotten about the ship.

"Monicandra has replied to my text about Montgomery being your fall guy," Shred chimed in, brandishing his phone. "Her team discovered a safe in that house you rented in his name. They got it open and found the fake evidence you'd prepared, intending to frame him for embezzlement if anyone noticed you were skimming from the company's profits. She's convinced her media contact to sit on the story for a bit while she gives Montgomery the heads up. I'm betting he'll spin the blame right back where it belongs—onto you."

"Uh-oh! Looks like you're damned whichever way you turn, Partridge," said Barron. "So, what are you going to do? Take your chances with the media and the justice system? Or drop off the map and take your chances with *her*?"

He pointed to Vicky, who was now standing with her arms crossed and wearing a decidedly predatory expression.

Wariness washed across Partridge's face. "When you say 'drop off the map', you mean...?"

"It means Pritchard and Glen Partridge both cease to exist," Barron told him. "It means that from now on you have one purpose in life, and that's to help us ensure the survival of the Nash'tcrcl race in whatever way we tell you to. It means we agree to keep you safe from your enemies in the outside world, *but*—and I can't say this often enough—only after you've called off the hunt, not just in Canada but all around the world. You started this massacre of innocents, and you're going to end it, or else."

"I can't," he said miserably.

"Can't? Or won't?" Shred demanded, showing his Nash'terel eyes.

As expected, the sight of them brought a clatter of words in response. "I would if I could but I can't. I'm not the mission commander."

"There's a commander?" A single stride brought Barron in front of the gnome, staring a promise of violence into his pale, upturned face. "Just how many of your kind are on this *mission*?" he hissed, drawing the final word out.

Glen Partridge might have been an explorer in his earlier life, Maury mused, but he was definitely not a military type trained to withstand interrogation. Shred and Barron had barely begun to pressure him, and already the gnome's forehead was glistening with sweat, and his knees looked about to buckle beneath him.

"More than me!" Partridge stammered, almost shouting the words. "What does it matter? They're embedded in the human population. I have no way to contact them, and you're never going to find them."

"Never say never, Partridge," Shred advised him with cheerful menace. "Especially when you're caught in a lie."

"I'm not lying!" he yelped. "I can't do what you want!"

"Well, in that case..." Barron took a step backwards. "All yours, Vicky."

"With pleasure," she purred, uncrossing her arms and looking her next prey up and down.

Partridge went even paler than before. "No, wait!"

"How many, *Mister* Partridge?" Barron thundered at him.

"Six!" The word seemed to leap from his mouth of its own accord. "Six of us managed to escape our home world before the infestation could claim us."

"Six of you," Shred repeated. "Is that five plus the commander?"

The gnome heaved a defeated sigh, then nodded wordlessly.

"And are all of you on Earth right now?" Barron persisted. "Or is the commander somewhere else, receiving reports from the planet's surface?"

"He's on the ship."

"Which is where, exactly?" Shred demanded. "Don't lie to us, Partridge. It's far too late for that."

"I don't know," he moaned. "None of us do. It's a precaution in case we fail and the *krekh* take us over. We can't let them onto the vessel."

The head of the snake, Maury mused. History did repeat itself, it seemed.

"Are the other four using *dashkra* detectors? Are they handing out the devices to Yeng assassins and paying a bounty on Nash'terel lives, as you've been doing?" Vincaspera cut in, her eyes flashing warnings.

"They might be. They could have developed their own version—I don't know. We each have our own territory to scour..." As his voice trailed off, Partridge was the portrait of misery.

"All right, that will do for now," Shred told him, but not out of sympathy. "Time is wasting. Call off the hunt in your own territory immediately, and we'll deal with the rest of it later."

"Immediately? That's impossible," he stammered. "It's going to take time to contact all my representatives and instruct them to stop paying the bounty."

Speaking deliberately, Vicky stepped closer to him. "The pawnbrokers, you mean?" Her next words came at him in a razor-sharp barrage. "While the Yeng continue to hunt and kill our children? That is *not acceptable!*"

Partridge stumbled backward, falling onto the sofa again.

"I—I have a list of everyone I've sent trackers to, back at my office. I could call them up and—"

"Not good enough!" Barron declared loudly. "In every organization, there's a way to transmit an all-hands alert in an emergency. Hotel switchboards have one. Security companies like Eyes on the World have one. And it's for certain that someone like you would have set one up for the *dashkra* hunt as well." Looming over the cringing figure in the middle of the sofa, he demanded in a voice that was part rumble, part roar, "So, what is it, Partridge?"

The response rattled out of him. "A batch—a batch email warning all the hunters to go to ground and—and wait for the all-clear."

It was a beginning. At the very least, it would buy the Guild enough time to locate all those tracking devices using Partridge's list of purchasers and execute a "product recall".

Maury sniffed the air. The gnome had finally peed his pants. He'd probably ruined the cushion he was sitting on, too. Vicky would not be happy about that.

"An email. And you can send it from your phone?" Barron growled directly into Partridge's ear.

His answer was a spastic nod.

"Good! Do it."

The collector accepted the phone that Shred had taken from him earlier. Under the laser-like gaze of four pairs of eyes, and with visibly shaking fingers, he opened an app and began tapping in text.

Meanwhile, Maury was thinking, *One down, four to go.*

Chapter Twenty-Six

◆

Three weeks had passed.

After demonstrating the *dashkra* tracker to the staff and trainees at the compound, Barron had sent them all home on furlough, with orders to explain to their families why their pendants had been left behind, and to warn their elders of the danger of having a bloodstone on their persons, at least until the current emergency had been declared dealt with. Of the twenty-three families who'd come through the rift to Earth, seventeen were represented in the current cohort. It was an imperfect way to spread the word, but Barron had seen no alternative, so this was the tactic he had gone with.

Piggybacking onto her mate's strategy, Vicky had conscripted everyone involved in Barron's program for her first experiment, to record how long it would take for the thirst to reassert itself—if, indeed, it did—once they stopped drinking the pure essence from Middlevale.

Meanwhile, Partridge's all-hands alert was having the desired effect. The frequency of reported attacks on Nash'terel by the

Yeng—in Canada, at least—had already begun to drop.

Monicandra had been told where Partridge's pendant collection could be found, and the Guild had moved quickly to scoop it up for safekeeping. Thankfully, there were far fewer bloodstones in his hiding place than they'd feared. It appeared that even with the technological assist, the Yeng remained at a disadvantage when it came to killing Nash'terel. Their distinctive odour kept giving them away.

Partridge's list of tracker purchasers had enabled the Guild to locate and neutralize a number of Yeng assassins, along with their devices. There weren't as many of these as feared either. (Apparently, Barron and Shred's first instincts about the gnome had been correct—he was as much an embezzler as he was an inventor.) However, he'd shipped the bloodstone detectors all over North America, making the clean-up operation rather time-consuming.

Plans were in the works to dispatch pairs of Nash'terel assassins to large cities around the globe, where they would quietly take up residence and begin gathering intel about possible *dashkra* collectors.

And Glen Partridge, also known as Pritchard, also known as the gnome, was dead.

Really dead, Barron assured Gershred via video chat, not faked this time. Slammed into a wall to stop his screaming after the baby caused Vicky's essence levels to drop suddenly and he saw her true form emerge. At least, that was what she'd reported to Barron when he'd called home from the compound to check on her the previous day.

Privately, Shred had been expecting something like this to happen. Vincaspera's thirst for vengeance was unquenchable.

Partridge's fate had been sealed from the moment her fangs had begun itching. All she'd needed was an excuse—and enough time spent in his company for him to give her one. Apparently, they'd been in the third floor apartment together, collating research data, when the incident occurred.

"Not that much of her was visible," Barron continued. "She was wearing clothing, after all. Essence instability in late-in-life pregnancies was one of the complications the midwife warned us about. Fortunately, we keep extra flasks on hand. Vicky found one and topped herself up. It took her less than a minute after that to revert back to human. No big deal. But Pritchard... He just lost it.

"I guess we shouldn't be surprised. Like you told him back at his office, he didn't know anything about the Nash'terel. Anyway, there he was, bouncing off the walls, scratching at his eyeballs and yelling at the top of his lungs, and Vicky decided she'd had enough. So, she deployed her *hainbek* and shut him up. For good." A pause, then, "Are you okay with that?"

Did he have a choice? It wasn't as though the Nash'terel could reverse time and change outcomes, after all.

...although a hainbek like that would certainly come in handy right about now.

"I suppose I am," Shred said with a sigh. "He did stop the hunt on this side of the Atlantic and give us his list of purchasers, and thanks to him, we know a lot more about the bloodstone now than we did before. Still, it would have been nice if she'd waited to kill him until after we'd wrung more out of him about the possible location of the ship. Finding it—and interrogating the commander—might have told us where to look for the rest of the mission team, saving Monicandra's people a lot of time and trouble. It could even have provided us another way off this world besides the rift. A plan B, as it were."

"Ah, well... What's done is done, Gordie. No way to undo it. But I'm wondering... Maybe, once the Guild have finished their mop-up, you and I could...?"

"...go looking for that alien vessel on our own? It could be sitting on the dark side of the moon, for all we know. Then again, the humans are very close to developing space travel, so I suppose it might be feasible in a century or two."

"I'd sure like to give it a try. Put a plan B in our pockets, like you said. And maybe a plan C if he was telling the truth about the star charts they found on the ancient planet. If we've developed a cure for the blood sickness by then, we could take it to other worlds. Save the galaxy, maybe."

Be heroes again. It was tempting.

"Let me talk it over with Maury and get back to you. Any news on the family front?"

"About Angie and Vicky, you mean? Nothing yet, and probably not for a while. The midwife wants Vicky to slow down and conserve her essence, which will seriously hamper her ability to travel to Middlevale, and it's unlikely that Angie will come down for a visit before the baby is born. So you can tell Maldemaur that he's getting his wish."

Now Shred was curious. "If Vicky can't go to Middlevale, does someone else harvest the essence?"

"Nope. It's done by the cult leader as part of a 'cleansing ritual' and it can't be delegated. I sure hope your partner's theory pans out, Gordie. Between the long drive there and back and the all-nighters in between, the harvest was a taxing exercise even before Vicky became pregnant. And after she's given birth, who knows when she'll be able to get up there again? We're going to stretch out our essence supply for as long as possible and keep our fingers crossed, for the next few months, at least."

Fingers crossed, indeed, Shred thought. Neither he nor Maury had experienced the urge to feed since their return home from Vancouver, ten days earlier. It was too soon to be drawing conclusions, of course. They would have to wait for more time to pass. However, if it turned out that pure essence was a way to kill or control the appetite of the *dashkra* in their blood...

The Nash'terel trainees and the humans from Middlevale might be able to socialize after all, perhaps even fall in love and create offspring together.

A race of human-Nash'terel hybrids. Imagine that!

"Two visits in one month. I'm honoured," said Laetitia, rising from her chair to hang up Monicandra's coat in the front closet. "But if you're not careful, people might think Justine Stoneman has returned to take up the reins of the media empire again, and we wouldn't want that, would we?"

"I know. I'll make this brief. Then I'll disappear again, I promise. I wanted to thank you for your help and ask for another favour."

Standing there with the coat in one manicured hand and a wooden hanger in the other, Laetitia narrowed her gaze. "We missed with Montgomery, but airing the embezzlement scandal did improve our ratings, and I guess I owe you something for removing the Glen Partridge irritant from my life," she allowed. "What's the favour?"

"I would still like you to approach the Yeng Council. Same proposal, different threat."

"Another common threat?"

"In eighty-four years, the rift is going to open between here and RinYeng, and an army of assassins will be pouring through it, to eradicate all traces of the blood sickness on Earth. This time they'll be targeting your people as well as mine. I realize a full alliance may be out of the question. Still, it wouldn't hurt to ask. At the very least, it would benefit both the Yeng and the Nash'terel to declare a truce between us so that both sides can focus on preparing to defend themselves against the emperor's purification campaign."

"Eighty-four years is a long time."

"For a human. Not for us. It's only been in the last sixteen years that Yeng on this side of the rift have shown open enmity toward the Nash'terel. We can stop it. We have to. If we continue looking for ways to weaken and undermine each other, we're only making it easier for the emperor to destroy both our peoples. Will you try to persuade the Council?"

She paused. "No promises, Mother," she said at last, "but if I can convince them the idea came from a Yeng... It just might fly. I'll do my best and let you know."

Monicandra nodded her acceptance and reached out to retrieve her coat.

Once back in her car, she permitted herself a satisfied smile.

Tisha wielded enormous influence on this world, far more than anyone suspected. If she wanted to forge a truce, there would be one. And from the truce would spring an alliance, and from the alliance an army. And then...

Patience, Monicandra admonished herself. She needed to take this one step at a time.

With that, the Nash'terel assassin put the car in forward gear and headed back toward the main road.

Bonus Story

Rocket Man, Coyote, and Oscar

*A*rrived in British Columbia two days ago, on the train.

Travis "Rocket Man" Fiore sat at his keyboard, glaring at the words on the screen of his laptop. They were the opening line of his first journal entry, and they weren't looking very promising. In fact, nothing about his life was looking promising right now. He was in the wrong place and knew it, had known it all along, had begged and pleaded not to be dragged out here, but had been ignored.

Now his life was totally messed up. He should have been back in Collingwood, working on skills with his hockey team and looking forward to the Junior draft. Instead, he was having to learn how to be an alien in order to fit into this isolated community in the wilderness. The other aliens wouldn't be fooled. They would take one look at him and know he shouldn't be there. And he couldn't explain to them why he was different because it was supposed to be a secret that he was half-human.

Bitterness welled up inside him and spilled onto the page:

I feel like that extra screw that's left over after something's been put back together. People know it needs to fit in somewhere, so they store it in a safe place until they can figure out where it belongs—which, by the way, happens almost never. I don't know whether to be sad or angry or just howl at the moon in frustration. No, wait, that would make me a werewolf, and I'm gonna be a fucking VAMPIRE. Fuck! Fuck, fuck, FUCK!!

He paused and reread the last few words. Save or delete?

No one else would be seeing this, so the hell with it. The 'F' bombs stayed.

The journal had been his mother's idea. She'd told him it would be for his eyes only, a good way for him to work through his feelings and make sense of things he found confusing.

Uh-huh. Like the fact that he would be recording his thoughts in a word processing file stored on a flash drive, instead of using a server and posting to social media like a normal person?

Grandpa M had warned him that the Nash'terel liked their privacy, but this went way beyond extreme.

It was ironic too, because his mother, Angie Fiore, was the computer nerd who'd set up the Middlevale website and intranet, and about a thousand people were merrily posting and blogging away on them, but now she was telling Travis he had to stay offline because the system wasn't secure enough for him to use. Like he was going to spill state secrets or something.

Really?!

This was bullshit.

Anyway. It was what it was, he guessed: his very personal blog with zero followers.

News flash: Those parent people from the video chats exist in three dimensions and they've got legs. Who knew? It was strange meeting them in real life. It was like running into an NHL star at the grocery store checkout counter and having a conversation. You know you're intruding into someone else's actual life, but they act like they're okay with it and you can't decide whether it's because they're really that interested in getting to know you or they realize they only have to put up with you for a short while so they may as well be nice to you.

He paused again. *Was* he only going to be in their lives for a short while? After two days, Travis wasn't sure how he felt about that, or how his parents felt. He'd gotten both kinds of vibes from them when they'd first met up in Vancouver. He and his dad had connected right away. Ken had cracked jokes and seemed genuinely pleased to have him around. Angie, on the other hand, had been way uptight and business-like with him from the get-go, as if he was a problem that needed to be solved by a deadline.

She'd seen him use his super power—sorry, his *hainbek*—to slam a Yeng into a wall. Had that made her nervous around him? It certainly felt that way. All of their conversations were short, and always about practical stuff, like was his room comfortable at night or how did he prefer his eggs cooked in the morning, which he wouldn't have minded so much if she'd just smiled at him once in a while.

My mother doesn't look any happier than I feel about me being out here. Maybe she'll change over time, or maybe I will. Maybe neither of us will but we'll get used to having each other around. Or maybe I'm trapped in the twilight zone for the rest of my life. In which case, just fucking shoot me now!!

It's Thursday evening, so I've been "home" for two days now, the extra screw stored for safekeeping in a cottage in the middle of nowhere, surrounded by lots of trees. I know I once lived here, because I've been getting flashbacks to when I was little. I remember the fireplace, but not the stove, which is electric and looks modern. The fridge is also different, and strangely bigger than I recall. Maybe it was a bar fridge back then. And I have vague memories of being in the same bathtub, but not in the current washroom. This place is smaller than my grandpas' house back in Collingwood, but it's warm, and I've got my own private space, a bedroom with a fair-sized window, unbarred, so I guess things could be worse.

Travis leaned back in his chair, recalling the drive from Vancouver, and the strange little building where they had had to stop and trade their truck for one with treads instead of front wheels. The "rec centre" looked plunked down in the wilderness as if it had dropped out of the sky, and riding in a cross between a snowmobile and a Hummer had felt like an adventure. Then they'd arrived at the cottage, and reality had smacked him in the face...

Walking back into it after being gone for so long totally creeped me out, though. They'd kept up all the crafts and drawings and stuff I apparently made years ago. Like I was kidnapped or died or something and they preserved my room exactly the way it was when I disappeared. WTF! First thing I did was tear everything down and put up my hockey posters instead. Grandpa M made me leave a lot of my stuff behind, so this still doesn't feel like my bedroom back home, but the creepiness factor has dropped by a lot. He's promised to ship me the rest of my things once he and Grandpa G get back to Collingwood.

I'm glad I brought my hockey gear. Dad has promised that I can try out for the local team, as soon as he's able to arrange it.

Travis turned and checked out the corner of his room, where his hockey bag and two new sticks sat, looking as if they were being guarded by Sidney Crosby. By his image on the poster, anyway. It showed him from the goalie's point of view as Sid was winding up to take a shot, and it made him look really fierce. That was how Travis tried to appear to the goalie when he was playing—shit-your-pants scary. Almost made him wish he could shapeshift his face as well as his feet. Almost, but not quite.

My mother has a part-time job at the library in town, and she uses a two-seater ATV to get there. Today she took me with her and introduced me to the people she works with. They're nice enough, I guess. Some of them said they remembered me from when I was four or five years old, but I think they were just making polite conversation. Nobody really recognizes anyone from when they were that young, not without aging their photo on a computer.

Met a new friend, maybe: He's a town kid about my age, named Oscar Carvey. Oscar volunteers at the library a couple days a week after school, so I offered to help him put away some books on the shelves and we hung and chatted for a while. He was easy to talk to.

Travis smiled to himself, remembering what Grandpa M had told him back in Collingwood: "*You'll be the new kid in the class, until you've made some friends.*" Apparently, he'd been right about that.

Oscar wanted to know what my parents did in the "outside world", so I told him what I'd been instructed to say in case anyone asked—that my father is a car mechanic and my mother uses computers to create special effects in the movies. Maybe that's even the truth. I have no idea. Don't much care, either, to be perfectly honest, as long as people believe it.

Then I asked him where's the best place to find pizza around here.

Turns out there's a bakery in town that will make the crust for you but you have to bring them the toppings you want on it. (Holy pepperoni, Batman!) I'd been warned to stick to "safe topics", because the presence of aliens on this world is apparently a huge secret, even from the people in town, who are all part Nash'terel and don't realize it. I wish I didn't either. This bloodstone is such a fucking weight around my neck!

Oscar doesn't play hockey. However, he told me he likes to skate on the pond at the edge of town whenever he can, and when enough kids show up with sticks, a shinny game will occasionally break out.

Dad says it may be a couple of weeks before I can try out for the Nash'terel team, and it's already been a couple of weeks since I was last on the ice. I don't want to lose my edge. So, next time my mother has to work, I think I'll grab some of my gear and ask her to drop me off at the pond. I'll practice my stickhandling and see if anyone else turns up.

When her shift at the library ended today, she took me to the town's education office to register me for home schooling and pick up the textbooks I need to complete grade 10 in B.C. I've been leafing through them. After the human anatomy course Grandpa M just put me through so I could change my appearance back to normal if my body tried to shapeshift, high school is going to be a snap!

It's Friday afternoon, and my mother is pissed at me for breaking some stupid rule that I didn't even know existed because she broke it herself just yesterday, and how fucking hypocritical is that!! (That's what I told her just before I slammed my bedroom door in her face.)

Now I'm in my room, staring at the cover of a textbook I'm supposed to be reading and waiting for Dad to get home from the training compound. She thinks he'll be pissed at me too, but I'm betting he won't.

Apparently, no Nash'terel are allowed to go into Middlevale, and that includes me. No reason given, that's just the way it is.

I guess Coyote didn't know about the rule either, because it was his idea to go down to the pond. We weren't doing anything wrong, just enjoying a little ice time, but the way she was carrying on, it was like we'd snuck into the actual town and gotten arrested for shoplifting and she had to come bail me out of jail or something. Even after I apologized for not leaving a note saying where I was going!

That part really annoys me, btw—being treated like I'm still a little kid and someone needs to track where I am at all times. She saw what I did to that Yeng in the alley. She knows I can take care of myself. She's the one who told me how safe I would be here. And I'm not five years old anymore, so what's the big fat hairy deal?!

As he closed the laptop, Travis replayed the day in his mind.

He had woken up that morning to find himself alone in the cottage. Both his parents had gone out. They'd left him his breakfast in the oven, and a list of written instructions on the table for what to do until one of them returned: math and geography until lunchtime, and English literature in the afternoon. Fine. It was a school day and he had the textbooks, so it was no sweat.

As he was drying his breakfast dishes, he heard the growl of a motor outside. Then it stopped. His first thought was that his mother had come back. However, a moment later there was a rather importunate knock at the door.

Wondering whether he might need to deploy his *hainbek*, Travis swung the door open and was met by a familiar face sporting an unruly mop of dark hair, a pair of mischievous blue eyes, and a huge, friendly grin. It was Coach Dagomir's son.

"Hey, Rocket Man!" Leo greeted him. "What's up?"

Travis quashed the urge to give him a welcoming hug and returned his smile instead. "Coyote! What are you doing way the hell out here?"

"We're moving to the west coast. Dad and I arrived yesterday. We're staying in the compound until Mom can join us. Anyway, I'm on my way to practise on the pond. Passing and stickhandling. It's kind of hard to do if you're alone. Want to come?"

Did he ever! But... "It can't be for very long."

"It won't be. An hour and a half, tops. I borrowed a two-seater snowmobile. It'll get us there and back real fast."

Just an hour and a half. And the math course was the same as the one he'd completed back in Ontario. As far as Travis was concerned, this was a no-brainer. He'd already taped both his sticks, so he grabbed one, along with his gloves and skates, threw on a warm jacket, and climbed aboard.

The rink was empty when they arrived, except for an old guy wearing a dark brown toque on his head, big rubber galoshes on his feet, and grey work pants topped with a matching fur-lined jacket on the rest of him. He'd been clearing the ice surface with a wide metal snow shovel. He stopped when he saw them pull up on the snowmobile, then came over to them while they were sitting on the slab of wooden bench, lacing up their skates.

"You're not from town, are you?" he said, planting the shovel firmly in the snow and holding the shaft upright by its handle.

"Nope," Coyote replied. "We're staying at the sports camp over there while our fathers train for the next Olympics." He jerked his head in the direction of the compound.

That wasn't the cover story the townsfolk had been told. Travis stiffened and held his breath, expecting to be called a liar and sent away.

But the man just raised his eyebrows and said, "Uh-*huh*. Well, I'm Max, and maintaining this rink is my responsibility."

"So, is it okay if we practise here?" Travis asked him.

"Long as you don't do anything stupid, it's okay by me."

Max stood off to the side while they skated a few warmup laps. Then they put on their hockey gloves and froze a couple of pucks, and he hung around, leaning on the handle of his shovel and watching them practise forward passing, drop passing, and deking around each other. The old man's gaze was appraising, even critical at times, but Travis hardly cared. He was just enjoying the sensation of ice under his blades and a hockey stick in his hands.

Rocket Man and Coyote went end to end, hard, until they were both dripping sweat and ready to call it quits. Max waited until they were back on the bench, exchanging their skates for snow boots. Then he strolled over and remarked, "You boys are pretty handy with your sticks. I'm guessing you've played for a while."

"In a minor hockey league, back in Ontario," said Travis without glancing up.

"Impressive!" Max said. "So you can pass and stickhandle. How's your shooting? Any good?"

Coyote puffed out his chest. "Good enough to play for the Vancouver Canucks!"

"Okay, tell you what," said Max. "You come back here tomorrow and I'll bring a net, and you can show me what you've got."

Travis wasn't sure he could sneak away like this two days in a row, but Coyote didn't hesitate. "Deal!"

It turned out they'd been practising for more than two hours. Angie was waiting for Travis when Coyote dropped him off at the cottage, and she was fuming. She knew where he'd been and with whom, because she'd passed by the pond on her way home to check on him and had seen them finishing up.

Travis should probably have thanked her for not roaring in on the ATV and dragging him back to the cottage then and there. (That would have been embarrassing.) Instead, seeing how mad she was, he'd gotten angry too. At first, the anger had remained in their faces, in the looks they gave each other while he cleaned and gelled his skate blades and she ordered him into the shower and watched him eat the lunch she'd made. Then voices were raised and accusations started flying, and he called her a fucking hypocrite and went into his room to study, convinced that the only people in the world who really understood him were back in Ontario, coaching and playing hockey.

I've done the first chapter of the math book—reviewed it, actually, since I'm repeating the course. Now I'm rereading Twelfth Night, *which is about a girl who is stranded in a strange country and has to pretend to be a boy so she won't be captured or killed. She falls in love with her boss, who's in love with someone he can't have. He sends the girl/boy to present a token of his love to this ice queen... who of course falls in love with the girl/boy and totally messes up everyone's lives.*

Right now I can honestly say that I understand exactly how they all feel.

I was right, sort of. He's not pissed at me. It's something worse. He's terribly disappointed. His words. And here I was, thinking we were becoming pals, when all along he was actually my father, acting like a kid so I wouldn't feel alone and miserable and do something stupid with my hainbek...

Travis stopped keyboarding, unwilling to relive the conversation they'd just had. Grandpa M's earlier words had come back to haunt him and were repeating on a loop inside his head: "*What about your parents, Travis? You have no idea how much they've missed having you in their lives.*"

Angie had missed him much more than he'd been willing to believe. Grandpa M hadn't been able to get through to him, but Ken had finally set him straight. It had torn Travis's mother up inside to part with him when he was five years old and she'd cried tears after each of their weekly video chats. And the first time they'd stood in the same room after that, he'd blown her off. Stripped all the happiness out of the moment for her with a grunt and a frown. Today he'd made his mother cry again, with angry words.

This was becoming a bad habit. Travis knew what the problem was—it was him. But he couldn't bring himself to say it. Instead, what had come out of his mouth was, "When she took me to the library yesterday..."

"She was showing you to her friends. She'd told them you were coming home and they remembered you and wanted to see you again. Little Travis, all grown up into a fine young man."

"I never knew—I mean, I just thought—"

"You thought what, Travis?"

"She bawled me out for breaking the rule, and I—"

"You threw it back in her face. She told me. Thing is, she didn't break the rule."

"Huh?"

"The Nash'terel from the training compound are not allowed in Middlevale because they're not part of the town. Your mother was born there and works in Middlevale, so as long as you're with her, you're allowed to be there. Otherwise, you're not. By going to the pond with Leo today, you broke the rule. And you disobeyed our instructions," he added. "You went off without leaving a note or telling anyone where to find you. I'd say your mother has good reason to be upset with you right now."

He was right.

"How do I fix this?" Travis asked.

"An apology would be a good place to start, followed by some kindness and consideration. You've got a fence to mend, son. I suggest you get to it."

Saturday is only half over, and it's already the best day I've had since coming here to the Little House in the Wilderness.

Which really isn't saying much, since the last few days have been so shitty. Still...

Last night I started mending that fence my father talked about. I apologized to my mother for being rude and calling her a hypocrite. I don't think she believed I was sorry, because she said, "Apology accepted," in that starched tone of voice people use when they want to call bullshit but they're too polite to do it, so they let you know they heard you, then they change the subject.

Warming up takes time, I guess.

When I told my parents about the deal Coyote made for us to meet up with Max at the pond, Dad frowned and my mother pressed her lips together, and I thought, Okay, colour me grounded. But they surprised me.

A breakfast loaded with carbs and protein was waiting for me when I woke up this morning. After I'd brushed my teeth and done all the usual beginning-of-the-day stuff, I was expecting Coyote to come on his snowmobile to try to spirit me away. Instead, Dad loaded my gear into the back of the snowhummer and drove all three of us down to the rink... and my parents stayed to watch me practise!

I could hardly believe it.

They'd brought folding chairs with them, and they sat there for the whole two hours, bundled up and cheering me on and drinking coffee out of insulated bottles, just like my grandpas had always done at the arena.

But that wasn't the best part.

For the first time since arriving here, I actually saw my mother smile.

My mother is radiant when she's happy. I mean that literally. Everything about her brightens as if she's about to give off a glow.

In that moment, I understood why Dad fell in love with her. And because no one but me is ever going to see this journal, I can be honest and say that I could feel myself kind of falling for her too. Is this normal for humans? For Nash'terel? What the fuck does normal even mean these days?

Anyway.

When we arrived at the rink, another surprise was waiting for me. Coach Dagomir and Coyote were already there, and Coyote was flipping wrist shots into a net they'd set up. It turned out that everything we'd done the day before was with his father's permission. In fact, there was no Max. That was Coach Dagomir, shapeshifted, scouting us for the Nash'terel team. He wanted to see what we could do when there was no pressure to perform, and he apparently liked what he saw. So now he was back as himself, with the blessing of whoever was in charge of the training program, to run an actual practice.

Coyote and I had a blast. Saturday meant no school for the kids from town as well. While we were doing warmups on the ice, a bunch of them showed up, most of them with hockey sticks, expecting to play shinny. These boys and girls looked to be anywhere from eight to thirteen years old. They stood around, staring goggle-eyed at us until Coach ordered them to join the warmup. They thought he was joking at first, but he wasn't. After the warmup, he put the kids without sticks to work chasing stray pucks while he gave a stickhandling clinic for everyone else.

Then we had a scrimmage, with the net at one end and two boots as placeholders at the other end. Nobody was keeping score. Every so often, Coyote and I slowed up on purpose and let one of the town kids take a shot on goal. Everybody had fun.

After the scrimmage, Coach organized a shooting skills competition using paper plates with numbers on them, suspended at different heights from the crossbar of the net. He made Coyote and me the leaders of a pair of mixed teams and we took turns trying to hit all five plates with five pucks in a row. Coyote's team squeaked through to a win at the end, and we had a noisy crowd cheering us on.

It felt like home ice. I almost didn't look at my parents. I wanted to keep imagining that my grandpas were there. If they weren't, I was afraid it would break the spell. But when practice was over I did turn and look, and I was glad I did.

My parents were both grinning from ear to ear. My mother was clapping her hands. Dad gave me two thumbs up. My heart felt huge inside my chest.

Best. Practice. Ever!

This afternoon, Dad is taking me to the indoor rink at the rec centre to watch the Nash'terel team practise without sticks. Because Coyote and I are still underage for the training program, we'll only have access to the ice surface on weekends, and only under Coach

Dagomir's supervision. In any case, I've got some catching up to do with controlling my hainbek before Coach will even let me try out. He and Coyote have both offered to help me with that whenever they can.

Today was Sunday. After breakfast, my parents drove me out to the pond to meet up with Coach and Coyote. This time, though, Dad didn't bring a chair for himself. He brought a pair of skates and put them on.

I had no idea he even owned ice skates. I must have been wearing my surprise on my face, because when he saw me watching him, he laughed. He's not a power skater or anything, but he's got some respectable skills. Coach put him to work managing the littlest town kids.

There were other parents there besides my mother. I'm guessing they were curious and maybe a little concerned about this older guy who had simply shown up and started teaching their kids the game of hockey. I hope they come to every practice. It's a lot more fun when you know someone's cheering for you.

Oscar Carvey came out too, playing with a borrowed stick and looking nervous about embarrassing himself on the ice. He didn't need to worry, though—he's tall and strong, and I could tell from the way he moved that he's a natural athlete. He and Coyote hit it off when I introduced them. He likes the nicknames we've given each other, but because they're the names of hockey teams we've played for, he isn't sure whether he qualifies for one himself. No matter. I think the three of us will be spending a lot of time together, doing stuff. Hope so, anyway.

The practice ended with a puck-handling race and a relay. Coyote's squad did well, but mine did it a few seconds faster. Now we're tied in points, 1-1.

Afterward, I found out that Dad had bought his first pair of skates right after hearing that my grandpas had signed me up for house league hockey. He'd been working at learning the sport ever since, so we would have something to share when I came back home. Hearing that made me fog up a little. I didn't know what to say, so I just nodded and hoped he wouldn't take it the wrong way.

In the afternoon, Dad called me down into the basement and showed me the entrance to a secret passage. We followed it to its end and found Coyote waiting for us with a huge grin on his face.

It was too early to watch the Nash'terel hockey practice, so we played chess in the common room of the barracks for a while. It was my first lesson. Coyote played the white pieces and Dad and I played the black ones, without hainbeka at first, then with.

Coyote's chessmen kept sliding off the board and mine kept jumping off, and we laughed each time it happened. But I know Coyote dumbed down his game—and his control of his hainbek—to make sure I would have fun learning how to play. Now I'm determined to catch up with him so I can beat him fair and square.

Anyway, dinner ended a while ago, and Dad promised me a chess match once this journal entry is finished, so guess what?

It's done.

I've been playing chess every afternoon for a week now, mainly with Coyote at our kitchen table, but Oscar has begun paying visits to my parents' place as well. He joins us on days when he's not volunteering at the library after school. From town to the cottage is a fairly long walk, but it's only one way for him, since my mother never minds giving him a ride back home. My parents like him a lot, and I have to say, it's been dope having friends I can hang with again! We're like the three musketeers.

Today was a library day. Coyote and I were standing outside the cottage, just getting some fresh air, when I noticed that he was wearing the same up-to-no-good expression as I'd seen on his face that first Friday morning.

"Want to blow your mind, Rocket Man?" he said. "Throw a snowball at me."

"Why?" I asked.

He was backing away from me. "Just do it. You're gonna love what happens."

I gathered a double handful of snow, pressed it into a ball, and let fly, directly at his chest. The snowball never reached him. It splatted in mid-air, like it was hitting an invisible barrier.

"Throw another one," he called. "Aim for my head."

I did. Same thing happened.

"What the fuck was that?" I said, walking toward him.

Now he was laughing. He told me he'd used his hainbek to create a defensive shield, and that it was the first thing his father had taught him when Coyote was old enough to become an apprentice. Sustained essence projection, it was called.

I was instantly jealous.

"I want to learn how to do it too," I said.

"Then you need to practise your control. And I will gladly help with that by throwing things at you, with force, as soon as you think you can block them."

I shot him a look. "Thanks a bunch."

That evening, Travis set up a target range in his bedroom, using a bunch of old toys from a box that he'd found in his closet. He would practise for an hour every night, he decided, until he could "pull his punch", knocking over each one with the same narrow precision as he'd developed scoring goals in hockey games, but without sending the object flying across the room.

Coyote had warned him that it would take time to develop the right amount of control. So had Grandpa G, more than once.

That was okay, Travis thought doggedly. It wasn't like his family was going to up and move him somewhere else anytime soon.

Apparently, Oscar's mother is the teacher who'll be marking my English assignments. She gave me a B+ on the one I turned in yesterday, about Twelfth Night. She agreed with me that people shouldn't judge others based on their appearance, but she thought I was too hard on the jerk in yellow gartered stockings, even if he was only interested in marrying up, and not hard enough on the characters who punked him. She's not a fan of practical joking, I guess. Good to know.

Moving on now to even headier stuff: a long poem about two kids climbing mountains, titled "David".

Spoiler alert: it doesn't end well for either of them.

I've been working on controlling my hainbek. Giving a hard mental shove to a puck on the ice or in the air (or to a Yeng in an alleyway) is no effort at all compared to stopping a shove halfway—or trying to, since I still haven't managed to do it. It's taking so much concentration that I'm actually working up a sweat when I practise. So far, nothing has changed. But it's early days, and I'm no quitter. I've increased my practice time to two hours a day.

Meanwhile, I've also had lots of schoolwork to do. David and Bobby have climbed their last mountain together and I have to decide on a topic to write about. Do I put myself in David's shoes and defend his final request, or do I explore Bobby's "ethical dilemma"? It's a tough choice. While I'm thinking about that, I can practise solving word problems using algebra equations, and study for my next geography test.

What are the main industries of the provinces of Canada? Fuck, I know that without even cracking the textbook. In the Maritimes, it's fishing, except for Prince Edward Island, where it's potatoes and Lucy Maud Montgomery. In Quebec, it's fashion, history, and tourism. In Ontario, it's mining in the north, agriculture in the south, and politics in the middle. In Manitoba, it's cold weather. (They don't call Winnipeg "Winterpeg" for nothing.) Saskatchewan has grain fields, Alberta has oil fields and beef ranches, and B.C. has trees. Lots of trees. And mountains, and movies. The Yukon and Northwest Territory have gold and diamonds. And Nunavut has seals and polar bears, which it's happy to share, especially with Manitoba.

See? I'm gonna ace this!

"Come on, Rocket Man! Knock it off its pins!"

Tensing to take the shot as he charged the net, Travis nearly tripped over his stick when his mother hollered this at him. Coyote just laughed.

Angie had become quite a vocal fan of the game in general, and of Travis's performance on the ice in particular. It was dope to be sharing his favourite sport with her, but she could be overly enthusiastic at times—like this afternoon, when he and Coyote were practising alone together on the pond and she and Ken were the only parents in sight.

"Help! Please!" a voice called out, and all at once a familiar figure was stumbling through the snow toward them. "I think they're going to kill her!"

It was Oscar.

Sticks clattered to the ice as three skaters and one spectator rushed to the edge of the pond to meet him.

"Kill who?" Ken demanded. "Where?"

"The cleansing ritual... Victoria Spears..." he huffed, breathless from running.

"Victoria Spears?" Travis echoed, feeling a chill that had nothing to do with the weather. "But she's my—"

"Yes, she is," Ken cut in, "and we're going to save her. Angie, throw our boots and skate guards into the snowhummer and bring it around here."

She gave him a grim nod and went slip-sliding back across the ice.

"She was struck down..." Oscar was gulping air and sobbing with fear, and he looked about to collapse. "...in the middle of the ceremony... she turned blue... grew horns and feathers... everyone rushed out, screaming about a monster... they've surrounded the building so she can't escape. If she tries—"

The vehicle pulled up beside him and Angie leaned out the window. "Everyone get in here, now!" she barked. "You too, Oscar! Let's go!"

Ken helped the human into the back seat, then swung himself onto the passenger seat up front and pulled out his phone. "Barron's at the compound," he told her. "You drive, I'll let him know. Oscar," he added over his shoulder as the snowhummer lurched into motion, "when Ms. Spears arrived to conduct the ritual this time, was she alone?"

"There was a man with her, but she sent him away. He wasn't happy about it. He said he had orders not to leave her side, but she told him she absolutely had to do this and it would break her most important rule if he stayed. Do you know what's happening?" he asked tearfully.

"Damn!" said Angie. "She is so stubborn. Yes, Oscar, we do know. She's inside the community centre, right?"

"Yes. Is she going to be all right?"

"She will be, as long as she's conscious and still alone," Ken told him. "Put your boots on, boys. I'm sending for reinforcements, but until they get here it's up to the four of us."

"You mean the five of us, don't you?" said Oscar.

Ken and Angie shared a significant look. Then Angie gave her head an emphatic shake no and Ken said, "No, I don't. It's four. When the snowhummer stops, I want you to find a safe place to be and stay there. We'll take care of this."

"No disrespect, sir, but no way. I stay with my friends."

Travis swallowed hard. He understood why Oscar needed to be protected, but... *fuck*! They were the three musketeers! "He can handle himself in a fight, Dad. And we might need him if there is one."

Ken let out a sigh and slipped his phone back into his pocket. "This discussion is not over," he declared. "Pass me my boots, will you?"

As the vehicle topped the crest of the rise and the town of Middlevale spread out before them, the community centre was easy to spot. It was the building with a thousand people swarming around it.

"How close can you bring us to the entrance?" Ken asked.

"Close enough," came the terse response. "But they'll let us through. I'm one of them."

"And I'm two of them," Oscar piped up stubbornly.

"Oy," said Ken.

The snowhummer rolled laboriously down the slope. Fortunately, the streets of Middlevale radiated out from its centre, giving Angie a more or less direct route to her destination. Soon, she was cutting across an open area adjacent to the town square, skirting the edges of an angrily muttering crowd.

A few of the men turned and gave the snowhummer's occupants drop-your-gloves looks as the vehicle passed by. Eventually, Angie pulled up and parked in the far corner of the square. She turned off the engine and took out her phone.

"It went straight to Vicky's voice mail," she reported a couple of seconds later. "We'd better hurry. And, Oscar—"

"You're not getting rid of me!" he warned her. "I don't desert my friends."

"They'll know he brought us here," Ken pointed out. "We can't just leave him outside."

"Okay. Fine," she said, snapping each word like a whip. "But Vicky is going to have a bird when she sees him."

"We'll figure something out," Ken assured her.

Coyote had been silent all during the ride. As they disembarked from the vehicle, Travis glanced over at him and saw a familiar, impish smile.

Oh, man, what a day! It's midnight and I'm still too wired to sleep.

We were the three musketeers defending the queen, just like in the movie.

Dad was our D'Artagnan. Or maybe it was Oscar.

Anyway—best of all—the queen's secret is still safe, and nobody got killed or outed.

Okay, backing up a bit...

There was hardly any snow in front of the community centre. Foot traffic had turned it into slush and mud right up to the front door. And my mother was right. The crowd parted to let us go inside.

Mom raced along a corridor and through half of a double doorway, into a large meeting hall. There was a wide raised platform in the middle of the room. The space behind it had been divided up into cubicles, using movable screens. Each cubicle had a chair and a cot. It reminded me of one of those donation centres that get set up during a blood drive, only with small metal containers instead of plastic bags. Some of the little bottles were scattered on the floor.

Dad called out to Vicky but there was no response, so he went from cubicle to cubicle to find her. A moment later he did, and we all hurried over to see how she was, including Oscar.

My godmother was in her true Nash'terel form. And she was unconscious. I knew from discussions with my dad that a Nash'terel couldn't hold their human shape if they were weak or injured, but she didn't look hurt to me, and I said so.

"She's not wounded, Trav," said Dad, "but she is very weak right now."

"She needs essence," Mom told us, "and she needs it immediately."

Coyote and I knew what she was talking about. We ran around collecting little bottles. Oscar had no idea what was going on. He just stood there with his mouth hanging open.

Dad found a filled bottle among the ones we brought him and pressed it to Vicky's lips. "Another couple of these should do it," he said. "They'll restore her human shape so we can get her out of here."

Oscar was backing away, shaking his head in disbelief. Meanwhile, I could hear angry voices, out in the hallway and coming nearer. The Middlevalers had finally worked up the courage to enter the building after us, and it didn't take a genius to figure out what they had in mind.

"I'm afraid we're about to have a fight on our hands," said Dad grimly. "Get ready to hold off the mob, kids. I'll join you as soon as I can."

Get ready for a brawl? Hey, I'm a hockey player. I was born *ready!*

If Oscar was having trouble processing what he'd already seen, watching Coyote and me use our hainbeka was going to totally blow his mind. But we were the three musketeers, right? It would all be good.

The grumblings from the corridor were growing louder.

We formed a defensive line across the front of the platform—Coyote, Oscar, and me, standing legs braced, facing the door, keeping ourselves between it and the cubicle where my parents and godmother were.

"Ever done this before?" I said to Coyote.

"Never off the ice," he replied. "But it shouldn't be that hard. Think of it as shooting practice, only instead of pucks, we're firing people into a net."

"You okay with that, Oscar?" I asked him.

"Depends. Shouldn't I have a stick or something?"

"Leave that to me," said my father's voice from behind us. "When the time comes, I'll get you one."

Seconds later, the door burst open and townsfolk were streaming through it. But they didn't attack right away. Instead, they clotted together just inside the entrance. It seemed like they didn't quite know what to make of us—three kids that many of them knew, standing on the platform and facing them down. They milled around and muttered among themselves for a moment. Then a burly guy with wavy red hair stepped forward and blared at us, "Bring out the monster!"

"There's no monster here," my dad called back to him.

"There is! We saw it with our own eyes!" shouted a woman's voice from the crowd.

Every muscle in my body tightened up, keeping my hainbek in check until it was needed.

"They're protecting it! Come on, what are you waiting for? We have to kill the monster! It's a stain on our town," the burly guy yelled to the others.

With that, a group of men surged forward, brandishing stuff they must have gone home to get. I caught glimpses of a couple of pipe wrenches, a large knife, a baseball bat, and what looked like a two-by-four. No guns, though. I was glad about that.

The burly guy was the first to reach the edge of the platform. I used my hainbek to toss him backwards into the crowd, his arms flailing. He took out three more would-be monster killers. Knocked them down like bowling pins.

It was a new sport for me, but, hey...

We divided up the space. Coyote protected the left side and I took the right. Oscar has his brown belt in a couple of martial arts. He took a ready-for-battle pose in the middle. There was a pause while the townsfolk got back on their feet. Then they all seemed to come to a decision together, and they rushed us.

Skinny man with glasses and a pipe wrench—kapow!

Blonde woman with an umbrella—sorry, ma'am, but my hainbek only has one setting at the moment. Down you go!

Heavy-set fellow with a... five iron? Really? Middlevale has a golf course? You're gone.

Twenty-something gal stepping up to bat—and yer out!

And so it went. I didn't see what Coyote and Oscar were doing, but they were obviously holding their own. And I was hainbeking like crazy and working up a sweat. After what felt like a very long time, I sensed someone coming up behind me. It was my father.

He stepped in front of Oscar and pointed into the crowd. All at once, a length of pipe flew up into the air, right into Dad's hand. He turned and handed the pipe to Oscar.

"As promised," he said.

For a moment, everything froze. Then the shock must have worn off, because the townsfolk came at us again, even angrier and more determined than before.

Dad got the same look on his face as Sidney Crosby wears on my poster. He pointed a few more times. After that it appeared as if the mob had turned to fighting among themselves, each using their improvised weapon to block the other townspeople's improvised weapons. Then they were screaming, and falling down, and shouting at one another to stop, please stop! And finally, they did.

In the quiet that followed, I could see what my father had done. He'd used his hainbek to turn some of the metal objects in the crowd into powerful magnets. Not just the weapons, either—one person's belt buckle had apparently been magnetized as well. Now all the pipes and knives and hammers were stuck together in clumps. Some of the townsfolk were helpless, unable to move. A few were bleeding, but no one seemed badly hurt.

"What manner of monster are you?" howled the burly red-haired guy.

Honestly, it sounded like a line from a bad movie.

"I told you once and I'll tell you again," my father said. "There are no monsters here."

"You're a liar! Victoria Spears—"

"—is not a monster! See for yourself!" said my mother's voice from behind us, and next thing I knew she was standing at centre stage, supporting my godmother with an arm around her waist.

Victoria looked pale and drawn, but definitely human. Dad hurried to bring her a chair. While he helped her onto it, Mom stepped forward and gave that angry crowd a piece of her mind.

We stood there, awe-struck, while she bawled them all out good and proper. I thought she'd been tough on me earlier, but I now realize that she was holding back. Anyone who can sharpen and throw words the way my mother can doesn't need a hainbek.

Go, Angie!

By the time she was done with those townsfolk, they were convinced that drawing the darkness out of their souls for so many years was what had caused Victoria Spears to transform before their eyes, and that it would take a shitload more purification ritual to restore them to a state of grace, so they'd better get started on it right away.

As for what they'd seen us do during the fighting: Mom sort of hinted that we might be the product of a classified genetics experiment—which was actually the truth—and since the Nash'terel cover story was that the compound was housing a top-secret government project, nobody questioned her on it.

I'm not sure how much of this Oscar believes. I'm just glad he's still my friend, curious about Coyote and me rather than scared of us, and that the three musketeers have come out the other end of this adventure intact.

In fact, we make such a good team that I'm sort of looking forward to the next one. And because of his martial arts skills, I think I know what Oscar's nickname should be: Ninja.

Rocket Man, Coyote, and Ninja.

Better watch out for these three, world—they're trouble!

Arlene F. Marks has been writing since the age of 6, and she has no plans to stop. A veteran teacher of the craft, she has authored two popular literacy programs for the classroom. Her short stories have appeared online and in print, notably in an anthology of reimagined fairy tales, *Grimmer Tales Volume One*. She is also the author of the Sic Transit Terra space opera series (from Edge Publishing) and *Adventures in Godhood*, her first of several recent releases from Brain Lag Publishing. *The Stragori Deception*, the next instalment of Sic Transit Terra, will be released later this year. Arlene lives with her husband on the shore of beautiful Nottawasaga Bay, where she spends time exploring imaginary worlds, collecting interesting-looking owls, and dreaming of one day having a tidy, well-organized office.

www.thewritersnest.ca